# The Last Iceberg

## Anne Ousby

*Best Wishes*

*Anne Ousby*

'I have heard the iceberg roar.'

David Rowbotham

Copyright @ 30 Sept 2012 Anne Ousby
All rights reserved
13:978-1484920497
10:148492049X

*All my gratitude* and love to Brenda and Ali for editing and reading this book for me.

I'm also indebted to Ben for getting 2000AD (the comic) when he was a kid. It was a race as to who read it first each week. I usually won! Thanks Ben, because without it I would never have met Judge Dredd and this story would never have been written.

"This novel introduces us to a sly, savvy voice from our future."
Wendy Robertson – author

"'The Last Iceberg' is a complex, thrilling, Dystopian read."

"This book is an unnerving glimpse into our future."

# The Last Iceberg
## Moon-time

*...There was something else in the hole with them, something that scratched and scraped as it slithered towards them over the rocky floor.*

*The child shrank back against her mother.*

*The woman whispered urgently into the blackness. 'Be brave, sweetheart, you must be brave.'*

*And the child tried – really she did.*

*Somehow she fought back the scream that was stuck in her gullet like a plug of sick terror; right up until the moment a dry, oozing coil crept over her foot and slowly encircled her ankle. She leapt up, beating wildly at herself, everything forgotten in the mad frenzy to escape this nightmare thing.*

*She could hear someone screaming and screaming...*

\*

By the time Maya hit the walkway it was wall to wall people – all shouting into their coms. Keeping her head down she elbowed her way through the yakkers. No way was she gonna be linked to her com like some moronic umbilicus. Suddenly a man barged straight into her. Jabbing her fists into his chest she pushed him hard and he staggered backwards, mouthing obscenities, but then he saw her. The light-weight body armour and insignia were a dead giveaway. Crime Operatives weren't known for their sweet dispositions and this CO wore her aggression with pride. The man flicked her an ingratiating smile before ducking back into the melee and disappearing. He left a balloon of rancid BO hanging in the air behind him. Something was happening up ahead. Frightened commuters flattened themselves against the walls as a phalanx of Elites came ploughing down the walkway towards Maya. She took a half step backwards. She never tangled with these baby-faced killers unless she had to. Elite troopers were selected for their brute strength and unwavering loyalty to Capa's beloved president – Lixir Matthews.

One young trooper, possibly thirteen with a badly pock-marked face, locked eyes with the girl as he yomped past. There was the briefest of hostile moments between them, neither of them wanting to be the first to look away. Maya was tempted to advise the boy on a suitable treatment for pusts but there just wasn't the time. She watched as he disappeared round the corner before going on her way.

At transroute level she leant against the wall and closed her eyes. She hadn't slept last day. Every time her eyelids drooped there it was again – the same freakin dream. She propped one dirty boot behind her on the pristine white uni-plas. She considered it her civic duty to contribute to the pollution of antiseptic Capa. Easing her aching shoulders, she ran her fingers through her sticky hair. She felt sweat trickling down her back. The temperature was still in the high 50s, even with air con.

Popping a can of C she held her nose as she drank. C was chemically mass-produced orange piss. At least that's what it tasted like, or what Maya thought it might taste like, had she been that desperate. Of course there was better stuff available, to those with the creds. Water traders were the richest bastards on earth. Talk was there was a gigantic berg, stashed somewhere deep underground ...the last one on the Globe. Rumour said the water from this berg was so good you'd die happy after one sip.

While she drank she flicked her wrist pad, accessing her cred balance. It was bad. She had to get a result soon or she was in deep trouble. Usually the Hot Phase was mass cred time for COs. Psychos freaked out as the temperatures soared and murder and mayhem exploded, but not this time. This time Capa was having an election and the city was crawling with troopers. What self-respecting nutter was gonna show with Matthews' beasties on the prowl?

*Vote for Matthews* posters were plastered everywhere. There had been some for a guy called Procter but as fast as they put them up they disappeared. Procter was what remained of the Opposition. Apparently, there was some really deadly virus that only infected you if you wanted to be the next president. She didn't know anything about Procter, except he was on the Real Food ticket. That got her vote, but she'd have voted for a rope snake if it meant getting rid of Matthews.

She shuddered. No snake thoughts. She concentrated on Matthews. The President owned the only div Station in Capa. Procter was lucky to get a daytime slot squeezed in between home-shopping and hundred-year-old toons. People got news nicely laundered and packaged in digestible chunks. No one really knew what was going on in the city and most didn't care.

Dropping her empty, she watched as a droid rushed out and chomped it before scuttling back to its hold. She aimed a kick at the annoying little tidy-up but her com vibrated just at that moment and distracted her aim. Kline of course. She ignored it. She wished she'd stayed in bed. This suspected poisoning job would be a dud like all the rest. Natural food poisoning, so no creds. CO's were paid by results. She pushed herself away from the wall and turned for home. A few hours sleep then she'd contact Central again.

The com again and this time she accessed. Kline's face grinned up at her through a curtain of thick blond hair. He was on board a transport. 'So? Where are you, Ma? Late night or something? Advise stay bedside.'

'You wish, Kline.' Maya said, leaning back against the wall and propping the other boot behind her. Two filthy boot imprints. Symmetry pleased her.

Kline pretended to look hurt. 'You know I'd always split the creds, Maya. We're partners.'

'In your dreams. And Kline? Get a haircut, um?' She closed, but not before she saw him turn and shout something at a little girl, running towards him. It was the horrible Poppi, and, as Kline grabbed her, her repulsive face covered the screen. What was it with the kid that made Maya so want to throttle it? And what did Kline see in her? Yeh, Maya hated Poppi and Lixir Matthews, plus the troopers, permit officials and top of the list, her duff shower.

Not for the first time Maya wished she wasn't so competitive because now she had to go on this rubbish job. She switched on her div and watched a toon as she waited for transport. Within moments an election broadcast interrupted. A blond bimboid in his late teens was being interviewed. Apparently this was Lixir Matthews. Maya shook her head in disbelief. Matthews had been in power all her life and before, and here he was miraculously reincarnated as a teenage sex God.

Switching off, the girl stared gloomily out of the thermi-plas at the night sky. No one lived Outside anymore. The blistering heat had driven the inhabitants of Capa East and the remainder of the Globe into Moon-time. The Polar ice-caps had melted and, after years of flooding, the river sources had dried up and the oceans were retreating between the fists of ever-increasing desert land masses.

She envied her predecessors. Okay, they had short brutal lives, but at least they breathed fresh air. Maya got permits for surface-shooting whenever she could, but it was getting harder all the time. The Tranch – a freak, violent wind – made the surface a dangerous place but that's what she wanted – the danger. Maybe she'd try for later tonight? She might even invite Kline. There was a new board she wanted to try out, but more than anything she needed to get that dream out of her head.

# *Lixir*

In the Presidential bedroom the real Lixir Matthews was watching the latest election div while he ate. He was sweating prodigiously in spite of several powerful fans directed at him and he mopped at himself with a large towel. The president wasn't a pretty eater and some of the steak had missed his mouth and was splattered on his bloated stomach and the bed. A big, ginger-rosette guinea-pig perched precariously on his pyjama-clad knee, claws cramponed in; poised to leap in whichever direction the next missed forkful went. Lixir sneezed suddenly and explosively, spraying meat in all directions. He blew his nose and dabbed at his streaming eyes. All this freakin cash spent on research at the Institute and they still hadn't come up with a cure for the common cold.

He glanced back at the div. The similarity between himself and this boy was uncanny but maybe it wasn't that surprising, considering the boy was his natural son. Of course Lixir had put on a bit of weight since that age and his once blonde hair was grey and thinning, but apart from that, they could have been brothers.

The Pool kept biog data on all the straws and it had been relatively easy to locate Blade – his stage name, apparently – in a Free Time complex, strutting his stuff. Said he was waiting for his big break. Too much make-up for Matthews' liking but you couldn't have everything.

Lixir watched his alter-ego perform through slit eyes. Sure he was confident and unassuming but he was also a money-grabbing little shit, demanding expensive clothes and repeat, repeat fees. Didn't the trond know how it hurt his Daddy to have to ex his sons, over and over again?

The President switched his attention to the young female interviewer and his eyelids drooped, allowing his meat-laden fork to sink towards his stomach. This was exactly what the guinea pig had been waiting for

'Aghh.' Matthews stabbed at the animal with his knife and it backed off growling, a piece of skin clenched in its sharp yellow teeth. The towel came in handy to staunch the blood. Lixir smiled indulgently through the pain. 'Lucky your daddy loves you or you'd be dead meat.'

The guinea pig twitched his whiskers. He liked this new taste sensation.

Matthews sighed. Party political broadcasts were boring, even when they were your own. What to do next? He lay back and shut his eyes. It was too hot to eat and he had heart-burn. Maybe he should cut back on the protein, get the old bag to follow a diet sheet? Trouble was he liked her food, it was tasty and comforting. Her cooking was the best thing about Fleur Matthews.

Matthews winced at the shooting pain in his chest. Freakin global democratisation. Freakin GSA. They'd never bothered with him before so why now? Elections? What was the point? He would win, everybody knew that. No, there was something behind this sudden Global interest in Capa. Matthews had his suspicions, and it was worrying, very worrying.

As the pain lessened he relaxed back against the pillows. No need to get paranoid. He was a genius and they were envious of his success. That's all it was, sheer jealousy. He picked steak out of his teeth as he considered what history would make of him.

Not that he expected the Globe to survive for that much longer, but it would see him out; that was the main thing.

He started to wheeze again and struggled onto his side. No wonder he kept getting colds, breathing in all this unhealthy re-cyced air. It was ridiculous. He was undoubtedly the most influential person on the Globe, yet he had to skulk in his bedroom like some naughty brat. However, his security advisors had been adamant. There were people out there who wanted him dead. Until he got Munro he had to be careful. There was no option, he had to stay in the palace until this farce was over and the GSA snoopers departed. You couldn't have two presidents knocking about, confusing the proletariat.

He sat up carefully. The pain in his chest had lessened. Maybe he could force down another morsel or two? As he ate he decided to visit the Pool later. He'd get the Pool Master to track down something from the same vintage. It was a hard one to beat. A perfect match of his considerable intellect and looks and her deviousness. He'd already had two 'presidents' from this batch.

Satisfied, Matthews' gaze returned to the delectable interviewer.

# Malcolm Blue

It was the beginning of the night shift and Malcolm Blue paused on the threshold of The Pool, allowing the blueness to settle about him. Everything in the Pool was blue, from the muted lights illuminating the computer decks to the pulsating straw reservoirs. The shimmering, quivering water patterns flowed fluidly across the walls and floors and ceilings – all blue.

Malcolm was Master of the Pool and all masters were named Malcolm. He had been selected at embryonic stage and transferred to an iso-globe where his developing foetus had bobbed gently amongst his contemporaries. Then at gestation he had been delivered to the State crèche, until old enough to be apprenticed to the old Master.

There was one secret that all Malcolms shared. They only saw in shades of blue. The blueness affected the eyes in the end. The only person Malcolm could tell would be the next Malcolm, who in turn would have the same incapacity. It was dangerous to have a defect in Capa. The President didn't like abnormalities.

This colour blindness didn't affect Malcolm's work because there was a failsafe system. All colour bands were kept in different vats, each bearing the appropriate classification, every straw numbered and entered in the computer files. However, to Malcolm they were all blue, or shades of blue, and he found their different hues fascinating and beautiful.

When the appointed time came, Malcolm had been proud to accompany the old Master to the Departure Lounge and press the Incinerator button. Afterwards the boy returned to the deserted Pool and selected the next master.

It was the Pool Master's job to nurture the new citizens of Capa. When he received notification, he would place the chosen in their dried-ice containers, and then carry them carefully to the iso-globe labs. It was always done with great solemnity. And sometimes, just before dawn, the boy would go and watch the tadpole-like embryos growing and developing in their iridescent, gently revolving transparent wombs. He especially loved watching the new Malcolm. He was convinced that the foetus's blind eyes were looking at him and the arm and leg buds were waving, communicating. If no one was looking he would wave back.

The object of the Pool was two-fold. One was to balance the status quotient and the other was population control. Both functions were crucial to the success of Capa: in fact they were vital for the survival of the entire planet. The Globe's resources were finite and to maintain a continuing supply of food and power meant strict reproductive control. All States had small populations. .

Capa East's population was one million but the figure was dropping year on year. The percentages for each banding were carefully regulated so that Capa society was a well-balanced pyramid. The Pinx were the predominant bed rock, covered with a finer band of Reds; then a wafer of Blus and finally a sprinkling of yellows, or Solitaries. Malcolm was a Solitary, and proud of it. It was the perfect social system, invented by their president, Lixir Matthews.

All Capa males were infertile except for specially bred donor males - like the President. Each embryo's provenance was recorded and kept in data banks. Matthews had hundreds of sperm straws in the Pool. It was very fashionable to have presidential off-spring.

Malcolm admired the president enormously. He considered Lixir Matthews to be the cleverest geneticist the globe had ever known. Who else could have invented SS? In the early days of Matthews' social experiment the Solitaries were prone to mental health problems. As the name implies these individuals had no emotional contact outside their crèche nurses and, as a result, many of these individuals grew up with psychiatric problems. There was the classic story of an eminent brain surgeon who lost his memory for three days because someone used his special laser scalpel and didn't put it back in the correct place.

Matthews couldn't afford to lose such skilled personnel – hence the introduction of Sensory Stimulation. An SS chip was implanted in a specific area of the infant brain, where it activated particular sensory reactions enabling the baby to `see' his mother, `taste' her milk; recognise her 'smell' and 'feel' her touch. Thus stimulated the individual would develop into a well-adjusted, sane citizen.

Malcolm's earliest memories were of standing on a chair beside the old Master looking down into the reservoirs, mesmerised by the movement of the water. He and the old man shared rooms adjacent to the Pool. Their needs were basic. They had creds to spare for luxuries but what did they need other than the blueness? One night, in a rare moment of communication, the Master had leant close and whispered in Malcolm's ear. "Remember, boy, you've been chosen to choose." And Malcolm remembered. He would always remember.

## Dan Young

In an integrated condo Dan Young was woken by a painful jab in the ribs. His wife was sitting up in bed pointing accusingly at the wall that separated them from the apartment next door.

'What?' Dan was still half asleep.

'Don't tell me you can't hear it. It's the kid. Tanya – stupid – Roberts. Listen.'

Dan could hear a child singing. 'It's her birthday. She's excited.'

'And when are you getting the air-con fixed?'

'Give us a chance, Rosie.'

'Well let's hope you do it before I die of suffocation. Integrated Condos? You can keep them. We were better off where we were.' The woman thumped back down on the bed and turned her back on him.

Dan rubbed his hand down her arm but she knocked it away. He knew why she wished they'd stayed in the Red Zone. In the red zone she could feel superior because she was a blu. Everything would be all right when he got Blu status. Rosemary would be happy then. He was feeling good and nothing was going to change that. 'Big night tomorrow,' he said, snuggling up against her. 'We're sure of an upgrade with Pete Roberts as our sponsor.'

'Your sponsor, Dan. I don't need one.' She moved out of his embrace.

Dan sighed. He had done extraordinarily well for a Red. Getting a job in the Institute was quite an achievement. Pete Roberts thought Dan must have been mis-coded. Pool mix ups had been common in the early days. All it took was a negligent Pool worker putting a straw back in the wrong bin.

Quality assurance had improved enormously since then. President Matthews had come to power on the slogan, "Making Quality Count." He had been a quality manager in the Pool as a young man.

Rosemary kicked out her legs in search of a cool spot and settled down to sleep. Dan was wide awake now. He slipped out of bed. There were some finishing touches to be done on his application.

As he dressed he looked at his wife. If only she had a friend. But she wouldn't make the effort and she discouraged their Emma from bringing any child home. It had come as a blessing when Anna Roberts had asked if Emma would like to join Tanya for Home Teaching. Anna wanted Tanya to explore and experiment and not be 'force-fed' facts from the State techno-labs. And Rosemary was only too glad to keep the creds they would have spent on school fees. The only thing that made his wife happy was shopping. When Dan got his upgrade they would be able to afford luxuries. Maybe that would make her happy.

## *Kline*

Kline was on the first Rat (rapid transport) of the night. It was no punishment for him to get up early. He relished the personal space it gave him back at the unit. He could be first in the shower for a start. All waste water was re-cyced and there was a definite after-taste of C if you got a mouthful of water. How disgusting was that?

At seventeen Kline was the oldest CO still living in the unit? Most operatives moved out as soon as they could and Kline desperately wanted a place of his own but until he could afford it he was stuck.

The boy was an optimist but he knew the score. He wasn't cut out to be a CO. Operatives were pre-selected but he thought there'd been some mix up with him. Law enforcers were ruthless and focused and he was neither. He was happiest doing his own thing – watching old films, socialising with his mates, doing a bit of sport and being with Maya Johnson. A smile crept over his face. Maya. He accessed her com. No response. He waited a few moments and tried again, knowing she wouldn't be able to resist it a second time. Her face appeared. She looked half asleep and bad-tempered. Nothing new there then. He hardly had time to say anything before there was a shout from the back of the transport and a child came racing towards him. She was dressed as a CO but the uniform was far too big for her. Kline yanked her into the seat next to him.

An angry voice came from the back of the Rat. 'Oi! Keep that kid in order or I'll report the pair of you.'

Kline pulled the little girl around to face him. 'What did you do?'

The child's eyes were wide and innocent. 'Nuffink. It wasn't me.'

'Don't lie.'

Poppi hung her head. 'Sorree.'

Kline had to turn away so that she wouldn't see his smile.

The man at the back was still shouting threats so Kline thought it best to apologise and ask questions later. 'Sorry, mate. But she's not been well, she's on med. It makes her a bit...unstable.'

'Unstable?' She's a freakin psycho. Only bit me on the leg, didn't she? Has she had her shots? '

Kline held up his hands to show he was sorry. The child tickled him and he let out a squawk of laughter.

Once the Rat had settled down again Kline looked severely at the little girl. 'You've got to promise that you'll behave when we get to the job, or I shall be forced to take extreme action.'

Poppi grinned at her friend, not believing the threat.

Kline's expression never faltered. 'You've got to learn how to behave, Poppi, or you're gonna get in serious trouble. I might not always be around to bail you out.'

The child was instantly serious. 'Why? Where Kline go?'

'Nowhere, Poppi, but be careful, that's all I'm saying. Okay?'

She nodded and switched on his pod, very loudly.

Kline grabbed it back. 'I thought you wanted to be a real CO one day?'

Poppi's eyes lit up. 'Poppi nine, when she ten, she CO.'

'But only if you behave. I shall be watching you tonight and if you do anything bad I'm taking your divs. *Mary Poppins* for a start.'

Poppi's eyes and mouth opened as wide as they could go.

'It's up to you. Okay?'

Kline liked Walt Disney too and he and his little friend watched them together. Poppi had acquired a huge collection from somewhere. He didn't ask too many questions about where she got them. Everyone pulled his leg back at the unit about Poppi but he didn't mind. He was fond of the kid. Poppi told him she was going to be with him forever He wasn't sure what Maya would think of that, he'd have to break it to her gently.

# *Maya*

Maya elbowed her way onto the first transport that came. It was *Pinx only* but so what? She wasn't making a colourist stand. She wouldn't be seen dead associating with `Society' freaks, no; all she wanted was to get to the job as quickly as possible.

Transports were air conned but the heat on this one was stifling and the stink of sweating bodies was overpowering. The only unoccupied seat was between two very pregnant women at the back. Maya eased herself into the space, trying to keep an air break between her and the women who were haemorrhaging sweat. Why would anyone choose to be pregnant in this heat? Creds of course. Most babies were bred in iso-globes but a few Blu and Red women paid for their offspring to develop in wombs, the old fashioned way. It was expensive but very fashionable and Pinx women were hired as surrogates.

Maya put on her head phones and accessed a game on her pod. Everyone was either bellowing at each other or shouting into their coms. But as long as no one tried to yak at her she didn't care. Within a few minutes she yanked her ear phones out and read the game description. *Exciting. Frightening? Difficulty + genius level.* Pinx brains. She stared out of the window as the buildings flashed by.

Capa had evolved around the skeleton of a $21^{st}$ Century conurbation and the brightly-lit habitations pulsed like fibre-optics on linked highways that looped and encircled the ruins of the old city. Above the walkways, but still hugging low, tubes shot off like spokes of a wheel. These were the Transroutes. In the distance Pinx towers speared the sky and dotted here and there were the domed admin, cultural, social and consumer centres of Capa. The presidential palace crouched at the centre; a massive egg-shaped building balanced on flying buttresses which extended on six sides.

The Pinx woman to Maya's left belched and popped a tab.

Maya's mouth puckered in disgust. Tabs were the staple diet of Capa, manufactured by Lixir Matthews.com. He had his greedy little trotters into everything. Maya bought re-con when she could afford it. Real Food was the best but you could only get that on the Green Market at astro-inflated prices.

The woman sucked noisily on her tab.

'God! How can you eat that muck?'

The woman pointed to her ears.

Maya shouted. 'Ever tasted Real Food?'

The woman wrinkled her nose. 'You kidding? They grow that stuff in shit. Anyway, who wants to waste time cooking for that lot?' And she pointed at the Pinx men. 'Get serious, girl.'

Maya caught sight of a massive alternately winking and smiling, hologram of Matthews as they sped by. 'So? You voting for that?'

The woman sniffed. 'Actually I'm a 'don't know.'
'

'What a surprise,' Maya sneered.

'One thing, girl, I won't be voting for your foodie. It's against the law. I'm voting for that...what's-his-name?'

'– Matthews?'

'Yeh, him.'

The woman leant across her and prodded her pregnant friend. 'Wouldn't say no to going ten rounds with Blondie Matthews?'

Her friend shrieked with delight. 'Too freakin true.'

'It's not really Matthews,' Maya said. 'It's an actor.'

'So chuggin what?'

The girl knew she couldn't win but it didn't stop her trying. 'It's illegal to use stand-ins for an election. The real Matthews is fat, repulsive, bald and smelly –'

'– Sounds like my Baz.'

Maya feared she might get trashed between the two hysterical women but eventually they settled back in their seats, wiping the tears away with the back of their hands.

The first woman was serious now. 'Na, he's done all right by us Pinx women, that…Matthews? Made life easier.'

Maya stared pointedly at the woman's swollen belly but the munching pinx ignored her. `You got banana flavour? Tastes like.... no don't tell me, it's on the tip of me tongue. Oh God. You know…what is it?'

Maya laughed unkindly.

The woman rounded on her. 'Think you're so big, don't you? Bloody COs. If you was mine, girl, you'd get a back hander. They never ought to let brats carry guns. How old are you? Twelve? Thirteen?'

Maya was furious. She was sixteen next birthday.

The woman hadn't finished. 'What you doing on our transport anyway? We could report you. Keep to your own sort. Stuck up tart.'

`Yeh,' the other woman leant threateningly over Maya, her fat arm sticking painfully to the girl's skin. 'We never asked you to get on our Rat.'

Maya peeled her arm away and hung her head. 'You're right. I was out of order. Sorry.'

The women glanced at each other, surprised.

Maya smiled sweetly at them. 'D'you mind if I ask you a question?'

'Ask away, girl. It's not your fault you've got no manners. You don't have a proper family or nothing do you? No one to show you right from wrong? Shame eh? What d'you want to know, love?'

Maya looked her straight in the eyes. 'I was wondering what it's like being an incubator for some rich bitch? Gonna be there at the birth is she? What? Course she will, got to make sure it's natural, hey? That's what she's paid for. And it *will* be natural, whatever happens. It'll be you and her and the pain. Whatever she's paying, ask for more, much more.'

The woman's mouth dropped open. Maya sighed contentedly and shut her eyes. The night had started badly but it was definitely looking up.

## *Fleur*

Lixir's delicious dream was cut short by a blast of red-hot air down the back of his neck. His bedroom door was opening slowly. There was only one person who would dare enter without knocking. Lixir bellowed, 'Come in if you're coming and shut that door.'

A woman scuttled in. She was small and wiry with a sly ageing rodent face, more like the guinea pig than the guinea pig himself. This was Fleur Matthews, the president's wife. If her looks weren't bad enough she was also a serial ticer, her head nodded, her mouth twitched and her hands clenched and unclenched. But the worst times were when she coughed. This triggered a bizarre, staccato dance involving her entire body. Matthews stayed well clear at such times; otherwise he was likely to get an out flung arm in his gut or somewhere even more painful.

Fleur dropped a pile of clean sheets on the bed and shoved the quotient documentation in front of him. He glanced at the papers as he scribbled his signature. 'Two biologists, Fleur? I thought we had two last month?'

His wife sniffed and looked away.

'What d'you do with them? Eat them?'

She tapped her fingers on his tray impatiently.

He hated it when she ignored him. Okay, she was in charge of the quotient and all things biological. He had his ...special project – but he was the President. He handed over the signed papers and watched her as she worked. It was oddly calming having her fussing around him. Her white button-through uniform crackled as she folded and straightened and smoothed. He quite liked *Nursey* weeks – some of her other personae were more disturbing. *Matron* was a bad one and *Queenie* – he didn't like to think about *Queenie*, not on a full stomach. He stayed well clear when that crown went on.

His wife was crazy of course but, unfortunately, it wasn't a congenital disease so he couldn't get her put away as a defect. She wasn't mad in the accepted sense. She was still an exceptionally good scientist and her intelligence was unimpaired, but she was totally off her head.

When they were students they had volunteered to trial the new SS technology. Unfortunately the experiments on Fleur had gone badly wrong. Instead of implanting the chip in her brain to unlock her senses, Matthews misplaced it slightly and it unleashed her subsequent deranged behaviour. She hadn't been particularly loving or giving before but since the accident she was totally alienated from him. It wasn't all bad though because it had given Matthews the idea for another use for SS.

Suddenly he was thrown back on the bed. Fleur had grabbed the pillows from behind him and was beating them to a pulp. The woman didn't look at him as she worked but he knew that her brain was spinning like a hamster's wheel. He would love to get rid of her but it was too big a risk. They'd risen from the gutter together, suffered the gene wars, shared terrible deprivations and done a lot of bad things in the name of science. She had secret files on him and if anything happened to her she had arranged for this information to fall into the enemy's hands. The Global State Alliance.

'Look at the state of you. You mucky devil.' Fleur slapped a wet flannel across his face.

'Ah that hurt.'

'You shouldn't be such a pig then. Who d'you think has to do the washing? Me? I work my fingers to the bone for you, you great lazy lump, and what do I get in return?'

He knew his lines. 'I'm sorry; I won't do it again, Nurse Matthews.'

Pacified, she expertly removed his soiled damp sheets and replaced them with pristine, crisp, dry ones. He lay back as she rocked him to and fro. Fleur hummed good-humouredly as she made the bed. Matthews was used to her mood swings. Old fashioned housework was her hobby. They had droids for all menial tasks but Fleur liked the hands-on approach.  Maybe that was why she liked dissections so much.

There was something about the insides of bodies that fascinated her. She used virtual-reality to keep her hand in but preferred live animals. The palace had animal labs which supplied her with all the mammals she could handle, plus his guinea pigs. Fleur hated guinea pigs. She was always complaining that they were lazy, highly-sexed animals with small brains and how she'd like to dissect them slice by slice.

Fleur had stopped humming and was scowling at a piece of uneaten meat on Matthews' plate.

Matthews speared it with his fork. 'Come see what Daddy's got, baby.'

The guinea pig's whiskered face appeared over the edge of the bed, the smell of meat giving him courage. He usually hid when Fleur was in the room. His black eyes glittered. Lixir tossed the steak high into the air and the animal caught it and demolished it in one gulp, then scuttled back to safety.

Lixir pushed the empty plate towards his wife. As she bent down he had a tempting view of her scrawny neck – one sharp twist would do it. As she straightened up he looked quickly away before she could read his mind.

She was smiling now. 'Seen the news, Lixir dear? Poisoned foodies in the Toy Museum?'

Matthews was immediately on his guard. When Fleur communicated directly with him it meant trouble. He tried to sound calm. 'Foodies', dear heart? D'you mean RF users? Surely there haven't been more tragic deaths?'

She winked at him.

He refused to be intimidated. This time he was confident that nothing could go wrong and he arranged a distressed look on his face. 'Poor, deluded fools. When will they ever learn, Fleur, um? Real Food is dangerous…' he saw her look at his empty plate, '…in the hands of amateurs. You have to be sure of the provenance, like in the palace biodomes. We're biologists, we know the toxins that exist in bad RF? They only have themselves to blame but I can't help feeling sorry for them.'

Fleur threw back her head and whinnied.

Lixir knew his eye was twitching. But there was nothing to worry about. She was winding him up. Intelligence was that Procter would be at the Toy Museum feast and now he was dead. Real Food for the masses? The man was mad. There was barely enough to go around the palace without dishing it out to everyone. True, he and Procter went back a long way. They'd worked side by side at the Institute. He was one of the original gang – old chums. Matthews prided himself on his tolerance but you had to draw the line somewhere.

He attempted a grave expression, 'Actually, Fleur, I have already heard the sad news about our friend Anthony Procter – '

` -- Procter? Procter's not dead, stupid. ' Fleur thumped the bed with glee. 'It's someone else, another "friend". You've got to guess, go on.'

Lixir bit his lip. 'What are you talking about? Of course he's dead. I – '

Fleur grabbed the remote and fast forwarded the news div. There were some general shots of the museum, the table, bloated bodies and then there was a close up of the face of one of the dead men. Matthews didn't want to look but there was something terribly familiar about the very theatrical eyes. No…please, it couldn't be. He sagged back onto the plumped pillows. His orders had been explicit. Blade was to be watched day and night and he was never to go anywhere, without a trooper-minder. He glanced back at the screen. The next shot was of another body lying face down beside the first, one arm thrown protectively over the other. The camera skidded away but not before Lixir saw the double helix tattoo. An elite Trooper. The div blacked out for a second and resumed filming, in another part of the museum.

Lixir's anguish turned to rage. 'Why didn't somebody tell me he was into RF?'

Fleur was smug. 'I knew but no one ever asks me. I'm only the President's wife, who takes any notice of me –?'

But Matthew's wasn't listening. '– It's that pathologist's fault. Huey Dipstick Montrose. He was supposed to be taking care of it for me. I'll murder him.' Matthews kicked back the sheets and swung his legs over the edge of the bed. 'Right you've ruined my night woman, now chug off.'

He planted his feet solidly on the floor and heaved himself upright. There was a sickening squelch. Without looking down he screamed. 'Well? What are you waiting for? I want another guinea pig here by the time I get back, and send in Scar. Now, get out.'

Fleur exited, leaving the door wide open.

Her voice came echoing back from the corridor. 'Oi, you! In there now. Piggy wants a word. Move.'

## The Toy Museum

Maya had to step over two bloated corpses to get inside the Museum. Medics were hurrying to get the deadies zipped up.

She glanced at the body nearest to her, clocking the twisted limbs, wide staring eyes and gaping mouth. There was something familiar about this guy. The second man lay face down beside the first, one arm flung protectively across him. Maya bent down to take a closer look but a trooper pushed her away with his gun and she moved on into the interior of the museum.

That's when the smell hit her. It was like a slap in the face. Nothing in Capa stayed fresh for long. Maya was used to the stench of decomposing bodies but this was something else. She stood for a moment, trying to decide what it was, while her eyes adjusted to the dim light. The museum had been closed for years but the shelves that lined the aisles were still piled high with toys. Stacked near the entrance were boxes of fluffy animals and dolls, plastic trains and toys and bikes, skate boards and games... *angry birds*. She had always wanted that. Maybe she'd *win* one on the way out?

The only light came from firebug spots that flitted overhead, homing in on body heat. One came on and fluttered annoyingly over Maya's head. Twenty or so hovered over a large table and chairs set up in the middle of the central aisle, where medics, div crews; troopers, COs and assorted state officials mingled.

The table shimmered in the flickering light, all honey and red and dark orange graining. A wooden table. Maya's fingers twitched. No one in Capa East – well, no one she knew – had a wooden table.

She'd only seen them on divs. All furniture was made in standard uni-plas – an indestructible material made to last from tube to incinerator. Maya couldn't take her eyes off that table. It must be worth a million at least. One day...one day she was gonna own a table. That was her ambition ... well, it was on the list.

She dragged her eyes away and glanced at the dead men sprawled in chairs and spread-eagled across the table. One of them was face down in a plate of food crawling with flies and the other had landed on an empty tin of salmon. Ouch! Maya caught the eye of a couple of medics she knew and grinned. They smiled back. It paid to keep in with these people. A lot of state employees didn't like COs.

One dead man was lying in a pool of bright pink, furry animals. Maya smiled wryly. A child was playing with them and she recognised the tousled head. Her com vibrated. 'What?'

Kline was standing behind Poppi and smiling broadly. 'At last. Thought you'd decided to take my advice.'

Maya snorted. 'That'll be the day. Did you have to bring that?' She was looking at Poppi.

Kline smiled indulgently. 'No one brings Poppi, Maya.' And then crossly, 'Hey you. I've told you. Put that back.'

Maya watched as Kline made the child return whatever she'd stolen out of the deadie's pocket. Kline looked stern but Poppi flashed him a cheeky smile and he ruffled her hair. Then he said something to the child and she made a face in Maya's direction and went off in search of someone else to annoy. Maya continued her appraisal of the SOC.

Kline came and wound his arms around her waist.

'Get lost, I'm working. Anyway I'm not talking to you.'

'Why?'

She ignored him.

'If it's about last night I – '

Maya spun on her heel and went to take a closer look at the table, fighting the impulse to wipe up a pool of spilled wine – it was going to leave a nasty stain. She ran her fingers lovingly over the silky smooth surface. Cherry wood she thought. The table was strewn with plates and dishes covered in the slimy blackish-green remnants of food. Now she knew what the smell was. In the middle of the table was a huge bowl of peaches, the furry skin of each fruit was growing another richer coat – in blue mould. Maya had eaten a peach once. It had taken half a week's creds but it had been worth it. Her mouth watered.

Kline was beside her again. 'So? What's it to be? *Kline and Maya* or *Maya and Kline*?'

'What?'

'Come on, Maya, we agreed last night. We're gonna amalgamate. What an amazing combo? Your brains and my looks. '

'I'm not a charity, Kline. Don't take this personally but you're crap at this job. Toughen up and I might reconsider. Now please, let the professionals get to work.'

Maya had noticed a chubby young man standing on the other side of the table talking into a strange looking com. Maya looked closer. No, not a com, a Dictaphone – one of those really old machines for recording stuff? Only one person she knew had ever used one of those. Maya arranged her face into a smile. 'Huey? It is you, isn't it? Huey Montrose? `

The man glanced up, not liking the interruption, but his shiny moon-face flushed with pleasure when he saw who it was.

Maya gushed on. 'This is such an amazing coincidence, Huey? I was only thinking about you the other night and here you are, in the flesh.'

Huey was so excited he couldn't speak. Maybe she shouldn't have mentioned flesh.

Maya hung her head and stared at him through lustrous lashes. She'd seen some bimbo do this on a div once. 'God, I am so embarrassed. You don't remember me do you? But why should you? I'm a nobody and you're a State Pathologist working for our beloved President Matthews. Totally out of my league.'

At last the boy's brain took over and, in his eagerness to get to her, he tripped over an upturned chair nearly knocking her flat. His arms went around her to steady himself and she got the full frontal of his rank body smell. She stepped away, smiling as she went, trying not to breathe in.

'Of course I remember you, Maya. We were fellow students at UCW. Maya Johnson is on file. I lost track of you. What happened?'

She thought his voice would have broken by now. 'I crashed out, Huey. Couldn't keep up with you high gumunsters.'

He grabbed her hand, his palm slippery with sweat. 'Not true, Maya. No. You had a good little brain. Untutored and undisciplined but nonetheless able.'

'Na, I wasn't cut out for all that thinking stuff. This job suits me better. I get to beat up anybody I don't like and get paid for it.'

Huey looked startled for a moment then he giggled – yes, it was a giggle. 'I'd forgotten your zany sense of humour, Maya.'

Had he actually said 'zany'? Maya slipped her hand out of his wet grasp and tapped his armband playfully. 'And look at you? Clever old Huey. I bet you've solved this one already?'

'I can't discuss State business, Maya, I'm sure you understand...' he saw her disappointment and lowered his voice, ' but...I'm sure I can rely on your discretion?' He darted a suspicious look at Kline, who was standing close by.

'Don't mind Kline, Huey. He's my business partner.'

Huey leant forward and whispered in her ear. 'Botulism.' He paused while she registered amazement, then he nodded in the direction of the tinned salmon. 'These real food addicts? When will they ever learn? The stuff's dangerous. They should stick to good old wholesome – '

'-- Tabs?'

'Exactly.'

Maya and Kline exchanged glances. They'd known what it was as soon as they saw the corpses. The last three poisonings had been the same.

'You're so clever, Huey, ` she said. 'I was beginning to think all State Pathologists were trond brains but it just shows how wrong you can be. `

Huey beamed. 'Look there's no time now, Maya, but you and I...we mustn't lose touch. I've always liked you, even though you were iconoclastic, but I'm convinced that the right man could do something with you. You have the makings.'

At that precise moment a trooper hurried up to Huey. There was much gesticulating and Huey glanced anxiously at the bodies by the entrance then he smiled apologetically at Maya. 'I've got to go. Places to be, bodies to see.' He was making a huge effort to appear calm but he didn't fool her, not for one minute.

'Who's the guy by the door, Huey?'

Huey darted a look at the impassive trooper and shook his head at her. His fear was tangible. He pressed something into her hand and closed her fingers around it. 'Come and see me soon. I could help you and I'm certain you could…do something for me. ` He licked his pink lips, leaving a spider's web of sputum dangling from the corner of his mouth.

Maya considered throwing up all over him but common sense prevailed. She watched his fat backside as he waddled away.

Kline came and stood beside her. 'So? We *are* partners?'

'Not. That was for Huey's benefit.' Maya was busy reading the address disc Huey had given her.

Kline looked over her shoulder. 'Hey! Maya Johnson's going up in the world. That GD's in a very exclusive neighbourhood.'

'You don't think I'm gonna actually see the perv, do you? What d'you take me for?' Maya wasn't smiling and Kline could hardly hear what she said next. 'Sometimes this job freaks me out.'

He put a fatherly hand on her shoulder. 'You know what they say, my dear? If you don't like the heat, stay out of the incinerator. `

'Aw, chug off, infant. `

Kline looked back at the table. 'Another one to put down to experience? `

Maya frowned. 'Four identical poisonings in a row, Kline? And did you see that creep? He was wetting himself.'

'It could have been a contaminated batch of salmon.'

'Yeh, but the question is who contaminated it? Was it an accident or was it …something else?' If only she'd been able to recognise the body at the door.

'No,' Kline was impatient to be off. 'The question is, do we watch a div or head for the free time zone?'

Maya was not going to be side-tracked. 'Think Kline. How convenient is this for Matthews? Procter is his only opponent in the election. He's on the Real Food ticket. Then suddenly people begin to drop dead from RF poisoning? Brilliant propaganda before the election? An incredible coincidence, I don't think.'

'Okay, it looks suspicious.' Kline was searching his pockets for creds. 'But there's no evidence, Maya. So? Are you coming or what?'

'Do what you like, Kline. I have to get a result. Kline? What are you doing?'

The young man had disappeared under the table. When he stood up he was grinning from ear to ear. 'You got the poor little mutt so excited he forgot this.' He held up a bag with H. Montrose written on the side. 'Now you will have to see him again.'

'He'll have to find me first.' Maya snatched the bag off Kline and looked inside. There were documents, the Dictaphone, and at least a dozen tapes. She snapped the bag shut and hurried towards the exit.

'I'm going surface-shooting, Kline. D'you wanna come?'

# Scar

The President was dressed but he'd forgotten his slippers and the *slap slap* of his podgy feet on the marble floor echoed down the corridors. Scar glided in front of him, surprisingly light-footed for such a large person. The palace workers they met pressed themselves against the walls. No one made eye contact with the President or the trooper, not unless they wanted the trooper's iron fist in their ribs.

As he stumbled along, the irate president barked out his orders. Scar dealt with them quietly and efficiently. The trooper's com crackled with feedback from outgoing and incoming calls. Scar's proficiency had a soothing effect on Matthews. He was fortunate to have this totally reliable, loyal trooper for an ally. And yes, their relationship, master and servant, had developed over the years into a close bond. Nobody would dare lay a finger on Matthews, not with Scar beside him.

Scar had been the first of his 'new' troopers. The citizens had been appalled at their ferocity and Capa's State Council had demanded their delicensing. The Council had some power in those days and Matthews had to obey but now Lixir did as he pleased and Scar was brought back into service. This trooper was his biological triumph.

Scar stopped and faced the president, waiting for him to catch up before speaking. 'We have a problem, Mr President. The pathologist H. Montrose has reported the loss of some vital documents.'

Lixir's heart was pounding. 'Vital? How vital?'

'Grade AA classification, Mr President.'

'Pertaining to what?'

'The recent RF poisonings – '

Matthews hit his head in frustration. '– I explicitly told the stupid, brainless idiot that nothing should be recorded. Update, Scar.'

'Montrose left his bag in the Toy Museum. Security says a CO picked it up.'

'When this circus is over, Scar, remind me to deal with those interfering tronds once and for all – '

The trooper waited.

'– But first things first. I want the information retrieved.'

'Intercept is on its way, sir.'

'Someone you trust?'

Scar nodded. 'With my life.'

Matthews was surprised. His commander-in-chief never gave that sort of personal endorsement. 'That good? Excellent. And of course Montrose and this freelance must be eliminated. Do we have a name?'

'M. Johnson, female, age sixteen.'

'What do we need freakin COs for? I told the Council a million times, troopers are more reliable.'

Lixir didn't wait for a response. He knew he wouldn't get one. That was another thing he liked about Scar.

They walked on in silence.

See? No fuss.

Matthews watched her as she walked. She must be in her forties now, although she didn't look it. Even from behind she was extremely attractive, sleek and strong, all rippling muscle and suppressed sexuality. She was dressed in black from her helmet to her long black boots. The only skin showing was on her face and this was unlined and smooth and very pale, almost translucent. Her eyes looked black too but, if you had the misfortune to get up close, you saw that they were deep, deep blue. She was big, in every department, like a warrior queen. She also had an amazing ability to turn into a sensuous, sexy female if she wanted. Matthews never tired of seeing some unsuspecting trond-brain try it on with her. She especially didn't like being asked where her scar was. The President smiled to himself. Only he knew that.

Matthews had never been intimate with her. Of course, he'd considered it but he wasn't sure he was physically up to it. She'd probably kill him. Anyway, he didn't like muddying his own pool. No, it was enough for him to have her around. To know that she was his. He got respect because of Scar.

*

Back in the presidential bedroom there was the sound of munching. The pile of squashed steak on the carpet was moving. The guinea pig ate as much as he could; stuffing his stomach until it was rock hard and hurt, then he trundled off to find somewhere to sleep it off. At least that was his plan but then he ran across the trail of prime meat which had been stuck between his meat-provider's toes. He couldn't resist following it.

## *Anyone for Angry Birds?*

Maya marched angrily down the walkway. A force 20 tornado was cast and all applications for Outside had been rejected.

What a night. No creds, no permits and now she had a mass headache. They could have caught a Rat but Maya needed to walk. Huey's bag and another smaller parcel were stowed in her backpack. It was heavy and getting heavier with very stride.

'Hey, who wants to get mushed in a tornado, Maya?' Kline had to run to catch up with her.

Why was he always so annoyingly good-tempered? Maya took a last longing look at the stars and the moon. Big, black, treble plasti-therm shields were coming down all over the city. Soon there would be nothing to see but white light. No sign of strong winds yet but that didn't mean a thing. The gentle breeze could turn into a raging storm in a matter of seconds and a bad storm could last for a week. They were safe in their hermetically sealed cocoon, but who wanted to be safe?

Kline was talking. 'So? What d'you think, Maya? Re-con? I've got enough creds if we don't go mad. Or maybe you'd like to come back to the unit?'

Maya watched him as he talked. He was a looker all right. A head taller than she was, his lean body was strong and straight. She resisted the urge to trace her fingers across his strong jaw line. He caught her looking at him and widened his eyes in mock horror. She smiled. Everybody liked Kline and she knew the female CO's envied her. She liked him a lot, really she did. They'd been friends since she was five. He was the nearest thing she had to family. And that was when, without warning, blackness closed in around her like a tight fist and she crumpled at Kline's feet.

*

*The child heard the noise again and clutched at her mother. There was something else in the hole with them, something that scratched and scraped as it slithered towards her. Her mother sat close, arms wound tightly about her and she whispered urgently into the blackness. 'Be brave, sweetheart. Please. You must keep quiet.'*

*

When Maya opened her eyes Kline was kneeling beside her, a stricken look on his face. 'Maya. Thank God. You okay?'

She made an effort to nod and he helped her to stand up. He kept his arm protectively around her.

'I'm fine. I haven't been sleeping too well lately, that's all.'

'Are you sure? You look terrible.'

'Thanks.' She moved out of his arms. 'Go home, Kline. I'll see you tomorrow.'

'What?'

'Something wrong with those?' She flicked one of his ears.

Kline's face flushed. 'You can't turn me on and off like a freakin shower, Maya.'

'Unfortunate choice of metaphor, considering mine doesn't do 'on or off'. I'll see you. Okay?' The need to be alone was overwhelming.

But Kline grabbed her arm, forcing her to face him, 'What the hell d'you want from me?'

Her voice was flat and unemotional. 'Nothing. Forget me. I'm bad news.'

'True. But it's my choice so don't push me away. I can help you, if you let me.'

'No you can't. No one can. I'm ...I'll destroy you. Get someone else. You keep telling me about all those women who fancy you.' Her attempt at humour didn't work. She touched his face. 'Kline, you know I like you but...'

He pulled her into his arms and kissed her. His mouth was warm and urgent and for an instant she thought that might be enough. When he let her go she stood staring at him.

He smiled confidently. 'Well?'

She wiped her mouth slowly with the back of her hand.

He spun around and walked quickly away, but Maya was already sprinting after him. She grasped his arm but he threw her off. 'I'm sorry, I'm sorry, Kline. I shouldn't have done that – '

.'– All those women and I had to choose Maya Johnson, Queen of Mean.' Kline's expression was grim

'There's always the brat.' It was out before she could stop herself.

'Poppi? She's nine years old for God's sake. What d'you take me for?'

'She's off her freakin head.'

'Yeh I seem to specialise in mad women.'

'Are you comparing me with that unhinged infant?'

'Sure she's a bit unstable but then who wouldn't be after what she's been through?'

'How long is she gonna cash in on that sob story?'

'She was left to rot in the tunnels, Maya. Somebody wanted her dead'

'Yeh, yeh, blub blub.' Maya was beginning to feel much better.

'She was two years old, Maya. Half starved, half crazy, couldn't speak.'

'So explain something for me, Kline. How come everybody thinks she's so freakin cute? You included. Does it bring out the paternal instinct in you? Hey? D'you want your own little Poppi?'

Kline was about to retaliate but he saw the look in her eyes. She thought she'd scored a point. He changed his expression to one of concern and patted her hand. 'Don't worry your pretty little head, Maya. You've got nothing to be jealous of. Promise.'

Maya snorted.

There was no stopping him now. He knew he'd got her rattled. 'And I do understand Maya, really I do, about your mood swings. It's that time of the month again, isn't it?'

'You'll be minus some of your oh-so-perfect teeth if you're not careful, boy.'

Kline's hand clutched his mouth protectively. 'Oh please, lady, not me loverly teeth.'

Maya laughed despite herself. 'Freakin *Mary Poppins*. I'm gonna trash that div one of these days.' He could always cheer her up. 'If I let you come back, there's one condition.'

'Say away.'

'We play *Angry Birds*.' And she patted the box in her backpack.

Kline was disgusted. 'Poppi's not the only thief around here.'

'I didn't steal this as it happens. That nice trooper on the door gave it to me. And I have first go, okay?'

The boy sighed. 'There's no hope for you. You're doomed. Good job, for you, we don't believe in hell anymore.'

The walkways were totally deserted now and Maya and Kline's footsteps echoed eerily as they hurried towards her mondo. When a tornado was cast all the good little citizens of Capa scuttled home, locked their storm-shields, watched divs and popped tabs.

As the two COs disappeared down a side tunnel a small figure rounded the corner, close to where they'd descended. Poppi was trailing Kline. She stood for a moment, then she took an almighty kick at the plasti-therm and screamed 'bitch' at the top of her voice, before running back in the direction she'd come, clattering her metal stick against the walls. The noise ricocheted against the shields and reverberated down the tubes until it ended in one final `ping' somewhere far away... and all was silence.

# *Malcolm in trouble*

'What d'you mean you haven't got them?' The President's face was purple with rage.

'The biogs and locations were destroyed as per orders, sir.' There was a tremor in Malcolm's voice but he wouldn't be intimidated. He was only obeying orders. 'They were forty years old this month – '

'– Destroyed? Destroyed? Who told you to destroy them?'

'It's in Section 334 of the manual, sub/para 19-201 of – '

Scar took a step towards him.

Malcolm's strong sense of fair play gave him courage, '...of Pool Regulations sir. I can find it for you if you wish. It would only take a moment.' Malcolm moved towards the computers.

Matthews shoved him aside. 'I don't need some smart ass quoting the rules at me. I wrote the freakers. And they don't apply to me, to my straws, or anything to do with me. Any trond-brain would know that. Now get into re-cyc and access.'

Malcolm stared at the president, as if seeing him for the first time. This was the man he had admired all his life. The only person he considered his superior. 'I'm sorry, Mr President, it's impossible. My orders are to keep records for forty years, anything prior to that time to be incinerated. I can't retrieve them, even if I wanted to. More recent data already fills many billion gigabytes of memory.'

Matthews was silent.

Malcolm took this for understanding. 'I was only doing my job, sir.'

The President struck him hard across the mouth and Malcolm staggered backwards, tasting blood.

Matthews followed the boy, fists clenched. 'Who do you think you are? You're nothing; you're less than nothing. You're an incompetent little shit and I ought to let Scar take you apart. But that would be too good for you. When's the new master ready? Well?'

'I...I...'

'Spit it out.'

'He's eleven months old, Mr President, a baby – '

'– Shut up. So, this is what happens. You sit at this computer night and day until you retrieve the data I need, got it? And I don't want any excuses. Now, get to it.'

The President and his trooper crashed out of the room, leaving the door swinging wildly on its hinges. Malcolm was too shocked to move. Maybe he'd dreamt the whole terrible scene, but he felt wetness on his chin and when he wiped it away he saw it was blood, dark blue blood.

The boy found a stool and sat down unsteadily. It was so unjust. He was good at his job – no, he was better than good he was...the best. There was only one Malcolm Blue and that was he. Had he not served the State faithfully all his life? "Incompetent?" The man had called him incompetent. And what was it all about anyway? What did it matter who the straws came from? What mattered was their viability. Each vintage had been kept in exactly the right conditions under the previous Pool Master and now himself. No straw died under Malcolm's watchful eye. They were his babies – his life.

It was all too much for Malcolm. He would never be able to forgive the president. He had done nothing wrong. It was he who had been wronged. With this self belief came confidence and Malcolm jumped to his feet. He would not even attempt to retrieve the destroyed data – he couldn't anyway. It was gone and Malcolm was glad. Let the President do his worst. He couldn't get rid of him until the new Malcolm was ten and that gave Malcolm plenty of time to punish the man for treating him so badly.

Before he had time to change his mind the boy went quickly to the Blu vat and took out one fertilised straw. He carried it carefully to the Pinx vat where he selected a Pinx straw, then he exchanged the coding on each straw, and put the Blu – now Pinx – straw in the Pinx vat and took the Pinx – now Blu – straw back to the Blu vat. He was shaking by the time he had finished but there was no going back. He was chosen, not Matthews or anyone else, he – Malcolm Blue.

# Disappointed

'Disappointed?' Rosemary's voice was shrill. 'That doesn't come close. My life is over.'

Dan tried to touch her but she knocked his hand away.

'My mother's organised a special celebration for us tomorrow at her GD. They'll all be there. All my family and friends. What am I going to say to them? How am I ever going to face them again?'

'They'll understand.'

'Oh yes, they'll understand. That you're a failure, my husband's a failure, my life's a freakin failure.'

'I tried my best, Rosie.'

'Obviously not good enough.' She stared accusingly at him, 'So what happened to the wonderful Pete Roberts? I thought he said he'd speak up for you?'

'He wasn't at work tonight, Rosemary. He had to look after Tanya.'

'Brilliant. So where was madam?'

'I wish you wouldn't call her that. Anna's a nice woman.' He was playing for time. 'Apparently she had to look after her mother. The woman's very ill, in hospital. Pete couldn't leave Tanya with a childminder, not on her birthday. Anyway, he wrote me a great reference.'

'Not great enough apparently.'

'He thought I'd get it, everybody did.'

'Except for the people that matter.'

Dan was grey-faced, 'Next time we're bound to –,

'– Next time? I'll be dead before then ... suffocation or...boredom. Is this all I'm worth? These four freakin walls? My father worshipped the ground I walked on and you promised him you'd look after me. Thank God he's not here now, to see how you've let me down. I should have listened to him. He said it could never work, me and you.'

Dan's voice was soft. 'You knew I was a Red when you married me, Rosie. I thought our love was beyond colour.'

'Grow up, Dan. This is reality, this…' And she spread her arms wide, '…this pathetic little box.'

Dan went to Emma's room and lay down on the bed, trying to blank his thoughts. It was Emma's sleep-over night for Tanya's birthday and he could hear the girls giggling through the dividing wall. It was reassuring. Emma was the one good thing in his life.

He was tempted to go and see Pete but Anna might have been released by now and he didn't want to intrude. Everyone had been talking about her arrest at the Institute. Dan had a sneaking suspicion that his application was refused because of his friendship with the Roberts. Of course he would never tell Rosie that but Matthews was making life very unpleasant for any Society supporters and they all knew that Anna Roberts was a party activist.

Dan wasn't political but he could see the injustices of banding. His work at the Institute had opened his eyes. He worked as Pete's senior technician and their remit was to screen embryos for genetic disorders before they were sent to the Pool to await selection. That had been fine at first but the directives had changed over the years and now it wasn't only genetic disorders they screened. They screened for intelligence, strength, size, passivity, breeding potential and most worrying of all, psychotic behaviour. They all knew what Matthews was doing but no one dared speak up. Dan wanted to resign but where else would a Red get such a well-paid job?

In the old days, Institute scientists were left to their own devices and so much of the budget was allocated to pure research, no questions asked. But that had all stopped now and the department only worked on state directives.

Forty percent of all children were solitaries now and the numbers were increasing. It was possible that within ten or twenty years' time there would be only 2% social children. The State-run training camps for troopers and COs were breeding grounds for anti-social behaviour. Adolescent children were notoriously difficult but when there was no parental control and the juveniles had access to big guns, it was a very scary scenario indeed.

Dan heard Rosemary moving about in their bedroom, opening wardrobe doors. He knew what she was doing. She thought he didn't know about her little secret but he had never minded. All he wanted was for her to be happy. He closed his eyes and fell into a troubled sleep.

When he woke he was disorientated and sweating. He went in search of liquid and found Rosemary curled up in front of the screen, half watching a news' div. She was much calmer and smiled apologetically offering him her hand. He took it and kissed it and then sat beside her, putting his arm around her. She snuggled into him.

He looked at the sreeen. It was a Society demo. Troopers were rounding up supporters and throwing them into transports. Rosemary sat forwards, two bright spots on her cheeks. 'Look at them. Serve the stupid fools right. *Equal rights?* Don't they know you can't argue with biology? If it's in your genes to be a Blu then so be it and if you're a Pinx then get on with it. The Pinx don't mind. Everybody's perfect now – in their own way.' And she smiled patronisingly at Dan.

Dan wasn't listening, he was re-winding the div. He froze the screen on a frame where a woman was being thrown into the trooper wagon. It was Anna Roberts. Behind Dan's back Rosemary settled back in the chair. She looked quite stunning when she smiled.

## On the run

Maya and Kline were laughing as she slid back her mondo door.

Huey Montrose rose guiltily from her bed, a skid of sweat on his upper lip. 'I've been waiting for you, Maya,'

Maya was furious 'How the hell did you get in?'

'No time for explanations. You have something that belongs to me – to the State?' He held out his hand. 'Hand it over and we'll say no more about it.'

Maya's eyes narrowed. 'Hey. Big of you, Montrose, considering you're the chuggin criminal here.'

'Cut the shit, girlie, give.'

Maya spun around. A trooper stood with his back to the door. It was the boy with the acne. There was the slightest flicker of recognition in the trooper's cold, contemptuous eyes before the mask settled back. The automatic he carried was almost as big as he was but Maya wasn't fooled by his size. These Elites were bred for their strength.

Montrose tried to assert his superiority. 'I'll handle this, Pox, thank you very much.'

But they all knew who was in charge here.

'Do as he says.' Kline's voice was urgent.

Maya backed away and pressed the button at her wrist. 'A class A crime has been committed; it's my duty to report to Central – '

Pox moved so fast that Maya only had time to fling an arm across her face before there was a thud, the door slammed and then silence. Maya peered out between her fingers. The trooper lay unconscious on the floor, her new Tranch board beside him, and Huey had disappeared. Maya examined her board for damage.

The colour had drained from Kline's face. 'What is it with you? All you had to do was hand over his freakin bag but oh no, that was too simple. The spanza could have killed you.'

'Not a chance.'

'I'm gonna lose my licence and I don't even want to think about what they'll do to me if he dies.'

Maya felt the trooper's pulse. 'He's okay.' She kissed Kline's worried forehead. 'Thanks. I owe you one. Don't worry, Kliney, Mummy will explain. It wasn't your fault.' She was searching Huey's bag. 'I wonder what the little rat was so frightened we'd find.'

'Leave it.' Kline jumped to his feet. 'Your pal's gone for reinforcements.'

Maya removed the shute cover from the disposal unit and jumped in, pulling Huey's bag after her. Seconds later her disembodied voice echoed up to Kline. 'Well? What are you waiting for? `

Kline hesitated, maybe he should stay, try to explain, clear his name? He changed his mind at about the same time automatic fire melted Maya's door into metal soup.

'What've you brought that for? ` Maya was waiting for him in the basement.

He was clutching her Tranch board. 'DNA – Maya, wait`

She was half way down the first tunnel when Kline caught up. She tore off her wrist pad and com patch as she ran, and hurled them away. Kline followed suit.

Most of Capa East was underground. Many of the commercial and industrial centres and service domes were down here and the passageways were full of people, mainly manual Pinx, going home from work. It didn't matter about the tornado down here. The workers hardly gave Maya and Kline a second glance. There were no Rats, but slow autopilot wagons circulated constantly. When they couldn't run any more they jumped a freight AP going in the direction of the city walls. Then, when the tracks ran out, they ran on again. Finally they stopped at a deserted surface lift. Kline was doubled up with a stitch.

'Maybe we've outrun them?'

Maya patted his shoulder reassuringly but they both knew they hadn't. Troopers had incredible stamina and tenacity. You couldn't outrun them. She and Kline needed somewhere to lie low, so that they could work out what to do next. They had to think their way out of this one. Brains were the only advantage they had over the troopers.

'I don't want to spend the rest of my life on the run, Maya.'

Maya grinned. 'At least it wouldn't be boring.'

'You're enjoying this, aren't you?'

'Well, you know what they say? '

'For Chrissake, woman, this is serious.'

Maya frowned. 'Kline, look ... what you did? It was totally brave. I won't ever forget it.' She kissed his worried face. 'Now let's get out of here.' She jumped into the lift and pressed the button.

Kline slid in beside her as the doors clanged shut. 'But what about the tornado --?' His words were cut short as the lift shot upwards.

They stepped out into a beautiful still, starlit night. The cool air was thick but breathable, so no need for vents yet. They set off at a jog. The moon was huge and bright and the air was speckled with glittering particles of sand. They put on their goggles. They must be very close to the city walls. An abandoned Pinx tower loomed up in front of them. Looking back towards the city Maya saw the lighted trans-routes and buildings. She hadn't been out this far for years. It felt fantastic.

A huge excavade rumbled towards them throwing up a breaker of sand. They watched as it lumbered past. They weren't concerned about being seen. These massive machines were driven by remote and the gangs of pinx inside would be eating and resting; going home after an exhausting night shift.

Gigantic sand dunes pressed in on the city from all sides, engulfing everything in their path. At sundown the city gates opened and the excavades trundled out, their colossal frontal plates repelling the outrider dunes. Each night there were breaches in the walls to be repaired, new defences to be dug and encroaching dunes pushed back. It was a never-ending battle and Capa East was on the losing side.

Maya and Kline ran until iron hoops tightened around their calf muscles. Then they broke into a disused sport's stadium as dawn was breaking. They found some old exercise mats and Maya slept where she fell, her head on Huey's bag. Kline stretched out beside her. He would keep watch.

## *Matthews*

Matthews lay slumped in bed, his food tray pushed to one side, untouched. It was steak and kidney pudding and jam roly poly with custard – real custard. He had his own Jersey cows. The food smelt delicious but he had no appetite. Scar stood beside the bed waiting for orders. Her expression was blank.

Lixir couldn't believe what Scar had told him. One of his Elite troopers had been bested by a female CO? That in itself would have been bad enough but, to add insult to injury, this criminal had escaped with the Montrose tapes. If the GSA got their hands on them it would be the end of Lixir Matthews and all his dreams.

Matthews knew Scar was suffering. She took the failure of any trooper personally. Matthews was glad he wasn't in this particular trooper's shoes.

'I trust you've got someone more reliable on the trail of this freakin CO?'

'She will be apprehended tonight, Mr President. My man will not fail again.' She saw Matthews' surprise. 'He knows the consequences.'

Matthews was satisfied. He knew as much as he wanted to know about the discipline of trooper camp. Anyone who didn't come up to scratch would be extremely sorry.

Scar continued her report. 'There is another CO involved, sir. A male; we have his biog if you wish to –'

'– I don't want his freakin life history, Scar. I want his life. What's the news on Montrose?'

'He is in his apartment.'

'You know what to do.'

'The SP has been eliminated.'

'Excellent. And the incriminating evidence?'

If Matthews had looked closely into Scar's eyes he would have seen the slightest of tremors pass before she responded. 'It has all been accomplished, Mr President.'

Matthews breathed a sigh of relief. He knew he could trust Scar. There was nothing to worry about. He pulled his tray back towards him. Shame to let good food go to waste.

## *Poppi meets Malcolm*

A tall thin boy wearing blue goggles slipped out of the Palace and walked quickly towards transroute level. Malcolm Blue wheezed as he hurried along, mopping the sweat out of his eyes with a sleeve. He looked ill and drawn. Both his hands were heavily bandaged and he held them protectively against his chest.

The goggles shielded his eyes from the harsh white, artificial light of the city. Without this protection he would have been as helpless as a baby. It was too jarring, too bright out there. Too not – blue. Malcolm only left the Pool in an emergency.

The Tradedome was a seething mass of buyers and sellers when Poppi arrived. She had taken her div off the chain and stowed it safely in her back pack. She hated not having it around her neck but it would soon be back where it belonged and it would have a friend.

Keeping her head down she dodged through the excited crowds. Some geek with blue goggles nearly walked into her but she side-stepped and moved on purposefully.

Her little mouth was set in a straight stubborn line. It was all Kline's fault. He said he would never leave her. So where was he? There was talk back at the unit that he was in trouble but she didn't believe it. She knew Kline wasn't the smartest but he had the ace CO with him. Maya freakin Johnson. The truth was Kline didn't care about her any more. He had abandoned her and she hated him.

When she got to the div store Poppi flicked casually through the latest catalogues. Her eyes were focused on the words but her senses were in free-fall. She chatted away to the dealer. He liked her. This kid was a good customer. She was a bit weird but, hey? All kids were weird. He turned aside to serve someone and in that instant Poppi saw what she'd come for. The Director's Cut, Mary Poppins div, featuring hologrammed dance routines. The little beauty winked up at her and in one fluid movement she wiped her nose with the back of her hand and palmed the div with the other. Then, when she was sure no-one was looking, she slipped it onto her chain.

She was totally calm. Nothing frightened her – well, there was that one thing, but she was working on it. Anyone watching her would never have guessed that inside her head she was floating way above the crowds. She felt as if she knew everything there was to know in the whole Globe and Universe. It was like she was the President or God or the top C O.

'Why d'you do it?' Kline had asked her once, frowning at her. 'You don't need to steal, you've got the creds, so why?'

Poppi had ignored him.

Kline had shaken her. 'Answer me.'

Poppi hated it when he was mad with her. 'I good thief,' she'd shouted. 'The best.'

'So you don't want to be a proper C O one day?'

This made Poppi take notice. 'When I ten I CO.'

'No way.' Kline had been the angriest she'd ever seen him. 'It's not gonna happen, Poppi. Not unless you stop thieving.' And he'd refused to speak to her until she'd promised that she wouldn't steal, ever again. She wanted to be good for Kline. He was her best friend but *ever again* was a long time wasn't it?

She couldn't remember anything before the unit, except for the rats. She still had nightmares about those huge, yellow-eyed creatures chasing her down long black tunnels – and the *scrit-scratching* of their scampering claws.

She knew that Kline had found her in the underground, traumatised and dying of thirst. She was dressed in rags and had a gold chain around her neck, threaded with an antique Mary Poppins div. She couldn't tell him who she was or where she came from, so Kline named her Poppi after the div. He took her back to the CO Unit and she'd been there ever since. For years Kline thought she was a mute because she couldn't speak.

Poppi's first real memory was that horrible night when they asked her to choose. She was called into Monty's office, where Kline and two strangers waited. Poppi tried to catch Kline's eye but he wouldn't look at her. The couple were staring at her as if she was going to die or something. Monty said she was a lucky girl because the man and woman wanted to adopt her.

The man was fat, with a round face. He smiled painfully as if it was tacked onto his face with rusty pins. The woman sat motionless, her long thin hands resting in her lap like dead things, except for when the finger-tips twitched. Poppi couldn't take her eyes off them. The man did the talking. He said they'd give her a home and advantages – whatever they were, but she didn't like the way they looked at her, like they were buying something and they weren't quite sure it was a bargain or not. They said Poppi would grow up with brothers and sisters, be part of a family.

Eventually the couple stood up and shook hands with Monty as if it was all settled. Poppi waited for Kline to tell them to get lost but when she looked at him he shrugged, like he didn't care.

The woman flopped her dead hand on Poppi's shoulder and the coldness of her touch was terrible. 'No,' Poppi leapt away and ran to Kline. She didn't cry or beg – Poppi never did that – but she would never go with these people. Her mind was made up. They tried to persuade her, even Kline tried – a bit, but eventually they gave up. The woman looked Poppi straight in the eyes as they left and there was something evil in that look. Poppi shuddered at the memory.

It was time to leave the Tradedome and Poppi made herself walk casually towards the exit. She couldn't wait to get back to the unit and watch her new div. She was relaxed, happy. See? She didn't need Kline. Poppi was okay on her own.

Suddenly a heavy hand came out of nowhere and grabbed her shoulder, spinning her around. It was a trooper – an elite. Poppi recognised the trooper's badly pock-marked face and pale, dead eyes. This boy had caught her stealing once before but Kline had been there and bailed her out. Her heart was thudding but she made herself grin. 'Hi, Pox. What?'

The trooper grabbed her bag and tipped the contents at her feet. Her div fell out and rolled away but before Poppi could grab it the boy's boot stamped down. He picked it up and thrust it into her face.

'This yours, girlie?'

She made a lunge for it. 'It's mine. Give.'

The trooper's fingers dug painfully into her flesh. 'Got proof of purchase?'

'You've gotta give.'

He dangled her beloved div just above her head. 'Go on then. Take it.'

She tried to reach it but he slipped it into his pocket.

'No', she shrieked. 'It's mine.'

'D'you think I'm stupid or something? You stole it. I saw you.'

'You never –' She stopped herself just in time. She'd been about to tell him the stolen one was around her neck. 'It wasn't me – '

'– Freakin liar.' The trooper spat the words into her face. 'I've been following you, ever since you left the unit.' He'd hoped the kid might lead him to her friend and the bitch CO but he'd wasted his time and she was going to pay for that. He was still smarting from the bollocking Scar had given him for losing the tapes.

'Call yourself a CO? You're rubbish. A pathetic piece of trash.' Poppi watched in horror as he drew out his heavy metal cosh. 'Time somebody taught you a lesson, girlie.' He was smiling now. 'And no freakin CO pretty boy to save you this time.'

Poppi didn't struggle, she went totally limp, and hung from the trooper's gauntleted fist like some broken puppet. The boy wasn't expecting this. He had hoped she would beg for mercy or cry or scream. This was something else and he needed to think about it. That one moment of indecision was all that Poppi needed and as he re-adjusted his grip, to allow for her dead weight, she threw her body sideways and squirmed out of his clutches. Then she head-butted him in the stomach.

'Pinx brain.' She screeched as she fled. People scattered as she ran. She wasn't looking where she was going and ran straight into the boy with the blue goggles. He was waiting to board a transport. Poppi was unhurt but Malcolm was winded. He bent double clutching his stomach, gasping for breath.

'What you? Blind?' Poppi yelled, looking nervously back over her shoulder. She knew she should get away but something stronger was telling her to stay. Pox had her div.

Malcolm tried to push past but she stood her ground. 'Please. I need to get this –' He watched in frustration as the train shot away down the track. Nothing was going right. He hadn't got what he'd been looking for in the Dome but a trader had advised him to try the West Zone. This was the underbelly of Capa where the green-marketeers hung out but Malcolm was desperate. He turned angrily on the child and grasped her arm. 'Now see what you've made me do? I shall be late now and it's nearly daybreak.'

'Why? Turn into toad?'

He shoved her hard. 'Go away, little girl.'

The 'little' girl's eyes narrowed. 'Chug off.'

The boy drew up his delicate frame so that he was looking down his fine, thin nose at her. 'Have you any idea who I am?'

The child gave him the once-over through slit eyes, 'Trond brain?'

'I am Malcolm Blue, Pool Manager of Capa East.'

'So? I Poppi. I CO in...soon, when I get ten.'

Malcolm turned his back on the unpleasant, illiterate little person.

Just at that moment Pox came crashing down the walkway and grabbed Poppi by the scruff of the neck. The kid fought wildly but this time the trooper wasn't going to let go.

One part of Malcolm's brain rejoiced that the rude little delinquent was going to be chastised but there was a softer side to Malcolm lately – a side he was having difficulty reconciling himself with, so when the girl cried out in pain he was compelled to say something.

'Excuse me. Is violence absolutely necessary?'

'On your way,' Pox snarled. 'Or I'll have you too, bug eyes.'

Malcolm laid a restraining hand on the trooper's arm.

Pox struck Malcolm's hand away, scoring a direct hit on the boy's most painful wound.

'How dare you.' The agony gave Malcolm courage.

The trooper was struggling to get cuffs on the wriggling kid or he would have silenced the interfering geek for good.

Malcolm was terrified of this brutish looking boy but he couldn't let this go. 'You've got the wrong person, Trooper. This child has been with me all afternoon. She hasn't been out of my sight. She's my…niece. Her mother, my sister, works in the presidential palace with me.' Malcolm showed his I D to the trooper. 'I'm the Pool Manager? You must release her instantly.'

Malcolm was as surprised by this speech as the trooper was.

Pox knew when he was beaten and he'd wasted enough time already. 'I caught her red-handed, citizen. She's a well-known thief.'

Malcolm looked shocked. 'Are you calling me a liar, Trooper?'

'No. But –'

Malcolm pressed home the advantage. '– We can go to the palace if you would prefer? Discuss the matter with the President?'

The boy dropped Poppi. 'My mistake, citizen,' he said, through clenched teeth.

'Well, don't be so hasty in future.'

Poppi scrambled to her feet and launched herself at Pox. 'Freakin, Spanza.'

Malcolm grabbed her. 'Shh, shh', he whispered urgently in her ear. 'We've got to get you home. Your mother will be worried.'

Poppi stopped struggling but Malcolm still kept a tight hold on her. He turned to go but she had other ideas. She pointed a dirty finger at the boy. 'He stole my div.'

Malcolm tried to pull her away but she refused to budge so he turned to the boy and held out his hand, hoping that the Trooper wouldn't see how his hand trembled. Pox took the div and threw it at the girl. There was murder in his eyes. The child grabbed the div and dived away down the walkway, laughing as she ran. Malcolm scurried after her, aware of the boy's eyes boring into his back.

The minute they were out of sight Malcolm fell exhausted to his knees. After a moment his elbow was jogged. It was the child. She was holding a can of 'C'. He was surprised she was still there but he took the liquid gratefully. While he drank, the child threaded her old div onto the chain with the stolen one. One shiny and new, the other old and tarnished. She looked very pleased with herself.

Between mouthfuls Malcolm muttered to himself, half delirious with pain and weariness. 'I should never have kept him. But what could I do? One bit of meat. Is that too much to ask? If he doesn't eat soon he's...he's going to die –I'

'-- What boy want?'

He'd forgotten Poppi was there and stared at her vacantly.

'What boy want?' Poppi asked again.

Malcolm sniffed, holding back the tears, 'It doesn't matter, it's too late.' He couldn't let the innocent creature suffer any more. He would make sure the end was quick and humane.

'I said "what"?' Poppi insisted.

'I have to buy some meat from somewhere but it's hopeless – '

The girl grinned. '– Meat? Easy. Come.' And she ran off down the walkway expecting him to follow.

Malcolm hesitated for a moment.

'Come,' she ordered.

And he stumbled along behind her, what else was there to do? He tried not to think about his screaming wounds and his aching, tired, flat feet.

His thoughts tumbled as he tried to keep the child in sight. If he hadn't stayed behind the night when the president had called him *incompetent*, none of this would have happened. Why hadn't he left the droids to clear up as usual? He should have ignored the pile of rubbish behind one of the smaller, reserve vats but, oh no, he had to clear up – efficient to the end. Imagine his surprise when the *rubbish* moved. Maybe he was hallucinating. After a moment he touched it with a finger. The texture was furry and indescribably soft, silky and warm. Finally a beady eye opened and regarded Malcolm. Malcolm had never seen a live animal before. The creature got to its feet, stretched, yawned and squeaked. It was communicating with him. Malcolm was entranced. It looked like some sort of rodent. But Malcolm didn't care what it was; he knew all he needed to know. He was in love.

The animal allowed itself to be picked up and Malcolm stroked his fur gently and tickled him under his chin. He squeaked again and burrowed his head deep into Malcolm's clothing. Malcolm shivered. He had never felt another living creature close to his heart before.

He locked up and carried the animal to his room. Safely inside he examined the creature. The animal's fur was a beautiful deep purple and Malcolm found a small brush and gently brushed the rosettes this way and that, marvelling at the way the whorls always returned to exactly the same pixel pattern. The animal fell asleep in his arms and Malcolm found him a cushion and gently laid him down.

Malcolm's hands were shaking as he accessed Pool regulations. He knew he must be infringing some rule but instead of worrying he felt exhilarated, like that first time the old Malcolm had let him transfer a straw on his own. Sure enough in sub/para 124, in the third volume of Pool rules 2291, it stipulated that No *animal should be allowed in or around the environs of the Pool. Flouting this rule would lead to immediate dismissal and cancellation of all privileges.* That was fairly unambiguous. Malcolm had never broken a rule in his life until tonight and he wasn't sure how he was supposed to feel. After a moment or two he did feel something, a sort of nervous knot starting in his stomach and moving upwards through his chest and out through his mouth, leaving his shoulders squared and his feet planted solidly beneath him. He felt taller and straighter and broader than he had ever felt before. He was the happiest he had ever been.

But that didn't last long because within a day Malcolm knew he had a serious problem. The animal would not eat. He spent a month's creds on RF – grains and fruit and other guinea pig delicacies – because that's what his pet was – a guinea pig. He'd looked it up and provided the food suggested. He had tried everything but the creature still wouldn't eat. The creature's once bright eyes became dull. His beautiful fur lost its lustre and began to fall out in clumps and he hid under a chair, eyes closed, making pathetic little distress calls.

Malcolm was desperate. He cut up a beautiful red apple. 'Come, baby. Try some for Daddy. It's good for you. See. I'll eat some first; then you.' Malcolm took a bite, going, 'Mmm, lovely,' but the animal didn't even open its eyes. The disappointed boy got down on his hands and knees and picked up the animal, holding him against his face. He could feel the guinea pig's tiny heartbeat. 'Please, eat,' he begged, and suddenly the creature turned his head sharply and sunk his sharp pointy teeth into the fleshy part of Malcolm's hand. The pain was horrendous and Malcolm thought he was going to faint. There was blood spurting everywhere and, when he looked closely, he saw that there was an actual piece of flesh missing from the side of his hand.

After bathing and dressing the wound Malcolm crooned to the animal. 'Come, baby. I'm not cross. Come.' And the creature poked his head out from under the chair, whiskers twitching and squeaked loudly and happily. His eyes were bright and he allowed himself to be picked up and petted. Malcolm thought the animal was showing genuine remorse for biting him but on the contrary the creature was hoping for another delicious morsel.

It took another four painful bites before Malcolm fully understood the situation and, although he loved the animal, there was a limit to how much of himself he was prepared to sacrifice.

## *A good idea*

Matthews lay on his bed trying to relax. He'd spent another fruitless night in the Pool, searching for a suitable replacement for Blade. His knew his blood pressure was high and he had a pounding headache. It was impossible to sleep.

Half-watching a div his thoughts went back to the Pool Manager. The boy hadn't accessed the deleted data yet and Matthews wasn't sure he was trying hard enough. Well, if the smug little freak thought he could play games with the President, he had another think coming. The problem was that the boy knew Matthews couldn't get rid of him – not yet. Too late Lixir realised that he'd made a mistake only having one Pool manager at a time. In future there would be several. He would see to that tonight.

Suddenly, he had a brilliant thought and he sat bolt upright, headache forgotten. There was an excellent way of making the Pool Manager suffer. Matthews was so freakin smart he frightened himself sometimes. He buzzed Scar and while he waited he thought about the stand-in problem again. Maybe he should come clean, appear in person to the GSA delegation, explain the situation and the threats to his life and throw himself on their mercy? But deep down he knew they wouldn't wear it and would be only too delighted to force him to resign and relieve him of his assets. He couldn't afford to alienate them, not yet. He wasn't quite ready to make his move. No, they could oust him if they wanted to, but for whom? He'd dealt with all the opposition candidates. Sadly, Procter had died tragically, only yesternight. Matthews made a mental note to send Mrs Procter his condolences.

At least the delegates would have nothing to complain about on the hospitality front. Fleur was in charge and she was an exceptionally thorough house-keeper. She'd been airing sheets and preparing rooms for weeks. The guests would be put up in the Palace, in luxurious apartments.

Of course there were other ways of keeping the delegates 'happy'. His medics had some interesting little drugs for such eventualities. But he would have to be discreet. These were powerful, astute politicians and they must suspect nothing. He banged his head with a podgy hand. What was he thinking of? He couldn't drug the delegates. They had bodyguards and their own medics.

So many things to worry about and the heat was frying his brain, plus Fleur was more annoying than ever. The woman seemed to thrive in hot weather, maybe she was a reptile and not a mammal after all? It wouldn't have surprised Lixir to see a forked tongue flicking out from between her yellow fangs. Even the new guinea pig was a disappointment. It was a weedy little runt that only ate finely minced steak, and spent most of its time quivering under the bed – even when Fleur wasn't there.

Matthews glanced back at the div. There was a 'Society' protest going on. Chuggin hell, didn't they know what an insult it was to him to have a bunch of weirdoes as the opposition? He'd destroyed five of their feeble coups in the past ten years. *'Love and integration?'* Not your fighting material at all. He despised the pathetic little freaks. *'No Purity laws?'* Trond brains. What the puny little do-gooders couldn't grasp was that for an efficient workforce you had to have able-bodied people. Occasionally some late on-set aberration went undetected but there were strict rules governing such eventualities.

The trouble started when misguided fools tried to hide defects and the State had to intervene.

Suddenly something caught his eye. A young woman was being man-handled into a troop carrier. What was a classy female like that doing mixing with that bunch of no-hopers? He might go down to the cells later, take a look at her. He needed something to divert him, but he'd have to be quick because they had to be shipped out tonight before the delegates arrived.

When Scar arrived Matthews swept past her, his original plan forgotten. He was on his way to the cells.

## *Defect*

Dan was exhausted. He'd done a double shift. As he let himself into their apartment the first thing he heard was Emma sobbing. As he hurried towards his daughter he saw Rosemary in their bedroom. She was reading.

'What's up with Emma?'

His wife carefully marked her page before closing the book. 'Need you ask? She's over-tired after that ridiculous sleep-over at the Roberts. I told you she shouldn't have gone. I've had to cope with her tantrums all day – on my own. There wasn't even school ...some sort of a mother she is.' Rosemary looked smug.

'Has something happened?'

'Haven't you heard? I thought everybody knew. I was going to buzz you at the Institute but I didn't think you'd – '

Dan was too tired to play games. '– Tell me for God's sake. I know Anna was arrested but Pete wasn't at work tonight. Have you seen him?'

'He's only got himself to blame. They wouldn't have taken him if he hadn't got violent.'

Dan sank down on the bed beside his wife. 'Tell me from the beginning.'

'Pete Roberts was arrested.'

'Why?'

'He tried to stop them taking her.'

Dan didn't want to ask the question but he had to. 'Tanya?'

Rosemary nodded. 'It makes me go all goose-bumpy, thinking about it. We'll have to take Emma for an examination, make sure she hasn't been contaminated.'

'The kid's got asthma not monkey plague. It's an allergic condition that affects the – '

'– Allergies can kill, Dan.' Rosemary's eyes were blazing. 'Why do you think the State eradicates all pre-deposed asthmatic foetuses? A century ago 50% of all adults in the Hinterland were suffering from some sort of allergy, 80% of all children Dan, that's a pandemic. Why d'you think the State culled pets and domesticated animals and birds and – '

Dan wasn't listening. He was trying to decide what to do.

Rosemary's eyes narrowed. 'You knew?'

'Of course I knew, we all knew.'

'Wait, wait. Are you telling me you deliberately allowed our daughter to mix with a…a defect.'

'Don't use that word'

'Are you mad? We'll be accused of colluding with criminals. You know the rules. All defects to be reported to the State within the statutory three month period post-birth. That's how we keep our gene pool pure. You work at the Institute. You know how it works.'

'Yeh, I know how it works, Rosemary, and it's wrong. Would you have given up our Emma if she'd had some minor ailment?'

'How can you talk about our beautiful wholesome child in the same breath as that… It makes me sick just thinking about it. My little girl sharing the same bed with that thing.'

Dan tried to shut his wife's voice out. He had to think. Somebody must have informed, but who? Theirs was a liberal Condo. He couldn't believe that any of their friends or neighbours would do such a terrible thing. Glancing up he saw the expression in his wife's eyes. She glanced away quickly but it was too late. 'Oh no please, you wouldn't do that, not to a little kid.'

'It wasn't me as it happens, it was Emma.' Rosemary picked up Emma's drawing book and thrust it at Dan. Emma loved drawing. She was very good at it. Dan flicked through the pages. There were lots of drawings of Tanya. Tanya in her party dress with a big plastic ring on her finger. Tanya eating her birthday cake and Tanya in bed with Emma. Dan got to the last page and was about to shut the book when something caught his eye. This last picture was different. Pete Roberts was in this drawing. He was standing beside the bed holding something and the girls were sitting up in bed. In all the others Tanya had a big smiley face but in this one her mouth was wide open in what looked like a scream. Dan looked more closely, no, not a scream, she was gasping for air. Pete was holding an inhaler in his hand.

Dan was too horrified to speak.

Rosemary squeezed his arm but he pulled away sharply. 'You mustn't be angry, sweetheart, I did it for us. It was my duty. I heard her the other morning having an attack and when I asked Emma she told me about the inhaler. We could have got into trouble if they found out. You'd never have been up-graded then. I had to inform Central. '

Dan dragged his wife to her feet. 'You reported Tanya to them?'

Rosemary broke away. 'I know where my duty lies. And one day you'll thank me – '

'– No. Never. I knew you were jealous of them but I never dreamt you'd do something like this. It's inhuman. And if you think this can help us then you're stupider than I took you for.'

'Stupid? How dare you. Right is on my side.' She smiled condescendingly. 'I know you can't help being soft-hearted, Dan. It's what first attracted me to you. But sometimes you have to be tough in this life, and I know what I'm talking about. She'll be well cared for, I'm sure – '

'– Well cared for? They'll send her Out. She's asthmatic for God's sake. There won't be any medication or shelter or food or love or...anything. How long d'you think she'll survive?'

'Surely you don't believe all those propagandist lies?'

'Is there anything you care about more than yourself?' He spat the words at her. 'Any little glimmer of humanity in that vain, acquisitive, superficial little brain of yours?' He threw open her wardrobe doors, ripped out the false partition at the back and hurled armfuls of new clothes onto the floor. 'I know I'm a Red, Rosemary, but I can do sums. I earn so much and we spend so much but for the last year there's been a deficit, a huge deficit. You've been hoarding all this...crap. Why? Does it make you feel good? Does dressing up in this trash make you feel like a Blu again?'

'You don't understand, Dan. I've always had a clothes allowance. I need to – '

'– Oh yeh, we all know what you need. All you had to do was ask. I only ever wanted you to be happy but I wasn't enough, was I? This,' and he held a dress in his hands. 'This is what you need...this bit of...nothing.' And then he tore the garment in two, as if it were paper, and tossed it at her feet. He piled all her outfits and shoes together in a heap and ignited a light stick.

Rosemary crawled onto the pile, covering the clothes with her body. 'Please, Dan. No,' she sobbed. 'Not my beautiful things.'

The flame reached Dan's fingers before he switched off. 'I want you to go now, Rosemary. It's finished. We're finished.'

She jumped up and ran to him. 'Don't be silly, Dan. Here, you've burnt your fingers. Let me see to it."

He shoved her away, 'I mean it. I want you out.' He was already pulling on his coat.

'Where are you going?'

'You'd better be gone when I get back. '

He went into Emma's bedroom. She was crying into the pillow. Dan took her gently in his arms. 'It's all right, Emmie. Everything's going to be all right.'

'It was my fault Daddy. I drew a picture and ...and – '

'– Listen to me. It was not your fault. Say it. Say 'it wasn't my fault.' Well? I'm waiting sweetheart, please, for daddy.'

The child looked up at him through tear-bright eyes. 'But the big men came, Daddy, and they took my Tanya away.'

Dan kissed the top of the child's head. 'It's okay, I promise you. Now dry those tears. We're going to see Mrs Thompson. You like her, don't you? You're going to stay with her until daddy gets back.'

'Are you going to get Tanya?'

Dan kissed her again and then he helped her get dressed. When she was ready he carried her back into the living room.

Rosemary ran to the door barring the way. 'Please, Dan, you don't mean this. You love me and I love you. Emma? You want to stay with Mummy don't you? Children belong with their mothers.'

Emma held out her arms to her mother and Rosemary snatched a kiss.

'We will be together again, Emma, I promise. You and me and daddy.'

Dan pushed past his wife. 'Don't even try to get her. She's mine; she's a Red and I thank God for it.' Then he strode out of the room.

Rosemary stared after them, tears running down her face. Then she salvaged what she could from her pile of clothes and started to pack.

# *Meat*

It was daybreak by the time Poppi and Malcolm got what they were looking for. Transport closed down during the day so they were forced to walk back to Central Capa. The place was deserted and even with the day shields down, the heat was terrible.

They could have done a deal sooner but Poppi insisted on getting the best price. When the dealers saw the eccentric weedy guy in the blue goggles they'd hoped for a profitable night but they hadn't bargained on him bringing the midget C O with him. They all knew Poppi.

Malcolm felt dizzy and nauseous in the pounding heat but Poppi bounced along in front. The palace was close by but the C O Unit was on the other side of Capa. Malcolm didn't know what to do. He couldn't abandon the child after she'd been so helpful but he had to get back to his room before the meat went off. However, he couldn't take the child to the palace with him because it specifically stated in the rules that the introduction of non-palace personal was strictly prohibited. Then he remembered that he didn't obey the rules any more.

Poppi was thrilled to be going to the palace and sang at the top of her slightly off-key voice. Something about `a spoonful of sugar' he thought, but sounds were distorted by the emptiness of the walkways. He would contact her unit later. They probably wouldn't care anyway – judging by the way they allowed the child to roam Capa. If it wasn't for him, she'd have spent the day in the cells.

He was surprised at how easy it was getting the child past security. 'This is Alice', he lied to the guard, looking the man straight in the eyes. 'My Pool security-chief's daughter?' And the door swung open. After all, what threat to the President was a little kid? Especially when she was so cute? Poppi dimpled at the man, then, as soon as he wasn't looking, she stuck her tongue out.

When they were safely in his room with the door locked, Malcolm called softly, 'Where are you, baby? Come see what daddy's got,' and a little twitching nose appeared from under the chair. The animal had caught the scent of meat.

Poppi took one look and screeched. The frightened animal shot straight back under the chair.

Malcolm shushed the frightened child – he didn't want to alert palace personnel. She climbed onto his bed and crouched there, hugging her knees to her chest and shaking uncontrollably. Her wide, frightened eyes never left the place where the animal was hiding

Malcolm used his most soothing voice – the one he used on his pet. 'It's a guinea pig, Poppi – Cavia cobaya – a rodent mammal. They're harmless little creatures.' Malcolm kept his bandaged hands behind his back.

Poppi wasn't listening; she was whispering something over and over again. Malcolm had to lean closer to hear what she was saying.

'Rat, rat, rat – '

'– No,' Malcolm reassured her. 'Not a rat. A guinea pig. I can show you a picture if you like. 'He's a friendly little chap. Come and be introduced.' She shook her head. Malcolm had wasted enough time and he crouched down on all fours and offered a piece of succulent steak to the quivering animal. The guinea pig shot out, grabbed the meat and demolished it in one gulp. Then he looked at Malcolm with an expression of such intense gratitude that the boy could have wept. The second piece went down just as easily and Malcolm was about to offer the third when he felt the child drop down beside him

'Not rat?'

'No,' Malcolm reassured her. 'Not rat.'

'Promise?'

'Promise.'

She took the steak and held it out on the palm of her hand. 'Come, guinea pig,' she ordered and the animal obeyed. Her hand was shaking but when the guinea pig took the meat and its rough little tongue grazed her skin, she laughed delightedly.

Malcolm sighed. He wasn't jealous of the child feeding his darling. He had provided the essential nutrients for the creature's well-being and that was enough for him. He was deeply satisfied.

The guinea pig ate his fill, then stretched out full length on Poppi's lap and looked up at her through black, glittering eyes. She gazed adoringly back at him. Malcolm found her the brush and she gently groomed the animal, while she sang quietly to him. If she stopped singing the animal squealed at her as if he wanted more.

Poppi kissed the animal's nose. ' Booty, booty. Orange boy.'

'Orange?' Malcolm didn't want anyone naming his guinea pig but him and anyway Orange wasn't a name.

The little girl gave Malcolm a surprised look. 'Colour, Boy, Orange.'

Malcolm was surprised. He prided himself on differentiating individual colours by their shade of blue and he thought his guinea pig was a deep reddish almost purple colour.

Poppi was busy rifling through the fruit bowl while the animal sat on her shoulder and groomed himself. Finally she found what she was looking for – an orange. She held it beside the guinea pig.

Malcolm saw the match immediately and laughed. 'We will have to call him Orange then, won't we?' And he reached out to take his pet from her. A deep scowl flitted across the child's face. Malcolm was puzzled, but then she grinned and passed Orange over. Malcolm took his friend and whispered into a shell-like ear. 'Hello, Orange. Are you happy now that daddy has found you some nice meat?'

'Poppi too.'

'Yes, you helped and we both thank you. Now, would you like to eat that orange?'

The child ate her way through the contents of his fruit collection. After that Malcolm prepared some vegetables and she held Orange while he cooked. It was the first proper meal Malcolm had ever shared with anyone. He only had one plate, knife and fork but Poppi ate with her fingers, out of the bowl. He had to stop her from eating it while it was too hot and he made a mental note to buy some more plates and things. Maybe she could come again one day and share some food with him. He'd found an antique site online, that sold all manner of eating paraphernalia.

After the meal Malcolm spread some soft bedding on the floor and the child lay down with Orange safely cuddled against her. They were soon asleep. Malcolm watched them contentedly. In his mind they were two of a kind, the young girl and the guinea pig. Both needed looking after. The girl's hair was a bit like the guinea pigs. Not so intricate or beautiful of course but similar. Maybe it was orange too?

Locking the door quietly behind him, he went to the Pool. There was something he had to do before he settled down for the day.

This time he switched a poet's straw for a mathematician's. The quotient for poets had rapidly declined lately and Malcolm thought it was time to have another. He also ignored a presidential directive to transfer a hundred Trooper straws to the iso-globes. Lately the president had been upping their numbers indiscriminately.

When Malcolm got back to his room there was a dreadful noise coming from inside. Not knowing what he would find he flung open the door. He was prepared for anything – well, almost anything. The room was full of dancing, prancing figures. There were penguins and a merry-go-round and wooden horses that broke off and joined a race with real horses. Malcolm stood transfixed. And there in the centre of the dancing singing group of people and cartoon characters were Poppi and Orange, both snoring.

What would they think of next? Malcolm leant over the sleeping figure and pressed the 'off' button on her div pod. And then he lay down, intending to think about all that had happened, but that was his last thought before he fell into a deep, satisfied sleep.

## *The ruby ring*

Kline woke with a raging thirst. He emptied his fluid bottle in one gulp. Maya was listening to Huey's tapes. There was a pile of them on the mattress beside her.

'Interesting?'

Her eyes were shining. 'Are you kidding? He wrote everything down. I'm gonna nail that bastard.'

'Matthews?'

'Of course, Matthews.' The girl jumped up. 'I'll fill you in as we go.' She saw the look on his face. 'Don't you wanna clear your name, Kline? Earn a lot of creds?'

'Yeah, but – '

'– If we get Huey to talk we've got Matthews.'

'You think the President's behind these killings?'

Maya pointed to the tapes. 'I know he is.'

Kline felt a bit happier. 'Okay, but we've got to be careful, yeah?'

'Sure. Got any tabs?'

Kline smiled. 'Thought you didn't like them.'

'Hand them over, boy.'

He got out a pack. 'So? We have bacon and egg...or rhubarb and custard?'

Maya wrinkled her nose and took one from each pack. 'Chew while you walk, Kline. Think you can do that?'

They emerged cautiously into a calm moonlit night. There was no one about. Kline was puzzled. 'Still no tornado?'

Maya popped a tab. 'Something's happening, Kline. I can feel it.'

'Paranoid or what?'

'Weather is never wrong.'

They waited for five minutes before breaking cover. It really did look as if they'd thrown the troopers.

Huey lived on the outskirts of the city, not far from their current position. They used the Teestrada, a dried up river bed, and now the main surface route through Capa East. It was a favourite location for surface-shooters and Maya had been out here a couple of times. Rusted cranes and warehouses still poked out of the sand on either side, marking the banks. Once it had been one of the busiest rivers in the Hinterland. Ships and oil-rigs had been built here for all over the world but the source had dried up and the sea had retreated to a day-span away.

Maya talked quietly and persuasively as they walked and Kline only stopped once to throw his arms wide as he argued with her.

The Strada was deserted. The surface was dangerous. There was always the chance of a freak tornado or sandstorm and the Tranch could take you unawares. And then there were the Tronds. Nobody had ever seen one and Maya guessed it was a story to keep people inside. The Pool had had its quota of disasters in the early days and Tronds were genetic mutations abandoned at birth and left to fend for themselves on the surface. The story went that they lived in holes in the ground during the day, much like the snakes and lizards of the desert, surviving on sector detritus.

The pair were enjoying the cool night air, when suddenly a convoy of armoured troop-carriers swept around a bend in the river and planed towards them on surf of sand. Maya and Kline hurled themselves behind a cannibalised vehicle and drew their guns.

The vehicles came abreast; then roared past, throwing up a wall of sand.

Maya had a fleeting glimpse of haggard faces staring out from behind barred windows. A prison convoy. The last wagon passed close to Maya and she saw a little girl pressed up against a grille on the back window. The child's small fingers clutched convulsively at the mesh. She had a plastic ring on her finger with a shiny red 'jewel'. Maya stepped out onto the strada and the child saw her. Then she was gone and the sand settled and silence returned.

Kline came and stood beside Maya. 'So? There's your tornado, Maya. Poor devils. I didn't know The Clearances were still going on.'

Maya couldn't speak. All she saw were those little fingers, knuckles white from hanging on, and that pathetic ring. Kline saw her expression and reached for her. She instinctively stepped into his arms. She couldn't tell how long they stood like that but it was so comforting.

But he had to go and spoil it by opening his big mouth. 'I've never held anyone like that before, Maya. It was like a totally a-sexual embrace wasn't it?'

Maya walked away, her mind clear of everything except the sheer physical effort of putting one foot in front of the other.

Kline was still talking. 'I guess that's what it feels like when your mother hugs you? Maya? Wait'

But Maya was long gone.

# Promises

It was almost day break when Dan found Pete Roberts. He was in a holding centre on the other side of Capa. Dan had been searching for hours and this place was his last hope. The small, hot room was packed with anxious people and smelt of sweat and panic. Dan elbowed his way through and touched Pete's arm.

Pete glanced at him. 'I've got a good feeling about this, Dan. I'm going to find her. I know it.'

Dan smiled encouragingly.

Pete clutched a remote as if it was a life line and stared up at a huge screen that covered the entire wall. The screen processed twenty enquiries at a time and Pete stood in line, beside other ashen-faced people, waiting for his heading to reach the top of the screen.

While they waited Dan asked if Pete had heard from Anna.

Pete shook his head. 'I've logged in their details, filled in the same data a dozen times; jumped through all the hoops, kept my temper and smiled when I really wanted to kill somebody – anybody. I've got to hold on for their sakes. Anna and my little …' He couldn't say any more.

'It'll be okay. We'll sort it.'

But Pete wasn't listening. He muttered something under his breath as he watched the screen. 'Daddy's coming, sweetheart. I promised you didn't I? Daddy never breaks a promise.'

And then the go-ahead asterisk flashed irritably beside Pete's details. *054/RE Young P.* Pete tapped in his wife's and daughter's names with trembling fingers. Both men stared up at the screen and Dan held his breath.

The response was instant. *Incorrect data. Negative information on Young/ Anna & Young/Tanya. No known matches in Capa East. The enquirer should re-define his request. Central MP Department is situated in Sector 6. Opening hours 20.00 – 22.00. We are here to serve you.*

Then the space went blank and another heading took its place. Pete stared uncomprehendingly at where his information had been. He tried to re-access but he couldn't. 'No that's mine' he shouted at the poor woman, beside him. 'No please, that's my space, it's mine. Tanya. Oh my God, Tanya.'

Much later Dan managed to get his friend home. Dan contacted his neighbour to make sure it was okay for Emma to stay the night, and then he poured Pete the first drink of many.

Pete told Dan what had happened over and over again as if by telling it Tanya was somehow still there with him. Early that night the troopers had broken down the door and dragged Tanya away and arrested him. At the jail Pete had pleaded with them to let him stay with his little girl but they refused. Tanya had been hysterical and clung to her father but they'd pulled her out of his arms and taken her away. She was starting an attack and he'd run after them with her inhaler. A hard-faced woman had taken the med but then they'd slammed the door in his face and he didn't know if they'd given it to her.

Dan sat up all night with Pete, letting him talk and trying to comfort him with lies.

## *The Penalty of the Peach*

The main gate to Huey's executive village **was open and the** gatehouse deserted. Maya and Kline slipped inside. Huey's place was easy to find. It was bigger and more flamboyant than any other building in the vicinity. There was an archway, bearing a coat of arms that led into a large courtyard. Nothing understated there. The apartment's frontage was decorated with ornate Romanesque columns and what looked like a solid oak door, with a huge wolf's-head knocker. It was all fake. Maya could tell without touching it. A trooper transport was parked outside.

The CO's were looking for somewhere to break in when they heard a blast of automatic fire and the sound of running feet. There was barely enough time to get behind a pillar when two troopers burst from the brightly lit habitation and drove off, leaving the front door wide open.

Kline grabbed Maya's arm. 'Did you see who that was?'

'Yeh. Our friend Pox. I told you he'd live.'

Kline followed Maya into the inner shell, sliding the screen across behind him. The facade was a plasti-therm cut-out, stuck to the exterior of a luxury mondo. The habitation was on three floors, all underground. Maya ran lightly down the first flight of stairs to a large atrium, with rooms radiating off. Huey's body was lying in an ever-widening pool of blood on the imitation marble floor. He had several bloody holes in his body and a sad look on his face, as if his sudden demise was a huge disappointment.

But Maya wasn't looking at Huey. She was staring longingly at the beautiful table in the centre of the room. She fingered it lovingly. 'Remember this, Kline?'

'Forget the freakin table, Maya', Kline pointed to Huey.

Maya feigned shock and horror. 'Oh my God. Has someone been hurt or something?'

He hated it when she was like that.

'Start here, Kline. I'll take the next level.'

She disappeared before he had a chance to ask her what they were looking for but within seconds her disembodied voice drifted up the stairs. 'Down here.'

The girl was standing in a large room housing a vast double door icer. On the floor beside the icer were cartons of tinned food, including salmon. Inside, the shelves were stacked with fresh meat, milk, cream, cheese and fruit and vegetables. On the bottom shelf was a carton of hypodermics, disposable gloves and a small iso-cube. Maya held the cube up triumphantly. 'Clostridium botulinum if I'm not mistaken'

Kline was impressed.

Maya turned the cube around so that he could read the label too, then she put it in her pocket and stuffed some bottled juice and two large succulent peaches into her backpack.

Kline frowned, trying to get his head around what was happening. 'Okay, so Huey was responsible for the poisonings, right? But then the troopers killed Huey because?'

Maya took the stairs three at a time, 'We've got to get out of here before they come back.'

Kline caught up with her on the next landing. He could move pretty fast when he had to. 'Why would they come back? They got what they came for. That creep Montrose.'

'Yeh they exed Montrose, but they came for something else too.' She waved the iso cube above her head. 'Luckily for us they've messed up but as soon as they get their dinosaur brains in motion they'll be back for this and...' she took off into the night, '...and us.'

'How long before we can stop running, Maya?' Kline shouted at Maya as they ran.

The boy couldn't see her expression but he knew she was smiling. 'It depends if you're talking figuratively or metaphorically, Kliney.'

\*

Montrose's kitchen looked as if the tranch had hit. The floors, walls and floors were covered in splashed and mashed RF. There were half open boxes and tins – their contents spilled everywhere – and the air was pungent with the rich aroma of a hundred different foodstuffs.

Pox smashed his fist into the side of the icer again, leaving another ugly dent. Den, his side-kick, winced. Pox shoved his hand out at the frightened trooper. 'I said get the evidence while I exed the pathologist, Den. So where is it?'

The boy avoided Pox's eyes.

'One little iso cube? How hard was that?'

The boy kept his head down and muttered. 'Sorry, Pox.' The fist came out of nowhere and Den folded up and slid to the floor.

Pox grabbed the trooper's collar and hoisted him onto his knees. 'Did I give you permission to use my name? You call me sir. Got that?'

Den looked up. 'Yes, sir, sorry sir,' he croaked.

Pox kicked him hard in the face. 'You will be sorry I promise you, very sorry, but first things first. Can you hear me? Good. We know where the cube is, don't we? You'll have to speak up, Den, I can't hear you.'

The trooper managed a hoarse whisper. His lip was split and his nose was broken. 'It's that freakin bitch CO and her oppo.'

'Yeh,' Pox took another kick at Den but the boy managed to roll away. 'First time you've been right all night.' Pox booted a carton of tinned salmon across the kitchen and the tins exploded in all directions. 'I hate freakin CO's.'

'Yeh,' Den tried to sound enthusiastic. 'Freakin COs.'

Pox got hold of Den and yanked him to his feet. 'If it wasn't that we're from the same squad I'd exe you right now and nobody would even notice, because you're a waste of space. What are you?'

'A waste of space, sir.'

'Now,' Pox said, screwing the trooper's ears painfully between his thumb and forefinger. 'This is what you do? I'm going after the bitch and you're gonna clean up here, and I mean totally. There will be no trace of RF anywhere and if that means you have to lick it clean with that horrible little tongue of yours then that's what you'll do. You leave one nano-speck of evidence and you get trashed, right? Now get licking.' Pox shouted over his shoulder as he mounted the stairs. 'And I'll be back, Den. Count on it.'

\*

Maya and Kline were back in the changing rooms. Kline had made a list and was striking off headings as they were dealt with. Maya was prowling up and down.

'Okay,' he said, stylus poised. 'Three. Huey was poisoning the RF users? But do we have a motive?' Kline wished he'd listened to all the tapes. 'He was investigating the deaths for the State, Maya, so why would he poison the people?'

Maya swung around and jabbed a finger at him. 'And who is the State, Kline? Um?'

'Matthews's a spanza, Maya, but he's a politician. It goes with the territory. Ever thought you might be a tiny bit paranoid about El Presidento?'

Maya's eyes were black with fury. 'Where've you been? That scum is capable of anything.'

'Okay, okay, calm down. But we have to prove his connection with the murders, that's all I'm saying. Cool, indisputable proof and...motives.'

'Okay, Kline, try to concentrate.' Maya talked slowly as if she was lecturing a young kid. 'It's in Matthews' best interest to discredit R F so that nobody will vote for Procter. Trust me. It's all on the tapes. Huey set up the real food venues supplied the poisoned food and attended the investigations as pathologist. He was busy, busy, busy and fortunately for us he was also very thorough. He recorded everything – and I mean everything. The dates of each murder, the amount of poison used, the venue, the names of the deceased...everything.'

'And he says that Matthews was involved?'

'No. Of course not. But Huey worked for Matthews, didn't he?'

Kline's forehead puckered. 'Why was Huey exed again?'

'Because of us. Matthews had to get rid of him before we got to him, in case he talked.'

'Poor little creep.'

Maya snorted. 'It's not very nice dying of botulism, Kline. You've seen them.'

Kline looked very pleased with himself all of a sudden. 'You've overlooked one important point.'

'Really? What?'

'If Matthews murdered Huey then why didn't his thugs get rid of the evidence while they could?'

Maya gave him one of her most patronising looks. 'Because they're pinx, Kline. They can only think of one thing at a time.'

'I've known some quite intelligent pinx.'

'Oh yeah?'

'Yeh.' Kline's attention was on his list again.

Maya peered out at the lightening sky. 'It's time to go.'

Kline frowned. 'The sun's coming up.'

For once Maya agreed with him and she opened her back pack and had a long drink of juice.

'They won't send troopers out in the sun.' Kline moved on to his next heading. 'Okay. What do we do if we can prove Matthews is involved in the crime? Do we shop him to the authorities?'

'No.' Maya offered Kline a drink.

'Because?'

'Because, he is the authorities.'

'Right, so we inform the GSA?'

'Not easy. Matthews will have them holed up somewhere and guarded by troopers.'

'Maybe Procter could get to the GSA? He's an election candidate. Matthews couldn't stop him from meeting them.'

Maya patted Kline's hand.

'What?'

'And how do we contact Procter? We have no coms. We threw them away. Remember? Anyway, he's probably dead by now and even if he isn't you can bet your sweet booty if we go anywhere near him we're finished.'

Kline was searching through his back pack and finally held up a hand-held com. 'Huey's not the only one who's into ancient machines. No GP

Maya. I knew this would come in handy one day.' He punched in some numbers.

'What are you doing?'

He put the speaker on so she could hear. 'Hi. I'd like the number for a Mr A Procter?'

The response was immediate. An analogue voice barked out. 'Name, location, political affiliation?'

'Mind your own freakin business.' The line went dead and Kline tossed his com back in his pack. He looked very pleased with himself

'Now we really do have to move.' Maya was packing up as she spoke.

'No need to panic, Maya. They can't track us. And at least we know now what the score is. So here's what we do, we stay here for a coupla until the GSA show, then we contact our CO mates, on my com, and they get in touch with the delegates and Procter too.' Kline was very pleased with himself. 'We're gonna be rich, little Maya Johnson'

'If we live long enough. Anyway what's with the `We'? I work alone.'

'I saved your ungrateful skin remember? Maya, what are you doing? I'm speaking to you.'

Juice was dribbling down Maya's chin. She held out the peach to Kline but he glared at her. Maya laughed. 'Baby. I'll share the creds, promise. Now enjoy.'

Kline wrinkled his nose in disgust. 'Trying to poison me?'

'Botulin doesn't develop in fresh fruit, Kliney. Your scientific knowledge is total crap.'

Kline took a step towards her and pulled her close. 'I'd rather taste your peach.' He kissed her chin, licking the juice, and then moved up towards her mouth. His eyes were shut. If he'd kept them open a moment longer, he would have seen the look of absolute horror flitting across Maya's face, before he experienced the briefest of blindingly painful moments and then oblivion.

As his unconscious body slumped to the ground, Maya came face to face with the trooper. She backed away, offering the peach. 'You should have some, Pox. No, really, fresh fruit is excellent for the complexion.'

'Shut your freakin mouth, girlie.' This boy obviously bore grudges. He motioned to her to unbuckle her gun belt.

Maya glanced at Kline as she obeyed. Blood was pouring down his face and he was so pale. Let him be alive.

Pox kicked her belt away and held his hand out.

She looked puzzled.

The boy's expression never changed. 'Three seconds. One…two….'

Maya gave him the iso cube. 'How did you track us down so quickly? I'm really impressed.'

Pox's blank gaze flickered at her. Well well, this boy could be flattered. She pressed home her advantage. 'Are you specially trained, or is it some inbred skill?' Whoops. His face shut down again. Maya smiled ingratiatingly. 'I'd really like to know how you did it. Is it some new tracking device?'

Pox nearly smiled as he stowed the cube. 'Never heard of footprints, girlie? Not so freakin bright are you? All the way back here from the Montrose house? Male prints and female ones – Blu female. Pinx bitches have feet like shovels. I've never had a Blu woman. I wonder what it's like.'

Maya smiled invitingly and offered the peach again. 'Why don't you try it?'

'Tapes, girlie.'

One day she'd ram that 'girlie' down his throat

'I said tapes. And then I'll decide what to do with you. You made trouble for me and I don't like that. My boss give me a freakin bollocking because of you.'

'And what if I don't give them to you? You can't afford to screw up again, can you, boy?' Maya had decided on a more direct approach.

The M13 was in Pox's hand before she saw him move. He really was very good.

'Dead or alive, bitch.'

He really did smile this time and she knew he wasn't bluffing. He was in no hurry. The main exit was covered and she wasn't going anywhere. The tunnel to the pitch lay behind her. One chance. Maya pointed to Huey's bag were it lay on the exercise mat, and as the trooper bent to pick it up, she spun on her heels and flew down the tunnel.

The sky was lightening as she burst onto the pitch. What had once been immaculate turf was now covered in hillocks of sand. The sun was on its burning way and Maya ran for her life. The trooper crashed after her, firing as he ran. It was hard work ploughing through the sand but Maya knew it was harder for him weighed down by heavy equipment. She zigzagged as she ran and ammo whistled around her. It was only a matter of time before she was hit but she kept going anyway.

Then, suddenly, out of nowhere she was plucked off the ground and tossed high into the air. The Tranch. Maya's first impulse was to fight the mighty wind but then her subconscious kicked in. In one smooth movement her board was under her feet and she crouched forwards, letting the rip-wind take her. She levelled out and headed towards where she knew the perimeter wall must be although she could see nothing but swirling sand. Within seconds the wall reared up in front of her. There was no time to take the board higher and she knew she would impact. Summoning her remaining strength she leapt upwards off the board, her hands searching for a finger-hold on the wall. The board exploded into a million pieces beneath her.

Somehow, she managed to hook her fingers over the top of the wall while bullets ploughed into the masonry all about her. Finding some purchase she thrust herself upwards and miraculously was over and falling. It was a long drop and she landed awkwardly, one leg bent beneath her. She heard the crack and passed out.

When she woke she had the taste of vomit in her mouth. There was a length of broken plast within reach. She used it as a crutch to lever herself upright then she hobbled painfully into the network of alleys that surrounded the stadium. It wouldn't take long for the trooper to detour and come for her and he would be moving fast.

She stared about her trying to blank the pain. This was Termite Town the most extensive Pinx area in Capa. Black towers pushed upwards into the sky and at ground level the surface was littered with wrecked transports and rubbish. The pounding of the massive air pumps blotted out any other sound and there was a terrible stink. The towers were aeration ducts. The Pinx lived underground and the putrid air was expelled through the towers and away. At least that was the theory, but the heavy foul air sank back down to surface level. Maya reached for her vent. The place was deserted. The Pinx would all be dropping exhausted into bed by now and even if she met some they would only help if she could pay them.

Her strength was almost gone when she found herself in a dead end. At the far end, the huge doors to a Pinx shaft straddled the street. The lifts were closed. Maya made it to the end of the alley then propped herself against the doors, easing the weight from her damaged leg. This was a bad place to be but she knew she was finished. She sank down behind some metal crates and closed her eyes, nausea and faintness coming in waves.

The burning sun was on her eyelids and she opened them as the giant shadow of the trooper leapt into the alley. The light behind him distorted Pox's slight figure into monstrous proportions. He was etched in black against the angry rising sun and he walked in the cocky way of all thirteen year olds, narrow hips thrust forward and legs moving stiffly from the waist. At any other time Maya would have laughed – this little half-man with the big gun. He knew she was there and came on slowly kicking every pile of rubbish, ramming his gun butt into every likely hiding place. Maya knew it was all over; she was too exhausted to fight and too disabled to run. She started to raise herself from the ground; at least she'd die standing up, but the sudden pressure on her leg sent her reeling backwards. For an infinitesimal moment Kline's face swam in front of her eyes and then her world was spinning into blackness and the pain was gone.

## Billy Boy

There were twelve adult prisoners shackled down the length of the transport. A young boy and a little girl stood pressed up against the back grille. Two troopers guarded the prisoners while two others sat up front with the driver.

It was deathly quiet in the wagon except for the synchronised lurching of the speeding vehicle, as it bucked in and out of the sand. Three prison transports had left Capa that night, but this one had picked up a puncture and now the driver was racing to catch up with the convoy. It was a bad idea to be caught out here on your own. Several prison details had been ambushed by rebs recently.

The prisoners sat slumped with their heads down, afraid and ashamed. They'd lived all their lives being reassured that they were just like everybody else, but deep down they'd always known they were different and one night they'd be found out. This was that night. They didn't speak or make eye contact with anyone. They were alone in their misery.

There was the young woman with a cleft palette, an old diabetic man, an autistic youth, a couple with glaucoma and a man with a congenital hearing disorder. One moment they'd been at home amongst their loved ones, safe and happy and now they were on their way to the Outpost. They'd all heard the stories of course but no one really knew what happened out there in the desert. The one thing they knew was that there was no hope. Not for them.

The little girl was crying. She had woken from a ragged, exhausted sleep but the nightmare was still there when she opened her eyes and she couldn't bear it. Great gulping sobs shook her little body.

The gaunt older boy squashed beside her whispered furiously. 'Cut it. You stupid?'

One of the troopers was already on his feet cursing, not caring who he crashed into or trod on, as he lurched down the fast moving vehicle towards the child. His face was a patchwork of scars and his nose was shoved to one side, as if it had been broken and not set properly.

Tanya saw him coming but she couldn't stop crying. She wanted her mummy and daddy so badly. She was hungry and thirsty and her little body was covered in bruises. It was airless in the wagon and she felt her chest tightening once again.

The trooper leant over a male prisoner, who was trying desperately to get out of his way, 'You? Yes you, mute.' He was looking straight at Tanya. She hid her face in her hands, her little shoulders shaking from the effort to stop crying. 'Shut your mouth.' He raised his massive gauntleted fist, ready to strike the child, 'Or I'll shut it for you.'

'Leave her alone. She's only a little kid.' It was the boy again. He stared straight up at the trooper, unafraid.

The trooper was surprised and pleased. Any excuse to beat a mutie was a bonus. He grabbed the boy and held him up, so that his feet dangled off the ground. Tanya watched through tear-bright eyes. 'Well, well, well, what have we here? A cocky little mute.'

The boy grinned from ear to ear. 'Yo, Squado.'

The trooper was so surprised he nearly dropped the boy.

The boy attempted a salute. 'I was at training camp with you, Squado. You were my lead trooper. Don't you remember me? Name's Billy?'

The trooper was confused. Mutants were scum, they had to be eliminated, but this was…this was Billy Boy. He remembered him. A good lad, had the makings, everyone said. The trooper lowered the boy to the ground, but still held on.

'We shared the same billet, Squado. You took me on my first kill. Blooded me yourself.'

'Yeh, so I did. Good times eh?' The trooper let Billy go and the boy brushed himself down.

'What are you doing on this –?'

'– Shh,' Billy put a finger to his lips and beckoned the man nearer. They stood very close, the boy on tiptoe, on a level with the trooper's chest. The man leant down to hear what the boy was whispering and the elec lock-tag, attached to the trooper's belt, dangled invitingly by Billy's hand. He was an exceptionally good pick-pocket. Squado didn't feel a thing as the tag was palmed to the nearest prisoner.

'Didn't they tell you about me?' Billy looked furtively about him, checking that no one was listening. 'I'm working undercover. No. Don't say anything. Don't look surprised. They mustn't know who I am. That's why I helped the little mute. Get them on my side, see?'

The trooper nodded, totally lost.

'Word is there's some high profile dissident here and my brief is to find out what's going on and then report back to the Big Man.'

The trooper mouthed. 'The President?'

Billy nodded. 'They're gonna attack the Outpost.'

Squado erupted. 'The freakin bastards.' But he saw Billy's warning glance and lowered his voice.

'But we were told this lot were all mutes. We've got orders to take them to the desert and – '

Billy smacked his head in sheer frustration. '– Freakin hell. Call your mate down, Squado, we need to talk, get this sorted, before we're all in deep shite.'

'I'll have to buzz Central first, check you out.'

Billy pulled a face. 'Yeh, do that, Squado, you know best.'

The trooper looked worried. 'What?'

'Nothing mate, you're the boss.'

'Tell me.'

Billy spread his hands in an apologetic gesture. 'I don't want to cause you no trouble but this operation is top secret.' And he made a zipping motion across his mouth. 'I wouldn't like to see my old oppo posted to desert patrol permanently.'

Squado was frightened. The troopers sent to the desert didn't come back and those that did were head-screwed. 'I'll contact them later. Yeh?'

Billy nodded reassuringly. 'Good man. We can sort this between us. What about the three up front? Solid are they?'

'Yeh, solid.' Squado was the trooper in charge on this trip. It was his first big assignment. He beckoned to the other trooper over. All their attention was on the matter in hand, so they didn't notice the change in the prisoners, the sudden alertness, the raising of heads, and the hope in their eyes and the tag going from hand to hand undoing their shackles.

Tanya had stopped crying and was breathing more easily. The med Billy had given her was working. She never took her eyes off her new friend as he talked to the nasty men.

## *Sonny*

When Kline opened his eyes it felt as if a huge bell was striking the hour in his head. He tried to move but his arms and legs were tied. Turning his head painfully he saw he was lying on a bed and there were other beds, identical to his, each with its prone occupant. Where was he? He tried to concentrate. He had no memory of what had happened. Had he been in a battle? If so where? And with whom? But if this was war he'd come off lightly. The other people were swathed in blood-soaked bandages, moaning with pain and the air was thick with the sickly smell of untended wounds. A few spot bugs flitted around the room and one fan rotated phlegmatically. The AC must have malfunctioned because the heat was stifling. Kline struggled to remember what had happened but the pain in his head defeated him.

Something moved at the foot of his bed and he craned to see what it was. An old woman was standing there, gently bobbing up and down and staring at him with bright, intense little eyes. Her hair was plaited around her head and she wore a glaringly white and starched button-through uniform. She caught his gaze and smiled, lips stretched back over her gums exposing long yellow teeth, and then she winked.

'All right, sonny?' She came and stood beside him. 'Only you don't look too good to me. In fact you look freakin terrible.' For some reason she thought this was extremely funny.

'Am I...is this...? I'm afraid I can't remember. Has there been an accident?'

The woman threw back her head and howled with laughter. 'You could say that. Yes you could definitely say that.' Then, in a matter-of-fact voice. 'D'you want to come and live with me?'

Fortunately for Kline he passed out at that moment. Fleur ordered a trooper to bring water and a bowl and then she set about making him pretty again. His only injury was the huge lump on the side of his head. She was in the middle of cleaning his face when she stopped in mid-wipe. Leaning forwards she stared closely at the boy. If anyone had been watching what happened next they would have been extremely surprised. Fleur Matthews – she of no feelings, other than angry and angrier – sniffed loudly. For her this was an act of extreme emotion. The trooper holding the water bowl was foolish enough to allow his mouth to twitch and Fleur kicked him hard, then she ordered him to bring the boy to her rooms. It took him a few minutes before he was able to obey her.

Kline dreamt he was propped up on cushions in a soft, cool bed with white clean sheets. This was a really strange dream. He felt his head carefully, it still hurt. Beside the bed was a table with food and drink on a tray. It was Real Food and tasted delicious. Kline ate ravenously. Did you get hungry in dreams?

'What's your name, sonny?' It was the old woman again. She was sitting in a chintz-covered chair at the bottom of the bed smiling at him. Her gnarled fingers plucked at the sheets. 'Go on, don't be shy, you can trust your Auntie Fleur.'

Between mouthfuls Kline searched his brain for a name – no, total blank. He spread his hands in a helpless gesture.

The woman patted his feet amiably. 'Don't worry about it, sonny. We'll have to make up a name for you until you remember your real one? Well now, let's see, what shall we call you? Umm? Charles? No. Mustafa? No. I know. What about Kline?'

Kline didn't think much of Kline but he sensed this wasn't the time to argue. Anyway, it was only a dream so it didn't matter. He carried on eating while the strange little woman fussed about piling his plate with more food, filling his glass and plumping his pillows. It had been years since he'd eaten steak and, dream or no dream; he was determined to enjoy it.

Only minutes after Kline had been moved, Matthews appeared in the cells. He looked around in disbelief at the prisoners lying in hospital beds and barked at the trooper Captain standing beside him. 'What's this, a freakin holiday camp? '

The trooper's expression never changed. 'Mrs President ordered all prisoners be brought to sick bay.'

Matthews gritted his teeth. Matron day. Fleur and her bloody boarding school fantasies, where everybody took their medicine like good little children. *'You may think I'm a cabbage but I'm not as green as I look.'* It had to be one of those bloody days.

Matthews walked from bed to bed tut-tutting to himself. 'Am I some sort of monster? No citizen in Capa East goes without. Everyone is healthy and has a roof over his head yet there are still these despicable malcontents. What's the matter with them?' He had stopped by the bed of a young woman with a badly bruised face. He recognised her at once. The woman on the div. His angry expression changed. 'Blu?' The trooper pulled up the woman's sleeve exposing the Blu coding. Matthews was immediately cheerful. 'Clean her up and take her to my rooms. I wish to interrogate her personally. Oh, and use the back door.'

Lixir was in a hurry to get back to his rooms so when a medic approached him nervously, he was angry. 'Well?'

The man took a step nearer and whispered in the president's ear. Matthews' face broke into a cherubic smile. He patted the man on the arm and then swept out, shouting over his shoulder, 'I want these beds empty by morning.'

The captain saluted. "Mrs President ordered a fire drill for 22.00 hours.'

'You heard me, Trooper.'

The man nodded. 'And the children, Mr President?'

Lixir's voice echoed back from the corridor. 'All of them, Trooper...especially the children.'

## *No choice*

Dan heard the news from a neighbour. The woman was still badly shaken. Apparently she and her husband had been returning home late, after a party, when they noticed Pete Roberts slumped against the wall beside their Rat stop. They didn't speak to him because they thought he was drunk. His eyes were red-rimmed and his skin was grey and greasy.

The shields were down and the lights were blindingly bright. The woman said Pete's clothes hung limply off him, as if he'd been sleeping in them for days. He was unshaven and gave off that pungent, sweet smell of the unwashed. In antiseptic Capa East this was not acceptable and she and her husband were wary of approaching him. All the condo knew what had happened to his family and they were very sorry for him but they didn't want to get involved. The woman stopped at this point in her tale and dabbed at her yes. Dan waited until she was able to continue.

She said Pete was clutching a piece of crumpled paper and finally it dropped from his fingers. Soon after that they heard a Rat approaching. The woman said she felt relieved. She wanted to get home and forget about Pete Roberts. It was too upsetting.

They could feel the onrushing air as the transport got nearer and nearer and the eddying wind picked up the paper ball that Pete had dropped and threw it high into the air and away, bouncing it down the transroute until it lay caught up in the track.

The Rat was on them when Pete suddenly sprang onto the track and raced towards the piece of paper. There was nothing they could do. Nothing anyone could do. The woman couldn't speak for a long time after this but eventually she handed a ball of paper to Dan. 'I found this afterwards,' and then she walked quickly away. Dan spread out the paper with shaking hands. *Tanya Roberts: Defect. Deported to Outpost: Sentence – life.*

*Munro*

The black ventilation blocks of Termite Town shimmered in the full-day sun and within one such tower, the Flume, Maya was waking up.

She lay on a hard bed in total darkness, the noise of ventilation pumps was overpowering. Her mouth was dry, her tongue swollen and she hurt all over. The smell of dried sick and stale sweat made her stomach heave. Wherever this was, there was no air con. She struggled to sit up but the sudden screaming pain in her leg forced her down again.

She tried to remember and saw the trooper's distorted shadow as it surged towards her down the alley. Someone must have pulled her inside the Pinx shaft before he got to her. She didn't have to move her leg to know it was broken. The next thought came unbidden. Kline. She fought to sit up again but this time a hand came out of the darkness and pressed her firmly back onto the mattress. Her mouth watered, she was going to throw up. She retched into the bucket held out for her.

Her eyes were getting used to the dark and, in the dim light, she could see the man sitting beside her. He offered her a cup and held it while she drank. As she gulped the liquid she looked at him. He was large and raw boned, unmistakably Pinx. He smiled when their eyes met but she looked away and lay back, closing her eyes.

The next time she woke a different man sat beside her.

'How d'you feel?'

Maya didn't answer stupid questions. 'Who are you?'

'I'm Munro and you?'

Maya ignored him.

Munro continued. 'Frankie tells me your leg's fractured.'

'Frankie? The Pinx? What would he know?' Maya tried to swing her legs off the mattress.

The man laid a hand on her arm. 'I don't think so.'

'You can't keep me here.'

He laughed grimly. 'Believe me, we'd all prefer you were somewhere else, but how far d'you think you'd get with a broken leg? Now please, I need to see how bad it is.' He tried to be gentle while he prodded her leg but the pain was terrible.

She clutched his sleeve. 'Look, there's someone… I had to leave him. He needs my help. All I need is an injection of – '

He was cutting away her boots. '– Start counting backwards from twenty, slowly'

She opened her mouth to protest, aware of a pungent, overpoweringly sweet smell and then, before she could count to anything, was asleep.

When she came round her leg was in a splint and the man was sponging her forehead. She felt light-headed, almost euphoric. Whatever he'd given her was good.

He saw that she was awake. 'It's a bad break I'm afraid. The rest of the damage is superficial – sprained ankle, bruising, and a lot of shrapnel-like wounds. I keep digging out uni-plas. What happened?'

'My board exploded. Look…Munro, how long before I can walk?'

'You're young and healthy, three, four weeks.'

'No. Look, I have to do something. Please.'

The man glanced at her, guessing that 'please' wasn't a word that came easily to her.

'I was with someone. In the sport's stadium, outside Termite Town?'

'Pinx City not Termite Town. It's a sensitive issue here. You don't want to offend the people who saved your life, do you?'

Maya didn't comment but everyone knew that Pinx were about as sensitive as re-cycled shit. 'D'you know what happened to him, to Kline?'

'I'm sorry. He was taken.'

Maya shut her eyes. He was sorry. God, it was laughable. All those years keeping herself to herself, not having relationships or emotions, not being political, not getting involved and now...

The man pressed a cup into her hand.

She drank automatically. Whatever it was it wasn't C.

'Not so fast, you'll choke.'

Maya wasn't listening. The liquid spilled out of her mouth and down her neck. She drained the cup, and then held it upside down, getting the last drop out with her finger.

The man laughed. 'Don't panic. There's plenty more where that came from.'

'What is it?'

'Water.'

'What? 'Maya felt her stomach heave. Nobody drank water. Not since the last typhus outbreak. The only safe water was chem, if you could get it. It cost a fistful of creds and then some. There was no way a Pinx zone would have chem.

'It's pure. You won't die.'

'But where did you get it?'

'You really are a nosy little kid. It was lucky for you that Frankie was late back from the walls. If it wasn't for him you would have been taken.'

'I haven't got any creds.'

'He doesn't want payment.'

Maya knew better but felt too weak to argue.

'He's not going to be the most popular guy around here either. The troopers will be back tonight to search for you. The whole Flume is being relocated.'

'The Flume? What the hell is that?'

'Questions questions. Get some sleep.'

True, she was exhausted and sleep would be fantastic but she didn't want to shut her eyes, because every time she did she saw Kline's face and that idiotic look as the Trooper's gun crashed into his skull. If he survived she'd make it up to him, she promised, on her Mother's grave.

*And she was there again…running, running along that dark corridor and they were getting closer and it didn't matter how fast her mother ran, because they were going to catch her…*

Maya called out in her sleep and Munro laid a damp cloth on her head. The med had done the trick. 'Sleep well, Maya Johnson.' Munro touched her tear-stained face; then drew up the chair and sat beside her.

## *A new presidential stand-in?*

Fleur Matthews crouched in the doorway facing Lixir. 'You touch a hair on his head and you're finished, piggy. '

Matthews was trying to get access to Fleur's 'boy' but his wife was determined not to let him anywhere near her patient. She wore an antique nurse's outfit with stiff, flyaway head-dress, starched apron and fob watch.

'I only want to ask him a few questions, dearest.'

Fleur ignored him.

Lixir didn't know what to do. He'd tried lying, he'd tried blackmail, freakin hell, he'd even attempted flattery. Bad move. She'd given him a nasty head-butt for that.

The president tried to look over his wife's head but she ducked and weaved with hypnotic agility, preventing any view of the interior. 'Clear off.'

'All I want is a little peep, dear heart. I promise.'

'Liar.'

President Matthews kept on smiling but a tremor on his upper lip gave him away. 'I could call Scar, Fleur.' And then more gently. 'But I don't want to do that. I don't want to upset you.'

Fleur narrowed her eyes. 'Then chug off, fatty. Go play with your bit of stuff and stop annoying me.'

She knew about the woman? But how?

Fleur smiled slyly. 'You tell me why you're so interested in him and I might let you in for five minutes.' She saw the immediate look of relief in her husband's eyes. 'But it's got to be the truth. You lie to me, Lixir, and you're pooped.'

Her husband never told the truth unless it was absolutely necessary. But these were very unusual circumstances. 'Okay, I'll give it to you straight. I have been advised, by an unimpeachable source, that your...young friend bears an uncanny resemblance to the late lamented presidential stand-in.'

'He does not,' Fleur was very angry. 'He's not a play boy.'

Matthews sighed. 'How many times? We don't have perverts in Capa East, not any more. Remember? We did away with all of that years ago.'

'You did away with it, nothing to do with me and don't you forget that.'

Matthews pretended not to hear her. 'We need someone to take over from that spanza who got himself killed in the Toy Museum, agreed?'

She didn't agree but he was holding her attention.

'If we don't find a look-a-like pronto, Fleur, we might as well wave goodbye to the good life. You know how much the rest of the world hates us? If they found out I've been using stand-ins all these years they'd hold free elections, get rid of my troopers. There'd be no status quotient. Yes, I thought that might interest you. All the work you and I put into setting up the model state, down the tube. You wouldn't like that anymore than I would. We'd be forced to live in an Oldium, along with all the bed-wetting, dribbling, and senile old gob shites. There'd be no dissections, no hobbies, no power and...' he could see he'd got her attention, ' and no Real Food.' That registered. He saw her expression. 'I promise you, Fleur. I only want to borrow him until the delegation leave.'

'And then you'll chomp him.'

'Fleur. You're not stupid. We can't have two presidents running about confusing people?'

'He's not to be exed.'

'Would I do such a terrible –? '

Fleur cut him short with a look of such contempt he was forced to look away. '– We'd never have got into this mess if you weren't so vain. It's been the ruin of you, Lixir. Your need to be young and sexy but you never were, even when you were young. You were always fat and flabby, double chin, double belly, double everything except brains. And we all know you never get anywhere with your females. You want to but you're not quite up to it, are you, dear? '

Matthews took several deep breaths. He hated his wife so much at that moment he could have slapped the white hot rage between two slices of bread and eaten it. He managed to hold on to his fury. 'It hurts me that you think I'm so superficial, Fleur. You know why I use a stand-in. There are people out there who want me dead.'

Fleur sneered. 'Oh, go stuff yourself. This is me you're talking to. I know you. The truth is you don't want women to see how fat and repulsive you are.'

Everyone has a breaking point and this was the President's. He grabbed his wife by the throat. 'You bitch. Take that back now or I'll – '

Fleur sank her sharp teeth into his hand, drawing blood. Lixir let go abruptly and jumped backwards, cradling his injured hand. '– You've blown it now, fatty. You can't have him. Try and take him and I'll destroy you.' She leapt inside her room and slammed the door shut. No one could get into her apartment without the code and she changed it every day. He knocked gently on the door. 'Fleur,

I'm sorry. Forgive me? You're my little wifey. We mustn't fight. I love you – '

'– You? You don't love anything except those freakin ginger rats and yourself. '

'Please, Fleur. Open the door. Everything I do is for you, for us, surely you know that. If I fall, then you do too. That's why I need your boy, we both need him. It's crucial for our beloved Capa. Now please, I have to see him before I can make my plans. I won't touch you. Cross my heart and hope to die.'

The door opened slowly and Fleur peered around it, keeping it between them, ready to jump back inside if necessary. The president spread his hands in an apologetic way and stepped away from the door. Fleur opened it wide and drew herself up to her full height, which was on a level with one of Matthew's chins. 'Right, this is the deal, take it or leave it. I loan him to you for the election and you swear not to harm him afterwards. We'll leave Capa as soon as the delegates leave and you'll never see us again.'

The President was stunned.

'Well?'

'You'll leave me?'

Fleur nodded. 'I'll need millions of creds of course – '

'– You'll go away, for good? I can divorce you?'

Fleur was getting exasperated. 'How many times, trond knob. So? Is it a deal?'

Matthews was stunned. The hag would leave him? He could have his pick of as many women as he wanted? He could play the field? Several dozen gorgeous young possibilities swayed sensuously into his mind. He felt giddy with excitement. But wait a minute, mustn't get too carried away. Weasel face was bound to have some trick up her sleeve. He tried to look forlorn but it didn't work. The corner of his mouth kept twitching. 'But, Fleur, what would I do without you? My soul mate, my – '

'– Shut your trap, worm. Is it a deal?'

He nodded, not trusting himself to speak and she stepped to one side. 'Inside before I change my mind.'

'One more thing, Fleur – not that I don't trust you or anything – but I don't particularly want to spend the rest of my life worrying about those secret files you have on me. I'd need to have them in my hands before I release the boy.'

Fleur let out an explosion of laughter. It welled up from the bottom of her laced up boots to the point on her starched nurse's hat. She had to lean on the door to stop herself from falling over from the sheer power of that laugh. Tears streamed down her face, leaving deep grooves in her thick, pan make-up. She held onto her waist, 'Oh no. Now I've got a stitch.'

'Can anyone share the joke, Fleur?'

His wife's eyes hardened. 'Come on, Piggy. This is me you're talking to, not that brain dead bitch trooper. This is what happens. You give us free passage out of Capa with enough creds to last us for the rest of our lives, in considerable style, and then, when we're somewhere totally secure, I let you know where I've hidden the files.'

Lixir opened his mouth to protest but Fleur quelled him with a look. 'There's no debate. That's my offer, take it or leave it,' and she prepared to shut the door again.

'Okay, okay I agree.'

She stood aside and put her finger to her lips. 'Shut the door quietly. My little boy's got a headache.'

## *Punishment*

Pox was in the punishment block at the Elite Unit. Scar let the young troopers loose on him first. Den had enjoyed getting even with his superior. Pox's face was a mass of bruises and his body was one ugly, purple welt. Two of his fingers were broken and some teeth had been knocked out.

Now it was Scar's turn and her fist plunged into the half-naked boy, the impact, breaking some ribs. Pox doubled-up with pain but he carefully straightened up and came back to attention. He knew he was nearly at breaking point but he held on grimly, determined to show true trooper courage. He was prepared to die, rather than beg for mercy.

Scar took something from her belt. The young trooper knew what was coming but his gaze never faltered. There was no pleading or defiance in his gaze, only blind obedience. He was an Elite and he had failed a mission twice. He accepted the punishment.

Concentrating all his remaining strength on thoughts of revenge kept him standing there. He promised himself that if it was the last thing he did, he was going to find that bitch CO and kill her, slowly and nastily.

The full squad of Elites moved in, forming a tight circle around the majestic woman and the slight boy. This was trooper business and they all knew what was about to happen. There was no sound except the laboured breathing of the suffering trooper. Scar raised the boy's arm searching for something – the double helix tattoo – then she fired the laser knife and brought it down.

### *Sonny gets the job*

Matthews stared in disbelief at the sleeping figure. This boy had to be Blade's double. The similarity was amazing. Fleur shook Kline's shoulder gently and he opened his eyes, blinking in the bright light. Damn, thought Matthews, he had brown eyes. Still that could be remedied. He was very pale; his head was swathed in pristine bandages, but tufts of blonde hair showed through. The boy tried to sit up but Fleur shook her head at him, and then stood behind him, resting her wrinkled claw tenderly on his shoulder. He had on a white, starched bed shirt and beside him on a chair was the dirty, stained body armour of a CO.

Matthews made a mental note to check this boy out.

Fleur's voice was soft, almost gentle. 'It's all right, Sonny. Don't be afraid. I know he looks horrible but he can't help it, he was born that way. It's my husband, the President.'

Matthews pushed his wife aside. 'What's his name?'

Fleur winked at Lixir. 'Don't know, do we? He's lost his memory. I call him Kline.'

Matthews beamed at the young man. 'Now er, Mr Kline, my dear wife's been telling me you've lost your memory. Most unfortunate. Still, not to worry, when the election's over my medics can give you a mind jolt.' Then to Fleur, 'Now dear, if you don't mind leaving us, this young man and I have some business to discuss. I don't want to worry your pretty little head with such matters.'

Fleur left the room and made straight for her broom cupboard.

Inside the bedroom Matthews was examining Kline. He walked round the bed slowly in one direction then again the other way, never taking his eyes off the young man for an instant. He couldn't get over the likeness. It was remarkable. In all probability this was another of his sons. Not such a limited edition then? He patted the young man's hand. 'Don't worry about losing your memory; it's most fortuitous, especially for you. It means you can concentrate on the job in hand, becoming me.'

As he talked, Kline only half-listened. His mind was struggling to remember something, anything; any little detail of his life, but there was nothing except a gaping hole where memories should be. His head ached with the effort but he was convinced there was something really important he should be doing and it wasn't listening to this old windbag. Matthews really irritated him. The woman was off her head but at least she seemed to be on his side.

Matthews' voice interrupted his thoughts. 'Well?'

Kline smiled 'I'd be glad to help you in any way I can, sir, but it doesn't sound quite legal, me pretending to be you.'

The change in Matthews was dramatic. 'Why you...' He grabbed Kline by the throat and squeezed hard. Kline fought to free himself. 'You'll do as I say understand? I'm the President. You may have wormed your way into that sad old hag's good books with your blond hair and girlie eyelashes but it doesn't wash with me.'

Kline's face was turning blue before Matthews let him go and his last thought before blacking out was that if this was a dream he'd rather be awake. As he slumped unconscious onto the bed, the door was thrown open and Fleur burst in, broom flailing.

## Billy in trouble

Billy's head was covered in blood and his bruised and swollen face was unrecognisable. One leg was bent grotesquely beneath him, obviously badly broken. The only blessing was that he was unconscious.

Squado had kicked him senseless before his mates managed to drag him off. They couldn't have one of their prisoners die on them. There'd be serious trouble back at headquarters; questions asked; creds docked, privileges denied. If there was any killing to be done you had to have special written permission. Rules and Regs that's what it was all about. Rules and Regs.

The rest of the prisoners had given up all hope now and sat deep in their own misery, hardly aware of the dreadfully injured boy.

The transport had pulled off the strada when the commotion began but now it accelerated back onto the road and sped towards the desert. The troopers had to deliver these mutes to the Outpost before sun up and get back to the city before they roasted in this metal box. Luckily for the prisoners this meant the troopers didn't have time to vent their anger on them too.

It had all happened so quickly. One moment Billy had been talking to Squado and the other trooper in a friendly manner, but then he had started to twitch and foam at the mouth and he'd collapsed to the ground. As he fell he knocked against Squado and the trooper fell heavily. As the other trooper went to help Squado the prisoners should have taken the initiative but they didn't. They were waiting for someone to take charge. And in that one moment of indecision the second trooper saw what was happening and got his gun out.

Billy could do nothing. He was having an epileptic fit. And when the angry Squado realised what had happened he attacked the defenceless boy. The little girl threw herself at the trooper but he knocked her aside with one swipe. She lay motionless under the seat.

Squado took one last vicious kick at the boy. 'Freakin hell. A mute in my squad and I never even knew. What's happening to the world eh? Wait till I get you to the cells, Billy boy I'll show you what a proper blooding is then.' And he spat at the boy before lurching back up the transport.

When he was back in his seat Tanya crept out and cuddled up against the unconscious boy, trying to warm him with her body.

## *Gola*

They came for Maya at sundown – four Pinx, Frankie amongst them. He smiled at her as he took his side of the stretcher but she looked away. It was still incredibly hot but they needed to be out of Capa before the troopers came calling. The whole place was being evacuated. Maya saw frightened men, women and children being loaded into transits. She closed her eyes. It wasn't her fault – she hadn't asked anyone to rescue her.

There were three transports waiting outside, each with rocket placements on top. Frankie jumped up into the cab of the one nearest them. Munro was waiting there with a group of young Pinx. Maya was stunned. They were troopers. There was no mistaking their shaven heads and strong muscular bodies. One of the girls grinned at her then lifted her bodily off the stretcher and into a vehicle, as if she were a baby. As the girl put her gently down on the pallet Maya saw the double helix tattoo on her shaven head – an Elite.

'Thanks, Gola.' Munro had followed the girl aboard.

'Pleasure, Munro. Pleasure.'

Munro gave Maya another shot – she needed it – and while she waited for the pain to recede she watched the Pinx as they loaded the transport with supplies and guns. Soon afterwards they set off. The vehicle lurched in and out of the sand and Maya had to cling on as best she could. Munro fixed a vent over her face, then one on himself. 'Bad pollution reports for tonight.' His disembodied voice echoed eerily.

'Where are we going?' The med was beginning to work.

'Out.'

Within minutes the vehicles were on the Teestrada and moving smoothly along. The transports had open backs and the gritty sand drifted in, covering everything in its white pall. A sandstorm was coming. Bad visibility was good news for them but a storm wouldn't deter the troopers for long. They had the latest SN but what Munro and the Pinx lacked in techno they made up with in flexibility. The troopers only reacted to orders and Munro was banking on them wasting a lot of time searching the Flume before they widened their search.

Once or twice an excavade reared up out of the murky light, huge head-lights piercing the swirling sand before being swallowed up again. The Pinx up top turned their guns to face the huge machines, while the pinx travelling inside held div phones and communicated with the excavades. These were friends.

Maya fought the soporific effect of the med and the rolling motion of the vehicle. She knew what she'd dream of if she slept. She made herself focus on Munro, studying his profile through the vent and tried to calculate his age – maybe fifty? She didn't know any really old people. Central Capa was for the young. Oldies moved out and settled in GD's, where they did whatever old people did, and when it was time they went to the incinerator. End of story.

There could never be over-population in Capa. The status quotient wouldn't allow it. One Blu died, one Blu was bred; one Red died and so on. When a couple wanted a child they applied and were vetted. If they fulfilled the criteria they were allocated a new child within their colour band.

Within each colour band there were sub divisions. Troopers were specially bred from Pinx straws and raised together in Troopergartens. And CO's were also specially bred but were Blus. Maya had been different. She was five when she joined the unit and before that she'd... The girl squeezed her eyes tight shut and made herself think about something else. The yellows. The yellows were a special band and each individual was genetically pre-selected to fulfil a pre-destined function, like the Incinerator man, the state officials; mathematicians; scientists, athletes, artists, poets and the debt man. Maya smiled grimly to herself. At least one good thing had come out of breaking her leg. The debt man couldn't get her in the desert. As her mind wandered she watched the Pinx. Some talked quietly as they checked equipment, others watched wrist divs, one or two listened to music and the girl called Gola was playing cards with some others.

Munro had been watching her. 'Never seen Pinx at play before?'

Maya shrugged.

'Fire away if you want to ask me anything, Maya. It's a long journey and we might as well use the time profitably.'

She turned her face sharply and stared at him. 'How did you know my name? '

'Everyone knows your name, Maya. You're famous. Or should I say infamous? You've been on every news' div for the past twenty-four.'

Maya swore out loud. Huey Montrose and those freakin tapes. '*I have you on file, Maya Johnson,*' and now the whole of Capa East had her on file. If he wasn't already dead she'd have enjoyed exing the creep.

Munro continued. *Maya Johnson enemy of the people. Rogue Crime Operative, murderer, extortionist.*

'Propagandist crap.'

'Of course.'

'And Kline?' Hope flared in Maya. 'They must have said something about Kline?'

Munro shook his head. 'You work on your own, apparently.'

Maya forced down her disappointment. She looked at Munro, blinking away the tears. 'So? What am I supposed to have done?'

'Poisoned a bunch of foodies at a RF feast? Plus an important election candidate – '

'Procter?'

Munro nodded.

So, they'd got Procter? It didn't surprise her. 'Anyone else?'

'Huey Montrose?'

Maya shook her head. 'Matthews was responsible for that plus all the RF killings and Procter.'

'Proof?'

She shook her head. It wasn't easy for the girl to admit she'd been beaten by a Pinx with a spotty face.

They didn't speak for several moments.

At last Maya said, 'So? My turn?'

'Fire away.'

'Who are you?'

'I told you, I'm Munro and I'm a member of the Society.' And before she could say anything, 'Yes, one of the original tree huggers, except there aren't any trees, are there? And we're on our way to the Society's base in the desert, my home for the past twenty years.'

'So why are you taking me?'

'We couldn't leave you for the troopers.'

'Why not? I might be a traitor for all you know.'

'You were a human being in need of help and that's all we needed to know. But – '

Maya smirked, ' – Oh yeh, there's always a *but*.'

'You're a CO, Maya, and we could use your skills. We need all the help we can get when we make our move on Capa.'

'I've got a busted leg, Munro. In case you hadn't noticed.'

'You'll soon be back on your feet.'

'One more gun isn't gonna make that much difference.'

'Every gun makes a difference. This GSA visit is the best chance the Society has to get rid of Matthews. We've been planning this for years. The man has to be stopped.'

'D'you think I don't know that?'

'Then help us.'

She shook her head. 'I operate on my own. So, you can drop me off at the next transroute.'

'If only.'

'Look. I don't give a toss what you think about me, Munro. I'm not,' and she pointed at the Pinx, 'one of your fan club. I'm a CO, that's how I live. I do a job, I get the creds.'

'We both want the same thing, Maya. Join us; help us put him on trial.'

'No way. You'll let him get away like you always do.'

'People have to know what he did.'

'Whatever.'

'We need him alive, Maya.'

'Alive or dead it doesn't matter as long as I get the creds.'

'People have to see what a monster he is. That way it might never happen again.'

The man and girl were silent, allowing the gentle swaying motion of the vehicle to calm them. When Maya spoke again she was looking at the troopers. 'What I'd really like to know is where they fit in.'

'They have more reason than most to hate Matthews.'

'And you trust them?'

'With my life.'

'And how much does their loyalty cost?'

Munro shook his head slowly. 'All they want is a better life for themselves and their people. But they still have time for you, a blu, one of the enemy? They still have love and hope but what about you, Maya Johnson? What do you have?'

'None of your freakin business.'

The man was on his feet. 'You ungrateful little brat. The entire Flume has been evacuated because of you. The Society has been put in jeopardy because of you but has anyone shown you any hostility? Each person on this transport is putting their life on the line for you. How dare you belittle them.'

'Don't worry I'll be out of your hair as soon as I can walk.'

'The sooner the better,' Munro shouted over his shoulder as he walked away.

Maya yelled after him. 'And who the freakin hell are you, anyway? Mr Mysterious with your hooded eyes and enigmatic smile? You've been watching too many old Star Wars movies, Obi Ben Kanobi.'

## *Freedom*

Kline was bored. He glanced disinterestedly around his room. It was very plush. All the décor and furnishings had been especially chosen by Fleur. She was okay – mad of course – but she made him laugh, especially when she did Lixir Matthews' impersonations.

The little woman had laid everything on to keep him amused. A consul with hundreds of buttons lay within reach. He had the best of everything, RF, fantastic clothes. All the booze he could handle. The one thing missing was his freedom. He might not remember who he was but he sensed that this sort of life had never been his. He needed to get outside, have some fun.

Plus, Kline loathed the coaching sessions. He was so sick of saying the same things over and over again. Matthews yelled constantly but that only made Kline more nervous and likely to fluff his lines. How was he supposed to remember all the freakin delegate's names when he didn't even know his own? Monsieur Xaviet from Euroville? Xaviet? What sort of a name was that? Heine Laroche from South Canton; Herr Rupert Dowstri the Second from Little America? Impossible. Trouble was Kline didn't want Matthews as an enemy. He'd seen enough to know that people who crossed Matthews, lived to regret it – or not, as was usually the case.

Flicking on the div he settled back. He still got pretty bad headaches. He was waiting for the cartoons but caught the end of the news. A girl's face covered the entire screen. She was about his age, slim built with spiky blond hair and a surly expression. Kline sat bolt upright. He knew her. He was positive he knew her. Screwing up his eyes he stared at the face but it faded and an older woman was being interviewed.

A voice-over droned. *Marge Procter found her husband dead in bed. He had been poisoned. The last person seen with Mr Procter – the Real Food candidate for the forthcoming election—was Maya Johnson. This terrorist poses as a Crime Operative and is armed and dangerous. Do not attempt to approach her if sighted but inform Central immediately. A reward of half a million creds is being offered for information leading to her arrest.*

Kline switched off and lay back. Maya Johnson. Maya Johnson. Maya Johnson. 'Come on, come on.' He hit the side of his head in frustration. 'Remember, stupid.'

At that moment Fleur scuttled in with Kline's clean clothes. She pushed the washing under his nose. 'Take a whiff of that, Sonny. Lovely eh?'

He obeyed but he wasn't thinking about the laundry. Should he ask Fleur about the girl? He decided not.

'Nothing better than freshly laundered clothes.' Fleur saw his expression. 'What's up?'

Kline sighed.

'Shall Mummy cook you something special for tea? Um? You choose go on.'

Kline sighed again. 'I'm not hungry, Fleur. It's this room, it's doing my head in.' He saw the look in her eyes and hurried on. 'I'm not ungrateful. You've done everything you can to make me comfortable but I need to get out of here, get some exercise.'

Fleur stood deep in thought for a moment and then suddenly grinned and pulled Kline to his feet. She hurried him out into the corridor. He opened his mouth to ask where they were going but she shushed him and led the way quickly to her broom cupboard. Inside she locked the door and led him into a smaller inner room. He hardly had time to take in his surroundings before she pushed him into a lift and they plummeted downwards. He was thrown against the woman and he had that prickling sensation of something half-remembered. There had been another lift somewhere? Where was it and who was with him? The girl with the spiky hair? Maya Johnson?

They emerged into the maze of passageways that ran beneath the palace. Fleur signalled for Kline to keep quiet and then set off at a trot. She was old but she was fit and he had a problem keeping up with her. He was out of condition and all the rich food was piling the weight on. As they jogged along Kline attempted to memorise the route but all the tunnels looked the same to him. The air was fresh enough and if this was his treat, it wasn't quite what he had hoped for, but at least it was different.

At last Fleur stopped and tied a handkerchief around Kline's eyes. Then she led him forwards. He heard a mechanical whirring sound and felt a blast of cool, almost icy, air on his face before the blindfold was removed.

They were standing in a gigantic chamber, lit by green phosphorescent light. In the centre of the cavern was an immense black block. It was taller and broader than any Pinx Tower and reached upwards and out of sight. It stood in a massive basin of bluey-green liquid and several small boats were tied up alongside a jetty at the rim.

Kline was speechless.

The old woman led him to the edge of the basin. There were cups on ropes at various intervals along the quayside and she dropped one down into the liquid and brought it carefully up. She offered it to Kline. He hesitated.

'Go on. Have a drink, Sonny.'

Kline trusted her but he was still nervous. It was unwise to drink anything in Capa that wasn't in a hermetically sealed container.

The old woman pushed the cup into his hands and smiled reassuringly. He sipped a tiny drop of the ice-cold liquid. It was the most amazing thing he had ever tasted. Cold
and refreshing with no after-taste of chemicals, sweeteners or artificial flavourings. He drank greedily, and then plunged the cup back, again and again, until he could drink no more.

Fleur watched him with delight. 'Good eh?'

'Freakin fantastic, Fleur. What is it?'

'Berg water.'

'Berg? What like an iceberg?' Kline knew what icebergs were. He'd seen them on divs.

Fleur nodded. 'Feast your eyes. This is the last one on the globe, and when it's gone that's the end.'

'The end?'

'Of the berg.'

'There won't be any more fresh water?'

'It'll see me out, Sonny. Not so sure about you.'

Kline let this thought percolate into his brain. No. He couldn't deal with this, not yet. He looked back at the berg. 'But where did it come from and how did it get here? I can't see any doors and how long has it been here and how long will it last and who gets to – '

Fleur wagged a finger at him. 'There are some things it's best not to know. Promise me you won't tell anybody you've seen it? Especially piggy? '

'Yeh, okay but –' Kline had his head on one side listening intently. There was a strange sound, a whispering, creaking and cracking and occasional louder report, like small gunfire. 'What's that?'

Fleur cocked her head. 'It's the berg. Talking to us. It's lonely. Hidden away down here in the dark; covered in a shroud. It wants to be free to roam the stretching blue of the oceans. It longs to hear the call of the albatross and the whale and see the Northern Lights again.'

Kline stared at Fleur. He'd never had her down as poetic. 'Any chance of getting closer?'

Fleur looked at her fob watch.

'Two minutes, please.' He jumped down into the nearest boat and started the engine. Fleur got in beside him and they moved smoothly out and across the melt water. Looking down Kline could see the bottom of the basin. It was very white, like marble.

When they got closer the noises were much louder. Kline reached out to touch the berg.

'No.'

Too late, Kline's hand was stuck fast to the frozen material.

Without hesitation Fleur leant over and ripped his hand away. It took away the entire surface skin on Kline's hand. The pain was excruciating. Fleur swore and smacked his face, hard. She was furious. 'Never, I repeat, never touch anything ice cold. Your scientific knowledge is abysmal sonny. Auntie Fleur will have to give you some lessons.'

The pain was horrendous but something popped into his brain again. Someone else had said something about his scientific knowledge before…only the word wasn't 'abysmal' it was…?

Back on dry land Fleur wound a handkerchief around the hand, blindfolded him; and then rushed him back along the corridors and into the palace. By the time he reached his room he felt sick and faint with the pain. Fleur gave him a shot and dressed the wound. Within seconds the euphoria of the med took over and he watched her affectionately as she worked. Not for the first time, he thought how fortunate he was to have her on his side. She'd be a scary enemy.

As she forced his hand into a glove, ignoring his shouts of pain, she lectured him. 'No one must know about this Kline? It's no good smiling at me like that. Promise me you won't let anyone see it?' She shook him and he nodded happily. 'It's serious, Kline. Watch my lips. If anyone asks why you're wearing gloves say…say it's a fashion statement.'

# *Attack*

The sandstorm was over and Maya lay awake. The Pinx were asleep, snuggled together, rolling backwards and forwards to the movement. The canvas sides of the transport had been raised to let in the cool night air and Maya caught glimpses of the clear night sky and the dry river bed. Skeletal cranes and ruined docks stuck out of the banks on either side as they barrelled along. The moon was waning but still bright and Maya imagined the river as it had been once, full of fast moving water rolling in from the open sea, accompanied by a cool breeze blowing straight from the Arctic.

Munro came and stood beside her. He obviously didn't bear grudges. 'My grandfather knew this when it was a real river. There were seal colonies all up the estuary. And dolphins. Amazing?'

Maya looked away. She did bear grudges.

'D'you need some more med?'

She was about to say *yes* when all hell broke loose.

**'Troopers. Troopers. South West.'**

The canvas sides came down and the Pinx grabbed their weapons. Two leapt out of the back of the wagon; some sprang up onto the roof, two hung from ropes, strung to the back of the vehicle, and Munro and Gola covered the sides.

Maya caught at Munro's arm.

He pressed a Rapid Fire pistol into her hand. 'Hold on tight, Maya. This will be rough.'

No sooner had he spoken than the rocket launcher on top went into action as the Pinx opened fire. There was answering fire, very close, and Maya steeled herself for impact. She knew how well armed troop carriers were. This old transport stood no chance against the latest State fire power.

But she was wrong. The next few minutes were extremely hairy but somehow they survived. One of the Pinx on the roof was hit and she heard the body fall but everyone else seemed okay. It was as much as Maya could do to stay inside the wagon. At one point the vehicle came to a screeching halt and reversed at high speed before going off in a completely different direction. Frankie certainly knew how to drive.

Maya lost track of time but it seemed that one moment they were in a full scale battle and the next it was over. The wagon came to a juddering halt and everyone bounded off. There was more furious gunfire and a lot of shouting and screaming and then…nothing.

It was uncanny after so much noise. The only sound came from the stiff tarpaulin that flapped against the sides of the transport as the wind caught it. Maya steadied the pistol against her shoulder and waited. If she was gonna die she'd take a few bullet-heads with her.

# *A new opposition candidate*

'Where's Mummy?'

Dan hugged his daughter to him. Rosemary had made no effort to see her daughter. It suited him but he hated to see his little girl so upset. His wife had come back when they were out and taken the rest of her possessions, but that was the last they had heard of her, apart from the message informing him that her solicitor was making a care order for Emma. He wasn't worried. He knew his wife well enough to know that the need was a momentary whim.

It surprised Dan how little he felt for his estranged wife. Once she had meant everything to him but now...Was love that shallow?

Emma picked up the black crayon and Dan watched as she drew the big black figures with huge heads and great gaping mouths and the little matchstick child, with a big red ring on her finger. He wished he had the power to wipe those terrible images from his daughter's young mind.

'Okay, prepare yourself.' He chose a bright red crayon. 'Daddy is going to draw you an elephant.'

Emma giggled. She knew he couldn't draw.

As he drew, Dan heard Mrs Thompson moving about in the bedroom. She had been staying with them since Rosemary's departure. Emma liked her, so it worked well, especially now Dan was so busy. And after tonight Dan wasn't sure where he'd be, or how long it would be, before he saw his daughter again.

Emma heard the noise too. 'What's Mrs Thompson doing?'

'She's packing a bag for you. You're going on holiday.'

Emma smiled. 'Where are we going, Daddy? Is it somewhere nice?'

Dan couldn't tell her he wasn't going with her, not yet. 'It's a lovely place, Emmie.'

'Where?'

He had to distract her somehow so he showed her his pathetic attempt at art. She giggled again and took the pad and drew a proper elephant.

As Dan watched her he was struck once more by the irony of his position. He had never been political. His parents had been kind, caring people, who had encouraged him to work hard and be happy. All he had ever wanted was to have a nice family and live a comfortable life. But then the troopers had come for Tanya and nothing could ever be the same again. The Purity Laws were a monstrous obscenity and Dan would never be at peace again, not until they were revoked and Matthews deposed.

After Pete's suicide Dan had followed in his friend's weary footsteps, trying to find out what had happened to Tanya and Anna. He knew it was hopeless but that didn't stop him until one night he was badly beaten by a trooper and thrown in a small metal cell. He thought he was going to die. A high status blu friend put his reputation on the line to get him released and Dan was strongly advised to forget the Roberts.

But he couldn't and that was when he had a visit from a tall, middle-aged man with a gentle reassuring smile, a man called Munro. And when he asked Dan to stand as the Society candidate he said *yes* without thinking. Dan was unknown to the authorities, Munro reasoned. There was a slim chance Dan might slip by unnoticed.

Tonight Dan was recording his first election broadcast. The GSA delegation was due in Capa and this was the Society's last chance to get Global opinion on their side. If Dan was caught it would be the end for him and anyone connected to him. That's why Emma was being sent away. If things went well he would be joining her in a few nights' time at the Society headquarters. He didn't know where this was.

Mrs Thompson opened the door. Time for them to leave. Dan picked up Emma and swung her around. She loved getting dizzy. 'Again, again', she squealed in his ear but he kissed her and set her down. Mrs Thompson took the child's hand and led her away quickly, before she had time to understand what was happening.

The door shut on her protest, ' – But my daddy? I want my daddy –' and her crying was lost in the louder noises of exodus from the condo.

Everyone was leaving. Each family had made their own secret re-location arrangements, so that if anyone was caught and interrogated, they wouldn't be able to betray their neighbours.

Dan picked up Emma's sketch pad and crayons and took them into her bedroom, and then he sank down on her bed to wait.

## *Pox*

Pox was looking for trouble. His pod was on loudspeak mode and he sat hunched in his seat, legs bent, filthy boots pressed flat against the seat in front, waiting for some Trond brain to complain. Pinx weren't allowed on blu rats were they? But he was a trooper, an Elite, better than any freakin blu.

But Pox's plan wasn't working. He had the back of the transport all to himself, as if someone had drawn a magic circle around him. The other passengers clustered together at the front, uneasy, ready for a quick exit. Pox looked truly terrifying. His eyes were blood-shot, his teeth were broken and his face was a rainbow mask of bruising.

The boy punched the back of the seat in frustration, tearing the last-for-ever fabric. Who was he kidding? Nothing could fill the void in his life. It was over. He wasn't an Elite. He'd been kicked out, lost his status, his mates. A jagged pain shot up his arm, reminding him of the worst humiliation. Easing back his sleeve he looked down at the suppurating wound where his tattoo had once been. He hadn't seen a medic, he wanted to get blood poisoning and die a horrible slow lingering death. That would show them? He tore a piece of fabric away from the seat in front and tossed the wadding all over the seat beside him. Show who? No one cared? His freakin life was over and it didn't matter a shit.

But there was one thing left. There was revenge – sweet, sweet revenge. He'd seen the Johnson female on the divs back at camp and joined in with the lads, boasting about what he'd do to her when he caught up with her. Two squads were out now trying to intercept but they wouldn't get her, he knew that. She was good, probably the best CO he'd ever come across. Most were rubbish. No brains and no commitment. Playing at being tough. But Johnson? She was something else. It was like it didn't matter to her. He'd seen the bleakness and indifference in her eyes and he'd recognised it.

One thing was certain. Whoever nailed her would get promotion – or maybe, in his case, even re-instatement. The Pinx took his feet down from the seat and straightened up – as far as his badly injured body would let him – but what if? What if he brought the CO in on his own?

The boy closed his eyes for a moment dreaming of the possibilities. He knew he had deserved to be sliced. No Elite failed twice, that was part of the code. Where he made his mistake was not killing the bitch as soon as he caught her. Instead, he had wanted to enjoy her. Stupid, stupid. He could have sex whenever he wanted it. No, he'd forgotten the rules of pursuit. Objective No.1 retrieve the info – done. Objective No. 2 disable or exe the perpetrator – no, no, no.

He got off at the next stop. Maybe he would get his arm looked at after all. He'd be useless if he was disabled. He had some creds put by, he could afford it, and there were always creds to be got, one way or another, through blackmail, bribery or whatever. He knew a medic who'd patch him up, no questions asked.

On the walkway people parted to let him through. Gone was his exaggerated trooper strut. He wasn't dressed like an Elite or armed like a trooper but there was something about him all the same. He had to be a trooper with eyes like that.

Pox made plans as he walked, the incessant pain in his arm making it easier to concentrate. He'd pick up his gear – he had a gun stashed -- and he'd be on his way. To where? To where he'd lost her of course. The place where he was born. The Flume.

## *The child*

*The child was alone. Tears streamed down her face, mixing with the sweat that covered her body. 'Mummy. Where are you? Please. Come and get me.' The terrible drumming was so loud she thought her ears would burst and then there was a light, a very bright light, and she ran towards it. Maybe it was the way out. But the light got brighter and fiercer until it was burning her, frying her...*

Maya's eyes snapped open. The rising sun was drilling into her eyes. Black shapes gyrated across her field of vision. She moved her head and looked around. She was in the back of the transport. Her tongue was stuck to the roof of her mouth and her leg throbbed horribly. From somewhere close by she could smell burning rubber. It left an acrid taste in the back of her throat. How long had they been gone? Were they all dead?

Pushing herself up into a sitting position she eased herself towards the side of the vehicle. She grabbed a corner of the canvas flap, pulled and came face to face with a trooper. His ugly scarred face and twisted nose were pressed up against the metal infrastructure of the transport. He was smiling at her. She went for her gun but it wasn't there. It must have slipped out of her grasp while she slept.

Somebody was clambering into the back of the vehicle.

It was too late to do anything, much too late, but it didn't matter, nothing mattered. Maya sighed. She felt totally relaxed, as if some huge weight had been lifted from her.

'Maya?'

The voice was familiar.

'Maya?'

'No', Maya moaned.

'Open your eyes,' the voice insisted. It was Munro.

'Leave me alone.'

Munro misunderstood. 'It's okay, you're safe now. I'm giving you a shot and then Frankie's moving you somewhere cooler.'

Frankie carried her outside and left her in the shaded doorway of a derelict warehouse, before joining the others. There was work to be done.

Maya could see everything from where she sat, propped up against the wall. The trooper was still beside the vehicle, staring inside. But dead men can't see, can they? And this trooper was very dead. The back of his head had been blown away. There were four other troopers sprawled nearby and there was a wrecked, burning trooper transport. The Pinx were salvaging what they could find.

Munro and Gola stripped the troopers of anything useful before dumping the bodies in a large pit. There were other bodies there too and these weren't troopers. Gola stood by with a flame thrower and, as the last body fell in, she ignited.

Maya heard a noise and peered into the black interior of the warehouse. Once her eyes got used to the dark she saw a group of people, huddled together. Some distance from them were two children – one on a makeshift stretcher and the other sitting close.

Gola came and handed out liquid. The people waited patiently and quietly for their turn, not looking at the Pinx or at each other. Afterwards Gola offered the liquid to the little girl but as soon as the child saw the Pinx she sprang at her. Gola grabbed the girl's arms. 'Okay, baby. Okay, cool it.'

The child wriggled out of her grasp and flung herself down beside the stretcher. Gola bathed the injured child's head and wet the lips. Whoever it was, was out cold.

After she'd finished she came over to Maya. Maya gulped the liquid down gratefully, wiped her mouth and looked at the Pinx. 'Prison convoy? Three carriers?'

'One.'

'Did you get them all?' Maya indicated the people.

'The troopers exed four.'

'What's the matter with the kid?'

'Been badly beaten.' The girl turned to go. 'Talk later,' she said. 'We've gotta get out of here soonest.'

'Gola?' Maya had never used a Pinx name before. It felt weird. The girl was surprised too. Maya pointed to a mark on the Pinx's face. Something hard had been pressed into the skin leaving an imprint. 'What's that?'

The girl fingered the mark. 'The kid had something on her finger, a ring I think.'

Maya was struggling to get up. 'Help me over, beside them. And leave the liquid, hey. I'll try to get her to drink.'

Gola helped Maya and sat her up against a pile of ammo boxes.

The boy was in a terrible state. He looked half dead but the little girl pressed his hand and the fingers moved. Poor kid. His nose and eyes and mouth were one huge sore. Trooper's work.

Maya offered the bottle to the child. 'Want a drink? You must be thirsty.'

The child looked away.

'What's your friend called?'

'Billy'.
That's a good name. I'm called Maya.'
Silence.
'Look, I'm sure your friend would want you to drink, wouldn't he? Is he your brother?'

The child shook her head, and then she grabbed the water bottle from Maya and held it to the boy's mouth. The water spilled out and down the boy's front. Some must have gone into his mouth because he started to cough and choke.

'Raise his head,' Maya ordered. The child obeyed. 'When someone has an accident, like Billy, you have to be very careful not to let them drink too much all at once, okay?'

The child nodded.

'There is something you can do to help him though.' Maya moistened a strip of cloth, torn from her bandaged leg, and handed it and the bottle to the child. 'Keep wetting this and let him suck it.'

The child solemnly followed Maya's instructions and just before Maya fell asleep she saw the girl take a swig of the water.

## *The Broadcast*

When Dan and his minder left the condo it was deserted. Several doors were open, offering glimpses of the abruptness of the families' departure. There were discarded toys and clothes, even a div playing – the ghostly cartoon images dancing across darkened walls.

The walkways were empty as they hurried along. When they entered a habitation on the other side of the loop two men detached themselves from the shadows. Security was tight. It had to be.

Everyone inside the makeshift studio was masked except for Dan.

A female voice explained. 'You have 60 seconds, Dan, then we re-locate.'

Dan saw the camera and waited until the red light changed to green. Then, taking a digi-print out of his pocket he held the picture towards the cam.

'My name is Dan Young and this is Tanya. She was six years old when the troopers came for her. Was she a criminal or a threat to national security? No. Her crime was that she had a medical condition, a very minor treatable condition called asthma, and for that she was taken from loving parents and banished for life. I'm the Society of the Tree candidate. Vote for me and no child will ever suffer like poor Tanya. Please, every vote counts. Your family may be genetically perfect but what about your grandchildren or your friend's children? What is happening in Capa East is a crime against humanity and Lixir Matthews is responsible. Do not vote this man in again. Vote for me, Dan Young. Vote for your children's future.'

Even as he put the picture back in his pocket the technicians were packing up.

## *Kline in Trouble*

When Kline woke Scar was bending over him, a murderous look in her eyes. He flinched, waiting for the punch, but it never came. She saw he was awake and stepped briskly away, her impassive mask settling back again. Had he imagined it? Pinx troopers were selected for their cold-bloodedness. They didn't have emotions. No, he must have dreamt it.

The woman was there to escort him to the studio. He felt light-headed and nauseous and the pain had come back with a vengeance. He couldn't flex his hand at all. He prayed Fleur would be there to give him some more med before he had to perform.

Scar waited by the door as he gulped down some liquid. Not as good as berg water – but nothing could be as good as that.

Kline watched Scar as he followed her down the passage. He really respected her physique. She was mass. He liked strong women. And then, out of nowhere, it happened. He punched the air with his good hand and shouted. 'She said *crap. Your scientific knowledge is total crap.* Crap, crap crap. Jubba Dubba. I've remembered something. I'm getting my memory back.'

Scar waited impassively until the excited young man was ready to move on again.

The President was pacing up and down the studio when they arrived, a scowl on his face. When Kline went to make-up and Scar reported Kline's returning memory, the scowl turned into a snarl. The bimboid couldn't get his memory back now, not before the delegates arrived. The President felt a distinct shooting pain up his left arm and must have registered it on his face because Scar led him to a quiet corner of the studio and got him a chair. After a moment the pain eased and Matthews relaxed.

It was no wonder he was stressed. The prison convoys were being attacked on a regular basis. His security services had failed to find out the location of the freakin Society headquarters. He had to get to them before they got to the delegates.

Matthews dismissed Scar. He wanted her to check that every dissident and deviationist had been shipped out.

It was surely the hottest night of the year and Matthews was sweating so much he'd given up trying to mop it up. He had a fan blowing warmish air directly on his face, so at least the sweat was drying up. A young PA hovered beside him, waiting to hand him water or towels or food. Matthews glared at the young man. Everyone was young, except him. He hated them all, for their bright eyes and clear cut chins and especially their appetites. They didn't even sweat like he did. He grabbed some liquid from the boy and poured it over his head, revelling in the thirty seconds of coolness. The boy stared longingly as the liquid evaporated on the president's hot blotchy skin.

Everything was going wrong. The female dissident had proved completely unresponsive. Said she'd rather die than be nice to him. Well, she would get that wish fulfilled. She'd be on the prison convoy tonight.

He half watched as Kline rehearsed. Actors were taking the parts of the GSA delegates but the idiot messed up every time. He forgot their names or he was confused about which country they came from.

Blade was Einstein compared to this one. Some of this dumb behaviour might be connected to the boy's brain injury but the President recognised a spanza when he saw one. It was even more depressing given that this boy was his flesh and blood.

The irony of the Kline/presidential stand-in scenario had long ceased to amuse Matthews. What did it matter if this boy was the CO who had helped steal the tapes with the Johnson female? Lixir knew it and so did Fleur, he suspected. Why else would she have suggested that the young man take the name Kline? The only thing that kept the President going was the thought that he could legitimately have the boy disposed of when the delegates departed. He had always planned to eliminate him after the election but now he had an official reason. Kline was an enemy of the State. And Fleur's threat? He'd have her killed and anyone else who stood in his way. The days of Mr Nice-guy President were over.

Reluctantly, Matthews left his cool corner and placed himself in front of Kline. This didn't help the boy's concentration one bit. Fleur had come in now and was seated near to her protégée. She watched Matthews closely. At that moment Kline got one of the delegate's names wrong again and Matthews leapt up, screaming abuse. Quick as a flash Fleur jumped between the frightened Kline and her ranting husband.

Fleur led Kline back to a seat and made him take a drink. She had slipped some med into the cup. He smiled weakly at her. When Kline was called for the next take, the pain was already receding and he had Fleur beside him.

Matthews was torn between the urge to tear Kline limb from limb and the need for a perfect take. He had to be word perfect for the delegates. Lixir fumed while the make-up artists fussed around the young man. They were obviously enjoying their close proximity to this good-looking boy. God. How Matthews hated his guts.

But, even if he got their names right, would this pretty boy be able to convince Global leaders that he was Lixir Matthews? These were hardened politicians who would like nothing better than to chew Lixir's ass and Kline would be speaking to them live? Okay, they called themselves peacemakers but Matthews knew what they were really after.

They wanted a slice of the action – his action. Somebody had been blabbing and Lixir intended finding out who it was.

His plans for global dominance were at a crucial stage. And the Berg? Safe in the underground dock. He sold water to whoever had the creds to pay the astro-inflated prices.

The young sexy interviewer leant over Kline and whispered something in his ear. Whatever she said worked because he cleared his throat and stared confidently at the camera. 'I am delighted and honoured to welcome you, our most honoured friends from the Global State Alliance, to Capa East's election. Our beautiful city is at your disposal. Please, go where you want; see whatever you wish, we have no secrets here, just an abiding wish to see our new world flourish.' Amazingly his speech was faultless and Fleur pranced about him on her thin little legs going 'yip, yip, yip.'

Matthews was seething with jealousy as the interviewer gave the boy a lingering kiss on the mouth, before slipping a disc into his hand. Her mondo number no doubt. Well someone was going to be very disappointed because Kline wasn't allowed out of the palace. It was the first time Matthews had smiled all night.

Now he could afford to be magnanimous, he grasped Kline's hand and pumped it up and down. Kline went as white as one of Fleur's starched sheets and yanked his hand away. Matthews frowned – what on earth? His wife got between them, trying to get her boy away but Matthews put a restraining hand on Kline's shoulder. The young man faced the president and Lixir saw the pain in his face. If the idiot was injured he wanted to know.

'What's the matter?'

'It's nothing, sir.' Kline put his gloved hand behind his back.

Matthews held his hand out and waited.

Fleur intervened. 'There's really no need, Lixir dear, I'm taking care of it.'

It was the 'dear' that did it for Matthews. He leant over his wife's head, grasped Kline's glove and tore it off. It had been a long time since he'd seen a wound like that but it was something you never forgot. He'd had an ice-burn once

Kline and Fleur looked at each other in panic.

Matthews was thinking fast. Thank God. The hag was dead meat. A traitor to Capa. She was at his mercy. The President faced his wife, a sly smile on his face. 'I don't think much of your nursing, dear heart. This injury needs proper treatment. I suggest you take our young friend along to my medics and get some skin cells implanted. We don't want him to have a scar do we?'

Fleur was speechless.

Matthews shooed them away. 'Off you go. The sooner it's done, the sooner he'll feel better.'

The President watched the pair as they hurried from the studio, the smile frozen on his lips. How sad; his dear little wife had just signed her own death warrant.

## *No going back*

Dan carefully smoothed out the flimsy piece of paper. It was amazing how much pleasure this little painting had given him. A scout had brought it back from Society headquarters. It was from Emma, a drawing of her standing beside a pillar, in what looked like a large cave. He would see this place for himself soon; because this was the night he was going to join her. He pressed the picture inside Emma's drawing book. It mustn't get torn or lost. He was taking all her precious things with him.

The door opened and a man stuck his head inside. He tapped his watch and held up five fingers.

Dan nodded at the huge Pinx. 'Yeh, be right with you, Denzo.' He was trying to wedge Emma's book into his already bulging back pack.

'Travelling light, chief?'

Dan wished Denzo wouldn't call him 'chief'. 'I'm taking a few things for Emma, you know, something from home.'

Denzo held out his hands.

'No, I can manage,' but Dan knew he couldn't, not really. He'd slow the others down if he was carrying too much.

Denzo flexed his muscles. 'There's gotta be some good come out of being born a Pinx, chief.'

They both laughed at that but Dan recognised the bitterness in the man's voice.

The pinx swept Emma's things all together.

'Thanks, Denzo, I really appreciate it.'

The man smiled and went out, shutting the door behind him.

Dan had never had that much to do with pinx before and although some were hostile and monosyllabic, most were like Denzo, completely relaxed and friendly. At first Dan had been surprised by their involvement in the Society. He'd grown up thinking that pinx were mindless zombies, fulfilling all the menial tasks of Capa without thought or complaint. How could he have lived for so long without realising that the pinx were the same as he was? All that angst about getting upgraded? It was so stupid. If only he'd met Denzo before. Dan smiled despite himself. If he hadn't married a blu he would never have recognised the inequalities of the system. So maybe there was something to thank Rosemary for after all?

His three pinx bodyguards were his age but that's where the similarity ended. They were big powerful men and he was slight and not particularly fit. Denzo worked in the thermal core power station and the other two worked in the desert, on the excavades.

They all had families, commitments, but they worked shifts, watching over him. They were risking everything for him. The sooner he was away from Capa the better – for everyone.

It was sundown when they left the pinx tower and brain-fryingly hot. Most people were still in bed and the few they met stared openly at the blu. One man, in particular, couldn't take his eyes off Dan and spat as he hurried by. Denzo moved threateningly towards him but Dan laid a hand on the pinx's shoulder. 'It's okay. No harm done.'

The man stood and watched them out of sight, contempt written all over his face.

Denzo shook his head despairingly. 'Ulysses – aka 'useless' Brantup. A freakin Trond.'

Dan smiled wryly. 'Not one of ours then?'

The pinx pulled a face. There were always people prepared to betray the Society for money or some favour. That was part of life in Capa.

Once underground, the pinx set off at a steady pace. Dan jogged along behind. They ran for five then waited for him to catch up, took liquid, then set off again. Dan's clothes were soon wringing wet and sweat flew from his hair and into his eyes. He made himself concentrate on Emma. How good it would be to see his little girl again. He wondered if they'd told her he was coming.

Exhausted as he was, there was lightness in his heart. He was getting out of Capa. No more waking up with that sudden rush of fear. Dan had no illusions about his importance to the Society. He was only there as a name on the ballot paper. It didn't matter that he had no chance of winning. All that mattered was that the people had a choice.

There was another reason he was glad to be leaving Capa. He hated putting his friends at risk. The troopers were everywhere and each day that passed was a day nearer to him being captured, endangering the lives of those who sheltered him.

It must have been time for another rest and as he rounded a corner he expected to find the pinx waiting for him. Instead they came racing back towards him. 'Troopers', they yelled as they crashed towards him. 'Go.'

Within moments the pinx men had overtaken him and Denzo scooped him up and flung him over his shoulder. A transport was coming up fast behind them. Denzo ran until he crashed to his knees, sending Dan flying over his head.

'Run.' Denzo gasped, as Dan scrambled to his feet.

He hesitated.

'Go, you freakin trond.' The pinx was facing the oncoming transport, a gun in his hand.

And Dan ran. He didn't look back. He was crying and swearing as he ran but he didn't look back. He made it to the next corner and heard a round of automatic fire and an answering volley. Bullets were pinging their way down the tunnels and around Dan's head but suddenly the firing stopped and there was silence.

Then the transport roared into life again.

Dan knew it was hopeless but he kept on going anyway. There was no alternative. He couldn't breathe, he couldn't think; his teeth rattled in his head. The other pinx were out of sight and he knew it was all over. Emma. He stood still and faced back down the tunnel. His hand was shaking so much he couldn't hold the gun steady and he watched as the headlights of the transport cross-hatched the tunnel walls as it roared towards him...

At that moment a large powerful hand came out of the darkness and pulled him off his feet and into a cleft in the passage wall. The trooper transport sped past and he looked up into the grim face of one of his other bodyguards.

When they thought it was safe to move they retraced their steps. Dan steeled himself when they got to where Denzo lay. He tried not to look but he had to. Denzo lay on his stomach. They'd run right over him. Dan knew he was crying but he didn't attempt to stop it; he couldn't.

At last they reached the walls and when they emerged onto the surface there were heavily armed transports waiting. Within minutes they were travelling out of the city and into the desert. The vehicles were crowded with people but Dan sat hunched at the back of the transport, avoiding eye contact. Another man had died because of him. Another good man. And what would happen to that man's family? He groaned aloud.

No one spoke. They had all heard stories of the desert and how people who ventured into the sands never returned. The sky was lightening and within the hour it would be daybreak. The dying moon gave the desert an unearthly flickering sheen.

Dan saw nothing but the ruined body of his friend.

## *Thief*

Poppi's hologrammed Mary Poppins div soon lost its appeal for Malcolm. He only had to hear the intro to one of the mindless song and dance routines to feel his blood pressure rising. The sound of Julie Andrews's clipped, formal pronunciation was enough to make him break out in a cold sweat. And there was no escape.

True the child had her uses. She was buying the meat for Orange and Malcolm had grown fond of her. He was attempting to teach her to speak properly. An uphill task. Strange that she could sing the words to all the stupid songs, especially the *supercalifragilistic...* thing.

No, it was definitely time she returned to the unit. He tried to reason with her but every time he mentioned it she changed the subject or ignored him or put on the dratted div. So, in the end it all came out badly. They were eating their meal and for once the div was off. One thing he insisted on. But she was humming *'Chim chiminy chim chiminy...'* under her breath while she shovelled the food in. She droned on and on until something in Malcolm snapped.

'You have to leave tomorrow.'

At first she didn't hear him and carried on eating.

'I can't stand it any longer. Poppi? Stop that noise. I want you to go back where you belong.'

The child gave him such a venomous look he nearly threw her out, there and then, but he didn't. He explained that he wasn't supposed to have people in his room and his work was suffering and the music was driving him mad. She just sat there tapping the table with a fork, as if she was singing in her head – which she probably was. After he'd finished she went and lay down on her bed. Orange snuggled in beside her and they were soon asleep.

Malcolm felt quite emotional but he knew he'd made the right decision. He had an early night too.

Poppi waited until she was sure Malcolm was asleep, then she packed her gear, stowed the meat in her back pack with all the 'C' she could carry and put Orange in her bag. Finally, she tiptoed to the door and let herself out into the sleeping palace.

\*

Fleur congratulated herself yet again on the installation of secret cameras throughout the palace. Without them she wouldn't have seen the child in the blind worm's room. Malcolm Blue, huh. Thought he was so big and he was nothing, he was a thing. She and piggy had made him.

The brat was called Poppi apparently. Fleur had taken an instant dislike to the child, probably because Sonny kept repeating her name in his sleep. But she was determined to cheer him up, so she would bring him a little present

Fleur watched as the child gulped down a bottle of C. The nasty little rodent stuck its head out of the back pack and licked the girl's neck, he was thirsty too. Fleur shivered, imagining that rasping tongue on her own neck – foul, dirty thing. The child held the bottle to the animal's muzzle and tickled its neck while it drank.

Fleur looked forward to getting her hands on the guinea pig.

When she looked back at the screen the animal was nibbling the fine hair on the nape of the child's neck and the child giggled delightedly.

\*

Fleur was more frightened than she liked to admit about Piggy's discovery that she and Kline had been to the Berg. She hated being at her husband's mercy, so this diversion was exactly what she needed to take her mind off things.

*

The brat tried another door without success. Didn't the little fool know that all the exterior doors were voice or pin coded? She was being drawn deeper and deeper into the palace, nearer and nearer to Fleur. As the child entered the corridor a few minutes away from Fleur's location the woman jumped up. It was time to put plan A into action.

Fleur adjusted her nurse's head-dress and smoothed down her pristine uniform and then picked up a pile of sheets. She left her room at a trot and made her way down the corridor, away from the direction that she knew the child was approaching from. When she was safely out of sight around a corner she stood still, then counted to thirty very slowly and said quietly to herself, 'Coming, ready or not.' Then she walked briskly back up the corridor to her broom cupboard, her white shoes click-clacking on the highly polished floor. She couldn't see, because the pile of washing reached up beyond her face, but she knew the child would be there in front of her. She imagined how terrified the girl would be. She fancied her looking desperately around searching for somewhere to hide. Should she run or should she stay? But there was nowhere to go. Her little heart would be beating so hard.

Fleur stopped at the doorway to her laundry room, and then she thrust out a hand from behind her pile of laundry and tapped in a code. The door swung open and she hurried inside making sure to leave it slightly open. Once through she pretended to hook the door close behind her with one of her little white boots, but she couldn't quite manage. *Come into my parlour, said the spider to the fly.*

Fleur went straight into the inner laundry room. She placed the sheets on the airing-shelves. She couldn't resist burying her nose in the freshly ironed material. Then she moved the pile a fraction to the right, allowing a glimpse of a button set into the wall and its accompanying red light which gently pulsated, casting a glow on the honey-coloured walls.

Fleur heard a slight noise from the other room. Ah, the child had taken the bait. The child would be hiding somewhere now, her mouth dry with fear.

When Fleur returned to the main room she saw the child's shadow on the wall. Fleur swept out of the room banging and locking the door behind her, then she raced back to her bedroom and tuned into the broom cupboard from her bedroom bug screens. While she watched, she grabbed her crown and handbag and squeezed into her jewelled slippers. It was time for Queenie to take charge.

The child was staring up at the screens in the laundry room. Fleur zoomed onto the screen she was looking at. There was Piggy snoring away in bed, then there were the interrogation cells and the prison hospital …and then the bedroom where Malcolm Blue lay. Fleur grinned; he was going to have such a shock when he woke up. Suddenly the child was looking directly into Fleur's eyes. She knew she was being watched. The girl couldn't locate the spy eye but she knew all the same and stuck her tongue out. Fleur grudgingly acknowledged another devious brain at work.

The girl disappeared from the screens and when the cam picked her up again she was standing by a long table, stretching down the entire length of the room. Fleur giggled. This should be good. Poppi approached the table and looked into the large specimen jars. She picked up some of the surgical knives and scalpels laid out on the surface and then leapt back, a look of horror on her face. There was an animal's dead body pinned out and it was slit open from the gullet to the tail. It was a guinea pig – a ginger rosette guinea pig. The child shrieked and ran to the exterior door and battered on it, trying to get out. Unable to, she ran into the inner room. It wouldn't be long before she found the button. It was time for Fleur to go.

The woman descended to the underground via her bedroom lift, then back along the tunnel to another lift door. She dived in and sat down at the precise moment the child pressed the button from above and the lift ascended.

## *Closing in*

Lixir was in bed eating a substantial breakfast. It was shepherd's pie and something called apple duff. He'd seen his medic and been given a clean bill of health. The pains in his arm and chest were stress-related apparently, so he was taking 'happy' pills. He felt better already.

The medic hadn't told him that he was being blackmailed by Fleur and had been strongly advised to ignore the President's very high cholesterol levels. Fleur was aware that Lixir's survival clock was ticking – or not as the case might be. Her husband's fatal heart attack must come soon if she and Kline were to get out of Capa alive.

In the meantime Fleur was at Lixir's beck and call and he made sure he becked and called a lot. He enjoyed seeing the little reptile squirm. He could relax now he knew who the enemy was. She wanted him deposed so that she could take over. Well, it would take more than Fleur Matthews to get the better of him and it was such fun toying with her. He could even afford to be kind to her and had given her his guinea pig. The creature had been a disappointment and apparently he was allergic to them. He hadn't coughed once since he'd got rid of the last one. Anyway, he didn't need pets now because, after Fleur's demise, his apartments would be open for all sorts of more diverting animal behaviour.

There was a discreet knock on the door.

'What?'

Matthews finished his mouthful before speaking. 'All secure at B dock?' Scar nodded. 'Excellent. So? What can I do for you?' Nothing could make Matthews unhappy tonight. Kline was appearing on news' divs regularly now and his handsome face flashed from buildings, all over Capa. He had been accepted.

Scar was holding a div.

Matthews nodded and she inserted and gave the remote to her master. Matthews accessed, and then took a large mouthful of shepherd's pie. He shouldn't have done that. He was mid-swallow when he realised what he was watching and started to choke. The food was jammed in his wind pipe. Scar picked him up by the scruff of his neck and hit him hard and accurately in the solar plexus. A wad of regurgitated food shot out of his mouth. Scar neatly side-stepped.

When he was able to speak again Matthews roared. 'Who the freakin hell is Dan Young?'

Scar put a biog into the president's hands and waited while he read. 'An elite squad is on its way to his habitation, Mr President.'

'And when you've nailed the freakin bastard, round up his family and friends...anyone that has ever known him, anyone who has ever known anyone who knows him.'

Scar was receiving. 'The last known address of D Young is de-habited, Mr President. The entire condo has been re-located, post air-conditioning malfunction. The inhabitants have been dispersed throughout the State.'

Matthews sank back on the bed and held his head in his hands. Scar waited patiently for orders.

## *Queenie*

As the lift door slid back Fleur smiled graciously at the astonished child and re-aligned her crown, which was a trifle on the large side.

'One is going down.' The old woman inclined her head imperiously and wafted at the child to join her. The last place Poppi wanted to be was in the underground, plus this oldie's head moved in a strange jerky way and the smile had too many pointy teeth in it, but what other option was there? Orange squeaked loudly in her ear, before burrowing deep down into the back pack. Poppi should have listened to her furry friend.

The woman tapped her fingers impatiently on the lift button. 'Hurry, hurry. Time is of the essence.'

And Poppi stepped inside. They plummeted down and within seconds had reached the bottom of the shaft. The woman didn't even look to check if Poppi was following but rushed off down a dimly lit tunnel, her shoes tapping on the rock floor. She hummed as she scuttled along.

Poppi ran after her. 'Hey? Old woman. What you?'

Fleur's step never faltered. 'No time for discourse.' Then she flashed away from the child, her thin little legs pumping and her head nid-nodding, like a prancing pony.

Poppi put a spurt on and overtook the old woman, then, when she was a few strides ahead she braked, spun on her heel and faced the old woman with arms folded and a stern expression on her little face. 'I said. What you?'

Fleur didn't check her stride but side-stepped the girl and was away again down the corridor, crown bobbing up and down like a piston.

At this point the child flopped down on the ground, too tired to move. Fleur screeched to a halt. 'Get up. I command you.'

The girl waved a weary finger at the 'queen'. 'Get freakin lost.'

Fleur raised her handbag menacingly and advanced on the child. If she had to knock the brat out she would. Suddenly Fleur froze. She had heard something.

The child heard it too and jumped to her feet.

Without a backward glance Fleur was off again faster than ever and Poppi was right behind her. The old woman disappeared around a corner in the tunnel and as Poppi flew after her she saw a small doorway, cut into the tunnel wall, and the old woman flapping her arms at her. 'Come on. Come on. Sluggish girl.' The child made one last huge effort and threw herself at the door at the exact moment the trooper transport roared into the tunnel behind her. The woman grabbed her and smacked the door shut.

She was the first to recover and before Poppi had a chance to react she snatched her backpack, emptied it and picked up Orange by the scruff of his neck. The animal tried to bite the old woman's hand but she held him firmly and he couldn't move his head. The child screamed and ran at her but then she saw what Fleur was holding in her other hand – a very sharp dissection knife.

'No you mustn't.'

The woman drew the blunt edge of the knife across the struggling animal's neck and then shook him. The animal wittered at Poppi. 'You are going to do exactly as I say, brat, or I saw this nasty little rodent's head off. Understand?'

Poppi nodded furiously.

The woman stepped backwards and pressed a light switch behind her with her elbow which lit up a long room with shelving from floor to ceiling, stacked with cages. Each cage held an animal or several animals. The air was full of the assorted smells and sounds of rats, mice, rabbits and guinea pigs.

'The animal stays here and it lives for as long as you behave yourself. His life is in your hands. And I won't have any insubordination.' Fleur smiled evilly at Poppi. 'Of course, I might slice him up anyway, for fun, but I might not. Say please your Majesty. Go on. Say please your Majesty don't hurt my vermin.'

'No. Not vermin.'

'Please don't hurt…' The old woman insisted.

'P…please. Don't hurt my Orange.'

Fleur threw back her head and roared. 'Orange? Ah. Sweet' and she swung the shrieking guinea pig around her head.

'You freakin bad. Poppi kill you.'

Fleur stopped swinging the animal. 'The only bad person around here is you. You're a disgusting little thief. I saw you steal the pig off the Pool boy.'

'Nasty peeper.'

'Be very careful girlie. I could throw you to the troopers any time I want.'

'Why not then?'

'Because, because I was…' Fleur bared her yellowing teeth at Poppi. 'I don't have to explain myself to a dirty little urchin. I am the Queen of Capa East. Fleur Matthews, the President's wife.

You might be useful to me, that's all. Otherwise, you and this nasty thing would be dead by now. D'you want him back?' She loosened her hold on the terrified animal and held him out to Poppi. As the child's trembling hands reached out for her little friend but Fleur pulled him back and squawked with delight. Then she did a little dance and quick as a flash put Orange into an empty cage behind her, locked it and pocketed the key. Then, grabbing Poppi's arm, she dragged her towards the door. 'He stays here and you're coming with me. Move. I haven't got all night.' And she dug the knife into Poppi's ribs.

As the door shut behind them the child took one last, longing look at Orange. He was pressed up against the bars, squeaking at her, entreating her to let him out.

## *Retribution*

The shock of waking up to find his beautiful guinea pig gone was something Malcolm would never recover from. 'Orange' he'd shouted, his voice crackling with panic. 'Orange? Come to Daddy. Look what I've got for you.' And he'd gone to the icer but it was empty. He got down on his hands and knees and searched under the chairs, behind the fridge, in the bottom drawer of his cupboard. 'Come, baby. Please. 'But there was no sign of the animal. That monster child had stolen his friend.

At last he dressed and opened up the Pool but it wasn't long before his assistants knew there was something drastically wrong with their manager. Malcolm was normally ultra efficient but that night he was distracted and irritable and kept making excuses to return to his room. He had to check one more time. Maybe Orange was hiding somewhere. But it was hopeless and Malcolm knew it.

His worried Pool team discussed what they should do. They considered alerting security about Malcolm's uncharacteristic behaviour but the boy had always been absolutely fair with them and had never treated them badly. However, a new directive had arrived for the Quotient, and Malcolm Blue was the only one authorised to make the selection.

Late that night, when the Pool was closed, Malcolm went back to the shady part of Capa and gave creds to all the RF dealers, promising more if they informed him immediately if Poppi tried to buy meat from them. They took his money but he knew they were crooks and anyway Poppi was too clever to go to them for food. But if the child wasn't buying meat from them, how would his darling survive?

With this terrible thought he dragged himself back to the palace and his empty, lonely room.

\*

Miss DeMontmerency – 'Monty' to the COs – was superintendent of Capa's Crime Operative unit. Everyone loved the tough woman, who regarded the operatives as her wayward children.

This was a very bad time for Monty. The very existence of the CO Unit was in question. President Matthews wanted to get rid of the unit so that his Elites could take over as Capa's law enforcers. Up to now Capa's Council had opposed this but Matthews' power base had grown and many of his opponents had disappeared or died in mysterious circumstances. Added to this, Monty's top CO, Maya Johnson, was missing along with Kline, and now she had this Malcolm Blue wanting to make a complaint.

She took her time checking the Pool Master's ID, while she tried to make sense of it all. Malcolm sat hunched on the edge of his chair shivering uncontrollably. Monty's lip curled – not your fighting material at all. He looked as if one breath of wind would blow him away. He caught her look and she gave him a thin smile. 'So? How exactly may we help you, Mr Blue?'

Malcolm hadn't changed the dressing on his wounds and blood was seeping through the material. His hair was sticking up in all directions and his blue visor wasn't quite centred. He looked like a drunken beetle. 'You have to do something,' he moaned pathetically.

The woman made a sympathetic noise. 'Of course, of course. That's our job isn't it? Perhaps you could give me details of the assault?'

'Assault? What assault?' The boy brought down his fist hard on the desk, momentarily forgetting his almost healed injury. He yelped with pain and then grasped the edge of the table and pulled himself up to standing. 'Three things,' he said, leaning towards the woman. 'One. You arrest the criminal. Two. I interrogate her. And Three. You punish her severely. Understand?' Exhausted he fell back into his chair.

This boy was obviously deranged. Monty kept her tone friendly. 'Do you know the identity of the offender, Mr Blue?'

'She's a CO.'

'But who?' Even as she spoke Monty had a horrible feeling she already knew the answer.

'About this high, short, scruffy, untidy tufty hair, can't string a sentence together? Called Poppi?'

'Ah' said the woman and sank back in the chair, bringing the palms of her hands together in front of her mouth, as if in prayer. 'It's a bit difficult, Mr Blue. You see, the child's not a registered CO yet.'

Malcolm looked at her coldly. 'So?'

'She's a little girl, Mr Blue, a very precocious one granted, but a child nonetheless and we have to make allowances.'

'I want her found and disciplined. It doesn't matter how old she is.'

'Did she do that to you?' Monty asked, looking at his hands.

Malcolm shook his head impatiently.

Monty was relieved. 'There are mitigating circumstances if you'd let me explain.'

Malcolm shot her an almost pleading look. 'I don't enjoy having to do this you know, but the fact remains that she's a thief and she can't be allowed to get away with it.'

The woman sighed. 'OK. What did she steal?'

'3,000 creds.'

Monty was surprised. 'You have proof?'

The boy nodded.

'May I ask what?'

'I saw her.'

'You actually saw her with the money in her hands?'

'I work for the State, madam, I live in the palace, and I see the President on a daily basis. Perhaps you'd like me to get him to endorse my credentials?'

'Of course not, but Poppi doesn't normally steal creds.' She stopped in mid-sentence, realising her mistake.

'So what does she "normally" steal?'

The woman sighed and pulled out a drawer in her desk. She counted out the creds.

'I don't want the money.'

'That's very generous of you – '

'– I don't want the creds. I want her.'

'She will be punished, Mr Blue.'

'I want her in prison.'

'Surely we can come to some arrangement.'

'No. And if you don't deal with it immediately, I shall have no alternative than to go to Central. I have no doubt the troopers will find her. '

'There's no need for that. Of course we'll handle it.' She spoke into her head mic and waited for a response, then looked apologetically at Malcolm. 'It seems that she's gone missing.'

Malcolm was already on his feet and making for the door. 'You've got until this time tomorrow, superintendent, and if you can't track her down you know what happens.'

Monty got to the door first. 'We'll find her but there are one or two things you should know. No please, hear me out. What you have to understand is that some young trainees here have …problems and Poppi is a classic case. One day she will make an excellent CO.' Monty rested her hand on the young man's sleeve. 'I promise you, she will be made to see the error of her ways.'

Malcolm knocked her hand away. 'Not good enough, not nearly good enough. That so-called child abused my hospitality and trust and she broke all the rules of common decency. She stole something from me that was very precious.'

'3,000 creds? That's hardly 'precious' is it? Not to someone like you? We're talking about a child's future here, her whole life. You send her to prison and she's finished. She'd never get a job with anyone, let alone the CO unit. Do you want to be the one responsible for that?'

Malcolm put his hands over his ears. 'Stop right there. Nothing you can say will make any difference. A crime has been committed and I want it dealt with. Isn't that what the CO unit is about? Arresting criminals? Isn't it your duty to protect the citizens of Capa? I expect to hear from you within twenty four or you will suffer the consequences. Do I make myself clear?' And then he crashed out of the room before the surprised woman could see the tears in his eyes.

## *Home*

Maya rode beside the injured boy and his silent friend. The child was calm now and sat close to Billy, clutching the pathetic scrap of moistened cloth. Moments before she'd been a wild animal. Frankie had tried to lift her into the back of the transport but she'd screamed and kicked until Maya suggested putting the boy in first. His stretcher was tied down to the pallet and the child clambered in and settled down beside him.

Frankie sent his wagon roaring into the desert. The sun was up and their liquid was almost out. They had to get under cover soon or they were all done for. They crested a huge dune, Frankie spun the wheel and they were plunging down and onto the bed of a huge wadi. They sped forwards between precipices of rock which towered upwards on both sides. There was shade down there. Within minutes the pinx up top started to whoop and holler. Gola and Munro and the others leant out of the sides and soon they were all pointing excitedly up ahead.

Munro beamed at the passengers. 'We're nearly there my friends, nearly home.'

All Maya could see was the dead end of the wadi. But as they got nearer she saw something else – a gigantic door cut into the huge dune wall. The door swung back as they approached, revealing a pitch-black interior.

The transports roared inside and when Maya looked back the doors were closing behind them, leaving them in total darkness. Their headlights lit a wide passage that wound steeply down, lights skimming whitish-grey walls. The surface was encrusted with some sort of shiny deposit that glowed in the dark. Eventually they entered a wide chamber where the other transports were being unloaded. People clustered about them.

Maya stayed with the little girl and injured boy. The rescued prisoners were helped down, but when two orderlies tried to separate Billy and the child the little girl screamed and screamed until she was allowed to go with the boy. She walked close to the stretcher clutching his lifeless trailing hand.

Maya was made to lie on a stretcher and Frankie and some others carried her to a door, guarded by two huge men dressed in full combat gear with missile guns. This door opened into another well-lit cavern. Down the centre were lines of giant rough-hewn pillars supporting the roof. Maya had seen divs of cathedrals and this was what this looked like.

After this cave they passed through another smaller door and then out and into sudden bright daylight. Maya gasped. In front of her lay a forest. For as far as the eye could see there were trees. Beautiful tall trees with mighty trunks; then smaller ones covered in blossom and others laden with fruit. There were birds singing and insects thrumming and the air was rich with the pungent, strange aromas of exotic vegetation and flowers.

They walked down a pathway between the trees. Branches covered in lianas, orchids and bromeliads hung low over the path. Frankie saw her amazement and grinned. She smiled back; meeting his eyes for the first time. 'Can I touch one?'

They set her down and helped her onto her crutches. She limped to the nearest tree and touched the trunk. The `tree' transposed itself onto her hands. She fluttered her hands through some `leaves' and the greenness criss-crossed her hands and arms. She moved further into the 'vegetation' and her face was a jungle.  It was a projection. Fantastic but not real.

## *Rachel Morta*

The Flume was the first pinx tower built in Capa East and it had won several design awards for its innovative layout and social infrastructure.

The black exterior of the tower gave a lie to its interior. There was a central core brightly lit with mondos radiating out on fifty floors, spiralling downwards. All of the apartments opened out onto this central area and the inhabitants used step-on lifts that rose and fell lazily in the core shaft. Some of the lifts serviced the ground level, some hovered at the fiftieth floor and some gently bobbed about between the middle floors, like plastic fish in an aerated tank. The resident pinx knew that at any time they could walk out of their door and be transported anywhere in the Flume.

In the central area, surrounding the lifts, there was a projected Garden of Eden. Exotic trees and flowers grew everywhere; the air was full of the noise of running water, the call of birds and the sound of insects. There was nowhere more beautiful in Capa and yet few people outside the Flume knew about it. Maya had only seen the service area.

This experiment in communal living had never been repeated elsewhere because Capa's council went over budget and it was too expensive to replicate. The received wisdom now was that pinx could be content anywhere, so why bother? True the building was in need of repair and some of the younger inhabitants thought it uncool but it was still a wonderful place to visit for the first time.

Pox hadn't been to the Flume for three years but he still knew every inch of the place and its inhabitants, the big-mouths, the grafters, the thieves and the greasers. He'd ask some questions, stamp on some faces and collect some favours. He might even look in on the old woman.

His confidence was surging back. He was good, he knew it and she had known it. That's why she'd trusted him with the Johnson job and he'd let her down big time. But never again. He'd show them all, especially her. He had to win back her respect. Okay, the Pres was supposed to be the big guy but Scar was the one. When Pox succeeded, she would give him back his tattoo and his pride.

He stepped onto a lift and descended slowly through the misty jungle, from the tree canopies and down the huge trunks towards the jungle floor. That was how he was spotted. A woman on the first floor saw him drifting downwards, his terrible appearance incongruous in all that beauty.

'Pox is back.' It didn't take long for word to get around the Flume. Pox still had quite a reputation. Nobody was likely to forget his rule of terror in the building when he was only eleven. But there was someone who was glad to hear the news and that was Rachel Morta, Gemmie's grandmother. She refused to call him Pox. He would always be Gemmie to her.

The night Pox arrived there was a lot of activity going on in the Flume. The people were coming home after the mass de-population when the troopers came to search for the CO. Most of them didn't know anything about Maya Johnson and those that did had gone to ground elsewhere, but there were still those who knew more than they were admitting. These were the people Pox was looking for.

Rachel Morta had lived all her life in the Flume. She had been a big, strong woman in her prime but a tough life had taken its toll. The old woman had a limp but she sometimes walked the 49 floors to ground level just to prove to herself she could still do it. She had a mass of white hair that she kept tucked under an old trooper cap and she dressed like a man. Some said Morta had been a looker when she was young but all she had left from that time were her eyes, which were deep blue. She also had a reputation. Nobody messed with Morta, not if they had any sense. She was as hard as plasti-therm but she did have one weakness

It had broken her heart when they'd taken Gemmie away. He was her only family. She'd had a daughter once but no one ever mentioned her. Morta wouldn't have liked it. Morta had tried her best with Gem but she was a woman on her own and had to work day shifts, so Gemmie spent a lot of time on his own. She wasn't there to keep him away from the bad influences in the Flume. Every tower had them, young girls and boys who did nothing but lounge about doing drink and drugs. Most of them grew out of it but Gem hadn't.

The boy became the youngest ever Flume gang boss and waged war against other tower gangs. The Flume's inhabitants were frightened to leave their apartments and eventually they signed a petition to get Pox and his gang zoned. It was very unusual for pinx to go to the council to solve their problems but in Gem's case it had been the only option. Zoning meant that he wasn't allowed within one kilometre of the Flume. If he broke the rule he would be sent to Trooper Boot Camp. Not a good place to be.

Morta did her best to help the boy and sent him creds but he was caught back at the Flume, visiting his girlfriend, arrested and sent to the camp. 90 % of the young people sent to TBC came out broken and totally screwed up; of the remaining 10% a few individuals were taken into trooper training. Gem was one of these.

The camp had been the making of the boy. He spent many hours in solitary and on punishment detail but nothing could break him. That was where Scar first saw him and she had the boy transferred to the elite training camp as soon as his sentence was up. She recognised his total fearlessness and the grudging yet burgeoning respect for the double helix. For Scar the elite's were her life. All troopers swore allegiance to the president and she was loyal to Matthews but if it ever came to the crunch Scar knew where her loyalty lay, as did Gem.

When Morta heard that her grandson was in the tower she felt the happiest she'd felt for a long time. But behind her elation was a small stab of fear. Elites never went on home-visits, not unless someone had died in the family and she wasn't dead, not yet – not till the fat Incinerator Man sang.

'Yo, Morta.' Gem lounged against the door, legs astride, an insolent smile on his face. He sounded like the old Gemmie but that was all that remained. His face was a mass of bruises and Morta could tell by the way he held himself, although he was trying hard to disguise it, that he hurt badly. There was also something in his eyes that hadn't been there before and she knew where she'd seen it. She steeled herself not to run to him and hug him.

'It's good to see you, Gem. Come inside. Are you thirsty?'

'My name's Pox. I'm not stopping, got something to do, okay? But I need some info.' He was trying to make his voice sound friendly but his words still came out like a threat.

The old woman looked away and brushed at the tears with the back of her hand. So, he still blamed her? 'What d'you want to know?'

'I need to find out what happened to the CO bitch? Johnson? Heard of her?'

'Hard not to, she's been on the news divs every day. Been exing foodies.' Morta had never been political. She knew Matthews was in power but as far as anything else went she had no idea what was happening. Her energy had all gone into survival. But even she had heard the talk lately. The younger pinx weren't so easy to keep down. They wanted equality, better jobs, non-segregated transport and education. They weren't content to put up with things. And there was a group of mixed bands who were trying to get new integrated policies through. 'The Society of the Tree.' This Johnson girl was supposed to be involved with this group.

Pox was impatient to be off. 'Got anything?' His arm was killing him. Freakin medic. He'd pay him a visit when he got back. Took his creds fast enough. Pox was worried it was going septic. The wound smelt bad.

'Can I take a look at that, son?' Morta missed nothing.

Pox stepped away from her, the shutters coming down. 'Have have you got anything for me? If not I'm gone.'

Morta wasn't frightened of him but she knew she had to tread carefully or he'd do something stupid. He was on the run again. Maybe not from the law but from something.

She sat down on a chair and pointed to the other one. 'You want me to tell you what I know, son, you'd better sit. And I'm having something to eat first. I've got some re-con and either you share it with me and we have a proper talk or I won't tell you a thing, understood?'

Pox sat down.

## *Malcolm becomes a daddy*

It was almost dawn and Malcolm prowled the empty palace, as he had done every night since Orange had been stolen.

There had been no word from the CO Superintendent or his RF contacts. The thief and Orange had disappeared into the underbelly of Capa East and Malcolm couldn't eat, drink or think about anything except his guinea pig. He seriously considered going to the incinerator room and throwing himself into the furnace – and that was still an option – but he would wait a little longer.

Malcolm's Pool staff were very frightened now. They knew that he had tampered with the straws. The whole banding system was being subverted and they knew the importance of colourist selection. They did their best to correct Malcolm's 'mistakes' but they had no idea how many straws he had changed. It could only be a matter of time before they were all sacked – or worse.

Malcolm was stalking the corridors near the crèche when he stood still, head on one side, listening. What was it? Maybe he had imagined it. But no, there it was again, the faint mewling cry of a baby. But this wasn't the full-on bawling of a hungry, healthy baby this was the cry of a sad, suffering soul, made more poignant by the silence. He had never heard a baby cry like that before.

Malcolm had a pass for the crèche and entered quietly, not wanting to wake the nurse. The long room was in darkness, save for the dimmed lights on the nurse's station. Long rows of cribs radiated out from the central point, containing hundreds of identically wrapped babies in identical, glass-sided cribs. These infants were the crème de la crème – yellow and blu band babies – pre-selected to fulfil some vital post in the State and all raised as Solitaries.

As Malcolm made his way towards the crying baby he read the labels on each crib he passed. 'Physicist', 'Micro-Biologist ', 'Genetic Scientist', 'Cellist', `Population Controller', 'Chemical Engineer', 'Professor of Eugenics', 'Professor of Parthenogenesis'... Without thinking Malcolm started to switch labels. At first one at a time, then two, then three until he was running up and down the aisles, plucking off a label here and sticking down a label there.

The room was spinning and he was light-headed with fatigue and hunger. He put a hand out to steady himself on one of the cribs and that was when he came face to face with the howling infant.

The child stopped crying and stared at the boy through huge, tear-bright eyes. But whatever he saw made him howl again, even louder this time, thrashing his little head from side to side as if he were in pain. Malcolm bent down and read the label. 'Pool Manager' age 11mths.' He took the child's hand in his and the instinctive curling grasp of the baby's fingers around his thumb was like an electric shock.

Without thinking he picked up the baby up and the child instantly stopped crying. Malcolm had never held an infant before and he clasped him tightly against his chest for safety, inhaling the sweet, warm smell. The child tried to wriggle out of Malcolm's arms. The boy readjusted his grip and placed one hand on the back of the baby's head to support him. He felt a raised lump under his finger and turned the child's head to see what it was. The

SS chip was put in at birth and the scar should be invisible by now. This mark was recent. Malcolm glanced at the surrounding cribs with their contented, sleeping infants and he understood. This child's chip had been removed.

'Put that baby down at once or I call Security.'

Malcolm jumped. He hadn't heard the nurse creeping up on him. The startled baby screamed again and the woman took him from Malcolm and put him back in his crib. That was when she got a good look at the interloper.

'Mr Blue?' She knew the Pool Manager. He often came by to check on the certification but she'd never seen him handle one of the Solitaries before. 'I'm sorry but I didn't recognise you. And you, of all people, should know the rules. No baby here should be handled unnecessarily. It is not conducive to the banding.'

Malcolm nodded. 'Absolutely correct, Sister, but I was …I was carrying out a scientific assessment on this child.'

The woman's eyes narrowed. 'Really? So why wasn't I told? They are my babies –'

'– Are you questioning the President's explicit orders, nurse?' Malcolm could sound very authoritarian when he chose.

The woman hung her head. 'I don't intend any disrespect, Mr Blue.'

Malcolm smiled condescendingly. 'I won't report you this time but, if and when I come again, I shall expect your full co-operation. Do I make myself clear? And I may come back tomorrow, at the same time.'

The woman avoided his eyes. 'Of course, sir. We shall expect you.'

'No one must know about this, except you.'

The nurse nodded resignedly. 'I shall see that I am here at this time each daybreak until you tell me otherwise, Mr Blue.'

'Good, good. Oh, and one more thing. Why doesn't this child have a chip?'

The woman looked at him, anger flaring in her eyes. 'I look after the needs of these babies I am not privy to – '

'– I won't ask again. Who gave the order to take out his chip? Well? I'm waiting.'

The woman muttered something under her breath.

'Speak up.'

She looked him straight in the eyes, 'I said, you did, Mr Blue.'

Malcolm was outraged. 'I did no such thing.'

'So why did the certification have your signature on it then? *Malcolm Blue, Master of the Pool.* That is you isn't it?'

.Malcolm was too stunned to react to her insubordination.

'And I don't care what you do to me, it was wrong. He was such a sweet happy little thing before but now…' and they both looked down at the tormented child.

Malcolm was near to tears, 'Who took him away?'

'Troopers.'

'When?'

'Two nights ago. It's not right…it's cruel.'

'I knew nothing about this. I would never have allowed it. Why would anyone do this to an innocent child?'

The woman shook her head despairingly and dabbed at her eyes with the corner of her apron. 'Why does anything happen in Capa?'

Malcolm left the distraught woman and hurried back to his room. He needed time to think. Was this a reprisal against him because he had thwarted the president? Surely the man wouldn't stoop to such petty callousness? But Malcolm had experienced the man's fury and had seen the ruthlessness in his eyes. The president of Capa was evil and yes, he could harm a baby if he thought in the long run it would harm Malcolm, and of course it would. Any Solitary without SS was a candidate for mental instability and in the Pool you needed your faculties unimpaired.

When Malcolm finally fell into a fitful sleep his dreams were full of crying babies, reaching their little arms out to him. He was lathered in sweat when he woke. His first thought was for the child but he had to put the baby out of his mind and get to work. He had a plan.

His team was delighted to have their old boss back and worked so hard that Malcolm let them leave early. Shortly after this he visited Baby Malcolm again, but this time it was before the child was put to bed. There was a different nurse on duty and when Malcolm asked where the other one was the new nurse pursed her lips and refused to answer. Undeterred Malcolm informed her that he was carrying out an ongoing scientific assessment on the child and he needed to watch the child at play. He knew she didn't want to let him but she had to obey. She took him to a small ante-room with two-way mirrors, adjoining the babies' play area.

Each zone was age and developmentally coded and there were about fifty crawling babies in baby Malcolm's age group. Malcolm wished he'd asked the nurse to point out his baby but as it happened this wasn't necessary. The child was wearing miniature blue visors and sitting on his own in the middle of the room, surrounded by the other babies, who played and laughed all about him, while he sucked his thumb and stared at them. No child approached him. Malcolm fought the impulse to rush inside and take the ridiculous glasses off the child and hug him but he knew that this would not be allowed and he would be reported. Once or twice baby Malcolm crawled towards a likely looking playmate but as soon as the other child saw him coming, it moved away and the baby wailed in despair. Malcolm made no attempt to wipe the tears away as he made his way back to the Pool. He couldn't go there again. But he did, the next night and the one after and the one after...until the magical night when the baby recognised him, smiled and gabbled away in baby-speak. Malcolm didn't understand every word but he got the general gist. Baby Malcolm was glad to see him and the feeling was entirely mutual.

At first the boy only stayed for a few minutes, then an hour and finally he informed the nurse he would be taking the baby back to his quarters for further tests. This did not please the woman at all. Malcolm knew there was a danger that she would report him but what other option did he have? His baby had to have someone to love. Without his chip he was an abandoned little soul.

The baby loved Malcolm's room and set about exploring as soon as Malcolm put him down. Malcolm watched in delight as the baby examined everything, putting things in his mouth, pulling himself up to standing, eating bits of apple and other delicacies that Malcolm bought for him and playing with the growing mountain of toys that

Malcolm had acquired. Sometimes, when he was sleepy, the baby would touch Malcolm's face gently, as if not sure he was real, and then he would gurgle contentedly to himself and close his eyes.

Each new word or action entranced the boy. He fed and changed and washed the baby. It was all perfectly natural. This child was his heir. Malcolm would always be with him to protect him and show him the way.

And he hadn't thought about Orange for a long time.

## *A Result*

Pox stuffed a wad of creds under Morta's pillow before stepping out through the projection and hopping a lift to the surface. There was something of the old Pox swagger in his walk now and his arm didn't hurt so much. Morta had dressed the wound and it was healing well. But best of all – and he patted the document tucked down inside his tight shirt – he had a result.

He had visited several old 'friends' while he'd been in the Flume. They had pretended to be well pleased to see him but he knew that they were wetting themselves. It made him feel good, that power he had over them. One or two weren't as frightened as they should have been and he'd had to remind them, but in the end he got what he wanted.

'Useless' Brantup had been in Pox's gang once and still had some glimmer of respect for the trooper. Useless was a well-known hard case. He hated anyone who wasn't from his tower and especially non-pinx. If anyone knew about Outsiders in the Flume it would be Useless.

The large, ugly pinx scowled at Pox. 'Never heard nothing about any Blu bitch but there was a Red a few nights ago.'

Pox pretended indifference. He didn't offer Useless a bribe. If this pinx was involved in exing some Blu or Red that was enough reward for him.

'The scum left before sun up, night before yesternight.'

'Who was he?'

Useless shrugged.

Pox pressed him. 'There's a guy called Young on the run. A member of the Society?' Was it him?'

Useless sniffed, 'Dunno. But he was with three freakin blu-lovers. Denzo Walter was one, but he got what was coming to him.' Useless smiled at this happy thought.

'What happened?'

'Your lot got him. I saw him...afterwards. Not much left but it was him right enough.'

'So that's it? The pinx got exed but you don't know who the red was, or where the CO's gone?'

'There might be more.' Useless smiled slyly.

Pox considered his options. He could beat this freakin low life to a pulp, but was it worth it? He needed to conserve his energy for what lay ahead, so he walked slowly away from the smirking pinx but Useless followed and grabbed his arm − the bad one. The ex-elite had the startled pinx by the throat before he knew what was happening.

Useless fought to get loose but Pox's grip was vice-like. 'If you've got anything to tell me, boy, now would be a good time.'

Useless was more than happy to talk. Apparently he'd gone scavenging after this Denzo character had got trashed. Useless liked mementoes but he was happy to give what he'd found to Pox. It was a kid's drawing. Pox took it back to Morta's. It didn't look much but he'd check it later when he'd followed up a coupla more leads.

Morta was looking at the drawing when he got back to her apartment. She said she recognised the place where the picture was drawn. It was the disused anhydrite mines, out in the desert. Her great-grandfather had worked there as a boy. Sometimes Pox loved that old woman.

Pox patted his pocket again and felt the reassuring outline of the folded drawing. He smiled. *Good things come to those that wait.* That's what Morta used to say when he was a kid. Once on the Rat he accessed elite headquarters and asked to be patched through to Scar.

\*

Pox stood rigidly to attention while Scar examined the drawing of the mines. This time they were on their own. At last she looked up. Was she smiling? 'You've done well, trooper.' Her voice was as flat and unemotional as ever. 'Re-instatement as an elite is secure, trooper...however there's one more test you must pass.'

'Anything, sir, I'll do anything.'

Scar motioned to the boy to raise his sleeve. The healed wound was ugly and still raw in places. Scar touched the wound and the boy flinched but kept his arm straight. She pressed harder and the room swam but he remained standing. Then Scar took something from her belt and, before he knew what was happening, an indescribable agonising pain shot up his arm. As he crumpled at her feet he saw blood pouring out of the opened-up wound.

When his eyes flickered open again he had a bitter taste in his mouth. It was blood; he had bitten through part of his tongue. He hardly noticed it; he was beyond pain, he was crushed. Was this some sort of cruel joke? He'd dreamt of re-instatement and praise and what had he got! Nothing – worse than nothing – more dishonour, more humiliation and more pain. Scar was staring down at him. He dragged himself up into a sitting position and nursed his arm defensively against him.

Her voice came from somewhere a long way off. 'Can you hear me Trooper? Nod if you can. These are your orders. You will infiltrate the Society terrorist cell in the desert and remain with them until they reach Capa. You will receive further orders from me, if and when the time comes. Understand?'

Pox nodded but his brain was in free-fall. He was to become a traitor? Mix with trooper rebels? His mouth watered and he thought he was going to spew. He swallowed hard and concentrated on a pool of blood on the floor to the left of his right boot. The nausea passed.

Scar continued. 'I had to...cut you again, trooper. The wound will protect you when you get into the rebel cell. Lie detection will be negative because, of course, your dishonour was real. But there is one lie you have to tell and it has to be convincing. You have to make the rebs believe that you hate the Elites and the President.'

Pox looked up, eyes blazing. 'No! Never – '

'– Remember how you felt when you were dishonoured; how you wanted to ex yourself; how you hated everyone, and me, in particular – '

'– I never – '

'– Don't tell me you didn't dream of revenge, trooper, because I won't believe you.'

'I did, I wanted it but ...not against you, or my mates...it was against her, that bitch CO! I still want it! That's what kept me going. The thought of getting her!'

Scar nodded slowly as if she understood. 'Good, keep that fire in your belly, trooper, but aim it at me. I was the one that knifed you! I let that rooky recruit beat you in front of your fellow elites. You hate me. Go on, say it.'

Pox got unsteadily to his feet. 'I...hate you! I freakin hate you! You and that spanza, Matthews!'

'When you leave here you will be taken to the city gates, where you will be fitted with a com patch; and wait for orders from me. You will not talk to anyone about your mission. Only contact me in emergencies. I will message you at 8am every day.'

Pox nodded.

Scar laid her hand on her tattoo and faced the trooper. He tried to put his hand on his arm but she took his hand and placed it on top of hers. 'Trooper, are you prepared to lay down your life for the President?'

'I am.'

'And will you uphold your sacred duty to your fellow elite brothers and sisters?'

'I will!'

Scar rested her hand on Pox's shoulder. 'You are one of us again, even without the double helix. And when you've achieved your goal you will receive full elite honours, in front of the entire company. You will be my second-in-command, Pox, and when I go to the incinerator you will take my place.'

Pox stared at Scar in disbelief. As she turned to go, she said something else. It was whispered but Pox heard it nonetheless. He remained at attention, even after she'd left the room, allowing the magnificent truth to sink in. 'I will,' he shouted. 'I will make you freakin proud of me!'

# *The Outpost*

It was nearly daybreak when Maya entered the ward. Everyone was asleep. Maya sat with Billy and the child most days now. It gave a focus to the otherwise mind-numbing boredom of life. Her leg was healing fast but not fast enough for her. She had to get back to Capa, find out what had happened to Kline and nail Matthews. There was nothing for her here and Munro gave her the creeps. Gola was okay – and Frankie. The irony of this didn't escape her. Before the mines she'd always considered pinx to be brain dead morons.

The little girl was perched on a stool beside Billy's bed, head resting lightly on the blanket. Billy's face was grey, except for the swirls of technicolor bruising that surrounded his sunken eyes. The boy had drips attached to both hands and the child's finger rested gently on his thumb, her 'ruby' ring catching the dimmed light and shining out.

The medics saw no harm in letting the child stay with Billy. She talked to him constantly. There were snatches of stories and nursery rhymes and lists – she liked lists – and counting. It was like a mantra, the way she counted slowly up to a hundred and then back to zero. No one knew who she was. The personnel records from her prison detail had been destroyed in the burned out transport. Maya was the only person the child tolerated. The CO gave the girl her inhaler and asthma med and brought her food and water.

The sleeping child's finger lost contact with the boy's thumb momentarily and she moaned fretfully in her sleep. Maya gently replaced her finger. What would the kid do when Billy died?

On her way back to the sleeping area she met Gola.

'Yo, Blu. Looking good.'

The pinx's grin was infectious and Maya smiled back. 'Yeh, getting there, Gola. You okay?'

'Freakin great. We get to kick Matthews' ass in a coupla. Hey. Munro wants to speak before you crash out.'

Gola saw Maya's expression 'Important biz.'

The CO reluctantly followed the pinx.

Munro looked up as she entered. He was watching a palm div. He pointed her to a vacant chair.

Maya perched on the edge of a table, holding her crutches out in front of her like a weapon. 'What d'you want?'

The man held the div out to her. 'Something you should see.'

Maya watched the small screen fill up with a face. A young, handsome boy with blond hair smiled out at her. Kline. She watched intently, greedy for more. He was talking to a presenter, being interviewed, but where? She noted the date mark – night before last. She glanced up at Munro, delight and relief flooding through her. 'Where did you get this? Pirate?'

Munro shook his head. He looked serious.

Maya didn't understand. What was wrong with him? Didn't he know how great this was?

'There's no nice way to tell you this. Your friend Kline? He's Matthews' new stand-in.'

Maya was on her feet immediately. 'That's a freakin lie.'

'I'm sorry, Maya – '

'– No way. He wouldn't do it…he couldn't.' Desperately she searched about for an explanation –

there had to be one – and there was. 'Oh yeh. Nearly got me there, Munro.'

Munro was puzzled.

'Ever since we met you've been trying to get me to join your Society, so you thought…you thought I'd fall for this crap.'

Munro shook his head. 'No trick, Maya. I showed you the div because I didn't want you to find out by accident.'

'You don't understand. He wouldn't do this, Munro, he couldn't.' She was pleading now. 'He's…Kline. There've gotta be thousands of pretty blond boys in Capa? This could be his clone or brother or father, whatever – I promise you this isn't him – '

'– We've checked with the CO training superintendent and she says it's him. We've checked with his CO friends and they say it's him. We've checked with the – '

'– Okay, enough.' She needed time to think. There had to be an explanation. Why would Kline do this? Maybe he was working undercover? No. He didn't do 'undercover'. She stared at the face of the person she thought she loved and felt hot tears gathering behind her lids. But she wouldn't cry, not in front of this man. She put the div on the table.

'I'm truly sorry.'

Maya wasn't listening. All she wanted was to be on her own, but Munro got to the door before her.

'I know this isn't the greatest of timing but there's something else, Maya. We're raiding the Outpost tonight and we need all the experienced help we can get. Are you up for it? I think you're fit enough.

Maya frowned at Munro, her mind elsewhere.

'You've heard of the Outpost?'

'What's this about, Munro? I've gotta – '

'– Matthews 'penal colony?'

Maya was only half listening. Of course she'd heard about the Outpost – where all the dissidents and defects were sent.

'So? What d'you say? We'll never have a better opportunity than this. I know you've had a shock but this would give you something positive to think about – '

'– I don't think so, Munro.'

'I thought you of all people would want to help.'

'What's that supposed to mean?'

'Nothing. So? What d'you say?'

Maya had grieved for Kline once and now she was grieving again, because this time he was lost to her, as surely as if Pox had really exed him. It was too cruel.

Munro's voice droned on, 'State troopers are over-stretched because of the election, so the place will be undermanned. Desert troopers already have low morale because they're on punishment detail, but they're still well armed and the fort is – '

'– Why are you telling me all this? I'm not interested, okay?'

'It's a dangerous mission but I thought that's what you wanted. A bit of action. But maybe I've got you all wrong – '

'– What? You think I'm afraid?' But she saw the triumphant look in his eyes and headed for the door. She desperately needed to be on her own. 'It's not an option. I'm going back to Capa, on my own. I've got…things to do.'

'Like getting Matthews and maybe Kline too? Or somebody, anybody, as long as it makes you feel better? Because your boyfriend's a traitor doesn't mean you've got to throw your life away on him – '

'– Let's get something straight, Munro, he's not my boyfriend and if he is a traitor I'll exe him myself. Okay? Now out of my way.'

'I thought you cared about these people. You sit with that poor child every day – '

'– That's different. I know her.'

'Really? Then what's her name? Where does she come from?'

Munro could be so irritating. 'I mean I know what she's going through. I don't know her stupid name. That's not important.'

The man sighed deeply. 'We all need to know who we are and where we come from. All of us, even you, Maya. That's what's wrong with Capa. Matthews wants to make us all anonymous, mindless creatures doing his bidding – '

Maya banged the door shut on his disapproval.

\*

She stayed in the 'forest' for a couple of hours and then she took out her palm vid and accessed. Yeh, there again. The smiley weasel, the freakin traitor. Kline! She zapped it off. He was at some shindig with the delegates. Standing there in his pretty clothes, handsome, assured, giving it some yak, yak. The camera took in the faces of his rapt audience. Kline, the golden boy, Kline the President of Capa, Kline the traitor!

She had to make some plans. She'd go back to Capa as soon as she could. Society personnel were travelling to and from the city on a nightly basis. There were special med supplies to be brought in and intelligence collected. She didn't expect or want any favours from Munro. All she needed was a lift to the West Gate and a gun.

Maya had forgotten about the raid on the Outpost, so when she entered the main cavern she was surprised by the amount of activity going on. Gola and the squad were in the thick of it, checking guns, stacking boxes of ammo, stretchers and supplies. Maya put her head down and hurried across the space but Gola spotted her and called out. Maya kept walking. The pinx ran after her and yanked her around to face her.

'Is it true?'

Maya stared blankly at the angry girl.

'I said is it true?'

Maya shook Gola off and attempted to walk away but the pinx blocked her path. Her eyes flashed. 'Okay, blu, what's the deal?'

Maya wasn't easily intimidated and she could have walked away but instead she searched about for an excuse. What was that about? Since when did she give a cred's worth of piss for what a pinx thought of her? She shrugged, 'I wouldn't be much use to the squad, Gola, not with this leg.'

'Hey that's a surprise, girl, 'cos I've seen you walking that treadmill and lifting those weights. I say this blu is fighting fit and ready to go.' Gola narrowed her eyes and rested a hand on her hip. 'You scared or what?'

So, here she was, strapping on a rapid-fire and stowing grens in her belt. Maya was going on the Outpost raid. She didn't understand why she was doing it. Munro's disapproval meant nothing to her — but Gola's? That was something else. When everything was ready they made their way to the entrance where three large Transports were ready, engines running. Maya leapt up into the nearest wagon using her crutches as vaulting sticks and saw a stack of boards. 'Hey? Who's the shooter?'

Gola jumped up beside her. 'Can you use one?'

'Can I spit a tab a hundred paces?'

'Pick one out – only not the pink one - that's mine!'

Maya never knew when this girl was joking.

'Might get to fly tonight, mass Tranch cast.' Gola continued.

Frankie was driving and there was a lot of good-humoured banter about his skills – or lack of them – as a driver.

There was a desert track to the Outpost but they travelled via the dunes. It was the usual Frankie ride and they all had to hang on, as best they could. Air quality was bad and they vented. It was a windy, cloudy night and the sand swept through the open-backed vehicles. Eventually the transports rattled and bumped into a cave. The vehicles would stay there under guard, and the squad would walk to the Post. Frankie was staying behind. Gola was in charge and he didn't question the order. Maya raised an eyebrow at Gola. She knew how good Frankie was.

'Too heavy. We'd have to dig him out all the time, ' Gola explained, as the squad fitted sand-flats to their boots. Maya and she did likewise.

They had to carry the missile launchers, boards and ammo with them and it was tough going. In places they sank up to their knees in sand, even with flats. True, Maya was fit again but her leg still ached horribly. At last they got to the lookout – a rock on the top of a dune. At least it gave some shelter from the sand-blasting wind. Maya got her first look at the Outpost through Gola's scopes. Even from a kilometre away the place looked grim. There was a huge perimeter wall surrounding a large open space, containing several buildings. She saw their roofs sticking out above the walls. There were gun emplacements topping the walls and earth works surrounding the compound. These were the spoil heaps from the quarries where the prisoners hewed stone. The stone was used for the groundings beneath Capa. There was no sign of life but maybe the threatening storm was keeping everyone inside.

Gola was alert. She was receiving and swivelled the scopes behind her. She looked and then handed them to Maya. The visibility was poor but, in the middle of an oncoming dust-cloud, Maya could see three transports approaching fast.

'Prison convoy?'

Gola nodded, 'Society supporters and mutes.'

Gola saw Maya react to the word but she wasn't apologising. 'That's what I've always called them, Maya, like you call us pinx!'

Maya didn't want to get into that. 'So, what's the plan?'

Gola smirked. 'Oh yeah! The Plan! OK gather round everybody. We attack the convoy, grab their transports; they open the gates, we get inside, rescue the prisoners, ex the guards then drive back to our wagons and away.' The pinx saw Maya's incredulous expression and pulled a funny face. 'Do you pray, blu? 'Cos if you do, then freakin do it now.' Then she strode off down the slope with the ammo. At the bottom she turned. 'Well, move it, and bring my board? Who knows, we might get lucky!'

Maya grabbed the boards and followed but suddenly her legs gave way in a deep sand drift. She toppled over but her legs were held rigid in the rock hard sand. Stretching out a hand she tried to push herself out of the drift. Her fingers went deep into the sand and came into contact with something soft and warm and moving. Maya knew what it was and snatched her hand away but not before she saw the triangular head rising up from behind the rock and saw the ropesnake's red and black coils. She froze as the snake slithered towards her. It rose up, ready to spit venom into her eyes. She tried to scream but her throat was dry with terror.

A machete came out of nowhere and the snake's head parted company with its body. Gola was grinning as she tossed the head away and stowed the still-wriggling coils into her back-pack. She put out a hand and pulled Maya out of the sand. She must have seen Maya'a fear but said nothing. Maya followed her down the slope.

The wind strength had increased considerably and within seconds they were in the middle of a violent sandstorm. The group split into two. One would ambush the transports and the other, including Maya and Gola, would get inside the fort and open the gates. They had ropes and power anchors. At least the weather was on their side.

Gola's group travelled light. The missile launcher and heavier weapons were set up facing the main gate and the other group toiled back down the road towards the oncoming prison convoy.

Maya had to fight every step of the way against the wind. There was nothing to think about but the sheer effort of putting one foot in front of the other. Her leg throbbed but she was coping. They rested against a smooth dune, took on liquid and in between the swirling gusts of sand they saw the sheer face of the walls towering above them. Even with their ropes it would take a long time to scale them.

They started off again and Maya hadn't gone more than twelve paces before the Tranch hit. It threw her off her feet and barrelled her across the sand. She was travelling so fast all she could do was pray she didn't hit a boulder. She caught glimpses of other flying shapes around her. Maya battled to get her board under her feet and then miraculously she was airborne. The wind was erratic low down but as she gained height, she entered the main pulse of the Tranch and shot upwards like a bullet.

Gola was ascending to her right and the other pinx flew all about her. They had to use all their skill to not hit one another. Maya could see the grins on the faces of the pinx as they swept under and over her and she knew she was grinning too. The old buzz was there but there was no time to revel in it. They had to get high enough to crest those walls. You never knew when the Tranch would die.

Maya saw Gola out of the corner of her eye. She was pointing to the walls. It was time to go in. They were high enough and as they swept forwards it looked as if they'd make it but then suddenly the wind dropped and they lost altitude. Now their approach was far too low. The walls came hurtling towards them. Gola screamed 'Abort!' Maya jumped her board at right angles to the wall but the momentum kept her going forward. She prepared for impact but at the very last moment her board reacted and screeched across the vertical face of the wall. Sparks flew and Maya waited for the board to break up but somehow it held. The next instant she was streaking out across the desert. Through a break in the clouds she glimpsed the lights from the prison convoy far below.

The Tranch was strong again and as she circled back towards the Outpost she saw one of their people hit the wall. She saw Gola and manoeuvred into line behind her. The pinx spiralled upwards, gaining height. Maya's board was good. It responded to the least pressure of her feet and as they rose she felt the old exhilaration. They were still shooting upwards and it felt as if the board must stand on its head and then crash back to earth.

At the top of their ascent Gola levelled out and there was the wall again, but this time they were high enough and within seconds they were skimming over the top and going down. They planed towards the ground and Gola pointed to a spot. They followed her in. Maya saw her friend land lightly, jump off her board and run in one smooth movement. Maya's landing wasn't so controlled but Gola was waiting to grab her. They dived for cover, expecting gunfire at any moment. The other five landed safely and soon they were clustered together behind the wall of the largest building. For the first time they saw the long one-storey sheds that must house the inmates. Gola sent two pinx over to them and then motioned for everyone else to follow her.

The first building was the trooper guard room and three troopers were seated at a table eating and watching a vid. They were surprised when a ropesnake came arching over their heads and landed in the middle of them and even more surprised when Gola shot them at point-blank range. The squad moved inside killing every trooper they met. They secured the building, and then Gola sent a pinx to open the gates. The rest of them moved on to the next building.

All of them were experienced killers and had seen and done things that still gave them nightmares but this place was part of the worst nightmare they could ever have. It was the punishment block. Maya would never forget what she saw there.

They found several dozen badly injured people in cells – men, women and children – but there were dead people there too and people who were about to die. They did what they could for the dying and then Gola gave them killer med.

No one spoke. There was no back-slapping or congratulating. If this was a victory then Maya never wanted to be at a defeat! Gola stayed behind when the rest of them emerged dazed into the courtyard. Maya turned to one of the other pinx. 'Where's Gola?'

He mimed a photo being taken.

The ambushed prison convoy was arriving, driven by jubilant pinx. All the troopers were dead and nobody had been injured in the attack. The prisoners in the huts were being helped out. No losses there. The pinx on the transports couldn't understand why their friends looked so glum. Everything had gone so well. They went into the punishment block to help bring out the injured.

There were about fifty people in all and ten stretchers to load into the three trooper transports and, although everybody was jammed in, nobody complained. Several of the fitter prisoners volunteered to walk and they set off back along the road, to where the pinx transports were waiting. Gola got in touch with Frankie and their three transports came to meet them.

Maya walked with two little boys. She held their hands. They were frightened of her but they would do anything this wild looking girl said, because then they might not get hurt.

The pinx took the body of their dead comrade back with them but they left all the other dead in the

Outpost. Gola ordered the missile launcher to blow up the punishment block. As they drove out into the storm they saw the flashing explosions and fires in the compound. One day they would come back and mourn those poor people properly but that would be for later, much later.

Frankie hugged Gola and smiled warmly at Maya. Once they got to their transports they were able to travel more comfortably back to the mines. The storm was lessening and the first rays of the rising sun crept towards them over the desert. Maya handed liquid out and saw that the boys drank. They were so petrified she didn't attempt to talk to them but she sat beside them and smiled from time to time. The prisoners from the convoy were in better shape than the inmates from the Outpost and one or two recognised friends or relatives. Maya watched as these tried to comfort those less fortunate. She looked up and saw that Gola had tears running down her face.

# *A Present for Kline*

Fleur prodded the unwilling child along in front of her. There were palace servants about now and each one dropped a curtsey to the old woman as they passed, as if she really was a queen. First rules of survival in Matthews' palace – be blind, deaf and a trond brain. No one gave Poppi a second look.

Fleur stopped outside a door with a crown embossed on its surface. She pushed the child inside and shut the door quietly.

This was Kline's room and he was asleep in a large bed, covered with fine white sheets, his blond head was resting on piles of pillows. Fleur tip-toed to the side of the bed, dragging the girl after her. The old woman lovingly brushed a strand of hair out of Kline's eyes and the child glanced down at his face. Then she looked again. A flicker of delight crossed her face before it was swamped by a much bigger one – of fury.

Kline opened one eye and saw a little urchin scowling down at him. Two divs dangled from a gold chain around her neck. He smiled, and then quick as a flash, she jumped on him, fists flailing. One little fist caught him on the jaw, knocking him back onto the bed.

'Bad, Kline. Leave Poppi.'

Fleur pulled the girl off and shook her until her teeth rattled.

Kline was sitting up in bed again, very much awake, and testing his jaw to see if it was broken. 'Whoa, Fleur. It's okay I'm fine...I think.'

Fleur dropped Poppi and the girl ran to the door trying to get out. It was locked.

'Who is she?' Kline was quite enjoying himself even though his jaw hurt. At least this was different.

Fleur frog-marched Poppi back to the bed, then yanked up her head by the hair so that Kline could see her face. 'Recognise it?'

Kline stared hard at the girl then shook his head.

'You've been saying her name in your sleep for days. Poppi.'

'Yeh, suits her.'

Poppi made a horrible face at him. 'You bad, Kline.' She went and flopped down in one of the big chairs.

'Poppi? No... doesn't mean a thing, sorry. But she called me Kline, so at least we've got that right. That was clever of you, Fleur. Guessing my name. Hey, maybe Poppi can fill in the gaps in my memory?'

Fleur smiled savagely showing her yellowing teeth. 'I don't think that's a good idea, sonny. Do you?'

Kline shook his head quickly. He wasn't stupid. 'It was really nice of you Fleur, to go to all this trouble for me.' Kline looked at Poppi again. 'Maybe she's a nightmare?' He thought this was quite funny. Poppi bared her teeth at him. He gave her a wink and she looked away in disgust. 'See? So cute.'

Fleur snorted. The brat's 'cuteness' has nothing to do with it. 'I wanted to bring you something to cheer you up.'

Kline watched Poppi picking her nose. 'Yeh, well thanks, Fleur, she has cheered me up, as it happens. What will happen to her now?'

'Easy come, easy go.'

'No. Don't get rid of her. I might remember. You know? Like I remembered 'crap'?'

Fleur sat on the bed and unwound the bandage from his hand. It hardly hurt at all now and Kline was able to stretch his fingers. The skin cells had taken well. Fleur cleaned the wound and dressed it while the little girl wandered into the room next door. 'Don't touch anything in there or I'll skin that pig alive.'

Later they found the little girl fast asleep on the floor, her head resting on the bottom shelf of the open icer. Remnants of RF were strewn about her, along with several discarded liquid bottles. Her face was smeared with juice and dirt and lumps of food were stuck over her clothes and hands. Fleur dragged the child away feet-first and slammed the icer shut.

'She was hungry, Fleur. Very hungry. Hey, watch her head.' Kline picked Poppi up and carried her into the bedroom and laid her on his bed. She snored, stretched and snuggled into the soft pillows. Kline was aware of her smell, a warm, pungent scent. Why did she hate him? That was very worrying. Maybe he was a paedophile? He didn't like that idea one little bit.

The child continued to sleep while Fleur helped Kline into his new clothes. This was the day. The 'President ' was due at the shuttle port in an hour – to welcome the first of the GSA delegates. Kline was quite relaxed about it. It was Fleur who seemed nervous.

'Run through the speech one more time, sonny. Just to make sure.'

## Success

The doctor had insisted that Matthews had bed rest and that was exactly what he was doing. He was expecting the tasty television producer any minute and he needed to conserve his energy. She was beautiful, intelligent and amenable, all the things he most admired in a woman. He had spent the last half hour preparing himself. Lixir had never heard the axiom 'less is more' and at this very moment his after-shave was probably being mistaken for a WMD by extra-terrestrials!

So, to say he was not pleased when his trooper chief arrived unannounced and insisted on seeing him on urgent business was a mass understatement. He was freakin furious! This woman consistently brought him bad news lately.

He scowled as she entered. 'This had better be important, Scar.'

Scar's impassive expression remained the same. 'The Outpost has been taken by reb forces, Mr President.'

'Full report, trooper!' Matthews's eyes were cold as he waited for his trooper's explanation.

Scar kept her eyes straight ahead. 'All the troopers have been exed, sir – '

The President sneered. '– A rag bag of sub-standard troopers won't be missed, trooper. What about the defects?'

'Released, Mr President.'

'And where were your men when this was going on?'

Scar's expression was stony. 'They are on duty at the heli-port guarding the delegates and the President...the presidential stand-in, sir.'

Matthews looked up quickly. Was she trying to be funny? No, she didn't have it in her. 'Are you losing your grip, trooper? Do you want me to relieve you of your duties? Get someone else in to head up my troops? Um?'

'Whatever pleases you, sir.'

'I don't want to side-line you, Scar, but I'm very disappointed. You've never failed me before. What's up? You haven't even pin-pointed the reb headquarters yet.'

'The geology of the terrain made it hard but – '

'– Excuses, excuses! That's all I get from you, Scar, and it's not freakin good enough! D'you understand what I'm saying? Well?'

Scar nodded.

'I know they're skulking out there in the freakin desert, it doesn't take an Einstein to work that out! They're planning to make their move on Capa! But where are they?'

Scar did look at the president now – straight in the eyes. Matthews was the first to look away. 'I've just received vital information as to the whereabouts of the rebel location, sir.'

'Then why in freakin hell didn't you tell me straight away?'

Scar offered the president a folded-up piece of paper. 'One of my men –' Scar couldn't hide the pride in her voice, ' – retrieved this from a dead terrorist. We believe it was drawn by Dan Young's daughter.'

Matthews spread the piece of paper out flat and gave it a cursory glance; then he raised an exasperated eyebrow at Scar. 'And this is it? Some kid's crappy daubings?' He scowled at the trooper.

The trooper stared over his head. 'If you look more closely, Mr President.'

Was she telling him what to do now? It had better be good or Scar might be on her way out. There were several other Elite Troopers who could step into her shoes. He glanced back at the drawing and saw a man and child standing in a dark place. A large cavern possibly. The man was Munro – rot his brains – and the kid must be Young's brat. Behind the figures were pillars stretching upwards, these were a light brownish colour and the walls were rough. He could see where machines had delved into the rock. Some sort of mine? So what? Then a thought exploded in his brain and memory-debris rattled down, all about him. Now he was excited. He knew where this was. It was the disused anhydrite mines! He had been inside them when he was a boy. They had been used for storing nuclear waste in the 20C. Matthews remembered standing beside his father in these caverns and staring up at the gigantic space. It was big enough down there to enclose the presidential palace and certainly big enough to conceal an army – several armies!

Matthews was out of his bed in an instant and throwing on his clothes. His wrist pad vibrated and he accessed. 'Not now! Tell her to get lost!' His brain was tumbling. Of course! Why hadn't he thought of the mines before? They were the perfect place to hide, they were vast, they were hidden in the desert and they were only a night span away from Capa. 'Collate all the relevant data and maps for the Mines.'

Scar nodded. 'The information is being processed, Mr President.'

'Good! Good.' Lixir felt more alive than he had for weeks. At last! He was back in charge. 'Move as many troopers as you can spare up to the Western gate. Put someone good in charge there. I'll meet you there when you're finished with the delegates. Have the heli-squadron on standby. I want every man and machine ready. We'll give the freakin terrorists a warm Capa East welcome. Oh and Scar? We need a trooper in the viper's nest. Have you got someone?'

Scar nodded.

'Deploy him.'

'There's a small problem, sir.'

'What?'

'He was dishonoured, sir, lost his double helix. But he has given us invaluable information and I know he won't fail you again.'

'Well, reinstate him, woman, what are you waiting for?'

'Thank you, sir.'

'You've done well, Scar. There might be something in this for you when we've crushed the reb scum.'

Scar lowered her eyes. 'I need no more honour than serving my beloved President.'

'Yes, yes,' he waved her away. How good it would be to be outside these four walls!

He hurried out of the room and Scar stood for a moment, squared her shoulders and then she was off down the corridor to Kline's apartment issuing orders as she went.

Fleur opened the door to Scar's discreet knock. 'You're early, pinx!' the old woman snapped. 'Wait there till I call you!' Then she banged the door shut in the trooper's face and spoke to Kline, loud enough for Scar to hear. 'If she was mine I'd have her neutered.'

Scar stood to attention outside the room listening to their laughter. She was smiling.

\*

Kline persuaded an unwilling Fleur to allow Poppi to stay in his locked room while they were welcoming the delegates. He put some divs out so that the kid would have something to do when she woke up.

Kline shut the door quickly so that Scar wouldn't see the child. Scar didn't miss much and stared at Kline for a fraction longer than was necessary. He promised himself that he would find somewhere safe for the child when he got back. Fleur had told him that Poppi was on the run but he didn't know the details.

When they reached the palace transroute level, the official state RAT was waiting for them. It was full of waiting officials and prominent citizens. Scar stood motionless beside the door to Fleur's VIP carriage, waiting for them to get inside. When they were properly seated and belted in, she got in with them and guarded the door. Kline noticed how her gloved hand never left the stock of her gun and she talked quietly into her com for the whole journey to the heliport.

Kline stared out at the beautiful city as Fleur ran him through his speech for the hundredth time.

'What's that?' he asked, pointing at a whitish glow at the horizon.

'The desert, sonny, not a nice place.'

He was like a child let loose in a toy shop. He asked Fleur so many questions that in the end she got quite shirty with him. She handed him over to Scar, who gave mono-syllabic answers to all his queries. She was also preoccupied but Kline didn't notice. If this was the place he lived in then he was a very lucky man.

## *Orange to the rescue*

In the end Fleur had nothing to worry about. Kline welcomed the delegation with the consummate ease of an experienced politician. His smile never wavered, his handshake stayed firm, he was sincere down to his socks and he delivered the speech as if he really believed it. He exchanged and received gifts and pleasantries with panache and smiled till his jaw ached. No one would have guessed that his eyes were full of the beauty of his city and his mind was occupied with questions. Who was Poppi? Who was Maya Johnson? And most importantly of all, who was he?

Fleur never left Kline's side and the incongruity of their supposed relationship gave rise to a few wry smiles amongst the delegation. After the formal part of the ceremony the delegates were transferred to the palace, where they could relax before the official reception that night. Kline and Fleur travelled with them but their Trooper guard had disappeared along with Scar. Kline was relieved. No Scar meant that the child would be safe in his rooms but the absence of troopers worried Fleur. When Kline asked what was the matter she snapped at him.

When they got to the palace Fleur hurried off to make sure the guests were comfortable; leaving Kline and the child watching divs. The child refused to sit near Kline but he knew she was keeping an eye on him. Once or twice she forgot herself and joined in with the songs until she saw him smiling. It was only when they both burst into *'A spoonful of sugar'* that she grinned openly. She had the most incredible smile. It made Kline happy just looking at her.

When Fleur returned they were sitting close together. The old woman smacked the child around the head.

'Ow freakin, bad.'

Kline was annoyed. 'What did you do that for? She wasn't doing anything.'

'Maybe not, sonny, but she's planning plenty.' Fleur dragged the girl to her feet.

'Where are you taking her?'

Fleur tapped her nose.

'You will bring her back? Fleur?'

Fleur nodded and hustled the girl out of the room.

'Watch out for troopers.'

The door slammed on Kline's words and the old woman and girl set off in the direction of Fleur's laundry room. Poppi dragged behind until she realised where they were going and then she bounced along excitedly in front. As they went down in the lift she took something out of her pocket. It was a piece of smelly meat. Fleur grabbed it and threw it away.

Fleur needed to be distracted. She knew Piggy was up to something but she had no idea what it was. Her information had dried up. You couldn't trust anybody in this freakin state. She should know. It was Fleur who had master-minded the Capa East security and surveillance unit. What she needed was a session on her bug screens but she couldn't leave the kid with Kline. She didn't want them getting too close. He was hers, no one else's. In retrospect it had been a bad idea finding the kid, she should have given her to the troopers. But she could still do that, after she'd had her bit of fun.

As she opened the door to the labs, the brat's guinea pig set up a high-pitched squealing which set all the other animals off. Fleur set the child to work at the far end of the room filling water bottles and feed tubes. Poppi worked quickly so that she could get to Orange but just as she was within reach Fleur grabbed the animal's cage and rattled it hard. 'Shut it. Nasty pig.' Orange was slammed backwards into the bars and lay quivering in a corner. Fleur turned to Poppi. 'I've got things to do, so I'm leaving you here. Try and escape or do anything stupid and I'll kill the thing. Understand?'

Poppi's lips were trembling as she watched Fleur exit with Orange.

Fleur had a frustrating time trying to locate Piggy on her bug screens. The cells, interrogation units, the Pool, Piggy's rooms, were all deserted. The place was like a ghost town. The only good thing was that the delegates seemed to have settled in well. Fleur contacted some of her informers and set them to work but she still felt agitated. She knew what would calm her down. A nice little dissection!

She held up the cage, so that the guinea pig's eyes were on a level with hers. 'Guess who's having a little operation today? Umm?' She chose a neat little knife with a long slightly curved blade. This was her 'filleter.' She could have done the dissection there and then but decided it would be more satisfying with an audience.

Fleur was humming as she opened the door into the animal labs. The room was in darkness. 'Come out; come out where ever you are.'

And Poppi did. She was balanced on a pile of crates behind the door and, as Fleur reached for the light switch, Poppi leapt onto her back. The pair crashed to the floor but Fleur was the first on her feet. 'I told you what would happen if you misbehaved.' And, before Poppi could do anything about it, she pulled Orange out of the cage and brandished the filleter.

'No,' Poppi screamed, her eyes never leaving that sharp evil-looking knife. The old woman nicked the animal on the neck and blood spurted down his fur. She was laughing and prancing about jiggling the animal up and down, so that droplets of blood flew everywhere. Poppi charged at Fleur, but Fleur dangled the animal just out of reach.

Fleur was enjoying herself so much, she wasn't looking where she was going. She stepped backwards and fell headlong over an upturned crate. The knife slipped out of her hand and the animal twisted free and shot away under a table. Fleur and Poppi dived for the knife and as they wrestled for it the filleter skidded away under another crate. Fleur grabbed Poppi by one of her fingers and bent it back.

'Ahh. Let go.'

'Not till you promise to behave.'

'Eat your boots.'

'Then I shall have to break your little pinkie.' Fleur increased the pressure slowly and agonisingly and, just as Poppi thought she was going to faint, the old woman let go and jumped away, clawing at something on her neck.

Orange was latched onto the back of Fleur's neck. The woman flailed at him but every time she touched him, he sank his long yellow teeth into the old woman's flesh.

Poppi watched with deep satisfaction. 'Good boy, Orange. Kill her.'

Fleur sank to her knees clasping her bleeding neck and moaning with pain and the animal jumped off and ran to Poppi. 'Taste nasty, Orange? Never mind. Poppi have nice meat for Orange.' Then Poppi kissed Orange on the nose and put him in her back pack. The old woman was still rolling around in agony and the child stepped over her and out into the corridor.

Through her pain Fleur heard the door slam and the noise as the brat scrambled the door code numbers. The very last thing Fleur heard before she fainted was, 'It's a jolly 'oliday with Poppi…'

## *What next?*

Malcolm took the baby everywhere with him. He'd bought a sling-thingy to carry him in. The child loved the Pool and the freedom of not having to wear his visor. Naturally he was extremely intelligent and he could say `Malcolm.' His version sounded like 'Ma, Ma' but Malcolm knew what he meant. He could also say 'yes' and 'no' but the best was to yet to come.

One night Malcolm was warming up the baby's bottle while the child explored his room, when suddenly the child shouted 'Ma Ma' very loudly and peremptorily. Malcolm turned to see the child standing on his own.

Malcolm knelt down and held out his arms. 'Come, baby. Walk to Malcolm. There's a good boy.'

The baby attempted to uproot one foot and fell over. Malcolm picked him up and he tried again. After several minutes of encouragement the baby took one unsteady step and then another before collapsing into Malcolm's arms. The boy caught the baby and swung him high. 'Clever baby, clever, clever, baby! You walked to Dad.' Malcolm sank down onto the floor, cradling the child in his arms. He was crying. The baby struggled to escape but Malcolm held him tight. This was the undoubtedly the happiest moment of Malcolm's life.

At that precise moment there was a loud banging on the door. Malcolm and the baby both jumped and the baby howled. No one knocked like that on Malcolm Blue's door and after the initial shock the boy was furious. He strode to the door, determined to give, whoever it was, a severe telling off.

The nurse from the crèche stepped forward and pointed at the boy. She looked very pleased with herself. Two large troopers towered behind her. 'You have infringed the banding code, Mr Blue. The President has been informed and you are to return the yellow to me immediately.'

Yellow? Yellow? This woman was calling his beautiful baby a ...yellow? He was so angry he reacted instinctively and as the woman leant forward to take his baby Malcolm put out his hands and shoved her as hard as he could. The women toppled backwards into the troopers and all three of them landed in a tangled heap on the floor. The nurse was a large woman and it took a moment or two for the cursing troopers to unravel themselves; by the time they had, Malcolm and the baby had disappeared.

Malcolm was flat-footed but it had never mattered before. It wasn't important for the Pool Manager to be fit. He ran as fast as he could and accessed the iso globe lab. The night shift was over and the room was deserted except for three thousand gently bouncing foetuses in their semi-permeable membranes. He got down on his knees behind a lab bench and pressed the child into his chest. 'Shh, Baby. We've got to be very quiet.'

The child gurgled and sucked Malcolm's shirt. He was obviously enjoying this adventure. Malcolm was gasping for breath. The baby was heavy and the boy's arms were already aching. Malcolm knew he couldn't outrun the troopers so he had to find somewhere to hide. He heard the troopers thudding past the lab, away from the Pool, so he counted to five then hurried back to the Pool.

He remembered the old Malcolm showing him a disused vat that had a small chamber inside, leading from an obsolete aeration duct. It was only a small space, but it would be large enough for the pair of them.

Malcolm forced the panel off the duct and wriggled into the chamber. He left the baby there then returned to his room and collected as much food and baby stuff as he could carry before climbing back into the duct and closing the partition firmly behind him. It was very hot and airless in the space and Malcolm knew they couldn't stay there for long. He would have to move at daybreak. He had no idea what he would do after that but there was one thing he did know, separation from baby Malcolm was not an option.

\*

Malcolm and the baby came out of hiding as soon as the last Pool worker went home. The baby was hungry and Malcolm was dripping with sweat. He had a terrible, throbbing headache. He wasn't cut out for all this physical stuff.

Malcolm crawled out backwards and the baby followed him. He was so glad to be out of that nasty little hole. Malcolm had made a plan of sorts while he was hiding. Obviously he couldn't stay in the palace, so he would have to find somewhere to live in Capa and get a job. Down there in that dark, hot little space, it had seemed a good idea. In fact anything to get him out of there had seemed a brilliant idea but up here it was different. He'd spent a lot of creds lately, first on guinea pig meat and then on baby paraphernalia. When the small amount he had left was gone what would he do? And it would have to be a job where he could take the baby too. He was only trained for one thing. To choose!

No time to work it out now; he needed to be somewhere else before nightfall and the troopers continued their search. Putting the baby in the sling he took one last long look at his home and exited by a service lift to the underground, where he jumped a slow-moving AP wagon and let it take him where it would.

He must have dozed off because when he woke the AP was in a siding and the baby was saying 'Ma ma!' very loudly. The wagons closed down during the day. They were solar-powered so the batteries were charged over day. Malcolm guessed they were on the outskirts of the city but he didn't want to venture Outside. He let the baby crawl about on the wagon while he tried to think of a plan. He was too tired and very soon he and the little boy drifted off to sleep. A sudden jarring motion woke him. The AP was on the move again. Malcolm collected the baby and all their stuff and got down from the vehicle as it lumbered off down the tunnel.

Malcolm looked about him. He was in part of the underground he'd never been to before and he didn't know what to do. He knew that the pinx lived on the outskirts of the city but would he be able to find work here? Or even people who would be friendly to him and the baby? Maybe he should walk back towards the centre? While he stood hesitating another AP came around the corner, going in a different direction. He climbed wearily on board.

## *Miracles*

When Maya thought it was safe to leave the forest she went in search of solitude. Fortunately the next cavern was empty and she was standing in the dark when suddenly a man and child came charging around one of the columns and crashed into her, knocking her over. Fortunately she fell on her good leg. 'Watch where you're going,' she yelled and the little girl burst into tears.

Dan helped Maya to her feet. 'Hey, we're really sorry. But there was an elephant chasing us, wasn't there, Emmie?' He picked up the little girl and kissed her on the nose. The girl stopped crying and wound her fingers in his hair. She watched the angry girl and sucked her thumb.

The man held his hand out to Maya. She ignored it. 'I'm Dan Young and this is my daughter, Emma.'

So this was the saviour of Capa.

He was rabbiting on. 'I've seen you before. Going into the hospital ward? Have you got someone ...in there?'

'No, I go there for fun!'

Dan held up his hands in apology. 'Sorry. I was ...talking, you know, making conversation.'

Maya wanted to get away. There was something about this man that made her distinctly uncomfortable. He smiled all the time. Creepy.

'Hey, I was very impressed with what you did –'

Maya looked at him stonily, refusing to make it easier for him.

'It was incredibly...brave.'

That was enough. She had to get away from him but he put a hand out, detaining her.

'I just wanted to say thanks. You brought some special people back for us. The wife and children of a ...very good friend and someone else, a lady we both love, someone from home. And we want to thank you, don't we, Emmie?' Dan was still floundering. 'And if there's anything I can do to help...after we're gone.' He was staring at her bad leg. 'You're injured so I assume you won't be coming with the rest of us.'

'I'm coming.'

'But if you needed anything, a friend or something then...'

Maya quelled the man with a look. What was the matter with everybody in this place? All this sugary niceness. She longed for Capa and all its straightforward nastiness. 'Yeah, whatever,' she said, and walked away.

Dan watched her go. Emma landed a big kiss on his cheek. 'Can we see Tanya's mummy now?'

'Yeh. You can see her every night.'

*

Later that night the Society's Council-of-War was in full swing and Munro, Dan Young and the other leaders stood on a raised platform, surrounded by a thousand or more of their supporters. All the council were middle-aged, whereas the members were young, mostly under sixteen and extremely noisy.

Everybody was there, except for those in hospital, on guard duty or out on patrol. It was only a matter of time before Matthews' spies found out where they were and they couldn't relax their guard. The mines were safe from air attack but a ground force was another matter.

Maya stood at the back. Gola had persuaded her to come. Maya wasn't a yak yak person but she couldn't help admiring these people. They were totally committed. Shame they had to die. They must know, as well as she, that they didn't stand a chance against Matthews and his troopers. Maya doubted that the Society's fighting force would even get inside the city walls, let alone talk to the GSA delegates, or the voters. Matthews would make sure his opponents were silenced long before they became a threat.

She would go with them to Capa but after that she was on her own. Nothing that Munro said to her had changed her mind. There were two objectives, one to get Matthews and... In her mind Kline had become Matthews, or at least his clone and equally guilty. She would never trust anyone again. That part of her life was over.

Suddenly there was a commotion at the back of the cavern and everybody craned their necks to see what was happening. Some men had entered carrying something between them. It looked like a body. Gola and the others crowded around.

Medics arrived and the body was taken away, then the meeting came back to order and Dan Young was next up. He looked so insignificant beside the imposing figure of Munro. Pity he was such a nonentity. He fidgeted with the pile of papers in front of him and then he cleared his throat and started his speech. The whole chamber went quiet. Maya had to strain to hear what he said. He kept his head down and read from his notes. Even from where Maya stood she could see him shaking. There was lots of 'Our *Capa*' and *'the tyrant Matthews*' and *'the evils of colour banding and the purity laws*' but she'd heard it all before from far better speakers than this inconsequential little man. The young audience started to fidget and someone shouted, 'Borin.'

That was when Dan Young looked up and they all saw the anger in his eyes. His voice was loud now, impossible to ignore. 'Yeh. It's boring. It's boring having your little girl taken from you because she's not quite perfect. Being branded an ignorant pinx all your life is boring. Not being able to have a baby unless you fulfil the criteria is boring. Eating and drinking crap to make some rich guy even richer is freakin boring. Having a job you hate because that's all your banding allows you. Being sent to the Outpost because you're a defect! Is that boring enough for you?'

The silence was so loud it hurt.

Dan gazed out at all the earnest young faces staring up at him. His voice was soft again but now the audience hung onto every word. 'The time has come to draw a line in the sand. If we can't live a better life then we must be prepared to die in the attempt. And, if you think that's boring, then God help you. God help us all.'

From somewhere near the back of the cavern someone started to clap, and then others joined in, until the whole place was a mass of waving, shouting people. The young ones clapped and yelled and stomped their feet. Maya nodded to herself. Not bad, not bad at all.

She met Gola on her way out.

The pinx smiled and linked her arm through Maya's. 'So Blu? What d'you think about Dan the Man?'

Maya shrugged.

'That good?'

'He'll get my vote.'

Gola laughed. 'Don't bust a gut will you? Hey Maya. I've been taking a look at the pinx they brought in?'

'Know him?'

'Yeh, as it happens. Gemmie something. Bad Boy. He was my mate's boyfriend. Had a bad reputation but she wouldn't listen. Found out for herself later, still got the scars.' Gola looked thoughtful. 'He's got mass sun burn and his arm…it's all pus and yuck. He was sliced.'

'Sliced?'

'I've seen one before…not nice. Trooper punishment. They slice off the elite tattoo with a laser knife.' Gola fingered the tattoo on her shaven head.

'What do you have to do to get sliced?'

'Disobey some rule. And there's lots of freakin rules.'

'So how come he was picked up? Just happened to be passing by?'

Gola laughed and punched Maya good-naturedly on the arm. 'You don't walk with an injury like that girl. The patrol found him, half dead, day span from here.'

'So really lucky then?'

Gola's forehead puckered. 'He's been dishonoured, Maya. Worst thing that can happen to an elite. I guess he crawled out into the desert to die.'

'Course he did.'

Gola heard the sarcasm and faced Maya, eyes glittering. 'It's the best it gets for a pinx, to be an elite. All your mates look up to you and your mates are your family, all you've ever known, since you were bred. It was the hardest thing ever for me, leaving the troopers.'

'So why did you?' Maya knew she had stepped into dangerous territory but it had been bugging her ever since she met Gola and the others.

The girl stared straight ahead.

Maya waited.

When Gola spoke again she fired the words at Maya, as if it was the only way she could say the things she had to say. 'There was a young kid when we were training. Younger than me. I liked him, he was a good kid. Not much up top, but then pinx aren't known for their brains are they? He stole some creds off a trooper. Not a lot but he got found out. There's a code in the elites. Never steal off your mates. They gave me a Rapid Fire and said 'use it', but I couldn't, so they said if I wouldn't do it, someone else would, and maybe not so nicely.' She drew a shuddering breath.

Maya wanted to put her arms around Gola, comfort her, but she couldn't. 'You did what you had to. You're not like them, Gola, they kill for fun.'

Gola looked coldly at Maya. ' Yeh, and what about you, Maya Johnson? What do you kill for?'

'Creds' Maya laughed, trying to lighten the mood and failed. She changed the subject. 'It still doesn't explain how this trooper 'amazingly' got picked up by one of our patrols.'

Gola had finished talking. 'I'm a pinx, Maya, you work it out eh, clever girl.' And with that she stalked off.

\*

The injured trooper was brought to Billy's ward. He was severely dehydrated but they thought he'd survive. He was on a drip and sedated so he wouldn't wake up for some time. The wound on his arm had been treated and it was responding well, so it looked as if they wouldn't have to amputate.

Everybody was crowded around his bed when Maya got to the ward. She waited till all the excitement died down before she took a look. The injuries looked convincing enough. The arm was a horrible mess and the face was one big burn. It was hard to see what the boy really looked like. Young of course, and slight, like so many of the elites. Maya made a stab at feeling sorry for this badly injured trooper but it didn't work  One less freakin spanza in Capa was what she thought, and then she went back to the ward. It was time for the girl's med.

Later that night, Billy opened his eyes, looked at his friend, smiled and then closed his eyes again.

# *Rats!*

Poppi wasn't singing any more. She and Orange were curled up in a crack in the tunnel wall. Beside her was a pile of stones and every now and then she picked one up and hurled it as hard as she could down the tunnel.

She'd lost all sense of time since she'd escaped from Fleur but her stomach told her she'd missed several meals. There was one can of C left. She offered Orange the last morsel of smelly meat she'd saved, but he took one sniff and backed off, grumbling at her. Poppi held the meat to her own nose and then hurled it into the shadows.

There was a scurrying and scampering in the blackness and Poppi grabbed Orange and held him tight. 'It's okay Orange. Poppi's here. Don't be frightened.'

The tiny, green pin-pricks of light were getting closer.

The child forced herself to think of something else. It would be daytime on the surface now and everyone would be asleep in their beds. Picking up another stone she sent it skimming over the rocky floor and heard the satisfying thud and squeal as it found its mark. The little lights switched off for a moment, only to return seconds later.

Orange stretched and scratched his ears with his back paws; then he squeaked at his meat-provider. He was very hungry. Where was his food? He jumped down from Poppi's lap. 'No. Orange. You mustn't.' She tried to stop him but he slipped through her fingers and scuttled away into the darkness. 'Nasty rats will bite you,' she sobbed into the void; then she grabbed her gear and some stones and stumbled after the guinea pig, her fear forgotten in her panic to get to him before the rats did.

Within moments there was a terrible screeching and squealing up ahead, as if something was being torn limb from limb. The light was very dim but Poppi saw the outlines of rats as they jumped and leapt and snapped about a larger animal – Orange. Poppi pelted stones at the outer ring, frightened of hitting her pet, and there were shrieks from the wounded rats as they fled. But the fight went on.

At last, when it was all over, Poppi ran to find Orange. She was crying so much she could hardly see. But there he was, lying on a pile of dead rats. She kicked them away and knelt down beside the animal, gently stroked his little head. 'Poor Orange. Poor Poppi's Orange.'

Quick as a flash he jumped away from her, his bright eyes alive with anger. He was in the middle of a delicious rat meal and he didn't intend sharing it with anyone. The delighted girl clapped her hands and then sat on her haunches and watched happily while the guinea pig stuffed himself.

At this point she happened to look up and right in front of her were two huge doors.

*

The AP that Malcolm and baby were on was full of empty crates. The train was slowing down and Malcolm peered up ahead. They were travelling down a side tunnel towards a solid wall, a dead end. Malcolm collected all his things together. Was he ever going to find somewhere safe? He was getting very low on milk and liquid. Maybe he should give himself up? It wasn't fair on the child lugging him about the underground like this. But he couldn't give the baby back. They would put the visors on him again and Malcolm would never be allowed to see him, or hold him, or kiss him...

He waited for the vehicle to stop but it kept going. What looked like a solid wall became two huge doors that were swinging open, allowing the vehicle inside into a large, brightly lit space.

Once inside, the wagon came to a halt at a loading bay. There were pinx waiting there and Malcolm climbed down on the other side of the wagon and watched, as the men and women unloaded the empty crates and filled the train with boxes of fresh fruit and vegetables.

When he got the chance Malcolm slipped away. It was easy to hide. The whole huge area was a jungle of plants, trees, crops, barns and workshops, and wherever Malcolm looked there was something new and delicious to eat.

Suddenly Malcolm had a terrible thought and looked down to where the baby was happily exploring the nearby bushes. When he saw Malcolm watching him he said 'Ma Ma' and fell backwards into a strawberry bed. What about him? What would a baby eat here? Or drink? Malcolm picked up the protesting child and set off to search the place.

## *Pox in the mines*

They said the injured trooper was awake and responding well to treatment, so he was to be interrogated. Maya watched as they set up screens. The truth drug was foolproof so they'd soon know whether this guy was genuine or not and Maya sincerely hoped not.

She glanced at the little girl. She hadn't taken her eyes off Billy since he'd opened his eyes. Maya wanted there to be a happy ending to this story but she was a realist. Billy's body had healed and his bones were mended but the mind was something else – another country. He had a tough little face, a thin pinched mouth, gaunt cheekbones and a thatch of lustrous black hair which the child spent hours brushing. She cut his nails, rubbed his back and pressed a damp cloth on his forehead when he got too hot. She had experienced love from somewhere. You didn't do that sort of stuff unless someone had loved you first.

Munro emerged from behind the screens and beckoned to Maya.

The trooper had his eyes open when she entered. Was it her imagination or did he stare a little longer than was necessary? She knew she was sexy but, hey?

Burn tech was amazing. Pink healthy skin was already showing through the scars in some places. His lips were still swollen but he looked almost human. Maya froze. There was an unmistakable trail of angry red spots covering the boy's chin and corralling his nose. She tried to be logical, loads of young troopers had pusts, but then, the boy looked at her again and there was no mistaking the naked malevolence in his eyes. This was Pox.

What to do now? She kept her face expressionless. It might be amusing to hear his story first. Having this freakin psycho at her mercy pleased her enormously.

'It seems that our young friend here has been through a dreadful ordeal, Maya.' Obviously, Munro hadn't seen the look that had passed between the two young people.

What was she supposed to do? Cry?

Then, as usual, Munro turned the tables on her. 'Do you know this boy, Maya? He says you do.'

Maya saw the flicker of anger cross the trooper's face. He didn't like being called 'boy' anymore than she liked being called 'girlie'.

The trooper had stolen her moment of glory but she could still make him suffer. She put her head on one side and pretended to take a long time making up her mind. 'Dunno, Munro. Troopers all look the same to me...but wait a minute. What have we here?' And she traced the angry, marching line of pimples across the boy's face. 'Yeh, hard to forget mass pusts like that.' Her voice hardened. She was done with playing. 'He's the spanza who took Montrose's tapes and the iso-cube ...if it wasn't for him we could have nailed Matthews...and he was the one that got Kline – '

Her hand was on her gun but Munro stepped between them, ' – Okay, relax.' Then he turned to the trooper. 'I want you to tell Maya exactly what you told me, Gemmie. Think you can do that?'

Maya knew her mouth had dropped open. Why was Munro talking to this low-life as if he were some sort of human being? But then the trooper retold the story of his dishonouring and Maya knew it was the truth. She wasn't sorry for him but she didn't want Munro to know what she was thinking. She wished the scum had gone to the incinerator

When the boy finished Munro raised a questioning eyebrow at her.

'Yeh, yeh. But what about all the people he exed? Montrose and all the others? And a freakin trooper did that to Billy.'

'Be fair, Maya. We can't blame every trooper atrocity on him. But we would like to know what happened to Kline, Gemmie.'

The trooper shrugged. 'I delivered him to headquarters, as per orders, and the next time I saw him he was on all the divs and hoardings. He's very popular. Seems to like being the president.' Pox glanced quickly at Maya, enjoying her pain. But she could wait for pay-back time.

It was extraordinary to hear this foul-mouthed trooper talking in such a reasoned, measured way. Maya had definitely underestimated him. She knew all about bad people, she'd been mixing with them all her life and this boy was truly bad, so how come Munro was taken in? She knew the answer. This was Camp Delightful where everybody loved everybody

She left Munro and Pox 'holding hands'.

When she got back to Billy's bed there was a lot of excitement going on. Billy was talking. All the medics were trying to hear what he was saying. Maya pushed her way through and stood by the little girl, who was listening to her friend. His voice was very soft and croaky. Eventually the child nodded and then solemnly scratched Billy's nose. He shut his eyes in ecstasy.

## *Agridome*

During the day in the agridome a deliciously cool mist descended on the plants at regular intervals. This particular day Malcolm and Baby were ambling through the vegetation enjoying the moist environment. The baby was tottering about pulling flowers and leaves off the plants and occasionally falling headlong into the lush vegetation. All the workers had gone home, so they could move about freely. He and the baby slept during the night. The boy wasn't thinking long term but this was an ideal hiding place for the time being. Especially now he'd discovered the milking parlour. All his baby's needs were met here. He didn't even need nappies.

He wasn't to know that he was about to meet an old friend. It was surprising they hadn't met before, considering they had arrived on the same day. However the agridome was a huge area covering many hectares.

Turning a corner Malcolm almost collided with Poppi. She was chasing after Orange, who was flitting through the bushes, hunting for small snakes and rodents. She was the first to recover and sprang away, but Malcolm grasped her shoulder before she could escape.

'So? We meet again. You nasty, little thief.' Malcolm tried to make his voice sound angry, but it didn't quite work.

Poppi stared at the boy. 'Who you?'

'Don't you dare. You know who I am. I'm the kind person who saved you from the trooper, remember? And how exactly did you repay me? Um? Shall I remind you?'

'It wasn't me.'

Malcolm looked about him. 'Where is he then? Did you eat him?'

'Nasty, Boy. Poppi love Orange.'

'Oh so you do know who I am? Show me the animal. I demand to know where my guinea pig is.'

'Poppi's Orange.'

'You stole him off me.'

'Boy thief too.'

'Don't be ridiculous.'

Poppi looked slyly at the child. 'What that then? Boy have baby?' She thought this was very funny and Orange poked his head out of a nearby bush, surprised by her sudden laughter. There was the end of a still-twitching mouse's tail slowly disappearing down his throat.

Poppi waited for Malcolm's reaction, ready to grab Orange and run, but Malcolm was laughing so much she smiled and picked up her pet. 'Boy have baby and Poppi have Orange.'

Later, over a meal of fresh fruit and carrots, the two runaways caught up on each other's adventures.

'Boy stole Baby?'

'No, he's mine, well he will be. He's the trainee Pool manager.'

'Trainee poo manager?' Poppi was in a very good mood. 'I shall tell him to say Poppi.'

'I don't think so. Babies find 'p' sounds very difficult, Poppi.'

Malcolm was amazed at Poppi's lucky escape from Fleur Matthews. He had never met the President's wife, he only knew her by reputation but she sounded as dangerous as the President, but with brains.

Malcolm and Poppi decided it was nice to have company and settled down to their life in the Dome together. The boy was intrigued by the innovative bio-technology that enabled green plants to be grown successfully underground. The habitat in the Dome provided a balanced biotic pest and plant control. Huge naturally lit areas contained heat loving plants, while other sections were in partial or complete shade and some had rotating light/shade programmes.

The cow byre was in a corner of the vast space. Cows ambled into the automatic milking parlour and ate, while the surface of their living area was cleaned and their waste re-cyced for plant fertilisation. There were three Jersey cows and a calf – a beautiful animal with limpid brown eyes. There was milk for all of them.

'Hi, cows,' Poppi said. 'I'm Poppi and this Orange.' Orange smelt prime rare steak and squeaked hopefully.

A young pinx boy looked after the cows and he was always the last to leave the Dome each morning. His job was to ensure that the animals had everything they needed for the hot day ahead and that the machinery was in good working order. One morning he looked up from his work and there she was – a sweet little girl – holding a furry orange animal.

'Hi', she said. Giving him her biggest smile. 'I'm Poppi, who you?'

He didn't stand a chance. Within minutes he was in the child's clutches and promised to bring her all the baby stuff she asked for. He also brought the news. Poppi didn't care about politics but she passed on the information to Malcolm and he got increasingly worried. Something big was happening in Capa.

## *Maya and Pox*

The night after he was interrogated Maya and Pox met face to face. They were in one of the narrow link-corridors between the main caverns. The trooper was walking slowly, his arm in a sling. Maya kept her head down, pretending she hadn't seen him but he blocked the path. 'We should talk, Johnson.'

How dare the freakin monster use her name. 'Move,' she snarled.

The boy shifted uncomfortably, 'I was only doing my job.'

She barged her shoulder into him, trying to force a way past, but he stood his ground, injured as he was.

He held his hands up, palms flat, placatory. 'I just wanted to say I'm sorry.'

Maya exploded. 'Oh that's all right then, as long as you're sorry. It doesn't mean a freakin thing. Sorry I exed you, I won't do it again. Sorry I stole your happiness and trashed your life. Pardon me. Sorry, sorry, sorry.' Then she gave the trooper the most deadly look in her repertoire.

The boy couldn't look her in the eyes. 'I was never on prison convoys.'

'Well, aren't you the lucky one? So where did you get your kicks then, boy?'

He rode the insult. 'I did what I had to – to survive. That's what I was trained for. Isn't that what CO's do?'

'Don't you dare compare me with you. CO's uphold the law in this corrupt, nasty, immoral little State. Your scum are nothing but killers for Matthews.'

The boy hung his head for a moment. Amazing actor, Maya thought. When he spoke his voice was a whisper. 'It's all over. They dishonoured me; made me crawl. I hate the freakers.'

Maya gave him a slow hand clap. 'But if you'd exed me and Kline, none of this would have happened would it? You'd be promoted by now, have your own little murder squad to play with?'

She saw his eyes flicker for an instant before the mask settled back. 'But I didn't exe you did I?'

'Are you telling me you spared me?' She didn't expect a reply. 'Do us all a favour pal, wriggle back into whichever hole you crawled out of and die.'

Pox watched the girl as she walked away. She wouldn't get to him, he wouldn't allow it. He could wait. There were more important things to think about than one pathetic bitch CO. It was time for Scar's com. He found a quiet spot further on and accessed.

## *The cool night air*

Lixir Matthews held up a fistful of white sand and let it trickle through his fingers. The cool night wind took the silica out into an arc, where it fell in a parabola of glittering dust. The President took a deep breath and stretched his arms up to the sky. The fresh air cleared his brain. Life was good. He had a very comfortable HQ in a disused warehouse beside the Teestrada. He had all the latest surveillance and communication devices at his disposal and a chef had come out too. Scar had arrived from the city and had brought her elites with her. Kline was doing his stuff with the delegates and Fleur was miles away making somebody else's life a misery. Life was exceptionally good.

His logistics people had pin-pointed the anhydrite mines and blanket surveillance was in place. All rebel movement was being tracked, West Gate was well protected and Lixir had the men and fire power to blow the terrorists away. But he was much cleverer than that. The sand scrunched behind him.

Lixir turned and greeted his trooper captain. 'Ah, Scar, good.'

Scar waited.

'Is your man in place?'

'Yes, sir.'

'Good, good. And he's totally loyal? I need a trooper who will obey my orders, without question, even if it means forfeiting his life by doing so.'

The woman didn't pause to consider. 'He is such a trooper.'

'Intelligence says that the rebels will make their move within two days. Their objective is to reach City Hall for a pre-election rally and lobby the GSA delegates before and during the election. They hope to win the election with this Dan Young creep! There's no chance of him succeeding but we have to be ready for all eventualities. With me so far?'

Scar nodded.

'Your man must travel with Dan Young into Capa and await orders. Understand?'

Scar nodded again. 'He won't fail you, Mr President.'

'Excellent.'

The trooper waited.

'Any news on the midget brain from the Pool?'

'I have a unit on his trail, sir – '

'– Stand them down, Scar. I'm glad the little incompetent's done a bunk. There are adjustments to be made in the Pool. He can freakin disappear off the face of the globe as far as I'm concerned.' The President handed Scar an official looking document. 'Get this to the new Pool manager. Oh and if Malcolm Blue turns up, exe him. Him and the baby.'

Scar took the document, saluted and left.

Matthews was hungry after all that brain work. He ordered his man to set a table out in the fresh air and watched the stars as he ate.

\*

After his meal the President called a final briefing with his chiefs of staff. They were waiting for him and as he swaggered in they rose to their feet and burst into spontaneous applause. After the noise died down Matthews seated himself and motioned for his staff to do likewise. He beamed at them and they beamed back. He liked the military mind, never happier than when it was kicking ass

'Well, ladies and gentlemen, this is the night is it not –? '

Heads nodded and medals rattled enthusiastically.

'– The night when the mighty power of Capa East is unleashed on the traitorous rebels?'

More smiles and nods.

'From this place...' And he paused and let the blood-thirsty devils wait. 'From this place you will return to your troops and prepare them...' He paused again, 'and prepare them...to stand down.'

At first the commanders thought they had misheard and looked at each other, eyebrows raised, waiting for clarification. Several of them allowed their mouths to stay slackly open.

The President smiled indulgently. 'Yes, I thought that might surprise you but I think you will agree that my new plan is brilliant.'

His advisors and chiefs of staff were experienced enough to know it was best not to question the President once he'd made up his mind. But a recently- promoted young commander was unable to hide his disappointment. 'But sir, we're ready to blast the rebs off the face of the globe.'

Everyone froze. Matthews stared at the outspoken youth for a moment, then he laughed, exposing all his teeth, and a communal sigh of relief passed around the room. Matthews glanced at Scar and she went to the offender and led him away. Matthews laughed again, and the rest of the men and women joined in. 'Ah, the impetuosity of youth.'

Several moments later Scar returned and the President continued. 'The entire rabble will pass into Capa East unmolested – '

There was an audible intake of breath but it ceased the moment Matthews looked up.

'— And then, as soon as their last transport is on the Teestrada, our forces will close in behind them, cutting off their retreat.'

An old general asked cautiously, 'We allow all their forces through, Mr President?'

'Going a bit deaf are we, General?'

Another brave man ventured a question. 'And when exactly do we attack, Mr President?'

Lixir smiled. 'Each battalion will receive written orders.' Matthews paused. His chiefs-of-staff waited for him to tell them his plan but he had no such intention. He didn't trust them; he didn't trust anyone except Scar. There were too many freakin traitors out there and anyway, he liked keeping them guessing.

'Might one ask what the ultimate objective is, Mr President?' The General again. The old fool definitely had a death wish. Well, Matthews was always pleased to make people's dreams come true

The President got to his feet, indicating that the meeting was over. There was a stunned silence followed by polite clapping. Matthews bowed brusquely as they exited. As soon as the doors were closed Matthews heard the frantic buzz of their conversation as they hurried away. He leant back in his chair and stretched his arms above his head. 'What news from Capa, Scar?'

'The pirate div station has been destroyed.'

'Excellent. Did you get the spanzas?'

'All exed, Mr President.'

'And has my package been circulated?'

'Every twenty minutes during prime time; then one-hourly intervals during day.'

'Good, good. And the delegates?'

'It's on continual loop on their screens.'

'That should do it. Next? The Pool?'

'Your orders have been carried out.'

'Good good. Any problems with the staff?'

'Nothing we couldn't deal with, sir. We have our own people in now.'

'Now to the main business of the night. Are the Elites in place?'

Scar nodded. 'Their orders are to take the mines and capture the dissidents with minimal collateral damage.'

'I want hostages, Scar, not freakin martyrs. We need to hold the trump card. And your trooper?'

Scar nodded. 'He will be travelling in the first wave with a group of traitor troopers plus the CO, Johnson.'

The President raised his eyebrows.

Scar saw his look. 'The criminal Maya Johnson, Mr President?'

'Ah,' now he remembered. 'I want to interrogate that one personally.'

Scar was silent and this time it wasn't appropriate.

'What?' The President looked up.

'I was hoping...' Matthews couldn't see her expression. 'I was hoping that the elites might be allowed to...interrogate Johnson. A trooper was dishonoured because of her. It seems fitting that we —'

'— As long as she gets what's coming to her. Now, Scar, I want you back in Capa tonight. The boy is at the delegate reception and I don't trust Fleur. Keep an eye on them. If anything happens you know what to do. We can't have the boid remembering who he is in the middle of his speech can we?' Matthews thought this was very funny and laughed so hard that all his chins wobbled in unison.

The trooper waited until the President was quiet again. 'May I also request we deal with the traitor troopers, sir?'

The President nodded. She was such a vengeful bitch. It was probably why he liked her so much. He leant back in his chair, easing his aching shoulders. The pain was still there, all the way down his left arm. Intuitively Scar placed her hands on the spot and gently kneaded the muscles. He smiled to himself as she massaged him. 'My plan is foolproof, Scar. Nothing can go wrong. And it all revolves around your man.' Scar stopped massaging for the briefest of moments and then continued. 'You don't think I'm going to lose the election, do you?'

The rhythmic manipulation never faltered.

Matthews's eyelid's drooped. It was quite tiring using his brain. 'Of course I'll win.' He muttered to himself. 'The populace loves me. It's all been worked out scientifically. Seventy per cent of Capa are pinx and pinx are selected for their unwavering devotion to me. Blus and Yellows will vote for me because they're greedy bastards and who cares about the Reds and assorted tree huggers and loonies?' Thus comforted, Lixir Matthews rested his head on his hands and fell deeply and contentedly asleep.

## *Memories are made of this*

Kline was worried. It was almost time for him to leave for the official delegate reception and still no Fleur or Poppi. He didn't trust Fleur with the child. He was on the verge of remembering who he was and he sensed that Poppi was an important part of the jigsaw. Kline had never felt comfortable with what he was doing. He knew Matthews and Fleur were bad people and the sooner he got out of the palace the better. He'd do the reception but if Fleur and the child weren't back by the time he got back, he was gonna split and chance his luck in the city. Maybe he'd bump into someone who knew him?

He dressed in the clothes that Fleur had laid out for him and ran through his speech in his head. Funny how he could remember all that diplomatic crud but he still couldn't remember who he was.

There was a discreet knock on the door. 'Come.'

Scar entered and stood waiting to escort Kline to the reception.

He smiled at her, hoping to distract her, but she had already noted Fleur's absence. She spoke into her com as she led him down the corridors towards the banqueting hall.

The huge room was full of people and Scar accompanied Kline to his position at the head table and then took her place directly behind him. The one thing Kline loved about being the president was the president's food. He might not remember what he ate before he lost his memory but his stomach did. If he hadn't been so worried he might have enjoyed himself. The div crew was there with the gorgeous interviewer – she gave him a lazy smile. And wouldn't you know it? He was seated next to the GSA president, Monsieur Xaviet from

Eurosville, who only spoke French. Kline had a trans-patch but it was hard to concentrate. There was a vacant seat on the other side of him for Fleur. Where was the woman? Monsieur Xaviet interrogated him about Capa's election and the social system and, although Fleur had trained him well, one or two questions floored him. He needed Fleur beside him, jogging his memory. And talk of the devil...

The old woman sank down into the chair beside him, breathing hard, as if she'd been running. Kline glanced at her. She looked terrible. Her face was grey and she had a blood-soaked bandage tied around her neck. Her ticing was ten times worse than usual and he moved his chair back so that he wouldn't get a flying elbow in his ribs.

'What have you done with her?' Kline hissed.

The old woman ignored him.

'If you've hurt her I'll – '

Fleur kicked him hard under the table. '– Don't threaten me, sonny. Forget the brat and do your job.'

But Kline wouldn't be distracted. 'I'm not doing anything until I know she's safe.'

Silence.

'I mean it, Fleur. Is the kid OK?'

'Is she okay? What about me?' She touched her neck and winced. 'She's an evil, vile little toad.'

'But where is she? Fleur?'

'In the underground. But as soon as this is over, I'm going to hunt her down and dissect her vein by vein.'

At that moment Kline was called upon to make his welcoming speech. He got to his feet, pushed the unruly strand of golden hair out of his eyes and looked confidently at the auto cue. Freakin great. It was facing in the wrong direction. Scar saw the problem and exited.

While he waited Kline smiled out at his audience. He was happy that Poppi had escaped and he wasn't at all nervous. There was a bowl of fruit in front of him, with a large succulent peach in the centre. He looked forward to sinking his teeth into it and that's when something exploded in his brain. A peach. Someone had offered him a peach once, someone he loved. Maya – Maya – Maya Johnson. A plug had been switched on in his brain and a tidal wave of information surged through him. Nothing could stop it.

Kline was remembering.

## *Happiness*

The news that Billy was sitting up in bed and talking spread quickly through the mines. Everyone had heard about Billy and his devoted little friend.

Maya had never seen the child smiling before and that in itself was a small miracle. It wasn't long before crowds of well-wishers arrived on the ward. Maya wasn't sure why she stayed but the boy was still important to her. She had watched his fight to stay alive. To have recovered from those terrible injuries showed what a fighter he was.

Some people couldn't get inside; so they stood in the corridor trying to catch a glimpse of the boy. Dan and Emma were there, and the woman Anna – the one from the Outpost. The Young brat said something to her and she smiled but her eyes pleaded, 'get me out of here.' Maya knew how she felt. The annoying kid was jumping up and down, trying to get a better view. When she couldn't, she grabbed her father's hand and pulled him through the crowd. Dan was apologetic but when the people saw who it was they let him through. Anna followed reluctantly.

Billy and the little girl were deep in conversation, oblivious to everything but each other. The boy laughed but it made him cough and the child tapped him gently on the back. As her hand rose and fell the light caught her 'ruby' ring and it sparkled brightly. There was a squeal of delight and Maya saw DanYoung's kid running towards the bed. Why didn't the idiot keep her under control? Dan shouted at her to come back.

Suddenly there was a crash as Anna slid to the floor. Dan knelt beside the unconscious woman and as Anna's eyelids fluttered open Dan whispered something to her. When she was ready he helped her stand. The brat was hopping about from one foot to the other, trying to talk to Billy's friend but the child was frightened and hid behind Billy. The boy said something to her and she peeped out. That was when the girl saw Anna. The child's eyes were huge and a tear ran down her cheek and into her mouth. Her tongue flicked out and she drank it but her mouth stayed open. She was panting like a frightened animal. Anna released Dan and took an unsteady step forward. The child clung to Billy's hand but he nudged her towards the woman. She took a step, then another and another until she was within reach.

The child put out a small tentative hand. The voice was barely a whisper. 'Mummy?' And then Tanya walked into her mother's arms.

## *Exit stage right*

'Say something, idiot.' Fleur dug her sharp nails into Kline's leg but he swatted her off. He refused to be distracted from this roller-coaster of memories. It was a fantastic ride and he wasn't alone. There was Poppi and his mates, there was the CO unit and Walt Disney and the peach and Maya ...his beautiful Maya.

Fleur's voice came from somewhere far away. ' What's the matter with you ? They're waiting. Say something.'

Kline leant towards her and his voice was steady and confident. 'I know who I am, Mrs President. I've remembered ... and if you harm one hair on that kid's head I'll exe you. Promise.'

Then, before she could do anything about it, he got to his feet. He had no need for an auto cue now. 'Most honoured friends, it is with great pleasure that I welcome you to Capa East for our election – the first for thirty years. I trust that you have a wonderful time in our little city and I encourage you to go anywhere you wish. No door will be barred, the palace laboratories, the Institute, the colour zones, the prisons, the interrogating rooms – they are all at your disposal. However...' He paused for effect. '...there is one small detail I should point out before I go any further. You see,' and he grinned at the surprised delegates. 'I am not the president of Capa East, I have never been the president of Capa East and I never will be the president of Capa East. I'm a stand-in, an impostor, employed by the real president, Lixir Matthews. The President is fat, old and a criminal. Deep beneath this palace there is a huge dungeon. And the prisoner? The Berg. Yes my friends the last Berg in the world. But some of you know that already don't you?' He looked hard at the delegates and several couldn't meet his gaze.

Kline saw Scar hurrying towards him. He didn't like the look on her face. He would have to be quick. 'Lixir Matthews is a murderer, a tyrant and a dictator.' And I am? My name is... 'And, from somewhere, his name fluttered down on a banner carried by bluebirds, while Judy Garland sang, "Somewhere over a rainbow ..." 'My name is Kline. I am seventeen and I'm a CO.'

He heard the thump as Fleur slid under the table. Strange He'd never had her down as a fainty type. Then, before anyone could react, he pushed back his chair, bowed to the stunned audience and walked slowly to the door and out into the corridor, where he ran like freakin hell to Fleur's broom cupboard.

# *Leaving*

Dan watched his daughter from the doorway of the children's ward. She and Tanya were playing cards with Billy. Emma laughed delightedly whenever the boy said something to her and gazed adoringly at him. Everyone loved this emaciated child. Dan was jealous. How pathetic.

Billy still needed rest but apart from that he had made an amazing recovery. Anna sat at the bottom of Billy's bed, supposedly reading, but she was really keeping an eye on her daughter. Tanya kept glancing at her mother, as if reassuring herself that her mother was real. She had worn a perpetual dazed expression ever since she and Anna had been reunited. One happy story.

The Society was making its move tonight. Dan had already said his goodbyes. He had told Emma he would be away for a few nights and had been almost hurt by the matter of fact way she had accepted this bit of news. She'd given him a big kiss but she wasn't tearful. Did he want her to be upset? Of course not. She would be with Tanya and Anna and Billy. How could he compete?

Anna had promised to look after Emma, whatever happened, and that was a huge relief. One thing less for him to worry about. At least they would be safe here in the mines. Matthews would be too busy dealing with the Society to bother with a few women, children and ill folk.

There was an escape route out of the mines but that would only be used in an emergency. Dan hadn't thought about what would happen when the Society was destroyed. His imagination refused to take him there. For the time being he was content to see his daughter happy and in the care of a loving woman. That was a lot more than most children had in Capa.

Munro came and stood beside him. 'Ready?'

Dan nodded and they walked away together. He didn't look back.

\*

There was a lot of frantic stuff going on in the main cavern. Guns and ammo were being loaded into transports and there were groups of people huddled around leaders getting their orders. Maya saw Gola's squad teaching some children how to use guns. To look at their faces you'd think they were planning a party.

Gola's squad was to be the vanguard of the attack and Maya was going with them. It felt good to be strapping on a gun again. She was now an official member of the pinx squad, as was Pox. The group treated them like their own. Maya would be sorry to part company with these people. They were the first real friends she'd ever had – apart from the traitor, Kline.

Maya watched Pox as he lounged beside Gola, one arm draped casually over the girl's shoulder, the other toting a missile gun. These were heavy bits of kit, but in the pinx's strong grip it looked as light as a toy pistol. A strong boy. He must be to have recovered so quickly from his grisly injuries. Pox was everybody's mate and even Maya grudgingly admired his performance. Because that's what it was. A brilliant performance. And he knew that she knew. He said something to Gola and she laughed out loud. Mr Congeniality. Even hard-nosed Gola was taken in by him, but not Maya – never.

Pox looked up, sensing her gaze, and returned her hostile stare with one equally as poisonous. This was the first time he had allowed his affable mask to slip, and she smiled triumphantly at him and raised a finger. Come back Capa Nasty, all is forgiven.

Their group was travelling in a SC. Scout Cars didn't have much in the way of fire power but they were fast and manoeuvrable. And guess what? Frankie was driving. As they waited to board, Pox was in front of Maya and she hissed in his ear. 'I'll be watching you, boy.'

He rested his hand on his hip. 'Yeh? I'm scared shitless, girlie.'

Then he looked away and said something under his breath to the pinx beside him. They laughed and looked back at her.

Maya was seriously considering trashing the spanza when Gola intervened. 'Hey, Maya? Munro needs to speak.' The CO was annoyed but Gola waved her away. 'Don't worry, we're not going anywhere without our favourite blu.'

Maya had kept well away from Munro since that day in the projection. It was hard enough coming to terms with what he had told her without seeing his concerned expression every time they met.

Dan Young was in Munro's room when she got there. He was dressed in body armour and held a hand gun very carefully between thumb and finger, as if it was likely to go off at any moment. Maya made a mental note not to be anywhere near him when the shooting started.

'What d'you want, Munro? We're ready to go.'

Munro carried on talking to Dan. 'So, I'll see you at the rally? And remember, keep your head down.'

Dan tried to smile.

When Young had gone Munro turned to Maya. 'I want to check you out, Maya, make sure you're absolutely fighting fit. We can't have any walking wounded. Okay? Plus I want to give you a shot. You're with Frankie so we know what that means.'

'I'm used to Frankie. I was with him on the Outpost raid, remember?' She'd spoken without thinking and her words hung like dead things in the air.

Munro broke the silence. 'Up to you. But you're not going anywhere until I've examined you.'

Maya sighed and sat obediently on the edge of the table while he prodded her leg.

'So? This is it, Maya.'

She knew what was coming.

'Thought any more about what we...discussed?'

What was it with him? 'Look. I don't know what I'm gonna do, Munro, till I find out what's going on, okay?'

'You've got to understand the importance of keeping Matthews alive – '

'– Yeh, yeh, you said.'

Munro held a hypodermic in his hand. 'Pull your sleeve up.'

She started to say she didn't need more med but saw the look in his eyes and knew it was useless. As he injected he said something that sounded like 'sorry' but she wasn't positive, and by then it was too late anyway.

*

When Dan told Gola he was coming with them she didn't seem too surprised, especially when he explained that Munro thought it better for him and Dan to travel separately. It made sense. Munro would be in the first transport behind the SCs, with other members of the council.

But Gola was very disappointed that their Blu was missing. She asked why and Dan said he didn't know. He did, but he thought it was best to be vague. Dan noticed the boy Gemmie looked a bit put out too. Maybe they were an item? Dan marvelled at the way life went on whatever the circumstances. Love and death, side by side.

It would be a lie to say Dan enjoyed the ride but it was certainly an experience and it kept his mind off things. It seemed that their driver Frankie and the SC were attached at the hip. The man made use of every bump in the terrain to leap forward, and every edge of dune to surf the sand, often on the tyre rims. Fuel was scarce and whenever he could, Frankie cut and they coasted down, going faster and faster until Dan thought they must crash. The pinx yelled excitedly and Dan smiled, despite his bruises. He glanced at their wild happy faces. Gola caught him looking and grinned. 'Going home, Dan.'

Their assignment was to get to the City Hall as quickly as possible and secure it for the election rally, where Dan would meet the delegates and address Society supporters. Their people in Capa were doing a fantastic job, keeping the populace up to date with what was going on. Gola's div from the Outpost raid had been circulated to every home and their support was growing

At that moment the SC dived into a huge hole and everybody crashed to one end of the vehicle. When they ploughed out Dan was laughing as loudly as everyone else.

'Hey, Frankie,' Gola yelled. 'You driving too smooth.'

Finally, they crested a massive dune and saw the lights of the city spread out beneath them. Frankie cut. The sky was clear and the sun was rising behind the city. It lit up the transroutes and walkways of the city and derelict buildings cast enormous purple shadows across the surrounding, lightening, white desert. No one spoke but when Frankie let out the clutch and they free-wheeled down a dune, they joined in one mass howl. ' Capa Capa Capa.'

## *Coming out of hiding*

Malcolm and Poppi had a routine. During the night all four slept together in the byre. Orange in Poppi's arms and the baby lying on top of Malcolm. The sound of the cows munching away was extremely soothing. Then during the day they wandered about at will.

Malcolm glanced at his watch again, worry lines etched between his eyes. He and Poppi were in the byre. Orange was out somewhere eating things. The animal was having the time of his life and only came back at the end of the day. He liked milk. Malcolm thought it probably helped him digest all the meat.

'He's really late now. What's happened?'

Poppi shrugged. She was talking to the baby. 'Say Poppi. P p p...Poppi.'

'Bobbi' the baby said, as clear as a bell, and the girl looked smug.

Malcolm would not be distracted. 'He's never late. Pinx are selected for their unquestioning obedience. There's something happening up there. Something important.' And he pointed towards the roof of the cavern.

Suddenly Poppi remembered the boy she liked. 'Where cow boy?'

Malcolm pursed his lips. 'What d'you think I've been talking about for the past hour?'

'Don't know. Don't listen.'

Poppi was getting on Malcolm's nerves. There was only so much Poppi-speak a sentient being could take. He had tried to teach her to talk properly but she had fixed him with one her looks and gone off singing some stupid song into the undergrowth. You couldn't have a discussion with her and he missed the stimulation of the Pool. Of course he loved Baby and he knew it would be dangerous for them to go back up there but he needed to find out what was happening. If only he could trust Poppi to keep an eye on Baby but the girl was unpredictable and he didn't like the way Orange kept licking the child's legs.

He tried to imagine someone else in charge of the Pool. He couldn't. After all, he had been chosen not them. If only there was a way for him to keep the baby and also be the Master? No, this wouldn't do. He would go back up there now, baby or no baby, and see for himself.

Poppi lay down to sleep with Orange and was soon snoring away.

Malcolm got a few things together. With any luck he would be back before the girl woke up.

As it happened, he wasn't and when Poppi saw he was gone she assumed he was out with Baby having his breakfast. She'd made a decision too. She missed her life as a CO. She missed her divs and she missed stealing. She loved Orange and life was easy down here but she needed more. The agridome was safe and warm and…boring. She could always come back if things got tough. It never entered her head to tell Malcolm. Poppi was in charge of Poppi. That was how it was.

## *So easy*

Gola's squad entered West Gate unmolested and drove onto the Teestrada. All their intelligence had indicated mass Trooper presence in this area but the strada was completely deserted. Frankie drove slowly and smoothly. No one spoke as they rocked gently together. Their senses were alert and their guns were drawn. Dan was sweating and it wasn't only because he was hot.

Gola caught his eye, 'Must have heard you were coming, Dan.'

'Oh yeh,' Dan smiled. 'They are so frightened of me.' What was he talking about? He knew, they all knew, that Matthews was playing some kind of game with them but it didn't seem to matter, there was still something glorious about entering their city like this, like heroes. The pinx were young, strong and ready to conquer the world and he was...well he was happy to be alive.

Frankie parked up outside a service lift and they spread out and searched the immediate vicinity. Still no sign of the enemy. Dan, Gola, Pox and half the squad made for the underground lifts. The others stayed on top to secure the area for the arrival of the main convoy, coming up behind them. Gola jostled Dan as she got into the lift beside him. 'Hey how hard was that?'

Dan couldn't hide his fear. 'We shouldn't get over-confident, Gola.' He dreaded going down into the underground again. Denzo would never be far away down there.

Gola snorted. 'Why not? This is your big day.'

They stood together against the rear wall of the lift, guns ready, facing outwards, but when they emerged into the tunnel it was deserted. It was getting very hot and Dan took a drink. The day raid was Munro's idea. He knew it would be hard for them but it would be even harder for the heavily armed Troopers. The squad wore the lightest of gear with double water bottles, slung across their chests.

Gola's group set off towards Central Capa. As they ran Dan saw his face plastered on the walls. Society supporters had been busy, even this far out. Gola tore down any remaining Matthews' posters that they came across and shredded them before tossing the bits into the air. Dan ran through a snow storm of his opponent's face.

He worried that he wouldn't be able to keep up with the pinx and after about half a kilometre he knew he couldn't. Gola was watching him closely when suddenly they heard a noise behind them. She shoved him against the wall, drawing her gun. It was an AP. Strange it was functioning in the daytime but it was lucky for Dan. They hitched a lift. Each new length of tunnel had to be checked for booby traps and mines but the AP travelled slowly so the pinx could reconnoitre and still catch up with the train further on.

At one point Gola and the others were up ahead, leaving Dan, his two bodyguards and Pox on the train. Gola had ordered Pox to stay. He was still recovering from his injuries and looked almost as done in as Dan. He hadn't wanted to stay on the AP but Gola was adamant and she was the boss. At that moment Dan heard something and looked back at the pinx. He saw him raise his hand to his ear. Was he receiving? There was no time to do anything about it because at that moment Pox leapt to his feet and yelled, 'Bail.' They dived off at the exact moment the train exploded into a million pieces.

Debris showered down on them as they were thrown to the ground.

Gola and the others came charging back and the white faced girl helped Dan to his feet. Dan saw her relief but she wasn't half as glad as he was. He was bruised but no one had been injured. They had had an amazing escape.

Gola patted Pox on the arm. 'Good one, Gemmie.'

'Yeh, thanks', Dan smiled at the boy. 'Thanks?' It sounded so inadequate. This boy had saved his life. The rest of the squad clustered around the trooper slapping him on the back. Pox smiled modestly.

The pinx with the detectors went on ahead while the rest strung out behind, walking carefully in each other's footsteps. Dan didn't mention seeing the boy receiving. It seemed churlish after the boy had saved his life.

Very soon Dan was too exhausted to think. As long as nobody talked to him or expected him to do anything, other than put one foot in front of the other, he was okay. They took on water as they went, secured each intersection, and then moved swiftly on to the next. The stamina of the pinx was amazing. Dan drank twice the amount of liquid they did.   Gola was in constant touch with the following group and Dan was delighted when she told him that Munro's party had safely entered the underground. They hadn't met any resistance either.

Incoming info from the surface was less reassuring. Intelligence reported mass trooper movements all over the city and wide-spread arrests of anyone vaguely associated with the Society. Word was there had been some sort of internal trouble within the Matthews' camp but no firm account had reached their intelligence yet. But any problem for the opposition was good news for the insurgents.

At last Gola called a halt and the squad waited while Dan limped slowly up to them. His legs had reached that stage beyond jelly when he wasn't sure they could hold him up anymore. He leant against the tunnel wall, getting his breath back. There were black spots jiggling in front of his eyes. At last, when he was able to focus again, he saw Gola pointing upwards.

'Thank God.' Dan wiped the sweat out of his eyes. 'Any chance of a dry shirt? I want the electorate to see me at my best.'

'Really? 'Gola emptied a bottle of water over Dan's head. 'You look beautiful to me.'

## *Beating*

*The child felt safe in her mother's arms but she could feel the woman's heart beating wildly against her as she ran. 'Sorry...sorry, Mummy, I didn't mean to –'*

*'– Shh,' the woman gasped, between snatches of breath.*

*And the child tried to blot out the noise of giant footsteps crashing behind them. She buried her face in her mother's neck, too scared to cry.*

*But the noise got nearer and louder and the woman couldn't run any more. She sank to her knees, her mouth open wide, fighting for air. 'Be quick, Maya. Find somewhere to hide.' The child hesitated, unsure of what her mother was saying. The woman put a trembling hand against the child's back and pushed her away from her. 'Run, Maya. Run very fast for Mummy. Please. Oh God, please!' And the sheer terror in her voice made the child run.*

The pounding in her head was still there when Maya's eyes snapped open. Munro was gone and the door was wide open. Maya glimpsed an empty, silent chamber beyond. They were long gone. She sat up and tried to stand. She was very unsteady – no doubt a side effect of the drug Munro had given her. Freakin Munro. She shook her head, trying to dislodge the pounding, but the rhythmic beating persisted, getting louder and nearer until finally, chillingly, Maya knew what the sound was. It was the clash of metal coshes against plasti-shields – the Elites were coming

Maya used up her entire repertoire of expletives as she collected her gear and stashed water and tabs. When she arrived in the main cavern it was full of panicking people. The menacing drumming was intended to terrify and it did. Some young guards were trying to organise a disciplined withdrawal to the escape tunnels, but there weren't enough of them, and they needed to get back to the gates.

One of the guards recognised Maya and grabbed her arm. He was about her age and very afraid. His eyes were pleading and she smelt his fear. Her reaction was to help defend the gates but he begged her to take charge of the civilian withdrawal and in the end she agreed. She remembered Billy and the child. 'Okay, I'll take over here. What's the plan?'

'Get them into the passageways and head downhill at all intersections.'

'Yeh. Then what?

The boy shrugged helplessly.

'Freakin fantastic. Did anyone get a message out to Munro?'

He shrugged again.

Maya hit her head in frustration but there was no point being angry. 'Okay I'll sort it; you get back up there.'

He looked apprehensively over his shoulder, 'I don't know how long we can hold them.'

Maya knew.

She selected some likely looking people, instructed them to gather a group each, collect all the liquid and food they could carry, and get to the tunnels. And to hurry.

On her way to the children's quarters she looked in on the hospital. The medics were already barricading themselves inside with their patients.

Anna and the other women were ready to move out when Maya arrived. The look of relief on Anna's face was palpable. 'I thought you were going with the others?'

Maya smiled grimly. 'Yeh, well there was a change of plan.'

'I'm so glad you're here.' Anna smiled but her mouth wobbled.

Billy saluted Maya. It was comical but Maya didn't laugh; she returned his salute, noting the explosives and RF tucked in his belt. A useful boy to have around. She left him to organise provisions while she got the children and women lined up. Emma chatted away as if it were some sort of adventure. As long as she was with her friends, it didn't matter. Tanya stood close to her mother, gulping in the air like a dying fish.

Billy and the girls led the way to the tunnel. Tanya clutched her friend's hand but kept looking back to make sure her mother was following.

Anna whispered to Maya as they walked, 'Promise me something?'

Maya knew what was coming.

'Don't let them take her – no, hear me out – use the med on Tanya and the others before they – "

'– Not now, Anna.'

'Please. Promise me.'

The desperation in the woman's voice got to Maya. 'Okay. But you've gotta stay calm. The kid's watching you.'

Anna took something out her pocket and slipped it into Maya's hand, and then the pair of them hurried after the children.

At the tunnel entrance there was a crush of people trying to get through the narrow opening. Word was that the outer doors had been blown and the surviving guards had retreated to the second chamber. The mine echoed with the sound of distant gun fire.

Maya pushed Billy to the other side of the entrance and they hurried the evacuees through between them.

When they were sure that everyone was through Maya told Anna to wait for them in the first cavern while she and Billy laid the explosives. The boy worked quickly and efficiently. When everything was set Maya withdrew behind a rock and tensed her finger on the detonator. 'Move it, Billy.'

The boy was standing at the entrance of the tunnel, his back to her. He didn't move. A huge explosion went off somewhere close by.

'Billy!'

The boy turned his head and she saw his face. His eyes were huge with grief. 'I'm not coming.'

Maya took a step towards him, judging the distance between them.

'Someone's got to stay on rear.'

'Don't be a trond, Billy. You'd be dead meat before you got within spitting distance of the spanzas.'

'I'm dead already,' the boy muttered. 'They took my life. Made me...made me do things.'

'– Forget it, Billy –'

'– D'you think I don't want to?' He spat the words at Maya. 'But it's in here all the time.' And he smacked the side of his head.

Maya was calculating how fast the kid could run. 'I can't do this without you, Billy. I need your help –'

He wasn't listening. '– If I wanted to get into trooper camp I had to ditch her. That's what they said. So I took her down there in the dark. I was gonna go back for her. Find somewhere safe for her but she didn't understand, how could she? She was screaming, clinging to me. I had to shove her away.

I hurt her. And then I ran. I could hear her crying for me, trying to follow me but I never looked back...' He couldn't go on.

Maya had no idea what he was talking about but she had to keep him talking. 'What about Tanya, Billy? She loves you. She needs you.'

He shook his head.

'I thought she was special?'

The boy's eyes flashed. 'What good would I be to her? A freakin mute? The only thing I can do is kill.'

Maya lost patience. 'Okay. Time up. Get here now or I'll –'

He turned and walked quickly away from her. Maya sprinted after him; punched him on the side of his head and dragged his unconscious body back into the tunnel and behind the rock. Then she pressed the button and the world erupted about them. She flung her body over the boy as white shrapnel zipped about and clouds of dust descended on them.

When it was quiet again Maya got to her feet. Billy was a white shape. He coughed and retched and tried to sit up. At least he was conscious. She hadn't hit him hard but he was still very weak. 'Hey, Billy. We did a good job.' The opening to the tunnel was totally blocked.

Maya flicked a couple of bugs and they lit up Maya's whitened hair like a halo and Billy's hard little face. 'Think you can walk?' She offered him a hand but he wouldn't take it and they set off in silence. He didn't look at her or speak to her. Well, she could live with that.

When they reached the cavern it was deserted except for three forlorn figures huddled together under one feeble bug. Emma screamed with delight and ran at Billy. Tanya followed more slowly with

Anna. Emma hugged the boy and jumped about until she was as white as he was. The little girl dusted Billy down. 'Billy's a ghost, Tanya, see.'

Tanya took Billy's hand and held it against her cheek. Then she looked up into his face and gave him a radiant smile before crying out in alarm. She had spotted the red mark on Billy's head, where Maya had hit him. The child tried to touch it but Billy winced and pulled away.

Maya smacked her clothes, throwing up a dense cloud of white dust. 'Okay, let's go.' She walked quickly away and the others followed. There were a few lost bugs flitting about in the tunnel and they latched onto Maya's party. Maya stowed their lights, conserving energy. It wasn't long before they overtook some of the stragglers from the main group. They were oldies, stumbling along as best they could. Maya couldn't wait for them. She had to get to the front of the evacuees. She shouted encouragement and reminded them to keep going downhill and then they were past them and away. It was hard to forget their haggard, frightened faces.

They ran until Emma fell down with exhaustion and then Maya pulled the child up onto her shoulders and they ran on again. Anna and Billy were taking it in turns to carry Tanya but Billy nearly lost his footing several times. How he stayed upright at all was a mystery to Maya. His face was bathed in sweat but he managed a flicker of a response when she smiled at him.

At one point the tunnel descended almost vertically and they slithered down on their backsides. They must be under the desert by now. The heat was crushing and the air was thick and dirty. Once they heard a huge explosion high above them. The tunnel entrance had been cleared.

Fortunately the tunnels were too narrow for transports but the troopers could run for hours without resting. Maya urged them on.

Shortly after this Billy was taking his turn at carrying Tanya, when his legs suddenly buckled beneath him. Tanya rolled away unhurt but Billy fell awkwardly and hit his head on a rock. He was out cold again. Emma screamed and Tanya knelt beside the unconscious boy, cradling his head on her lap. Anna poured some water between his lips but Tanya took the liquid bottle off her mother and moistened the edge of a piece of material then bathed his head. In a few moments Billy opened his eyes and smiled weakly up at his little friend.

Tanya regarded him seriously. 'You've been overdoing things.'

Maya smiled despite herself. They waited until Billy could stand and then they walked on slowly. Maya had no idea where the rest of their group was. The tunnels criss-crossed and the others might have chosen different paths, on different levels. There was no noise now except their footsteps and the occasional slough of dislodged gravel.

Coming to the bottom of another steep incline, the tunnel levelled out into a large space with four exits. There were a dozen or so women and children huddled together in the dim light. Elizabeth and the boys were in this group and Emma found some of her friends. It was comforting to see familiar faces.

All the passages leading out of this cavern were on the same level but Maya postponed the decision about which way to go until they'd all grabbed some rest. Her instinct told her to go on but she saw the fatigue on the faces of the children and knew it was pointless. They sank down on the hard rock floor, took liquid on, ate tabs and fell into an exhausted sleep.

# The Rally

When Gola's squad arrived outside Capa's City Hall they were welcomed by excited, cheering supporters. Dan was dirty and dishevelled, surrounded by equally filthy pinx but no one seemed to notice. It was an unofficial holiday and whole condos had turned out for the rally. All colour bands mixed good-naturedly, waving 'Vote for Freedom' banners and wearing Tree insignia.

The hall was a magnificent plasti-therm sphere set like a jewel in a courtyard full of projected plants and fountains. Gola and Frankie spear-headed their slow advance through the throng of people. Dan's bodyguards stuck close to him. Any one of these smiling, enthusiastic people could be an assassin. When the squad got inside, a wall of applause hit them. Everyone was on their feet yelling, 'Dan, Dan, Dan, Dan,' and that single word resonated around the space and out into the courtyard and down the walkways, like a pounding bass drum.

The people of Capa knew nothing about Dan Young but they knew they didn't want Lixir Matthews any more. The President had treated them with contempt. He'd tricked them with stand-ins and they'd all seen the Outpost div. And besides, Matthews was old and Capa was a young city. It didn't like oldies. Matthews had encouraged the cult of youth and ironically it was this youthfulness that would defeat him. It didn't matter that Dan was short and ordinary against the towering squad of pinx. He was their man, their hope for a new and better life. They pushed forwards eagerly, trying to catch a glimpse of the next president of Capa.

The GSA delegates were already seated on the platform when Dan eventually mounted the steps.

Another huge cheer echoed around the hall. Everyone could see their man now. He shook hands with President Xaviet and the delegation and finally took his seat, centre stage. Gola, Frankie and the bodyguards flanked him, while the others placed themselves strategically around the hall. Pox stood two rows back from the platform.

Dan's smile was frozen and his heart was pounding but he was happy to be there. He had never expected to get this far. His friends were beaming too, but Gola was talking into her com and Dan followed her gaze to the top tier of the hall. He saw indistinct shapes and knew what they were. Pinx snipers. They couldn't drop their guard – not yet. A contingent of Matthews' troopers lounged threateningly around the perimeter walls of the hall, their black helmets reflected in the plasti-therm.

Gola caught Dan's eye. 'Piece of cake?'

Dan poured himself a drink. His mouth was so dry it took some time for the liquid to force its way down his gullet. As he drank he stared out at the crowd. All of these people here because of him? It was amazing, surreal. He looked at his watch. Where was Munro? Behind him Gola was receiving and as he watched he saw her eyes widen in horror.

'Gola? What is it?' He clutched her arm.

The girl was immediately relaxed and smiling. 'Hey, nothing. You worry too much.'

'Where's Munro?'

'He'll be here in five.'

'And he's okay?'

Gola patted his arm. 'Relax. Everything's good.' She talked slowly as if she were reassuring a frightened child. Dan recognised that tone. He had used it often enough with Emma…Emma. He had to believe he'd see her again one day. He made himself grin at the pinx. Five minutes. He could wait five minutes, couldn't he?

Almost immediately there was a disturbance at the back of the hall. A tall figure was pushing its way through the crowds towards the platform but it didn't look like Munro. And there was another figure, a smaller one, behind the first. The taller of the two was a trooper, an imposing female, and the other was an old, fat man, dressed in a bizarre formal uniform with plumes and medals. The cheering came to an abrupt halt as they advanced and the silent crowd parted to let them through. When they reached the platform the trooper helped the man up the steps. He was gasping for breath and flopped into the nearest chair.

Dan heard the whisper. 'Lixir Matthews. Lixir Matthews...' Was it possible? Most people, including Dan, had never seen the real president before. Everybody craned their necks to catch their first sight of the President of Capa. Matthews sat, oblivious, staring down at his podgy sweating hands, getting his breath back.

The people didn't stay silent for long. Someone shouted, 'Like your dress, ducky' and a couple of people laughed and then the whole crowd joined in. They jeered, they whistled, they stamped their feet, they shouted and they shrieked with laughter, until it felt as if the whole of Capa was enjoying this old man's humiliation.

Matthews ignored the rabble and looked coolly about him, marking down the names of those he recognised in the crowd. He had a good memory. Then, out of the corner of his eye, he saw Dan Young get to his feet. He held up his hands for silence and the mob obeyed instantly. As Young sat down again he gave Matthews a half-smile of sympathy. The President struggled to stop himself from grabbing the little runt and strangling him on the spot. But he must be patient. He couldn't do anything in front of the GSA, not yet. He concentrated instead on the satisfaction he would feel when Dan Young found out that his precious daughter was at his mercy. Then he'd see who could be magnanimous.

Didn't the little worm know how deeply offensive it was for him to have such an unworthy opponent? Lixir was the most powerful man in the Globe and Young was nothing, a Red, a non-scientist; a lackey. Matthews felt his heart beating wildly. He mustn't get over-excited but the heat pressed down on him like a mighty weight, suffocating him. Maybe it had been a mistake wearing this uniform. He had wanted to show the GSA that he wasn't afraid of them or their pet poodle, but the material was thick and stiff and smelt of something extremely unpleasant. It had been one of Fleur's little finds. Thinking of her cheered him up. At least the old bag was done for. After his re-election Fleur would be sentenced as a traitor to the State and sent to the incinerator. That thought could sustain him through a lot of over-heating. He was also looking forward to killing Kline. He should never have taken the imbecile on to begin with but he'd been desperate. Kline's memory return couldn't have come at a more inconvenient moment. He would be hunted down and exterminated along with all the other traitors.

Matthews glanced at the delegates. Spineless nobodies the lot of them. They'd be running home soon, their tails between their legs, and the fate of Capa forgotten.

He wasn't worried by the Outpost raid's bad press. His div company was putting out constant footage of Society 'atrocities' with substantiated evidence. It wouldn't take long for those manufactured images to become the truth in people's minds. Matthews knew all about implanting thoughts. He was an expert in that.

His mistake had been in not completely crushing the Society when he had the chance. He should have exed Munro years ago but instead the man had stayed right under his nose, causing trouble, stirring up malcontents. Well no more Mr Nice Guy. This time the Society would be totally annihilated and then it would be the Globe's turn. The age of Lixir Matthews was about to begin.

Looking up Matthews found himself staring straight into Monsieur Xaviet's eyes. The man was sneering at him. He had always hated him, ever since Matthews had refused to cut him in on the grain trader scam. But the president of the GSA would get his…cut very soon. Matthews could guarantee that. He looked at his watch. It was time.

He leant back in his chair. 'Everything ready, Scar?'

The response was immediate. 'Affirmative.'

'Where?'

'Second row, centre, Mr President.'

Matthews got his bearings. Ah yes. He couldn't pinpoint his man exactly because they all looked the same, but there was a group of ex-troopers close to the platform. All of them wore the Tree insignia. Nothing marked Scar's trooper out as different. It was the perfect disguise.

'And the signal?'

"Most illustrious friends and world statesmen, sir – '

'– There's no room for mistakes, Scar.'

'He's the best there is.'

'Okay, get moving.' When he glanced back he was surprised to see the trooper still behind him. 'Didn't you hear me?'

Scar nodded. 'I wanted to clarify what happens afterwards, sir.'

Matthews could feel the sweat prickling under his armpits. 'After freakin what?'

'After the…elimination?'

Matthews threw back his head and laughed, a real belly laugh. Several delegates looked up in surprise. He had guts this Lixir Matthews, if nothing else. This man could be going to prison for a long time if found guilty of the charges levelled against him.

Matthews wiped away the tears and looked at Scar. The trooper was really very funny. He beckoned her nearer, so he could whisper. 'He gets exed, Scar. He's a freakin assassin, isn't he? He's public enemy number one. What did you think I'd do with him? Give him a medal?'

'Exed?'

Matthews was beyond patience. 'I've given you an order.'

'He could escape, sir.'

'No chance – '

'– He could leave the city?'

'No –'

'– Elite would never talk – '

The President swivelled around and caught the trooper's arm. 'Anyone can be made to talk, Scar. You included. Now get to it.'

Scar's voice was soft. 'I understand, Mr President, but who does the – '

'– You of course, trond brain. Or maybe you want me to do it?'

At last Dan saw Munro's unmistakable figure hurrying towards him through the crowd. Anyone who knew Munro would have known there was something wrong but Dan was too wound up to notice anything except the reassuring presence of his mentor. Gola and Frankie glanced worriedly at each other.

There was one other person who noticed the strain on Munro's face – Matthews. The President and Munro knew each other well.

Munro slipped into a seat beside his protégée. His face was smiling now. 'Sorry about that, Dan?'

'Is something wrong –? '

'– Everything's fine. Are you ready?'

Dan attempted yes but it came out as a squeak. He had no saliva in his mouth and his tongue lay stranded at the bottom of his mouth. Munro handed him some liquid and Dan drank gratefully.

'They'll love you, Dan. Just be yourself.'

Dan did a thumbs-up. Be himself? Not a good idea. He had to be someone else, some other Dan Young, from a parallel universe maybe? That made him smile – a bit.

Munro got to his feet and waited until the hall quietened before he swept his arms out in an embrace. 'Welcome GSA and welcome Capa.'

The crowd roared back.

'The Society thanks you for your support and good will. And now it is my very great pleasure to introduce the next president of Capa East. Vote for the Society. Vote for Dan Young.'

The people rose as one and clapped and cheered. Eventually Munro held up his hands for silence and in that still moment Dan got unsteadily to his feet.

'Friends. I'm an ordinary man, a Red. I have a child. I had a decent wage, a reasonable standard of living and a loving family but then one night the troopers came for my neighbours' daughter and my life will never be the same again.'

He didn't have glamour, he wasn't a great orator. He was an everyday man, telling it how it was. The audience listened in silence and sadness, because Dan Young was speaking for himself but also for them – every one of them. When he sat down there was total silence for a moment before the applause threatened to take the roof off.

Pox was in the zone. He heard the noise but he wasn't there, he was somewhere else, looking down on himself. All his senses were heightened as adrenaline pumped through him. This was his moment; the one he'd been waiting for all his life. The moment he would make Her proud of him. His eyes swept the hall and yes, there she was, on the left hand side of the stage, and her eyes were on him.

When his com vibrated he glanced at the pinx beside him, checking he wasn't being watched. The ex trooper was yelling and screaming like everyone else. Pox was smiling too as he listened to Scar, his delighted expression never changing. Then he looked back at the trooper-chief and nodded imperceptibly. He was ready.

Lixir was breathless and dizzy but if he could hold out for a few more minutes it would be all over and he would be able to take off this freakin coat. He glanced at Scar. She was in place. It was time. He took a deep breath and rose to his feet.

'Friends.' His voice boomed out but most of the excited crowd didn't hear him. Those that did didn't recognise yesterday's man. Lixir Matthews was old Capa and they were already in the new one.

'Friends,' the man continued, refusing to give up. A few more heard him this time and shushed their neighbours. When there was a semblance of quiet Matthews walked slowly to the middle of the stage, standing to one side of Dan Young. The President's coat was stained with perspiration. Deep troughs of dark sweat showed under his armpits and down the centre of his back and as his head moved, glittering droplets of moisture spun from his hair like beads on a string. The old man clasped his hands in front of him as if in prayer. 'Please, I beg you. Indulge an old man. Allow me to say a few words? 'He coughed and this very human action made the crowd more tolerant. What harm could it do, to let this sad oldie speak?

'Thank you, thank you, you're too kind.' The President smiled. 'It's fitting that we're gathered here tonight, in this beautiful hall, built in memory of my dear father –'

'– Get on with it, granddad,' Someone shouted good-naturedly.

But Lixir Matthews was not going to be hurried. 'It was built by my dear, dead, lamented father, the founding father of Capa East – '

' – Another Matthews' bastard.'

Matthews was still smiling. He would have his revenge against all these shiny-faced traitors jeering up at him. He beamed out at his persecutors. 'I love this city and if that is a crime then I am guilty. I have made mistakes but we're all human my friends and how many of us can say we've never erred? Um?'

The crowd muttered impatiently.

'I did away with poverty and hunger. I provided well-paid work for everyone. I banished illness and suffering. But...' And at this point he stopped and stared out with a look of deep sadness, '...but it wasn't enough was it? And now you want a younger man, a new hand at the helm. And tomorrow when you vote I shall bow to your wishes. Lixir Matthews' chapter is coming to a close. Long live Capa East, my beautiful city.'

Here was a sentiment the people could relate to. And the crowd replied in one voice. 'Long live Capa East. Our beautiful city.'

Matthews' eyes searched the crowd, looking for that one face. The spotlight dazzled him and he couldn't see the assassin but he was there all the same and that knowledge was enough.

Matthews continued. 'Tonight I feel a mixture of emotions. Happiness that our beloved State will be in the capable hands of Mr...Young but sadness too, because I must leave you after so many years.'

Huge cheers echoed around the hall.

'But you will make your choice tomorrow and my presidency must surely come to an end. I bow to whatever fate awaits me. I may be many things –'

'– A freakin spanza for one,' someone yelled

'But I have never been a coward and I will face up to whatever charges are levelled at me.'

Then, slowly and with great dignity he faced the GSA delegates. 'I would like to take this opportunity to thank the GSA and especially my most illustrious friends and world Statesmen...' He started to cough again. Someone offered him a drink of water and he drank and replaced the cup on the table. 'I must apologise I seem to have caught a summer cold...'

Even his enemies had to admire this man's composure.

He started again, 'My most illustrious friends and world Statesmen.' It sounded as though every syllable was wrenched from him and Matthews obviously thought the same because he repeated those words again. 'Most illustrious friends and world Statesmen...'

And that was when a single shot rang out and Dan knew he was dead.

## *Kline and Poppi*

Kline's original plan was to locate the berg cavern and hide out until the excitement died down, but he was lost. He'd tried every permutation of left and right he could think of. He was sure it was left to begin with, left, left, then immediately right and straight on for about a kilometre but he kept returning to the place where he'd started. So he closed his eyes and walked forwards very slowly, arms outstretched in front of him, as if he were blind-folded.

And that was how Poppi saw him as she swooped around the corner, in hot pursuit of Orange, who was chasing dinner. She screeched to a halt.

Kline opened his eyes and thought he must be hallucinating, because he'd been thinking about Poppi and hoping Fleur hadn't exed her. And then, here she was. She was a good kid and he wanted to explain everything. There was so much he needed to know. Where was Maya for a start? He knew she was alive, he'd seen her on too many divs to think otherwise. He kept imagining what it would be like to meet up with her again.

Poppi folded her arms and glared. 'What you?'

'Give it a rest, Poppi. Have you got any C?' His mouth was so dry he could only croak.

She pulled a face.

'Please, Poppi, no games. You know who I am. I'm your friend, Kline. Now give me something to drink.'

'Kline? Don't know Kline.'

'Okay okay. You're angry with me and I don't blame you, but I couldn't help it. I got hit on the head and lost my memory.'

'Memory?'

'Yeh you know, when you remember things from when you were little?' Kline moved closer to the child and she tensed. 'I need a drink, Poppi. Please.'

She ignored him.

'I'm dying of thirst.'

'Good'

'I told you. It wasn't my fault. Please, just a little drink.'

'What give?' She held out her little dimpled hand.

Kline was not in the mood to haggle and he grabbed the bottle and drank and drank, until it was all gone – not enough, not nearly enough.

Poppi pummelled Kline with her fists. 'Nasty thief, Kline.'

Kline held her off with one hand. 'Oh? So you do remember me after all?'

Poppi wrenched herself free and ran off. She'd seen Orange. Kline chased after her. He was desperate not to lose her. She seemed to know her way around down here. She stooped down and grabbed a furry ginger animal that was eating a rat; then she was away again, laughing over her shoulder at him. 'Come, sluggish boy.' She disappeared down another tunnel and he went after her. And then it happened. He felt a blast of cool air on his face. Rounding a corner, he saw Poppi standing in front of two huge doors straddling the rock face.

She looked at Kline. 'What this?'

'Ah, that would be telling, Poppi. But let's say I think we're gonna have all the water we'll ever need soon.'

The child banged her little fists on the door but Kline pulled her away. 'You'll never get in like that.'

'You're right there, sonny.' The voice came out of the darkness followed by a huge sneeze.

Orange squealed in alarm as a small figure jumped out in front of them. It was Fleur and she was holding a laser sword. Quick as a flash Poppi released the frightened, squirming creature. 'Go, Orange. Go away from Poppi.' The animal didn't need telling twice and streaked away down the tunnel and out of sight.

Fleur made a slicing cut at the animal as it fled, but she missed. Thwarted she jabbed the sword at the girl, expertly slicing through the webbing on her back pack, so that it fell to the ground. The frightened child jumped away and hid behind Kline. 'Don't worry, brat. I'll find your pet for you later. He and I have some unfinished business.' Fleur smirked. 'They're wonderful little gadgets these,' and she hacked the blade through the air, leaving an arc of burning light in the dark tunnel. 'Total precision. I could cut your lying tongue out before you could even shout, *it wasn't me*. But I don't want to hurt you... not yet.'

The woman looked terrible. Her neck bandage had come undone and the blood-spattered white material trailed about her. Her uncontrolled movements had become so exaggerated she looked as if she was building up to some mighty volcanic eruption.

She turned to Kline. 'You didn't really think you could ditch me did you, sonny? I've been waiting for you, ever since you ran away. I might have guessed you'd get lost but you've brought the brat with you so I'll forgive you. Two birds with one stone?'

Poppi pushed Kline towards the old woman. 'Get her, Kline.'

Kline dug his heels in. He had no wish to tangle with a laser sword. 'What do you want, Fleur?'

'What do I want?' She tut-tutted. 'I'm disappointed in you, sonny. I thought you understood.' She sighed and looked away but when she looked back her eyes were intense burning pinpricks of yellow. 'I want what's owing to me. Why d'you think I saved you, eh? Because you're pretty?' She laughed. 'I could have any pretty boy I want. No, you're my ticket for the future. You're going to look after me when I'm old, like any dutiful son should.'

Kline shook his head sadly. She really was off her head.

'Don't you believe me?'

'You're my mother? No way, Fleur.'

'It's true.'

'You're crazy.'

The little woman pretended to look hurt. 'To be rejected by your own child. 'Tis the bitterest pill.'

'You're sick Fleur – '

She smiled sweetly. '– True. Of course I didn't actually give birth to you but – '

'– So you're my…my…?' Kline was floundering.

'– Biological is the word I think you're groping for. What's up? Don't you like having a mummy? Um? I knew the minute I saw you lying there in the prison hospital. You were one of a very limited edition. Piggy has exed most of your batch now but he's not getting you – I am. That great fat thing looked a lot like you when he was young. But not to worry, sonny, you've got my genes too, so maybe you won't turn into a disgusting old lecher.' Fleur saw Kline's stricken face and laughed. 'Now, off we go, there's no time to waste.' Brandishing her sword she herded Kline and Poppi in front of her towards the door. She pressed a lever, punched in some numbers and the doors slid open. She pushed them forward and followed them closely. The doors closed behind them.

\*

Malcolm waited until the staff left before letting himself into the Pool. At least they hadn't changed the door codes. All the Pool personnel were strangers and the layout of the Pool had been altered beyond recognition. He felt uneasy, as if he was an intruder. He stood for a moment, allowing the blueness to calm him. There was no hurry. He had all day to investigate his domain and the baby was sleeping peacefully in his sling.

But it only took a few moments for Malcolm to realise there was something dreadfully wrong. Only one of the vats was pulsating. He ran to each of them in turn but the story was the same at each one, flat, sterile water and no straws. Malcolm accessed the main data base and saw that whole tranches of straws were missing. He ran a shaking finger down the screen, checking and double-checking. It wasn't just old straws but new ones; whole swathes of colours had been eliminated. According to these records only specialist pinx straws were being kept…Troopers.

At first Malcolm thought it must be some terrible mistake made by inept Pool workers but no, here was the authorisation. Matthews' signature code on every new quotient directive. The President was raising a whole new generation comprised entirely of trooper pinx. There would be no new specialist citizens, no Reds or Blus or Pinx, no babies for families, only troopers. Malcolm shivered. In all his years in the Pool the status quotient had always been balanced precisely, that was how it worked. This was a travesty.

The boy's brain was in free-fall as he hurried to the iso-globe labs. He was prepared for what he'd find but nothing could have prepared him for the reality. Every holding bay was full, every foetus labelled Trooper Pinx. Capa's finely balanced social pyramid was in ruins and where had the other foetuses gone?

There were tears running down Malcolm's face as he remembered baby Malcolm at this stage and how he used to wave his little arms and legs at him. He took the sleeping baby out of his sling and hugged him, inhaling his sweet smell.

## *The end of everything*

But Dan wasn't dead and the only thing that hurt was his head. He put a shaky finger on the spot and his fingertip came back bloody. But it was nothing, a scratch, where he'd hit his head when he'd dived under the table. He was alive. It was incredible.

Instants later he was grabbed and hustled away. People were screaming and running in all directions. He saw Frankie lifting a lifeless body onto the table and caught a brief glimpse of the victim's face. The man had a bullet hole in his head. Munro was crouching over him, frantically searching for lifesigns. The man was Monsieur Xaviet.

Dan was taken to a side room, with two of the squad outside to guard the door. While he waited he tried to make sense of what had happened. Monsieur Xaviet had been sitting two seats away from him, beside Munro. Matthews had been making his speech; so maybe he had been the intended victim? So why had the assassin killed the Frenchman?

The door opened and Munro hurried in.

'Is he dead?'

Munro nodded.

Dan sighed. 'Someone else dead because of me.'

Munro shook his head. 'You weren't the target, Dan. The murderer was a trooper and they never miss.'

Dan didn't understand. 'But why? Why would Matthews ex the president of the GSA? I'm the candidate, Munro. I'm Matthews' opponent. I was the one he needed to kill.'

Munro clenched his fists. 'I've been such a fool. The moment I saw him on the stage I should have known. He would never have come here tonight if he intended killing you. It would have been far too dangerous. Don't you see? You were never the target.'

'But he's murdered the GSA president. That's good for us isn't it? I mean obviously it's really sad but it lets us off the hook? We've got Matthews where we want him. The GSA will have to support us now.'

Munro didn't look at Dan. 'The assassin was one of ours.'

Dan thought he hadn't heard properly. 'What?'

'He was our man.'

'But you said it was a trooper.'

'The trooper we rescued from the desert? Gemmie.'

'Gemmie? No. He was with me all day, with Gola's squad? Freakin hell Munro, he saved my life. 'Then, too late Dan remembered the boy receiving on the AP. 'I'm the idiot, Munro. A total freakin idiot.'

'He had us all fooled. All of us except Maya. We should have left the scum to die. '

'Are you absolutely certain it was him? Maybe he was – '

'– No. We all saw the bastard. He took out his gun, aimed and fired.'

'But why? It doesn't make sense. How does Matthews benefit from murdering a GSA man?'

'If we are responsible for assassinating their president, is the GSA likely to support us?'

Dan was on his feet. 'Then, we have to find the traitor and get him to talk.'

Munro sat with his head down, utterly defeated. 'It's no good.'

'Who've you got after him?'

Munro looked despairingly at Dan, 'Gola, but it doesn't make any difference. It's over, Dan. We're finished.'

'No. Don't say that.'

'The delegates are convinced we murdered their president, so what would stop us from murdering them too? They're already on their way back to the shuttle port. They'll be leaving the city tonight.'

'But when we win the election – '

'– What election? Didn't you hear me? It's over, we're…over. Matthews has won.'

'What's the matter with you, Munro?'

'There's something else …something you should know.' Munro took a deep breath. 'The mines have been taken. One of our men managed to contact us before they were overrun. The Elites attacked soon after we left. A few of our people escaped into the tunnels but it's only a matter of time before they're all captured – '

Dan grabbed Munro's arm and swung him round to face him. '– No. It's a lie. Tell me it's a lie. Not my Emmie, please, not my little girl.'

There was nothing Munro could say.

Moments later there was gunfire from somewhere close by and a squad of Matthews' troopers burst into the room. Matthews swaggered in. 'Munro? So it really is you? I thought you were dead.'

'I wish you were.'

The President looked hurt. 'Not nice, Munro, not nice at all.' Then he tried to look sad but it didn't quite work. 'Unfortunately I have an unpleasant duty to perform. I have to arrest you and your stooge for the murder of Monsieur Xaviet, the much lamented, late president of the GSA.'

'The killer was one of yours.'

'Really? Then prove it, dear boy.'

'I demand to speak to the delegates.'

'Too late, much too late. You know what these foreigners are like? They're already running home, their pacifist little tails between their legs.'

'In that case you have no jurisdiction.'

Matthews smiled. 'They have washed their hands of Capa, Munro. They don't care what happens here now. I can do what I like.'

Suddenly Dan launched himself at Matthews, managing to get his hands around the President's neck before a trooper knocked him unconscious.

Matthews was gasping for breath. 'Take them away. Take the freakin spanzas to the cells. I'll deal with them later.'

# *Trapped*

Maya had her hand over Billy's mouth as she woke him. The boy stiffened but when he saw the CO he relaxed and nodded. She removed her hand and cupped her ears.

Billy heard it too. He mouthed, *Rock fall?*

Maya shook her head.

The sound seemed to be coming from somewhere up in front of them but in this labyrinth it was hard to tell. The troopers should be behind them but Maya knew there might be short-cuts or even circular routes. Matthews' men would have maps and could have cut off their escape route – anything was possible.

Billy held up three fingers. Maya wasn't sure but held up five. Either way they were both surprised, because if it was troopers then surely there would be more? Maya attempted to pinpoint the exact position of the sounds. Finally she pointed to the tunnel directly in front of them. Billy nodded and waited for Maya's orders.

The girl was in a quandary. They could make a run for it down one of the other tunnels but what if she chose the wrong one? The troopers might have planted a few people up front to panic the evacuees into disclosing their location. Maya decided to stay where they were, at least until she had a better idea of what was going on.

They woke their people quietly and split them into two groups. Billy was in charge of one and Maya the other. They moved them into the two remaining tunnels. That way at least some of them might escape. Maya and Billy didn't have to tell them to be quiet; each face wore the same strained, frightened look. Even Emma sat as close to Tanya and Anna as she could. They could all hear the sounds now.

Maya and Billy shared out the remaining liquid and tabs, and then they drew their guns and squatted at the entrance of their tunnels. Billy was with Anna, the girls and some others and Maya was with Elizabeth and the other women and children. Anna sat behind Billy, hugging the two little girls to her. The woman caught Maya's eye and she nodded. Anna sighed. She knew the CO would keep her promise.

They stowed all the lights. Just before they were plunged into total darkness Maya saw Billy's face. His gaunt little features were transformed by the fire in his eyes. Maya knew he wouldn't let them down. Then there was nothing to do but wait.

## *A job well done?*

Pox was carried along with the hysterical crowds as they stampeded for the exit. The trooper tore off his Tree insignia as he was swept along. Gola's mob would be on his trail soon but he had a head start.

Outside the building people were unaware of what had happened inside and were still pressing forward, trying to get into the building. So, when the frightened citizens came reeling out, they met a wall of enthusiastic supporters pushing the other way. It was total anarchy.

Dodging through the melee, Pox made for transroute level. Morta would hide him and when things quietened down he would contact Scar and begin the rest of his life. He felt amazing. He was the best and he knew it. It had been a perfect execution. The trooper wanted to be somewhere quiet on his own to re-live the kill, frame by frame, but that would have to wait till later.

He looked about him as he jogged along, shaking his head in cynical disbelief. One little shooting and the inhabitants of Capa went mental. A woman grabbed at him as he ran. His hand went automatically to his gun and she backed away, fear in her eyes. Lucky for the woman, Pox was on a high, so he gave her what passed as a smile. 'I'm security. Can I help?'

She was reassured. 'What's happening back there?'

'A Society assassin has exed the president of the GSA.'

The woman ran back to her friends and he saw their stunned faces as she passed on the news. Word of mouth, you couldn't beat it.

On board the Rat it was the same – rumour and counter-rumour. Pox settled back to enjoy himself.
*Was the Society trying to take over the world?*
*Matthews isn't that bad.*
*He's a harmless oldie.*
Pox laughed out loud at that one.
*Maybe he didn't do those terrible things?*
*It could have been the Society, a put up job.*
*I've heard they've arrested all the ringleaders.*
*Capa doesn't need trouble from the rest of the Globe,*
*Better the devil you know...*

Classic. Pox wasn't political. It made no difference to him what spanza was in power. He was trained to do a job and he did it, end of story. There was only one thing that mattered to Pox. This time no one noticed him as he drifted down through the trees to Morta's flat. Now he was the watcher. On every floor there were groups of terrified people shouting and gesticulating to each other. He could taste their panic. Pox let out a deep sigh and straightened his aching body. He was responsible for all this mayhem and it felt freakin fantastic.

He was still smiling as he pushed open the door to his grandmother's flat. Morta was seated at the table, her back to Pox, but there was someone else sitting opposite the old woman and, as he came through the door, the other person rose. It was Scar and she was holding a gun. It was only when Morta turned her head that Pox saw her mouth had been taped and her arms tied. The old woman's eyes said *run* but he closed the door and walked calmly to the table and sat down.

Scar nodded imperceptibly at the boy and pushed a document across the table towards him, and then she placed the gun to her head and squeezed the trigger.

## *The last Straw*

When Malcolm staggered out of the specialist crèche he had to lean up against the wall to keep upright.

But it wasn't long before the horror he felt became outrage. All those tiny cribs empty, each baby sent to the incinerator. Matthews must be made to pay for this. Malcolm had to do something – but what? Tell someone, but who? He had never had any relationship with anyone outside the Pool and inside, any communication was purely boss-worker based. He had to find a citizen who had the power to use the information he had and bring the President to book for his crimes. Malcolm could testify but he wasn't an orator. He needed somebody the people trusted, someone they would listen to. That was when he remembered Dan Young.

When he emerged on the surface the world had gone mad. Screaming, hysterical people ran in all directions. Malcolm had to hang onto Baby or they would have been knocked down. Malcolm had forgotten his visor and blinked owl-like in the intense light. At that moment a young boy rocketed into him.

'I know you.' The boy said.

Malcolm squinted at him. 'Are you talking to me?'

'You better make a run for it, mister.'

Ah, now Malcolm knew who it was. It was the cow-herd from the agri-dome. Malcolm was about to tell him off for neglecting his charges but then he remembered he had more important things to worry about. 'What's happened here?'

'Been a killing. One of the delegates.' The boy was busy shredding his 'tree' banner as he spoke. 'And I was gonna vote for them.' He continued after a moment. 'My girls all right then?'

'Perfectly all right, no thanks to you.'

At that moment a detail of troopers came marching towards them and the boy pushed the half-blind Malcolm into a doorway. They watched as the men surged past, herding two stumbling prisoners along in front of them.

'That's Dan Young', the young boy muttered, pointing to the smaller of the two. 'The Society's candidate?' The boy smiled in a self-satisfied way. 'He'll be getting what's coming to him. Dirty murderer.'

'He killed someone?'

'The president of the GSA.'

'Are you sure? This Dan Young killed the delegate?'

'Na, he didn't do it. He got some trooper kid to do it. But he was wearing a 'Tree' badge; so he must have been one of theirs right? My old man said they were too good to be true. Na, I'm gonna stick with Matthews. You should see him. He's a pathetic oldie. No way could he have done all the stuff they said he did.'

Malcolm grabbed the surprised boy by the scruff of the neck. 'Matthews is a monster. He has to be stopped. Tell that to your "old man", boy. Tell him, tell everyone, President Matthews has incinerated a whole generation of Capa babies.'

The boy's eyes widened. 'Incinerated?'

'Terminated, murdered, exed. He is the worst sort of murderer, a coward. He kills defenceless babies for fun. Go on. Run away, boy. Tell them all.'

The boy didn't need to be told twice. 'Okay, okay I'll do that.' And with that he fled.

Malcolm pressed onwards. The crowd was thinning now, but there were still a few dazed Society supporters talking desperately to each other. A woman called out to him as he passed. 'Mr Blue? Wait a minute.'

Malcolm screwed up his eyes, trying to see her properly.

The woman smiled nervously, 'I ...I used to work in the State crèche? We met when you came to...' Her voice petered out. She had spotted the baby. Her sad expression was transformed. She touched the sleeping child's downy hair. 'I'm so glad you've got him. I lost my job because of you. But it doesn't matter; I was going to leave anyway. I couldn't stand it anymore. They were doing such...dreadful things.' Her eyes filled with tears. 'All those innocent little babies...' She looked longingly at the child. 'Do you think I could hold him – just for a moment?'

Malcolm handed Baby over.

The woman smiled gratefully at Malcolm over the child's head. 'We hoped the Society were going to win this election and then the President would be stopped but it looks as if that – 'And she looked around furtively ' – that evil man is going to get back in. I don't want to live any more if that happens.'

'Is it true a Society supporter assassinated the GSA man?'

The woman's eyes flashed. 'He was dressed like one but why would the Society want to kill the very man who could help them? No, Matthews was behind the murder. That's the only explanation. And now he's going to win the election – '

'– No, Matthews will be exposed, I promise you.' Malcolm was surprised at how confident he sounded.

'But they've arrested the Society leaders and the GSA is leaving Capa. Matthews has us at his mercy. There's no one to help us now.'

'There's me.' Malcolm saw the incredulous look on the woman's face but he didn't care. 'If I can get through to the delegates and explain that the assassin was working for Matthews, they would have to help us. All I need is someone to get me through to the heli-port.'

'And you have the proof?'

'Not exactly but I'm sure I can persuade them.'

Hope died in the nurse's eyes and she looked uneasily over her shoulder. 'It's time to leave, Mr Blue. They're rounding up Society supporters. Most of our friends have been arrested already.' She handed the baby back to him. 'Where are you staying?'

He hadn't thought that far ahead.

'Come with us. At least you'll have somewhere to sleep and I could help you.' She rested her hand on the baby's head.

Malcolm went with her. Where else was there to go?

*

Dan shuffled along behind Munro, his feet moving automatically, his mind in some other place. Emma

They were thrown into an already overcrowded holding cell. A large man pushed his way through to Munro's side. It was Frankie. He tried to smile but his mouth was bloodied and twisted and he had several teeth missing. 'I think she got away,' he whispered to Munro.

Frankie saw the despair in his friend's eyes.

'If anyone can get him Gola will.' Frankie was trying to sound positive.

Munro nodded and then the two men talked quietly and urgently together. Once or twice they looked over at Dan but he was oblivious to everything.

## *Truth or lies?*

Maya had no idea how long she sat in the darkness straining her ears for the slightest sound. Sometimes it went quiet for minutes and she would shift her weight, easing her stiff shoulders, but then it would start up again. Maya had been in dangerous situations before but this was different. This time she wasn't just looking out for herself, she was responsible for these people – people she'd grown to like – like Billy and the child and the woman, Anna.

Now she could hear individual footsteps and a couple of times there was the sound of someone slipping on the gravel. Finally, out of the darkness, on the far side of the cavern, emerged one, two…three shapes, lit by a solitary, dying bug.

The group had reached the centre of the cavern when the smallest of the group collapsed. Immediately a flash of incandescent light arched over the fallen figure, lighting up the face of a young girl. The person holding the laser sword was a small, old woman. The fiery light lit her wizened face and she glared down at the child, her eyes bright with loathing. The third person was in the shadows. As the woman swept the sword jerkily closer to the child, this figure leapt between them and Maya saw who it was.

'I told you, Fleur, you hurt the kid and I'll exe you.'

'Out of my way, sonny, or I'll stick you too.'

Maya's heart was pounding so hard she felt sure they must hear her. She rubbed her eyes. Was she hallucinating? He couldn't be here. It was impossible.

She watched as he pulled the child to her feet and placed her behind him. His voice was strong and confident as he faced the woman. 'We're not moving until you tell us where we're going.'

'You'll do as I say.'

The child's voice rang out. 'Freakin bad. Poppi kill you.'

'One more time, Fleur. Where are you taking us?'

'That's for me to know... now move.'

The boy stood his ground. 'No way. Our water's out and we're going back before it's too late. I suggest you come too. Unless you want to die down here.' Then he grabbed the girl and walked quickly back to the tunnel they'd come from. The old woman didn't hesitate; she let out a blood-curdling scream and raced after them. The sword was aimed at his back.

There was a shot and the laser clattered harmlessly to the ground and extinguished. The bug chose that exact moment to die and there was absolute silence for a moment before a child's voice cut through the blackness. 'Who that?'

## *Malcolm meets Gola*

The girl-trooper prodded Malcolm along in front of her with the gun. Okay, they had to fool the guards but Malcolm wasn't sure that his hands had to be tied quite so tightly. He had pins and needles all up his arms.

'Move it, you pathetic flat-footed trond.' Gola shouted in his ear, deafening him.

He was about to protest when she jabbed him hard in the back and he staggered forwards.

'Sorry,' she hissed. 'We're being watched.'

The first check-point had been easy but they couldn't expect the next one to go so smoothly. Their story was that Malcolm was wanted for questioning by GSA security. Malcolm was supposedly one of the gang who had master-minded Monsieur Xaviet's murder. There was an official-looking document in Gola's pocket that would pass for genuine, as long as nobody thought to check up on the details.

Malcolm had met up with Gola at the nurse's condo. It was a fortuitous meeting because Gola was on the trail of Monsieur Xaviet's killer. However, Matthews' hit-man had gone to ground. All Gola could do was wait for information from her people and the waiting was killing her. So when she heard Malcolm's plan she readily agreed to join forces with him. She could get Gemmie later.

She would never forgive herself for trusting the trooper and now Dan, Munro, Frankie and the others were taken. Malcolm didn't have a clue what she was talking about, but he was extremely relieved that she was on his side. He had never had anything to do with a pinx before and this Gola was formidable.

At least his baby was in good hands and he had set off in good spirits. Maybe, if he'd known what was in store for him, he wouldn't have been quite so pleased with himself. As they got closer to the perimeter wall of the heli-port they saw the second check point. It was guarded by two burly troopers. The men watched them closely as they approached.

Gola whispered. 'I'm gonna give you a slap, be ready.'

But Malcolm didn't have a chance to draw breath before she knocked him clean out. He came to as she was dragging him roughly to his feet. 'Sorry,' she said. 'Bit too hard.'

The troopers watched in amusement. 'What you got there, trooper? Animal, vegetable or mineral?'

Gola smiled grimly. 'He's a freakin traitor. The Pool master.'

'Traitor eh?' The biggest and ugliest of the troopers moved forwards menacingly. 'We don't like traitors do we?' He asked his mate. 'Like those freakin traitor troopers? We're gonna see to them.'

His companion rubbed his spade-like hands together. 'Yeh, see to them all right.'

The first pinx took out his cosh and thumped it into his palm, never taking his eyes off the petrified boy.

'I'd like to oblige, chief, but I've got orders and he's gotta be able to talk.' Gola gave Malcolm a push in the middle of the back that sent him on a collision course with the man.

The trooper didn't move until the very last moment and then he shoved his cosh into Malcolm's kidneys as he stumbled past. Malcolm curled up in agony.

Gola laughed and handed over the papers. The trooper could hardly take his eyes off the girl. She was very attractive when she wanted to be. As he glanced down at the documentation she stepped closer to him. 'Tell you what, chief, if there's anything left of the spanza when they've finished with him, I'll come back this way, um? Let you have a little...fun. How long you on for?'

The man rolled his eyes. 'Who knows? It's freakin mad out there. Talk is she's dead.'

Gola looked puzzled.

'The top bitch. Scar? Our Commander in Chief?'

'What?' Gola's surprise was genuine.

'Yeh, bit of a nightmare if you ask me.'

'Who's up for the job?'

'Talk is Pox.'

Gola was stunned. 'Freakin hell.'

The man handed the papers to Gola and stood aside. He was talking into his com as she yanked Malcolm upright and waited for the gates to open. Gola made Malcolm run, even though he could hardly put one foot in front of the other. 'Scar dead?' She shouted at the dazed boy. 'Things are looking up for us after all, eh Blue? What d'you think?'

He couldn't think.

They were close to the terminal buildings now and the cordon of transports made an impenetrable circle around the heli-pad. Two shuttles were taking off and several more were waiting for clearance, powering up. People were scurrying about but there didn't seem to be any clear-cut command at work. There were several foreigners, who Gola took for the delegates, surrounded by burly men with searching eyes and extremely large guns. Gola pushed Malcolm towards the nearest group; then she made him wait, while she went up to talk. She was immediately surrounded by GSA security and within moments she and Malcolm were hustled away for questioning.

'Over to you', Gola whispered to Malcolm as an imposing man, with an arm full of braid approached them.

'You have important information for the GSA?'

Malcolm nodded weakly.

'Connected with what?' The man was looking at his watch, estimating how much longer he would have to stay in this rat trap.

'Concerning the unlawful killing of the GSA President and...' Malcolm painfully drew himself up to his full height, '...and crimes against humanity committed by the President of Capa East, Lixir Matthews.'

# *Trust*

'Maya? Lights? ` Billy's voice was urgent.

Maya flicked some bugs and sent them skidding across the space to where Kline and Poppi bent over the old woman. Maya and Billy walked slowly towards them, guns drawn.

Kline heard them coming and grabbed the fallen laser sword.

'It's okay,' Billy shouted. 'We're friends.'

Maya could see him clearly now. There was no mistake. It was him. She felt as if some huge weight was pressing down on her. Her finger trembled on the trigger. *Kill him*, her head screamed. But she couldn't. She was in another place and he was beside her, his arms around her and the smell and touch of him was so real.

As they came closer Kline lowered the sword and his look of wariness changed to one of absolute disbelief and then delight. 'Maya?'

'Check the oldie, Billy.'

Kline took a step towards her, his face bright with joy. 'Maya? This is freakin fantastic – '

Maya whipped around to face him, the anger and hurt making her voice ugly. '– One more step and you're dead meat…Mr President.' Her gun was aimed at his head.

Kline sighed. 'Ah – '

'– Yeh, *ah*.'

'You're not gonna believe what happened to me, Maya – '

Maya cut him off. '– No, I'm not.'

'Come on, Maya, this is me, Kline. I wouldn't do anything like that unless I had to.'

'Nothing you can say will save you, Kline.'

'Even a condemned man gets to defend himself.'

Why was she wasting time yakking? *Kill him.* 'Okay, Kline, let me guess. You were abducted by aliens and forced to impersonate the president? Or maybe you lost your memory and it was all a terrible mistake? ...or you took drugs and you really did think you were the spanza? – '

'– I did lose my memory as it happens. It's true. Ask Poppi...yeh Poppi can tell you. Poppi? Tell Maya about me losing my memory, Poppi?'

The child didn't like Maya and she certainly wasn't going to talk to her.

Kline dug her in the ribs. 'Poppi, please, tell Maya...'

But Maya wasn't listening, she had to kill him now – while she still could. She brought her gun up to shoulder level but before she could squeeze the trigger something rocketed into her, knocking her off her feet. It was Poppi. They crashed to the ground and Kline kicked Maya's gun away. Poppi was only half the size of Maya but she was a ferocious little fighter.

Eventually Kline grabbed the child. 'Okay that's enough. Let her up. I said that's enough.'

Maya jumped to her feet breathing heavily.

Billy's voice cut in. 'Somebody tell me what's going on or I'm gonna shoot the kid.' The boy stood, legs astride, his expression grim. His gun was against the back of Poppi's head. Kline moved away from the gun and Maya picked it up. Billy looked at Maya. 'Well?'

'He's the spanza that's been standing in for Matthews.'

Billy pushed the girl towards Kline, so that he and Maya had them both covered.

'Execute them.' The old woman was sitting up, cradling a bloody arm. 'Go on, what are you waiting for? I order you to kill them.'

Poppi kicked out at the old woman.

Kline grabbed her and stared at Maya over the child's head. His eyes were pleading. 'I lost my memory, Maya. When I was hit? You must have been there when it happened. They used me as a stand-in for Matthews but I got my memory back two days ago, and since then I've been on the run –'

'– I don't believe you.'

'It's the truth.'

Billy glanced worriedly over his shoulder. Maya understood. They both knew how far the sound of gunfire would travel down here. She would deal with Kline later. 'Okay, time to go.' She spoke to Kline. 'Where does the tunnel go that you came down?'

'Back to Capa.'

'Poppi go to Capa now.' The child was already trotting towards the tunnel.

'Who's the oldie?'

`Fleur Matthews.'

Good news. The old woman might come in handy if there was any bartering to be done. 'How bad is she, Billy?'

'Not. I winged her.'

Kline flashed Billy one of his lazy, self-assured smiles. 'So it's you I have to thank for saving my life? Billy? Thanks, thanks a lot.'

Poppi pushed herself in front of Kline and gave Billy one of her specials. She liked the look of this boy. She didn't blame him for putting the gun against her head. He wouldn't have shot her.

They got everybody together and Tanya and Emma ran to Billy. Poppi watched them through narrowed eyes. Anna and the others were relieved that everything was okay and pleased when Maya told them they would be returning to Capa. There was some hope in their tired eyes now but Maya knew that their troubles weren't over, not yet. Her first priority was to get them to safety and then she'd deal with Kline. She should have left his lying, traitorous carcass down here to rot, but there wasn't time. She glanced at him and he smiled. True it was a rueful smile but she knew he thought he'd got away with it.

Kline couldn't take his eyes off her. She was so gentle and caring with these people. He'd never seen her like this before. She was lean and dressed in dirty, ripped clothes but she was still his Maya, his beautiful girl. 'So what's the hurry, Maya? Debt collector on your tail?'

'Troopers,' Billy answered, as he pulled Fleur to her feet. He was glad he hadn't exed her. He respected Oldies. She leant towards him and spat in his face.

Maya handed around liquid and they set off, Poppi taking the lead. Maya came next with the others. She lit the last of the bugs and they spread out along the tunnel, lighting the way. Kline followed, dragging the unwilling Fleur along on a rope. After a while she dug her heels in and refused to move; so Kline slung her over his shoulder. Billy brought up the rear. Maya looked back and saw them talking once or twice. Billy could look after himself but she hoped he wasn't giving too much information away.

As she jogged along Maya's thoughts went round and round. Kline looked the same, same face and smile, same ...everything, but Matthews might have used a mind jolt or torture or ... anything. She couldn't trust him, she mustn't. But he'd been Fleur's prisoner. So maybe his story was true? Pox had hit him very hard. He could have lost his memory...it was possible.

It was very tiring walking uphill, especially as the further they climbed the hotter it got. The evacuees were all exhausted but they knew the troopers were behind them and fear kept them moving. Some of the smaller children had to be carried and Emma was asleep on Maya's back, her head nodding to the rhythm of Maya's stride. Tanya walked beside Anna. Sometimes she stopped and stared back to see if she could see Billy.

There was still a feeling of urgency and threat but the thought that they were going home gave them all heart. Maybe, just maybe they were going to escape. Maya hoped that some of the other escapees would find the same tunnel. Perhaps if she got this lot out she could go back for them? She laughed out loud at that and several people looked at her in surprise. But then Maya had a grim thought. What if the Society had been defeated already? After an hour or so the tunnel levelled out. It was easier walking but they had to be careful where they trod because the cavern floor was deeply rutted by two huge parallel fissures. It looked as if something incredibly large and heavy had been hauled along, tearing out the path. The tunnel got wider and wider until the sides and the roof disappeared totally. Poppi was up ahead when suddenly she let out a whoop of excitement. Maya hurried to catch up and felt it too – a wonderful cool breeze on her red-hot skin. But Maya's delight was short-lived because there in front of her, barring their way was a precipice of solid rock. It reached sideways and upwards and out of sight. Kline had led them into a dead-end.

Poppi was prancing about singing.

No one else spoke.

When Kline arrived he was smiling. He calmly set the old woman down and eased his aching arms. Fleur immediately flew at him, fists flailing. She screamed, 'Don't think I'm finished with you, Sonny,' and charged straight through 'the wall.'

Maya was stunned, but before she could do or say anything Billy came panting up to them. His face was grey and he was gasping for breath. He pointed back down the tunnel and they all knew what he meant. The troopers were coming.

Kline walked to the wall and rested one hand on the 'rock'. Every eye was on him and he grinned. 'All you have to do is say the magic words – '

Emma shouted ' – Izzy wizzy let's get busy,' and Kline disappeared through the wall, closely followed by Poppi. It only took a few moments for everyone else to follow suit. Only Maya remained behind.

'Maya?' His voice.

She moved closer to the wall.

'Are you waiting to say *hi* to the troopers? His hand appeared through the middle of the wall and beckoned to her. The girl grabbed it, and yanked the laughing Kline back on her side.

'You and your stupid, stupid games. These people don't need some spanzoid trond-brain doing magic.' She shoved him roughly aside and marched through the projection. 'Any freaker could see what it was. Sensory Projection Architecture? I've met the guy who invented this.' She knew she sounded petulant but she couldn't help it.

If she was surprised by the projection, then she was utterly dumbfounded by the Berg. She stared transfixed at the huge black, block of ice, in its lake of melt water, and heard it creaking and whispering to her.

'It's the Berg, Maya. The only – '

'– The only one left in the world.' Everyone knew about the Berg. But it actually existed. She dragged her eyes away. No time for Bergs. Not now, but one day – it was definitely on her list.

Billy was setting up a gun placement. Their people were hurrying across the cavern towards another set of doors on the far side. The entrance to Capa's underground. They had to make sure the evacuees got a head start before the trooper's broke through the projection.

Poppi was hopping about in excitement, wanting to be off, but not wanting to leave Billy yet. Maya grabbed her. 'D'you want to be a real CO one day, Poppi?'

The child nodded suspiciously.

'If you do something for me I'll put in a good word for you with Monty. Deal?'

Poppi narrowed her eyes at her enemy. 'When?'

'As soon as. All you have to do is show Billy and the others the way to the agridome.' Maya had been planning to take the group to the dome from the moment she knew they were headed back to Capa. She had been taken there by her parents when she was little. Strange she could think about them so easily now, now she was so close to avenging them.

'Poppi busy.'

'I thought you liked being with Kline? You'd have the creds to buy all the divs you want.'

'Keep loads of guinea pigs,' Kline added.

Guinea pigs? What was Kline on about?

'Okay,' the child said, immediately making up her mind, and then she ran to catch up with the people. She shouted imperiously over shoulder. 'Billy boy, come.'

Billy's mouth was a stubborn line and he pointed to Kline. 'He can go.'

'No, Kline stays with me.' Maya ruffled Billy's hair. 'Don't make me knock you out again.'

The boy didn't smile.

She drew him aside and whispered. 'I can't trust him, Billy. That's why I want you to go. You know I'd choose you if I could.' Then out loud. 'You're the only one who can do it. Poppi likes you, but watch her, okay? She's...well she's Poppi, and when she's got something on her mind she's unreliable. When you get to the dome, settle the people and wait for me.' She saw his disappointment. 'Tanya and Emma and the others? They need protecting, Billy. And if we don't come, then ...you're in charge, okay?'

The boy knew when he was beaten and handed Kline his gun.

When he was gone Maya turned to Kline. 'Make one wrong move and you're dead.'

'I'm not a traitor, Maya. What do I have to do to prove it to you?'

But she never had a chance to answer because at that moment the troopers arrived on the other side of the wall. Maya and Kline tensed, ready to put a bullet into the first man that came through. The troopers obviously didn't know that the wall was a projection but it would only take one person leaning against it to find out. They heard the pinx fall out and pass around rations. They could even hear their conversations. If Maya had put out a hand she would have touched them. But she didn't. She could wait.

## *Call the Incinerator Man*

Scar's body lay slumped across the table, her helmeted head resting in a pool of blood studded with flies.

Pox untied his grandmother and un-taped her mouth. They lifted Scar onto the bed. The boy's thin mouth was a gash of grief. 'Why did she do it?'

The old woman shook her head uncomprehendingly.

'She was gonna ex me, but then...then... I don't understand. I did the job, Morta. It was freakin perfect. She said she's reinstate me. She said...I had to make her proud.'

The pair of them stood on either side of the bed looking down. They knew the procedure. Call the Incinerator Man and get a slot – the sooner the better in this heat. They'd both done it many times. Cadaver carriers arrived in minutes. It was straightforward, routine, and unemotional.

At last, Morta moved away from the bed and rummaged through some drawers, while Pox read the document Scar had given him. It was authorisation for his instatement as the next Elite commander-in-chief. He could barely read the words through his tears. He read it twice, not believing it, but there was no mistake. There was her official stamp, next to the President's. Numb with grief he watched his grandmother examine each item, until she found what she was looking for. She put it in Pox's hand and closed his fingers around it.

He waited until she left the room to contact the Carrier and then he opened his hand. It was a digi print, the sort people used for family photographs in the olden days. Pox put it on his pod. It was a picture of a young woman holding a baby. She was smiling down at the infant and she was very beautiful.

Morta came back into the room.

'I always knew.' Pox's voice was soft.

'What?'

'That she was my mother.'

'How could you? She didn't even know herself, Gemmie, not after he – '

The boy punched his fist into his open palm. '– So, why didn't she kill me?' Then softly again. 'Because I was her son.'

'But she didn't have …memories, Gemmie. He took them away. Left her with nothing but a space for him to fill.'

The boy glared at the old woman. 'What you saying? You mental or what?'

'I was nothing to her, Gemmie and I was her mother.' Morta moved to the bed. 'There's something you should see.' She removed her daughter's helmet and parted the hair. The boy stared down at a scar that stretched from one ear to the other.

'He did that.' Morta spat out the words. 'Matthews. Experimented on her, made her into a machine. Stole her life and put pain and duty and whatever he wanted in its place. Your mother was the first one, Gemmie.'

The woman moved away from the bed and replaced everything in the drawer. 'She was the first trooper from the Flume, the first in our family.' She touched her cap, 'This was hers, she gave it me, the day she got the scar…before, before she forgot who I was.' Morta took off the cap and placed it on the table, beside the document that Scar had given Pox. 'You should have it now.'

Pox didn't move.

Morta continued, 'She was so happy when she was promoted, couldn't wait to start her new job. One night she was my daughter and your mother, next, she was…nothing, no one…a thing. She came back once to pick up her stuff and I never saw her again until now.'

Pox wanted to touch the scar but his fingers wouldn't move. He whispered. 'She did know who I was, Morta, you're wrong. She…cared about me, that's why she didn't ex me. Don't you see? Her orders were to eliminate me after the killing. Matthews couldn't chance me being taken. That's why she came here, to finish the job – but she couldn't – '

The old woman sighed deeply. '– Whatever. I'm going to have a drink, d'you want one?'

Pox shook his head.

When the old woman returned he was gone and so was the cap.

Morta washed Scar's face and brushed her hair – her beautiful black hair – making sure it covered the scar. Afterwards, she drew up a chair and held her daughter's hand while she waited for the Carrier.

## *Normal service has been resumed*

Only hours after the assassination Lixir Matthews broadcast live to the frightened citizens of Capa.

*Friends, this is Capa's darkest hour. Our esteemed ally, the president of the GSA, has been gunned down in cold blood. And who committed this terrible crime? A Society supporter. Yes, I was astonished too but there are many witnesses to this cowardly act. Why? Why indeed? You thought the Society was Capa's friend but alas, now you see them in their true colours. These power crazed rebels will not be satisfied until they have taken over the Globe. I have no alternative but to declare a State of Emergency and to cancel the election. It grieves me to do this; it goes against everything that I hold dear, but needs must. I am proud to say that the assassin is dead and his co-conspirators arrested. Their trial will take place tomorrow night, televised live. So please, bear with me. Life will get back to normal as soon as possible. Keep indoors until further notice. There are desperate people out there, wicked men who would stop at nothing to further their despicable ends.*

At this point the sweating President signalled a break. He gulped some water and popped a pill under his tongue.

When the broadcast continued Lixir was composed again. His affable appearance was reassuring to the people. How could anyone who looked like your granddad be the monster the Society had painted?

*I know there are those amongst you who are fearful for the future but I will not punish the innocent. Even the poor misguided souls amongst you, who are Society sympathisers, will not be chastised. I offer a full amnesty to anyone who reports to their nearest Trooper check-point within twenty four. No harm will come to you, or your families. You have Lixir Matthews' word on that.*

Now his smile disappeared and he hung his head. *I too have made mistakes and I hope you can find it in your hearts to forgive me...'* The camera tracked his trembling hand, as he took a drink. *'I swear that I will never use presidential stand-ins again. I have been too private; too withdrawn. From now on I will be available to you - my people. And lastly...'* and here the president got to his feet and put his hand on his heart. *'...I vehemently deny all the charges brought against me. Do I look like the sort of man who would condone the killing and torturing of little children? The sort of loathsome creature that the Society would have you believe?'* He looked away then and wiped at his eyes. *'I would never, ever, do anything to harm little ones, and it hurts me deeply to be accused of such dreadful atrocities.*

When the broadcast ended the President's advisors and the div crew gave him a standing ovation. The only slight annoyance was the news about Scar. Killed herself they said. Not likely. No, Matthews was sure it was some internecine rivalry in the Trooper camp. He was sorry, Scar had been a loyal servant – until recently when she seemed to be losing her focus. So possibly it was time for a new broom to go with his new regime. But he needed her replacement in situ as soon as possible. Apparently Scar had left instructions as to her successor – efficient to the end. Matthews made a note to send presidential condolences. Untypically for a trooper, Scar had a family, so there might be someone who remembered her.

And then, putting Scar out of his mind, he concentrated on more important issues. The Society's days were numbered now that he had Munro and Dan Young. He was waiting to hear that all of their people had been taken and then he would destroy them all. The Society would never recover from such a defeat.

Incoming intelligence reported mounting unrest all over the city, hence the abruptness of the trial. The sooner the better, before their supporters had time to re-group. With their ringleaders dead or banished he would be able to deal with the Society riffraff at his leisure. There would be no amnesty for Society members.

Matthews settled back in his chair and kneaded the sore spot on his shoulder. He hoped the new CIC would have the same healing hands as Scar.

## *Last Chance*

Gola stood with her back to the boy, looking out of the window. Malcolm sat hunched at the table, all hope gone. If he was executed, the baby would be orphaned and the Pool would be contaminated forever. They had tried everything they could to persuade the delegation that Matthews was behind the assassination. When the interrogator had asked for proof and they couldn't give it, they'd been locked in this room.

Malcolm lifted his arm to wipe away the sweat that was running into his eyes and had a sudden strong blast of Baby smell. It was on his sleeve. He held the material close to his nose and inhaled. Had he told the nurse about the special banana flavoured cereal that the child liked so much? And where would she get fresh milk? And why hadn't he told her about the Agri-dome? Malcolm cursed his stupid arrogance. He'd been so confident that he could get the GSA to change their minds. All his life he had been in charge and he expected people to obey him, without question. Who did he think he was? He was a pathetic, weak little know-it-all. He looked at the girl. She had more intelligence and general competence than he would ever have. He had been trained like an automaton to do one task and one task alone. A service droid could do what he did.

At that moment the door opened and a guard motioned for them to follow him. Gola pulled the shaking boy to his feet. It was hopeful wasn't it? Following rather than being led? But perhaps this was the dignity given to the condemned? Whatever the judgement he would plead to see Baby one more time.

Gola squeezed his arm. 'Okay, Blue?'

He nodded.

The guard led them to a large room where several men were clustered around a table. They looked up as the two were brought in.

One of the men spoke to Malcolm. 'So? You're President Matthews' Pool master?'

Malcolm was furious. How many times did he have to tell them? 'No. I'm Capa's Pool master. Matthews is an abomination in the face of humanity...a traitor to his scientific background...a vile murderer of innocent babies – '

The man held up his hands, ' – And you? 'He spoke to Gola, 'You were one of Matthews' genetically selected troopers but have changed allegiance to the Society. Correct?'

Gola nodded. 'I hate the spanzo too but I haven't got so many ...polite words to say it. The trooper camps make kids into unthinking killers. They don't stand a chance. Either they become bullying psychos or...or they're out of it.'

"Out of it?"

'The Incinerator man comes calling.'

'I see. So how exactly do you explain your...transformation, Trooper?'

Gola leant threateningly towards her interrogator. 'I am not a freakin Trooper. Got that?'

'Gola,' Malcolm warned.

But nothing was going to stop her. 'You want to know why I left them? Okay, I'll tell you. They made me do something so...bad I had to split, or top myself. But,' the girl's voice softened, 'I got lucky. D'you want to know why? Because that was when I met Munro.'

'Ah, Munro.'

'And I don't give a freakin shit what you do to me, but Munro? He's the best.'

Before Malcolm really knew what was happening he was on his feet beside her. 'In ten years time Matthews will have the biggest, most ruthless army since Genghis Khan. No one will be able to stop him. Is that what the Globe wants?'

'Please,' the man indicated that they should both sit down.

'Genghis who?' Gola muttered, as she plonked herself down beside Malcolm.

The man was talking, 'We have been aware for some time of the threat Matthews poses to the Global States but he is a very powerful man and the GSA isn't militarised. We believe he's responsible for Monsieur Xaviet's murder but is there enough resistance in Capa to support GSA intervention? We could only lend token assistance at this stage.'

This was something Gola did know about and Malcolm listened with growing admiration as she explained her party's strengths and weaknesses. The GSA could call on united help as peace keepers but they could not be seen as aggressors. They talked for what seemed like hours and Malcolm dozed off once or twice. It was lovely to shut his tired, strained eyes. He woke up with a jolt as Gola was pulling him to his feet. The room was empty and there was a lot of activity going on outside.

'Okay, Mr Blue, time to rattle some cages.'

Malcolm didn't like the sound of that but he followed her anyway. The GSA organised transport for them and, as they waited to get clearance at the perimeter gate, Malcolm hunched down in his seat. He didn't want to meet those two troopers again. But they weren't there. Two men, equally as large, were on guard, but they were wearing GSA arm bands. Malcolm sighed and closed his eyes. He really could sleep now.

## *Pox in Charge*

There were two troopers lounging on either side of the Presidential palace entrance. They'd done a double shift and were hot, hungry and mean. They watched through slit eyes as a slim boy, in an old trooper cap, approached them.

Luckily for them Pox was in a hurry. He flashed his official pass and the two men came to attention so fast, their spines cracked. This boy was their new Commander In Chief. They didn't need to read the document he thrust in their faces. Freakin hell. This was Pox. Every trooper had heard about Pox. The Elite who had been sliced twice and survived the desert – in daytime.

Did the Commander want them to accompany him to the presidential suite? No. Did he need anything? A change of clothes maybe? Anything? No, no, no. All he wanted was the directions to the trooper crèche and the men's assurance that they wouldn't tell anyone that he was in the building. Their Commander asked if they understood – they did.

When Pox arrived at the crèche the noise was deafening. Each crib contained a small, open mouth screaming. The nurses wore ear-defenders and didn't notice Pox until he leant over them. His mouth was smiling but his eyes weren't. They jumped to their feet. This boy looked like something from their worst nightmare. His eyes were bloodshot; his clothes torn and an ancient trooper cap was pulled down over a badly pock-marked face. He mimed for them to take off their earphones and pointed to the cribs. 'Why are they crying?'

One nurse spoke up. 'They always cry, sir – '

'– Why?'

'Trooper babies cry, sir. It's natural. It doesn't hurt them.'

Pox grabbed the woman and twisted her arm sharply behind her back, she yelped with pain. 'That didn't hurt you, did it?' He jabbed a finger at the nearest crib. 'Bring that one here.'

The nurse obeyed.

'Hold him.' The woman held the frantic infant while Pox ran his finger over the back of the child's head. 'What's this?' He pointed to a tiny raised scar, a thumb print long.

'The SS entry point.'

'In freakin English, bitch.'

The terrified woman could hardly get the words out. 'Sensory stimulation implantation, sir...' She saw Pox's look. 'It's a technique that uses parts of the child's brain to encourage certain thoughts and feelings – '

'– That don't belong to him?'

'Yes, that don't belong to him.'

'Are they happy *thoughts and feelings?*'

The woman kept her eyes down. 'I only work here sir, I'm not responsible.'

Pox took the baby. The child stopped crying and watched Pox through huge tear-brimmed eyes. 'Once this...stuff is done can it be undone?' He saw the nurses' confusion and put the child gently back in its crib. Then he put a finger to his lips. 'No one must know I was here. Understand?'

The women nodded their heads violently.

When Pox got outside he threw up. What was happening to him? Those kids didn't mean anything to him. No one meant anything to him.

Not now. He ran a trembling finger over his shaved head, no scar, no mark at all. He was one of the lucky ones, wasn't he?

*Safe*

Poppi was in a hurry to find Orange but she had to keep waiting for the stupid people to catch up.

'Take it a bit slower, Poppi,' Billy ordered. 'We've got some tired people back here, okay?'

They set off again, only more slowly this time. Poppi would behave for Billy. He didn't treat her like an annoying little kid

Billy again. 'How much further?'

'Dunno,' she shouted. But it couldn't be far now. She didn't mind being underground now she wasn't frightened of rats. Where there were rats Orange wouldn't be far behind. And she was longing for a creamy drink of milk in the Dome. After that she had things to do. She had to find the animal lab and set all the caged animals free.

She didn't think about Kline. She didn't concern herself with things that were happening elsewhere. She liked him, of course, but she had Orange now and... she looked back at Billy. The girl who didn't speak was walking beside him. Someone should teach her to say things. Poppi had learnt, so she could. That kid was lazy.

'Billy? Come to Poppi. On own, no child.' She stopped in the middle of the tunnel and waited for him, her hands on the place where her hips would be one day.

'What's up?' Billy looked worried as he hurried up but then he stopped dead in his tracks. He was staring at the chain around Poppi's neck

'Walk with Poppi,' she wheedled.

'I can't do that. I have to look after everyone.' His eyes were still on the div. Poppi saw what he was looking at and her hand went protectively to the necklace. What was the matter with boy? 'Poppi go,' she threatened.

'No you won't' he told her. 'You promised.'

She made a face.

'Poppi? Where did you get that? The div? And the necklace?'

'It's mine,' Poppi was confused. Maybe this boy wasn't so nice after all. 'You can't have it.'

He held her arm lightly. 'I don't want it, Poppi. But where did you get it? Please. Can I see?'

Poppi tore herself away and ran off down the tunnel.

He went after her, determined not to lose her. He needn't have worried because suddenly, there she was looking at something in front of her and when he reached her he saw it too. It was the entrance to the agridome.

Poppi enjoyed all the people thanking her for finding the agridome but she kept a wary eye on Billy.

\*

Maya changed hands and stretched her cramping fingers. She glanced at Kline. Sweat was trickling down his face but his eyes never left the wall. She had no idea how long they'd been there but the sounds from behind the projection had stopped a long time ago. Of course, that didn't mean the troopers had gone away. They could be sleeping, or waiting for orders. It would only take one of them to lean up against the wall to discover their secret.

Maya breathed evenly. This was how she liked it – just her and the enemy. She looked at Kline. Was he the enemy too? Suddenly Maya tensed. There was a noise. A sort of scrabbling, scuffling sound, not loud but persistent, and it came from the other side of the wall. Maya took a step backwards, legs braced, gun steady. This was it then.

Kline moved beside her. 'If this is the end,' he whispered. 'I want you to know I love you, Maya. I've always loved you and I'm not a traitor.'

She didn't respond. Her eyes were full of tears but they never wavered from the spot where she expected the troopers to come through. If she'd glanced down she would have seen the orange nose that popped out at the bottom of the wall. Kline saw it first and swung his gun down. They both watched as a set of twitching whiskers emerged, followed by a pair of beady little eyes and then a whole body shot through. A little ginger animal scuttled towards Maya, squeaking loudly.

Maya took a step backwards. 'What the freakin...?'

Kline put a warning finger to his lips and then he ducked through the wall. After a moment his voice came back to her. 'All clear Maya.' And she followed him into the deserted chamber. The only sign that the troopers had been there was a pile of empty C cans.

The animal was waiting for them on the Berg side. Kline bent down and picked it up, keeping his fingers well away from the teeth. 'Haven't you seen a guinea pig before, Maya?'

Maya put her hand out to touch the animal.

'I wouldn't do that – '

Too late. Maya swore and wiped her bloody finger on her sleeve.

Kline tried not to smile. 'He belongs to Poppi – '

'– Really? What a surprise.'

'Friends?' He held out a hand to her but she ignored him. She had to keep her mind clear for what lay ahead.

The boy sighed and stowed Orange in his back pack. They filled their water bottles from the berg melt and Maya took one last wistful look at the huge iceberg. Then they set off into Capa's underground. Maya led the way.

\*

Poppi went wild when she saw Orange and after kissing him all over she carried him to the nearest bush and watched, with deep satisfaction, as he shot off in search of his dinner.

Shortly after this Poppi slipped out of the Dome. She knew that Orange would be safe while she was gone but the animal saw her go and this time he wasn't going to be left behind. There was someone else who saw her go too but Billy didn't tell anyone.

\*

The fugitives had made themselves at home and were enjoying the fresh fruits and vegetables of the Dome. There were no pinx workers except for the cow boy, who gave them the latest news, including the assassination, arrests and the trial of the Society ringleaders taking place that night. Maya knew that Matthews would somehow be responsible for what had happened. It didn't give her any pleasure that Munro and the others were taken. She pushed Gola and Frankie and the others to the back of her mind. There was no time to worry about them now. She had to get Matthews before it was too late.

As soon as she could, she and Billy made their plans. They waited until Kline was distracted and then they jumped him, trussed him up and tied him to a tree.

'Maya? Why are you doing this? I can help you. You can't get Matthews on your own.'

'Watch me.' She couldn't look him in the eyes.

'I thought you were the one with brains. If I was a freakin traitor why didn't I betray you to the troopers back there in the Berg Cavern?'

It was a good question. Why hadn't he? Because he had something more important to do? Like? Her brain hurt from thinking and she switched off. Turning her back on Kline she collected her stuff. Billy was in charge now. She had done all she could for these people. Billy wished her luck and she hugged him, then she said her goodbyes to Anna and the others and hurried to the door. She didn't look at Kline.

He shouted 'Maya', as she walked away and the hurt in his voice stayed with her for a long time.

After Maya's departure Billy and Anna made sure everyone was comfortable. Billy gave Kline some tabs and fresh fruit. Kline hadn't eaten for a long time.

'Do you think I'm a traitor, Billy?' He asked, between mouthfuls.

Billy shrugged. 'It doesn't matter what I think.'

'I lost my memory, when I got hit. Why won't anyone believe me?'

'Because Capa is full of liars.'

'Yeh but Maya knows me. Or I thought she did –'

'– Where does the kid fit in?'

'Poppi?'

Billy nodded.

'She's a trainee CO, at the unit,' Kline answered, not wanting to get side-tracked.

'She seems very close to you,' Billy persisted

'Well, I'm her adopted family I suppose. I found her down here when she was a little kid – about two years old? She couldn't speak, didn't know who she was or where she came from. I took her back to the CO unit and she's been there ever since, plaguing the life out of me. Now can we get back to me? – '

'– Did she have the necklace when you found her?'

'Yeh. Look Billy what's this all about? Maya could be in real danger and I could help her. All you've got to do is untie me.'

'Was the div on the necklace when you found her?'

'Freakin hell, Billy. What is it with you?'

'Tell me.'

'Yeh, the Mary Poppins div was on the chain when I found her.'

'Have you watched it?'

That made Kline laugh. 'Only about sixty million times.'

'Tell me all about her and I might let you go.'

So Kline told Billy everything he knew, good and bad. How Poppi was a thief and even about the couple who wanted to adopt her. But when he'd finished Billy still didn't let him go. He was a liar too.

## *Your turn next!*

It was midnight by the time Maya emerged on the walkway — usually the busiest time of the night in Capa. But tonight she had the place to herself, except for the heavily armed trooper squads that swept by on their way to the City Hall. She stepped into side corridors until they passed and then tagged along behind.

City Hall square was packed with Matthewite supporters, all wearing Matthews' rosettes and carrying banners. Maya felt highly conspicuous until she stole a cap with *We love Lixir* on it and joined a long queue waiting to get inside.

She took a swift look about her and immediately saw Pox ahead of her in the line. He had his back to her and was wearing an ancient trooper cap but she would have known him anywhere. He must have sensed her eyes on him because he turned and saw her. He looked different, older. His eyes were set in huge pools of purple fatigue and he was dirty and unkempt. There was no swagger in this Pox. She tensed, waiting for him to make his move, but he sniffed, wiped his nose with the back of his hand and looked away. After a few moments he left the line and disappeared amongst a group of Matthews' groupies, all screaming, 'We love Lixie,' at the tops of their stupid shrill voices.

Maya didn't have time to work out what that was about because she saw troopers up ahead checking IDs. She ducked out of line and slipped around to the back of the hall where she found a service lift. She exited in a deserted AC control room beneath the City Hall and found what she was looking for — a waste disposal shute accessing the hall.

It was hard work climbing up the slippery tube. She kept sliding back until she worked out how to brace her knees and arms against the smooth sides. By the time she reached the top she was exhausted and dripping with sweat.

There was a fat old guy in the room, looking at himself in a mirror. Maya looked for the exit but he must have seen her in the glass and turned to face her.

\*

Kline waited until the exhausted boy's eyes fluttered shut and he fell into a deep, almost unconscious sleep. He was one tired boy. The COs hands had been free for some time but he hadn't wanted to confront Billy. He sensed that the boy would rather die than disobey his orders and he didn't want to have to kill him.

Everyone was asleep now and Kline stowed Billy's automatic and stepped carefully over him and out into Capa's underground.

\*

Kline had only been gone a few minutes when Billy opened his eyes. He was as sure as he could be that Kline wasn't a traitor and Maya needed all the help she could get if she was going after Matthews. Billy didn't need a gun for what he was going to do. He trod softly to where Tanya and Emma lay curled up beside Anna. They would be safe until he got back. He didn't want to leave them but there was something he had to do.

As he made his way out of the Dome there was no sound except for the gentle pattering of moisture on the leaves as the irrigation system kicked in.

\*

Kline carried priority passes for most places in Capa and the guards at the City Hall entrance weren't looking for presidential stand-ins.

He slipped inside and joined a group of screaming adolescent girls halfway back from the stage. Once in position he looked for Maya. She wasn't there. She had to be. He scanned the crowd again and again but there was no sign of her. He tried to stay calm. Maya would be all right, she could look after herself. So where was she? *Act natural Kline.* He could hear her lecturing him. He forced himself to grin at the young girl standing next to him.

She flushed with pleasure and dug her friend in the ribs. 'Oh my God. He's chuggin gorgeous.'

Kline concentrated on the stage. There was an impressive throne-like chair set up in front of a huge solid, highly-polished wooden table which held an assortment of food and drink. Kline knew all about presidential perks and his mouth watered. The table looked familiar and then he remembered. It was the one from the Toy Museum – the same one that Montrose had liberated.

Suddenly the girl beside him bent down and hurled something at a plasti-therm booth at the foot of the platform. When he looked he saw a box of missiles at her feet. She was handing them around to her friends. The *thud thud* as the rubbish hit the screens was like far-off gun-fire. The girl offered Kline one and he took it. It was some sort of compressed uni-plas. He turned it over and saw *Matthews.com* written on the back. This man thought of everything.

Kline looked back at the booth and saw that each partition contained a prisoner. Service droids seethed in a frenzy around the base of each compartment trying to demolish the ever-growing pile of missiles. Kline guessed the people were Society leaders.

At that moment there was an ear-splitting communal scream to the left of where Kline was standing. *Lixir Lixir. We love you.* The noise came from a group of trainee Troopers – Matthews' special girl squad.

\*

One girl in this group was an elite and although she joined in with her companions her eyes never left the prisoners. Gola didn't need to see their faces to know the pain her friends were suffering. Munro and Dan Young were slumped low in their seats; even Frankie's huge frame looked crumpled and defeated. If only there was some way of letting them know they were amongst friends. Gola's eyes swept the crowd. Many of these Matthewite supporters were not what they seemed. Turning her head slightly she spoke softly to the boy standing behind her. 'Still with me, Blue?'

Malcolm's eyes were dazzled by the bright lights and all he could see was a tuft of hair sticking out from beneath Gola's helmet. His heart was pounding. GSA and Society forces were in position inside and outside the Hall. The man who had called him incompetent was about to be brought to justice and he, Malcolm Blue, had played his part in the depraved monster's downfall. He'd have some fine stories to tell Baby when he grew up.

\*

Lixir Matthews was in his dressing room, artfully arranging his thinning hair over his scalp, when a young girl appeared out of nowhere. She was wearing a *We love Lixir* cap. Matthews was furious. Someone would pay for this security balls-up. Had he not given explicit orders not to be disturbed until the trial was due to start? Every minute away from those infernal lights was a bonus. However, taking a second glance, he saw that the intruder was a looker. A bit grubby and sweaty but there was a wildness about her that appealed to him enormously. He decided to excuse the gross abuse of protocol and smiled graciously, holding in his stomach. 'Can I be of assistance?'

She stepped towards him, a puzzled look on her face.

He was sure he knew her from somewhere.

'Who're you?' she asked rudely. 'Do you work for Matthews?'

He was too astonished to reply. Who the chuggin hell did she think he was?

Maya didn't have time to waste on morons and went to the door. 'Yeh, well thanks for the info, granddad.'

Matthews could move fast when he had to and he got to the door before her. How dare she think he was some oldie. He puffed out his chest. 'Have you any idea who I am?'

'No. That's why I asked you.'

Her attractiveness was fading fast. 'I am your President, Lixir Matthews.'

The girl's hand flew to her mouth. Good. Now she was properly terrified. He kept the stern expression on his face while he waited for her grovelling apology. There would be time for forgiveness later.

However when she finally took her hand away she revealed a mouth open-wide in a huge grin. 'You're Matthews?' she spluttered. 'Really? You're not kidding me? I mean. I knew you were old but...' She couldn't go on she was laughing so much.

Matthews could feel his blood pressure rising. She'd blown it now. He would call the trooper guard. Maybe she'd find that amusing too?

But then she did the weirdest thing. She took a step towards him holding out her arms, as if she wanted a hug. He was confused but automatically moved towards her. He was never one to turn down such offers. Quick as a flash, she thumped him hard with the palms of her hands and sent him reeling backwards into a chair.

He watched in growing panic as she tore off her cap and hurled it away. That done she hitched up a chair and sat down facing him. She wasn't smiling now and that's when he remembered who she was. 'You're that renegade CO...Johnson? Maya Johnson... Kline's sidekick...the freaker.' He didn't see her reaction to this because he was busy digging himself out of the hole he'd just dug for himself. 'But that's all in the past now, my dear,' he babbled. 'I'm offering amnesties to all Society sympathisers. You and Kline will not be harmed, you have my word.'

The girl's lip curled. 'Your word, Matthews? Oh yeah, very funny.'

'What do you want exactly?' His confidence was growing. His people would be coming for him at any moment.

'I think you knew my father?' The girl's voice was soft and menacing. 'He worked with you, in the Institute?'

That made Matthews sit up. 'Johnson? Of course, Jack...Jack Johnson, we were old chums...' His words ended in a squeak because he suddenly remembered what had happened to Jack Johnson. And when he looked at the girl again she was holding a gun.

'And Munro? And his family? And all those other *old chums*? What happened to them, Mr President?' Still the same quiet, deadly voice.

Matthews' treble chins were wobbling with fright, 'Please don't,' he gabbled. 'A lot of things happened back then that I regret now. They were difficult times. We were fighting for survival.'

Maya leant closer and he smelt her sweet sickly breath. He looked away but she stuck the muzzle of the gun into his jaw and he was forced to look into her expressionless eyes.

'And my mother, Mr President? What happened to my mother?' There was a tremor in the voice now.

'It wasn't my fault,' Matthews' pleaded. 'It was Fleur – she didn't want to share the Crick prize with anyone – she's a very dangerous woman. I feared for my life.'

Maya leapt to her feet, sending her chair toppling backwards. 'You sent my mother to that place for some freakin prize?' She grabbed Matthews by the throat and half dragged him out of his seat.

He was choking. 'Please, please. You don't understand. The Crick prize is the best it gets… And I didn't kill your mother. I swear. Not personally. She was sent away. But I never killed her.'

Maya dropped him abruptly and he collapsed back onto the chair. She took a step away and levelled the gun at his head.

He shut his eyes. This was it then? But the seconds dragged by and nothing happened. He opened one eye and then the other. She was still there but the gun hung loosely from her fingers. She was looking at him but he knew she wasn't seeing him. Her face was wet with tears and she was shaking. When she focused back on him all the hate in the world was concentrated in that one look. 'I'm not gonna ex you, Matthews –'

'– Oh thank you, thank you,' he gushed. 'I'll reward you. I promise, you won't be sorry.'

She swung the gun up and jabbed it viciously at him. 'Don't say anything, Matthews. I hate your freakin guts so much but Munro's right; killing's too good for you. You have to pay for what you've done. Everyone has to know what a freakin monster you are.' She drew a long, shuddering breath. 'All my life I've blamed myself. I thought it was my fault. I thought I'd betrayed her. But it wasn't me. It was you. You were too much of a coward to kill her yourself but you did a worse thing. You sent her to that…to that… obscene, filthy place. I've been there, Matthews, I've seen it…I'll always see it.'

While she was raving Matthews' brain was spinning. He would only get one chance and, at the exact moment he lunged for her gun, the door was flung open and a trooper burst in. The boy knocked Maya to the floor and then cuffed her to the chair.

It all happened so quickly Matthews could hardly take it in. He was alive. His heart was pounding but he had survived. Euphoria swept through him. He waved the trooper away. 'Take her and put her with the other traitors. Oh and good work. You will be well rewarded –' but the President's words died in his throat because the trooper was at the door scrambling the access code. Matthews rushed at him but the boy side-stepped him and the President tripped and fell. The trooper turned Matthews over with his foot and stared down at him. That's when Maya saw who it was.

Pox ignited a laser knife and Matthews scrambled into a sitting position, holding his hands protectively over his face. He stammered, 'I'll give you anything, only don't…please don't.' The boy swept the knife down, narrowly missing Matthews' hand and the President scuttled away on all fours. 'But you're a trooper,' he yelped, backing into a corner. 'All troopers are loyal to their President. You must obey me.'

Pox walked slowly to the man and planted a boot on either side of his body so that Matthews couldn't move. He whimpered. 'I'm an old man, please don't hurt me.'

Quick as a flash Pox sliced the knife across Matthews' hair. It didn't touch his skin but he was shaved to the scalp. The boy grabbed a handful of cut hair and tossed it high into the air, so that it fell about Matthews like Presidential confetti. Then Pox sliced again and the President's smart jacket fell away from his body in two precise segments. Matthews scurried into another corner and screamed at the advancing boy. 'Tell me what you want. I'll give you anything.'

The boy kept walking. 'Too late. You took the only thing I ever wanted.'

Matthews was desperate. 'Who are you?'

Pox drew himself up to attention. 'Your new Commander-in-Chief reporting for duty, sir. My mother was Scar.'

'Your mother?' This time Matthews' trousers parted from his podgy little legs and then Pox picked Matthews up by the scruff of the neck and forced the man's head into an arm lock. 'I wasn't there when you sliced her. I was only a baby but I've seen the scar – it was mass. I know how to make a wound like that. I've been trained well.'

Matthews was blubbering now, all hope gone.

Maya screamed, 'Pox. No! We need him. He's gotta stand trial.'

But the boy wasn't listening. The knife came slowly down towards Matthews' face when, suddenly, the door disintegrated and the room was full of troopers. One moment Pox was there and the next he was gone.

\*

When Matthews finally made his late yet triumphant entry into the Hall – several stiff drinks and a new suit later – his adoring supporters went ballistic. They approved of their President's new radical haircut.

The President was on a high. He had survived two horrific attempts on his life. Spanzoid medics, what did they know? There couldn't be much wrong with his heart. He was beginning to believe his own propaganda. Lixir Matthews was invincible? He waved and smiled at the cheering crowds. He was delighted with the large turnout, his people had done well. It would have been expensive but worth every cred.

\*

Kline only had eyes for the three people preceding Matthews. A slight girl was being hustled along between two guards. It was Maya. She was white-faced and one side of her head was covered in blood but she was alive and that was all that mattered. They shoved her into one of the holding cells.

The boy picked up a projectile and hurled it. Maya heard the crack as it crashed against the screen but she kept her eyes down, ignoring the hostile, jeering crowd. Kline threw another missile as hard as he could and this time she did flick a look of loathing in his direction. This time she saw him.

\*

Matthews tossed some nibbles into the air and opened his mouth to catch them. Several missed and fell onto the platform. He didn't notice, he was too engrossed in congratulating himself on choosing the City Hall as the venue for the trial. It appealed to his warped sense of humour. The place of Dan Young's supposed triumph would serve as the venue for his humiliation and defeat and subsequent demise. Matthews glanced at the pathetic prisoners. Young hadn't said a word since his arrest and even Munro and the Pinx were subdued. The deal was they confessed to everything he accused them of, or he would ex the mine captives, one by one, starting with the Young brat. He hoped they would liven up during the cross-examination. It wouldn't be much fun if they didn't put up a fight. Still he had the girl now, so that should add some interest.

The President checked the autocue. If he'd looked to the right of it he would have seen a familiar face.

*

Kline was trying to work out what to do next. He knew Maya wanted Matthews dead but he'd never be able to get a clear shot at the spanza in this crowd. That was when he spotted the kid weaving towards him through the crowds, searching for something. When she got within reach he grabbed her.

Poppi struggled wildly. 'Let go, Kline. Orange.'

He might have guessed it was that animal again. 'Forget him, Poppi, there's more important stuff to do.'

The child fought to get loose. The girls on either side of him stared. Kline couldn't afford to be noticed.

'Baby, ' he crooned, smoothing Poppi's wild hair. 'I told you to stay at home but you love your daddy

Matthews so much you had to come, didn't you? Didn't you?' he insisted.

Poppi looked about her and understood. She relaxed and Kline squeezed her hand gratefully. 'Stay close to me, I don't want you getting lost. Okay?'

Poppi twisted her mouth into a *yes* and stood quietly but her eyes continued to dart everywhere.

When it was safe he whispered, 'Where did you lose him?'

'In the animal place. Poppi open nasty cages.' At that moment the child's face lit up. She'd spotted Maya and heaved a missile at the partition.

Kline grabbed her. 'You'd better behave or I'll …' his voice trailed away. There, on the inside of Maya's partition, were four letters, written in bright red blood. **N O X M.** Her eyes pleaded with him through the bloody message.

\*

Maya was pretty sure Kline had seen and understood the message. Considering what had happened she didn't feel too bad. Her head was bleeding but it was only a flesh wound.

She was trying to work out what had happened. Why would Pox want to kill Matthews? It didn't make sense. She looked to where Kline stood, head and shoulders above a group of little girls. He wasn't a traitor. Another missile hit the screen and she glared out at the offender, and that was when she saw the other prisoner crouched in the corner of her cell, moaning and rocking backwards and forwards.

'Dan?'

No response.

Maya touched his shoulder. 'It's me, Dan. Maya? Maya Johnson? From the mines?'

Dan looked at her, worry lines puckering his forehead. He was making a huge effort to understand what she was saying.

'Are you okay, chief?'

He put his head in his hands and wept.

Maya knelt beside him, holding him against her. 'It's okay. She's safe – '

But Dan wasn't listening. '– That monster's got my Emmie. He's going to kill her.'

'No. she's okay I swear. She's with Tanya and Anna and Billy – '

'– No. They're all dead and it's my fault.'

'We escaped through the tunnels. She's in the agri dome with Elizabeth and the others.'

Dan grabbed the girl's arm and his fingers dug painfully into her flesh. 'If you're lying I'll kill you – '

She shook him off. '– Cool it, Dan. I don't lie.'

Then she hammered on the dividing wall to get Munro and Frankie's attention. They didn't need to hear every word to know what her message was. Munro looked out at the crowd for the first time and immediately saw Gola. Frankie spotted other members of their squad and the pair of them squared their shoulders and sat up.

\*

Matthews noticed the change in the men. It was worrying. Maybe he should have questioned the girl before putting her in the pen? She'd been in the mines so why hadn't she been taken prisoner with the others? Did that mean that some of the rebs had escaped? If so, she would know where they were hiding.

He half-turned, expecting to find Scar standing behind him. Damn the woman, she couldn't have killed herself at a more inconvenient moment. His direct line of communication had broken down and he had lost touch with the heli-port and the whereabouts of the delegates. There was no word on the Young child, even though he'd claimed that she was in his hands, and now he'd discovered Scar's replacement was a lunatic – a dead lunatic by now, he hoped.

Matthews shivered. It was probably delayed shock. Understandable after what he'd been through. He looked about him. Bullet proof screens protected him on three sides and snipers were positioned at every vantage point in the hall. He made himself concentrate on the sea of happy faces staring up at him, adulation on their faces and popped another delicious meaty nibble.

\*

Fleur lay flat in an AC shaft, halfway up the wall, facing the platform. It was a tight fit, and it had taken her a long time to wriggle into position but now she had a perfect view of Piggy through her telescopic lens. Sonny was an unexpected bonus. It was fitting that they should die together, father and son. The mini-rifle was a favourite of hers, small yet deadly. In this confined space her erratic movements were controlled and she would have a steady hand. The duct acted as a superb tic-corset.

When Piggy was dead Fleur would take her rightful place as Queen of Capa. Why should he have all the fun while she did all the hard work? From now on she was concentrating on number one. Capa was going to run to Queen Fleur's beat and she was going to have a lot of fun.

From somewhere far away she heard the applause reaching a crescendo. She would wait for Piggy to start his pathetic speech and then ...oink oink.

\*

The producer cued the audience and Matthews rose to tumultuous applause. He felt confident and relaxed but, when he opened his mouth to speak, nothing came. He cleared his throat and tried again – nothing, not even a squeak. He took a deep breath and smiled at the faces beneath him. *Stay calm and the vocal chords will remain elastic.* He held his breath to the count of five, and then let it out slowly. He did this three times but his eyes were streaming and when he looked down at the eager little faces turned up to him, they coalesced into white blobs, all bouncing and jiggling together, like balloons caught in a net. And then he experienced that familiar dreadful tickling at the back of his throat and nose. This was the excruciating yet delightful pre-sneeze sensation that he loved and loathed in equal measure.

When it came Matthews sneezed into the meaty morsels, firing them like grape shot over the stage and front rows of the audience. He sneezed into the microphone, deafening the crowds and then he sneezed onto the TV lens and the picture disappeared under a coating of gunk.

He knew he was in the eye of the storm and had a few precious moments of respite. All he had to say was, 'My most loyal and devoted subjects,' How hard was that? He took another deep breath and …sneezed again. This time the force propelled him backwards into his chair and as he collapsed into it he saw a movement down by his foot. It was an animal – an orange guinea pig. Of course. That was why he was sneezing – it was the freakin pig. The horrible rodent was rooting about, feasting on discarded titbits.

Matthews kicked out desperately but Orange growled, standing his ground. Matthews picked up a plate and hurled it but he missed and it exploded into a million fragments across the stage.

That was when Poppi shrieked and sprang away from Kline. She had to save Orange before the fat oldie stomped him.

As it happened this was just what the insurgents needed. The perfect diversion. Every eye in the hall was riveted on that one small figure, charging towards the President. Several troopers drew their guns but they didn't dare shoot, they might hit their chief. This indecision gave Society infiltrators and GSA personnel the opportunity to move swiftly into place. The sniper troopers were taken out and Gola gave the signal for each ex-trooper to move forward carrying a missile gun.

\*

In the AC duct Fleur was laughing so much she started to tic convulsively and catastrophically...

\*

Matthews' whole being was centred on the approaching great granddaddy-of-all sneezes. And when it came, the mighty impetus shot him out of his seat, flinging him against the bullet-proof screen and bouncing him backwards. His flailing hands snatched wildly for something – anything, to stop his fall. He managed to grab the corner of the table and clung on desperately. All his weight bore down on that single point. There was a tremendous c*rack* as the leg gave way and the magnificent table rose up majestically, like the prow of a sinking ship, and then crashed over on top of the President.

Some say they heard Matthews shout as he fell, 'My most loyal and devoted citizens.' But whether he did or didn't is of no consequence, because, as he fell, the corner of the table struck him a mighty blow on the side of his head and Lixir Matthews – President for life – was dead.

The stage was a bomb site, littered with wrecked furniture, broken screens, smashed china and glass. And in the centre of all this devastation lay the huge upturned table with the President's arms and legs sticking out grotesquely on either side, like some nightmare turtle. There was absolute silence for a moment and then someone started to clap and a few cheered and finally the room exploded with joy.

\*

Within minutes the President's trooper guards were taken or surrendered and the Society leaders were freed and surrounded by delighted, back-slapping supporters.

The girl beside Kline was now screaming, 'Long live Dan Young.' She glanced at Kline and shrugged apologetically but Kline wasn't looking at her. There was only one thing on his mind. As he fought his way towards the stage Kline passed one weedy little guy squinting into the bright lights. As Kline watched him, a powerful girl trooper threw her arms around the boy, kissed him soundly and then lifted him off his feet and swung him around. They were both laughing and shouting.

\*

When Billy found Poppi she was stretched out on the platform, too exhausted to move, her bloodied fingers clutching the div around her neck. She had been digging for Orange in the debris. Her eyes were squeezed tight shut and tears had scoured salty channels down her dirty cheeks. At first she didn't feel the light touch on her shoulder, she was too deep in her own misery.

'Poppi?'

She looked up. Billy was kneeling beside her, eyes wide with pity. He lifted her gently into a sitting position, so that her back was propped up against him, and wrapped his arms about her. 'It's okay Poppi. Everything's okay. I'm here and I'm never gonna leave you again. Promise.'

She didn't hear the words but she felt the warmth of him. Taking a deep breath she closed her eyes. 'He's dead, Billy. My Orange is dead.'

He rocked her backwards and forwards and as he did so the gold chain around his own neck fell forwards and sparkled in the stage lights. It was exactly the same as Poppi's.

\*

Malcolm went off happily to be reunited with Baby, promising to meet up with Gola later. He would go straight to the Pool and reinstate some form of balance to the quotient.

\*

The Society div crew was already filming a live interview with Munro to be broadcast immediately to the people of Capa. Society supporters were on their way to release the prisoners from the mine. Frankie had volunteered to drive Dan Young to the Dome – he'd liberated a trooper transport. Dan had a com pressed close to his ear. He was speaking to Emma and it was doubtful he would ever get that smile off his face.

Later that night Dan would broadcast to Capa flanked by Munro, Frankie, Gola and the GSA delegates on one side and Emma, Tanya and Anna on the other. He would abolish the Purity laws. The few elites still loyal to Matthews were holed up in their units, preparing for a last stand. But Gola and her friends were in touch with all the Trooper squads and many of the troopers were defecting. The Society promised an amnesty for any trooper or citizen who handed in their weapons.

The opposition died with Matthews' death. His erstwhile spies had no real allegiance to anyone but themselves and the malcontents would remain disaffected whoever was in power. Most of the rich blus headed for the shuttle ports, hoping to get away before the gates were closed. This exodus included Rosemary Young and her mother. They had investments in Offshore Little America and would be able to sustain a comfortable life-style in a new country.

\*

It didn't take long for the wonderful news to spread throughout Capa and the citizens came out in their thousands to celebrate. In every zone and within all colour bands the walkways were jammed with dancing, laughing people. People were burning their ID's and having colour codes removed. Young couples were thinking the impossible; planning their families. In the Flume the inhabitants partied their way up and down between the levels and projections.

\*

Morta sat alone in her room and waited.

\*

Maya stared at what remained of Lixir Matthews. Somewhere in her head she was aware of the pandemonium going on around her but the sounds were deadened, as if she was hearing them from a long way off. It had nothing to do with her. She felt nothing. No relief, no anger, nothing. Yes, he was dead, the monster was dead, but what now? Would it bring back all the people he'd murdered? Her mother and father? Those poor prisoners in the desert and God knows how many other unknown, unmourned innocents?

'Johnson?'

He was only a few metres away from her. He had a gun aimed at her head.

*And suddenly it didn't matter, nothing mattered. Maya was totally relaxed, as if some huge weight had been lifted from her. And she felt her mother beside her, her arms about her, keeping her safe.*

The boy's thin face was grey with exhaustion and grief. His eyes were red-rimmed and half-closed against the painful brightness of the light. There was a livid welt on his forehead, where the battered old trooper cap had dug into his flesh. He was breathing quickly through his mouth and his chest fluttered, like a kid trying to stop himself from blubbing.

He took a shaky step towards her. 'Got to do this,' he muttered. 'Got to ex the bitch CO. That's what she said. Rules and regs see? You've gotta obey rules and regs. Without them you…you…' A tear inched its way down his cheek and he had snot on his nose. He swiped a dirty sleeve across his face and sniffed. 'Can you hear them?' he asked, suddenly, looking over his shoulder.

She waited.

'I hear them all the time, in here,' he tapped his head. 'All the time.' His look was pleading. 'D'you hear them?'

She nodded and took a step towards him.

He tensed his finger on the trigger.

'Do it, Pox,' she said.

'Gemmie,' he said softly. 'My name's Gemmie.'

\*

That was when Kline saw her. She was facing him but her eyes were on the boy standing in front of her. He had his back to Kline and looked like one of the reb Troopers. 'Maya!' Kline yelled, waving both arms above his head. 'Over here.' She didn't hear him but the boy turned his head a fraction and Kline saw who it was.

As he leapt towards her he drew Billy's automatic. 'Dive, Maya,' he screamed. Kline's finger tightened on the trigger. He had to do this...

Pox saw him coming and the indecision in his eyes. He raised the gun and took aim.

'No!' Kline hurled himself forwards.

Pox was smiling as he pulled the trigger but then he was falling and blood was spurting from a bullet hole in his head. He was dead before he hit the ground.

Kline came to a halt beside the boy's body, staring down at his gun. Had he done this? He was conscious of someone talking to him. It was the girl he'd seen hugging the guy.

'You okay?'

He nodded. 'I think so.'

The girl curled her lip as she looked down at Pox. 'Saved me the trouble didn't he? Shame though 'cos I'd have enjoyed exing this Gemmie boy.' She looked at Maya. 'Glad you're okay, blu. Catch up with you later? Got things to do.' And she disappeared into the crowd.

Maya was on her knees beside Pox. The trooper's cap had fallen off and she was putting it gently back on his head.

Kline knelt beside her. 'I thought he was gonna kill you.'

'So did I.' she smiled faintly.

'I don't understand.'

'Poor kid.'

Kline was shocked. '"Poor kid?" This is Pox, Maya, remember? He tried to ex me and he sure would have loved to ex you.'

She turned a stricken face to him. 'He couldn't help being what he was, Kline. Matthews made him. He made us all.'

Kline pulled Maya gently to her feet and she stepped towards him, one hand outstretched. He took her hand and kissed it and then he pulled her into his arms. 'I'll make you forget all this, Maya. I promise.' She rested her weary body against his and closed her eyes. Kline glanced over her head at the bits of the President he could see. This man had been his father, according to Fleur. Kline wondered what he was supposed to feel.

'He's got away with it, ' Maya muttered against his chest.'No one's ever gonna believe what he did. Not now.'

'Not true,' he whispered, turning her so that she saw the people going mad with joy. 'They know, we all know.'

'I hope so,' she said. 'I truly hope so.' And then she leant back against him and they stood quietly together, while the world changed about them.

\*

If Poppi had had her eyes open she would have seen the whiskery face that suddenly appeared over the ledge of the demolished table. Orange saw his meat provider and squealed loudly. Poppi opened her eyes and shrieked. She grabbed the animal and pressed her face against his muzzle, crooning to him. She was in ecstasy and so was he. He had found the biggest meaty morsel he had ever seen in his life and it was clamped in his jaws. He would never let it go.

Anne Ousby lives on the Northumbrian Coast in England. Her stories have been published in anthologies and broadcast on BBC radio. Her stage plays have been performed widely in the area, and a television drama, 'Wait till the Summer Comes', was broadcast on ITV.

Her first novel 'Patterson's Curse' was published in 2010 by Roomtowrite www.roomtowrite.co.uk . And her second novel 'The Leopard Man' was published in 2012.

Made in the USA
Charleston, SC
20 May 2013